Re/D

Doms o

Michele Zurlo

www.lostgoddesspublishing.com

Editor: Debora M. Ryan
Cover Artist: Anne Kay

Published by
Lost Goddess Publishing LLC
www.lostgoddesspublishing.com

A Note to Readers:

Misconceptions about Daddy Doms and littles (D/l or DD/l) are very common. Even in the BDSM community, they're frequently a misunderstood subset. The relationship between a Daddy and a little is not the same as between a father and daughter, and there is no age play involved—that's something else entirely. Many words have different meanings depending on the context, and that's what is happening with the "Daddy" title. In Latino cultures, *papi* is slang for a hot guy, but it also means father. In this case, "Daddy" serves a similar function.

Like any worthwhile dominant, a Daddy Dom is a responsible alpha male who feels a driving need to take care of his submissive. He's playful and indulgent, walking that fine line between spoiling and reining in his submissive. Daddies will typically give their littles chores or tasks to complete with the purpose of fulfilling his little's goals and needs. For example, if she struggles with self-esteem, he might task her with writing a list of her positive attributes, and he might punish her (often a spanking or corner time) for putting herself down. He's a protector, an emotional sanctuary, a mentor, and a teacher—and a boyfriend, husband, and lover.

Littles are women who sometimes feel like part of them is still a child. They may identify with a specific age or the age may be fluid. When stressed or if they need to decompress—or even for no reason—they can regress into "little headspace." It's a safe place where they can relax and have fun and forget about the real world. They might blow bubbles, color, or watch a child's movie or TV show—whatever appeals to them. Littles tend to have a childlike spirit and an underlying innocence. They're generally happy and upbeat, and very playful, even when they're not in little headspace. It's important to note that they're grown women with all the wants, needs, and complications that come with adulthood.

The sex in a D/l relationship is no different from sex in a vanilla or BDSM relationship. The kinks are separate from the D/l dynamic and are specific to the people involved.

Littles are very complex, high-maintenance women, and Daddies are the Doms who love maintaining them.

Re/Defined
Reading Order

Re/Bound

Re/Paired

Re/Claimed

Re/Defined

Acknowledgements:

This book would not have been possible without some key people who helped me with research and revision. I'd like to thank the members of The Speakeasy for their support and The Loving Dom for starting the group. Thanks to John K., Celeste King, and Ruadon King for allowing me to interview them, and thanks to Sherry Dove and Celeste for beta reading from a little's perspective. Additional thanks to Karen and Michelle M. for their tireless reading of my rough drafts—all of my rough drafts. I couldn't have done this without the light of your brilliance illuminating the errors and WTFs in my manuscript.

Sherry—the daisy is for you.

Chapter One

The flyer for the free seminar had simply read *Life Keep Smacking You Down? Tired of Always Losing Out? Take Control of Your Destiny.* Brian liked the message. Simple and direct, it didn't use fancy language or promise the moon. He'd found it under his wiper blade as he left work for the last time. Halfway through his shift, the plant manager had called him upstairs.

Downsizing, he'd said. Government cutbacks and rising retiree healthcare costs.

"If the motherfuckers would just die, everything would cost less." Brian hadn't meant to say it out loud, and he'd scrambled to cover his mistake. He hadn't spent four years in the military protecting his fellow citizens to disrespect them like that. The manager had merely nodded and reminded Brian to punch out or he wouldn't be paid for the day.

Days like this, he should find an N.A. meeting, but Brian was too pissed for that crap. Balling the flyer in his fist, he spat in the direction of the glass fabrication plant, and then he threw the paper missile to the ground. He bypassed the meeting and went straight for his favorite dealer's usual hangout. After the shit month he'd endured, he deserved an escape.

Miguel Lawrence watched the parking lot from the window of the plant manager's office. This wasn't his castle, but there was no doubt he was the king. He sniffed the cigar he'd light up as soon as he got to his car, and he reveled in his power. "That wasn't so bad."

Jeff, the manager of the fabrication plant, snorted, but he didn't try to plead for leniency again. "Good employees are hard to find."

"That's true." It was even more difficult to find someone with the correct profile. Miguel needed capable, skilled men who possessed key weaknesses. Brian Gartrell had worked hard to get his life back together, but he was too volatile to keep it that way. It was just a matter of time before he blew it, which needed to happen before he'd be desperate enough to fall into Miguel's trap. Yes, his organization needed men like Brian, and men like Jeff made it happen. Jeff hated doing this, but he had no choice because Miguel only had to make a phone call to destroy the man's life. And after the unexpected competence of the FBI over the past several years, he was down several key players.

"You're going to ruin his life, his wife's life, and his kid's life." A whiny edge crept into Jeff's indirect protest.

Miguel shrugged. "Minor inconveniences. You did well today. You'll be rewarded."

"Just stay away from me," Jeff said quietly. "I want nothing more to do with you. We're done. This never happened. I don't know you, and you don't know me."

Miguel watched Brian crumple the flyer and toss it to the ground. He smiled widely because the man had read it first. The seed was planted. "I'll need one more. You know what to look for. Call me within a week with a viable candidate."

"You're a fucking prick, you know that?"

Finally, Miguel turned away from the window. Brian had driven off, and one of Miguel's lackeys followed. He regarded Jeff with the full force of his stoic glare. "We all make mistakes. You're just upset because I know how to profit from them. Give up seeking redemption, Jeffy. Join my organization full time. I'm always looking for good men, and you're one of the best talent recruitment specialists I've come across. It's a gift you're wasting in this hole."

With that Jeff looked away, unsuccessfully hiding his guilt and disgust. Miguel laughed. He'd always been great at pushing his little brother's buttons.

Chapter Two

"You haven't known him long enough to move in together." Jordan Monaghan barely refrained from grinding his teeth and growling. His youngest sister had graduated from high school two weeks prior, and she was spending a week with him in Michigan before heading back to Wisconsin. This afternoon, he'd taken her to an engagement party. His friend Malcolm was finally tying the knot with his submissive fiancée. The pair had a five-month-old baby, and Darcy had wanted to wait until she lost the baby weight before scheduling the wedding. Malcolm had humored her to a point, and then he'd set the date, saying she looked fantastic and didn't need to shed another pound.

Jamie flipped her long dark hair over her shoulder. "We've been going out for over a year, and if Mom and Dad don't have a problem with it, I don't see why you do."

Their parents did have a problem with it, and they hadn't known how to handle it. As the youngest of five kids, Jamie was also the most headstrong and the least reasonable. Flabbergasted when their daughter had announced her plans, his parents had offered to pay for her trip to come see Jordan. As the oldest, he had been blessed/cursed with the responsibility gene. It helped that he had a dominant personality with a penchant for taking care of people.

"Jamie, so much changes in your first year of college." That was the year he'd discovered BDSM, and he'd met his first mentor, a Domina named Rachel. His high school girlfriend had not embraced the lifestyle, and they'd eventually parted ways. "Give it a year. Don't be in a rush to move in with somebody. That's a huge decision, one that shouldn't be made hastily."

This time Jamie rolled her eyes. "A year, Jordan. We've been together for thirteen months. That's longer than you've ever had a girlfriend."

While that was true, it wasn't a fear of commitment that kept his relationships short. It didn't take long to determine a woman wasn't your soul mate. He had a strict rule about not having sex in the first three months, and he was big on communication, which meant he got to know his girlfriends thoroughly. It infuriated him that he wasn't able to get through to his sister.

As he watched her lick barbeque sauce from her fingers and ignore his concerns, he tried to reformulate his strategy. Of course his brain short-circuited as soon as Amy Markevich, sister of the bride-to-be, showed up with that cute smile and a stack of pink boxes. She stopped at the buffet table and set up a three-tiered stand. Darcy went right over and hugged her sister. Jordan watched, delighting in the way Amy's face lit up when she was happy. Today she wore one of those dresses that wrapped around her body, the lemon yellow fabric hugging her dangerous curves and highlighting her breasts. They were more than a handful, not that he'd had the pleasure of measuring exactly how much more. The neckline plunged down to show cleavage, and Jordan shifted to give his boys breathing room. Those delectable curves continued, drawing his eyes over her hips and down her legs to the matching yellow Mary Jane's on her feet. Each shoe sported a white daisy on the buckle.

He'd looked for Amy when he'd first arrived, but he hadn't found her. Amy was an event planner, and part of her wedding gift was to plan the engagement party and the wedding. Malcolm had told him that Amy had gone to pick up the desserts. Most of his friends were under the impression that he liked Amy for her taste in pastries. Don't get him wrong—while he had a distinct weakness for her cupcakes, it was nothing compared to what he felt for Amy.

Six years separated them. He'd never dated an older woman, but Amy didn't seem like she was thirty-two. She had an air of innocence and naiveté that drew him, a moth to her flame.

Punctuated by moments of insight, her sometimes flighty demeanor left most people scratching their heads when they tried to understand her. Jordan had no problem recognizing and appreciating the multiple sides of her nature. She had a gorgeous face, with blue eyes that were perpetually happy, and straight brown hair that fell past her shoulders. It was silky and soft, and he had yet to find a good excuse to touch it. His reasons thus far had been mostly lame—engineered accidents that made him look a little klutzy. And that body—*holy shit,* it just didn't quit.

"Earth to Jordan."

He forced himself to look away from Amy's delicious figure and focus his attention on his sister. "You were saying?"

She jabbed a thumb over her shoulder. "Your buddy moved in with his girlfriend a couple months after meeting her. Now they have a kid, and they're getting married."

"They both finished college and have successful careers. There's no comparison." Before she could argue, he stood and held out his hand. "Amy's putting out cupcakes. We'd better get some before they're all gone."

Jamie let him pull her up. She regarded him with an amused grin. "You weren't drooling like that over cupcakes."

"Shut up, Jamie."

The cupcakes hadn't been finished on time, meaning Amy had to leave the party to pick them up. She didn't mind. Not only had a vendor donated them—they were hoping she'd use them at her other events—but her parents were in town for a couple of months. They planned to stay until after Darcy's wedding, and then they were off to explore the northern states in their new RV. Amy could only spend so much time with her parents before they annoyed her. Luckily they had Darcy's adorable baby to distract them. They spent most of their time *oohing* and *ahhing* over Colin. When they weren't with the little one, they were hounding her to find someone and settle down like Darcy had. If they only knew that Malcolm was a Dom, they'd stop urging her to find a nice man like Malcolm to marry. They hadn't exactly been understanding with Darcy's last fiancé, also a Dom. Neither had Amy, and she regretted letting her ignorance drive a wedge between her and her sister. At least now they were back to being best friends. Darcy was one of the only people who accepted her—quirks and all—and Malcolm did as well.

Setting up the cupcakes didn't take long. A crowd gathered before she finished, each person hungrily eyeballing the goodies on the three-tiered stand. She giggled at their undisguised interest. "You don't have to wait for me to finish. If you see one you want, go for it."

Many people flashed a grin in greeting as they took what they wanted and skedaddled. Malcolm, her brother-in-law-to-be, took a bite and closed his eyes as he savored the taste. He was tall, dark, and handsome, and they'd become good friends over the past year. "Damn, Amy. I don't know how you do it, but you always manage to find the best sweets." He finished his cupcake and took another one. Amy wasn't going to comment when he started in on that one. Malcolm grinned and swallowed. "I'm eating it for Darcy. She said I had to get her one, and then she said I couldn't let her have one because she's trying to lose weight. This is how I compromised."

Darcy had been the first one to greet her, and she'd already taken off with a cupcake. Amy merely nodded. "There's plenty for everybody."

"Great to know." Dustin Brandt, Malcolm's friend, leaned in to look over the selection.

Amy pointed to one. She knew Dustin's weakness. "Double chocolate with a mocha crème filling."

He flashed a dimpled smile as he grabbed it. "Thanks."

"Where's mine?" Layla Hudson, a tiny, petite blonde clutched Amy's arm and jumped up and down. The woman was close with Darcy, but over the past year, she'd become one of Amy's friends as well. She and Dustin had recently moved in together.

Along with Keith and Trina, that made three couples Amy knew who were in D/s relationships. The more she saw and read, the more she understood that she was thoroughly a submissive. She might run her own company, and life had thrust her into the role of big sister, but at heart, she wanted to submit to somebody. But not *anybody*. She wanted to find the right man first. Malcolm had been helping, introducing her to friends or vetting potential dates she met through a kinky dating service, but she had yet to meet anyone with whom she felt a connection.

Turning, she spotted Jordan Monaghan coming her way. At 6'5, he towered over everybody there. His long, shaggy black hair emphasized his sharp features. Jordan had an air of danger and authority that only enhanced his handsomeness, but it also made people take a step back and move out of his way. Amy had initially found him intimidating, but his warm and welcoming demeanor had barreled through her defenses, albeit a little too well.

This was the kind of guy who made her nipples pebble just by being nearby. Amy fantasized about Jordan and nameless men who looked like him, but who wanted her. As if the age difference wasn't enough, Jordan Monaghan was totally out of her league. To prove her point, he towed a tall, thin brunette with him. She was pretty enough to be a model, the exact type of woman who was perfect for him.

"Hey, Amy." He released the model to greet Amy with a heartfelt hug. His arms felt so good around her, and she let herself enjoy the brief press of his hard body against her softer one. "I see you brought the good stuff."

She handed him the box. "Since you weren't in the initial swarm, I left a banana cream in there for you."

He accepted her offering with a pleased smile that made her heart beat faster. "Amy, I want to introduce you to my little sister, Jamie. She's visiting this week from Wisconsin."

Her relief was momentary as she reminded herself that she wasn't Jordan's type. Too old and too plump, she'd be lucky if she landed a middle-aged business man who had a soft heart and a firm hand. Still she could close her eyes and pretend, couldn't she? Wasn't that what married people did—closed their eyes and pictured their partner as someone younger and more attractive? As long as she didn't accidentally yell out the wrong name, she'd be golden.

Remembering her manners, she grasped Jamie's hands in hers. "It's lovely to meet you. Are you visiting long?"

Jamie smiled and squeezed Amy's hands, acknowledging the friendly gesture. "Just a week. I leave in two days, which is a good thing. I think Jordan's getting sick of me always being underfoot, and his bachelor pad isn't fit for company."

Jordan's brows drew together in a menacing scowl. "It's cleaner than your bedroom."

Laughing, Jamie slapped a hand on her brother's shoulder. "Clean? It's barren. There's nothing around to suggest anybody lives there. No pictures, no curtains, not even a pair of socks on the floor. It's unwelcoming. You need a girlfriend, or at the very least, a good female or gay friend who will help you make your apartment homey."

"Socks on the floor isn't welcoming; it's gross."

Yep, they were siblings all right. Amy laughed. "Jamie, would you like a cupcake? I didn't make them, but the person who did is an incredible baker."

"You're a pretty fantastic baker." Jordan extracted his cupcake from the box and finished it in two bites. He savored and swallowed. "Though this is also very good."

"I see chocolate mint," Jamie said as she went toward the dessert table.

Jordan had a crumb on his chin, and without thinking, Amy brushed it away. The undercurrent of electricity that happened at the brief contact was only on her end, but she enjoyed it anyway. He had stilled to let her groom him. "Thanks."

The easy smile and the warm way his deep brown eyes sparkled were all the gratitude she needed. A small blush heated her chest, and she barely suppressed the urge to fan herself. "No problem."

He seemed to lean in, like he wanted to tell her something, so she did the same. Her breast inadvertently brushed against his hand as he brought it up, probably to make sure no other crumbs were stuck to his face. The awkwardness cancelled out the thrill of accidental contact.

Pink tinged his cheeks as he pulled his hand away. "Sorry."

Amy shrugged off the non-event. "No big deal. My girls go wild sometimes."

He laughed, a quiet chuckle that warmed her core.

Later, as the celebration was winding down, Amy went around to the tables and collected the bottles and cans people had left lying about. Anything not returnable went into the recycling bin, and anything returnable needed to be rinsed and put into bags. As she stopped at a table near the back of the yard, she overheard Jordan and Jamie arguing. Apparently Jamie wanted to move in with her boyfriend, and Jordan objected. Amy smiled at how protective he was of those he loved, but she also recognized Jamie's impatience. She didn't want to hear Jordan's opinion. Amy sympathized with them both. She'd once stepped over the line by telling Darcy how to live her life, and the result had been a deep rift in their relationship. Jordan meant well, as had Amy, but he was going to alienate his sister if he kept this up.

"I lived with a guy in college," Amy offered. "We'd been together for almost a year, and I think we both thought we'd be together permanently."

Jamie's gaze flicked to Amy's bare ring finger. "What happened?"

A short laugh bubbled out as Amy sat down next to Jamie. "You never truly know a person until you live together. We tried hard to make it work, and so we kept at it for the whole school year. I think we were both relieved when summer came and we got to have some time apart. That was the hardest thing—the assumption that because you're living together, your social lives have to be intertwined."

"Marc never tells me I can't hang out with my friends. He likes to hang with his friends too."

Amy nodded. "Hopefully your friends like his friends, otherwise things could get awkward. My ex didn't like my best friend all that much, and both relationships suffered. It was difficult to be in the middle and know they were tolerating one another because they loved me."

"Why did you break up?" Jordan's eyes flashed, and Amy realized she wasn't doing a good job of supporting his argument.

"I think not really having space to ourselves was bad. We rented a room in a house with six other people. Looking back, I should have rented my own room. That way I would have had a place to go when I needed to be alone to study or just to gather my thoughts without worrying that someone was going to come in at any time." Amy set a hand on Jamie's wrist. "If you're going to do this, get your own room. Even if you never sleep there, you know you have a place where everything is yours, you don't have to share closet space, you can change your clothes without worrying your boyfriend is going to bring a friend in, and you have a place to go for when you fight. You will have disagreements. That just happens in a relationship, especially when you're sharing space."

While Jamie thought about that, Amy ventured a peek at Jordan to see if he was pissed that she hadn't taken a harder line with his sister. He snorted. "She's eighteen. She's too young and inexperienced to live with a guy. He's a year older, so it's not like he's just starting out."

"I'm an adult, Jordan." Jamie snarled the words at her brother. "It's my life. You're just jealous because you haven't found a woman who will put up with you trying to control everything she does."

Amy had wanted to defuse the situation, not escalate the war. "I didn't think universities allowed freshmen to live off campus?"

"Most don't," Jordan said. "She's going to community college."

"Oh." Amy peered at Jamie. "Darcy and I both spent our first year at community college. Living at home with our parents wasn't too bad, and we both worked and saved enough so that we didn't have to work during the school year. We had summer jobs, but that was it. Let me tell you—having that kind of freedom is priceless. I had a lot of friends who juggled work and studying. It was tough. Some dropped out."

Jamie glared at her. "Of course you're on his side. You think I need a Daddy to tell me what to do."

Jordan's lips pressed together, and his face darkened. Amy wasn't sure why Jamie's comment upset him so much. She scrambled to think of something that would appease them both. "You know, being the older sibling is hard. One day your parents bring home this adorable little baby, and they tell you that you're responsible for protecting her—and you take that duty very seriously. Fast forward eighteen years, and she's grown up, but you've programmed yourself to protect her at all costs—even if it damages your friendship with her. It's hard when your baby sister grows up. Goodness knows Darcy has wanted to kill me many times because I've offered unwanted advice or tried to talk her out of something because I didn't think it was the best idea. It's taken a long time and a lot of work, but I've learned to let her make her own decisions. We're so close today because I finally learned to listen to her, and she learned to listen to me. It's a different kind of relationship that's taken us almost ten years to develop. You have to give Jordan some time to acclimate. He loves you, and he has your best interests at heart."

The anger seemed to drain away from Jamie. Next to her, Jordan visibly relaxed, and Amy hoped she hadn't overstepped her bounds. She sometimes stuck her nose where it didn't belong, and she didn't know if Jordan would tell her she'd gone too far, or if he'd just decide he liked her less. An orange butterfly flittered above nearby flowers lining the edge of the yard. Momentarily forgetting where she was and who she was with, Amy gasped with excitement and half rose from her seat to follow the insect's path with her gaze.

"Is that a monarch?" Jordan asked.

Amy's attention snapped back to Jordan and Jamie. Embarrassed at having been caught getting excited over a bug, heat traveled up Amy's neck. "Yeah. They're so pretty. I haven't seen one yet this year."

Jamie smiled like she had a secret. "That doesn't mean I have to do what he says."

"No, but you should at least have the courtesy to really listen and try to understand his concern." Turning to Jordan, she put her hand on his wrist, and she felt him relax even more at her touch. "And you have to try to come to terms with the fact that she's an adult who is going to make mistakes no matter how hard you try to stop her. If you want to be the person she turns to, then you have to learn to treat her as a friend instead of a child. She's not at all submissive, Jordan. She's too much like you for that."

"Amy?" Darcy called from across the yard. "I need you."

With a grin, Amy excused herself. She hoped what she'd said helped.

Jamie's smirk was almost too much to bear. Jordan frowned. "What's that look for?"

"You *really* like her. I think she likes you too. Notice how she scrambled to make you happy with how she supported your argument against me moving in with Marc. If she wasn't nursing a crush on you, then she wouldn't care about your opinion." Jamie's expression, if possible, grew even smugger.

"That 'Daddy' crack wasn't necessary." Not for the first time, Jordan regretted sharing his identity as a Daddy Dom with his sister. Though they'd discussed it at length and he was confident that Jamie understood, he didn't think Amy was aware of the nuance.

The smirk dropped from Jamie's face, and she peered at him with genuine concern. "She doesn't know?"

"No, she doesn't know. She's very innocent when it comes to these things."

"Well, she's very knowledgeable about other things."

He thought about the things he didn't know about her—like the fact she'd lived with a man before—and it only made him want to get closer to her.

"She's probably right." The resignation in Jamie's voice pulled him from his thoughts. "I should get my own room. Or maybe consider staying home with Mom and Dad. They have very reasonable rules, and they won't mind if I don't come home every night as long as they know where I am."

Jordan knew his parents would mind, but they wouldn't make a big deal out of it. He'd done similar things when he'd visited home during breaks from school or the military. Relief flowed through him that she was at least willing to consider other options. He smiled at his baby sister. "We do have a pretty cool set of parents, don't we?"

They'd stayed long past the end of the party, though he knew that Malcolm would tell him if he was overstaying his welcome. Giggles came from the center of the yard. Jordan looked up to see Malcolm, Mal's brother, and their father clearing away tables. In the space they'd created, Amy spun in a circle, arms extended. In each hand, she held a bubble wand. Angelina, Keith and Trina's 4-year-old niece, raced after the trail as she tried to collect bubbles without breaking them. Corey, the thirteen-month-old, toddled around on unsure legs and snatched at bubbles. Amy's mother held five-month-old Colin so that he could wave his arms and shriek at the bubbles. Several more kids ran around, but they were ones Jordan didn't know. In the center of it all stood Amy with a carefree and joyous smile. She laughed with delight at the kids' antics.

Jordan's attention focused on Amy. He loved the undisguised joy emanating from her. Darcy came by to grab the recyclable bottles that Amy had been collecting. Jordan stood. "Jamie and I can help."

"Thanks," Darcy said. She handed him an extra bag she had stuffed into her pocket, and she regarded him with eyes as clear and blue as Amy's. "I didn't want Amy to do any more work. She planned and put together this whole thing. It's a fantastic present, but I just wanted her to unwind for a bit. She loves blowing bubbles and playing with kids, so I handed her a bottle and asked her to keep them entertained. She'll make a great mom one day."

Jordan agreed, but he didn't see her behavior as indicating she wanted to have kids. "That was very nice of you. She needs time to unwind." *And let loose her inner little.*

Chapter Three

Looking in the mirror, Brian saw a man in his mid-thirties with wire-rimmed glasses and a receding hairline. When he'd cared about his appearance, he'd kept his hair clipped close to his head. He didn't want to be one of those pathetic assholes who tried to fight genetics. Bald was coming, and he was going to greet it with dignity.

Only now that his life had gone to shit, he didn't give a flying fuck about his appearance. Gone was the boyishly round face with the laughing eyes and mischievous smile. Dark circles were perpetually imprinted under his eyes. Full of nervous energy, he no longer slept unless he passed out.

He wouldn't even leave the abandoned and dilapidated house he called home if he didn't need to find another dealer. His had been arrested, and with the three strikes law, Brian was unlikely to see him again.

Head low, hands in his pockets, Brian cruised the likely areas. On one corner, some asshole shoved a flyer into Brian's chest, forcing him to take it. A glance showed it was the same flyer as the one he'd found two months ago on his car. Six weeks ago, he'd sold the car to score more crack, at which point his wife had left him, taking their daughter with her. *Can't get ahead?* This time it had an address, and it offered coffee and food. Since he couldn't find a dealer, maybe he'd get some java to tide him over.

The place wasn't too far away. It was in what had been an abandoned store. Brian pushed the door open to find the interior dimly lit, which was great because bright light sucked. Several people sat on folding chairs. Others stood. They all had a homeless look about them, and they smelled worse than he did. Or he'd gone nose-blind to his personal stench. A sweep of the place revealed no other obvious addicts. Fuck. He helped himself to a plastic cup of lukewarm coffee and a stale donut before anybody could kick him out.

"Hey, man."

Brian turned to see a silver-haired guy who was perhaps twenty years older. Time had been kind to his face, and the muscles bulging from his short-sleeved shirt warned Brian against trying anything physical. Withdrawal always made him cranky.

"Nice night for a walk."

That wasn't the comment Brian had expected. "Yeah. I guess."

"Forgive my directness, but you look like you've fallen on hard times." The man regarded Brian with patient expectation.

If he was a priest or some kind of do-good pastor, then maybe Brian could play on the man's sympathies and get some cash. "Yeah. Lost my job cause of the fucking government. Wife left and took the kid. Got evicted."

He nodded knowingly. "Come into the back room. We have better food there."

Over the course of the next few hours, Brian found himself pouring out his life story to this stranger who never offered his name. When he finished blaming corporations, the government, and wealthy people for all the world's ills, the man said, "I have just the thing, my friend." He went to a drawer, took out a pouch, and handed it to Brian. It contained two rocks of crack, Brian's favorite medicine.

Cautious and greedy, Brian took it. "How much?"

The man shook his head. "Gratis."

Nothing was ever free, but now that Brian had salvation in his pocket, he wasn't going to dwell on that. He stood. "Thanks."

The man held up a hand. "Not so fast."

Sonofabitch. There was always a catch.

"Day after tomorrow, there's a rally." He handed a card to Brian. It had a black-and-white outline of an eyeball on one side and an address on the other. "I think you'll find a lot of like-minded people there."

Brian took the card and tucked it into his pocket. He didn't give two fucks about other addicts, but if this was a place where he could score more crack, then maybe it was worth his time.

Chapter Four

The next day, Jordan took his sister to an exhibit featuring Diego Rivera and Frida Kahlo at the Detroit Institute of Arts. She patiently contemplated the art and listened to the docent leading the tour, and she seemed to really enjoy the exhibition of local art. It featured the work of a woman who used crayon shavings to make images, and it occurred to him that perhaps Amy might enjoy this excursion. Afterward he took Jamie out for a late lunch.

"I know a great in-line skate place." He hit the button on his fob to unlock his truck. Tomorrow was the last day of her visit, and though he'd been able to wrangle a lot of time off, he'd worked four of the seven days she'd been there. "And Ann Arbor has a kick-ass Hands-On Museum."

Jamie got in. "You know I'm not into kid stuff anymore, right? I don't skate, I don't want to go to the zoo, and I don't want to make a tornado inside a plastic bottle. How about we do grown-up stuff? It's a college town. Let's go to a dance club. You can flash your badge, and maybe we can get in for free."

He sincerely didn't want to take his sister to a club. The idea of watching her shake her ass and flirt with men who had more testosterone than sense did not appeal to him. "I'm sure you'll spend enough time at clubs in the next few years that you won't miss not going this one time."

She threw him a cheeky grin, and mischief sparkled in her dark brown eyes. "Or we could call Amy and see what she's doing. I liked her, and I'm afraid we'll all grow old and die before you make a move."

"You're such a drama queen. I like to take my time and really get to know a woman before I tell her about my kinks."

Jamie snorted. "You'd get farther more quickly with 'Hi, I'm into you. Call me Daddy and do what I say' as doing it your way.

Women appreciate honesty and directness, and she already knows you're a Dom."

"Is Marc?" Not only did he want to change the subject, but if his sister was this serious about a guy, it was time he switched from urging caution to mining for information.

"Didn't you find that out when you did an unauthorized background check using FBI resources?"

He shot her a dry look. No sense in denying it. "He came up clean, and our records don't contain that kind of information unless he has a criminal history or ties to certain organizations."

"Aww, poor baby. It must be killing you not to know." Her voice dripped with false sympathy.

He didn't reply. Silence would get her talking faster than more questions.

"No. We're not into that stuff, though that's not to say we won't eventually experiment. I hope he doesn't turn out to be a Dom because I know I'm not submissive. I wouldn't mind tying him up and making him squirm."

Jordan switched to mentor mode. It was the only thing that could save his sanity. "Safe, sane, and consensual. Always discuss and plan out a scene and be aware of the dangers and how to deal with them. If you're going to try bondage, have scissors or pruning shears nearby, something with enough strength to cut through the rope."

Jamie didn't say anything, but when he stopped at a light, he found her staring at him with wide eyes. "What in the world makes you think I want to talk to you about my sex life? I was trying to embarrass you into dropping the topic, and you turn into a fountain of information. No, Jordan. This isn't happening."

Pleased to have the upper hand for once in her visit, Jordan laughed heartily. When he finished, he squeezed her hand. "If you decide to explore kink and you aren't comfortable talking to me, at least ask me to give you the name and number of someone reliable and trustworthy to talk to, okay?"

Her face flamed red, but she nodded.

The ringing of his phone brought Jordan awake. He grabbed it and answered before that last dreamy image of Amy, naked and kneeling, faded from his brain. "Monaghan."

"Remember those reports from Chicago about the rash of crimes tagged with that eyeball symbol?"

He blinked, clearing the cobwebs of sleep from his brain as Brandy Lockmeyer's question penetrated. "Yeah." The report had caught his attention because graffiti had also shown up at the scene of an execution-style murder of a city council member from a Chicago suburb. His gut had told him it was practice for something larger.

"Wixom police nabbed someone in the act of robbing a gas station last night. They caught him drawing the eyeball on a wall with permanent marker."

Sitting up, Jordan glanced at the digital clock across the room to find it was just after eight in the morning. "Copycat?"

"I don't know." Brandy exhaled. Jordan pictured her sitting in her office, toying with a pen as she considered the angles. Chief Lockmeyer was one of the smartest women he knew. They'd met seven years ago when he'd been a nineteen-year-old daredevil with Special Forces, and she'd been on a secret mission that had gone sideways. He'd extracted her, but most of her team had been killed before he'd arrived on scene. Though she'd been shot, she'd fought at his side, and four of them had made it out alive. That had begun a friendship that almost nobody understood, mostly because they were not and had never been romantically involved. Once she'd rejoined the FBI, she'd badgered him to finish his degree and apply for a job. It had taken a few years, but he'd eventually followed her.

"You want me to check it out." It wasn't a question. She wouldn't have called otherwise.

"I know it's your day off, but I really need your gut on this one."

Jordan's instincts frequently hit the bulls-eye. "My sister leaves this afternoon."

"They're questioning him soon. Take Dustin and just watch. If you think it's nothing, then we'll let it go. It shouldn't take more than an hour."

Nothing was that fast. He snagged his jeans from where he'd thrown them across the foot of the bed and shoved a leg in. "It better not. I'm taking her to lunch and the airport."

"Of course." Her grin came through loud and clear. "Thank you for doing this."

His next call was to Dustin. "Chief called. She wants us to observe an interrogation. I'll text you the address and meet you there."

Dustin sighed. "I was going to take some comp time today. I bought a new spanking bench, and I wanted to surprise Layla when she gets home from work."

"I plan to be out of there no later than eleven. Jamie leaves today."

"Sounds good. That'll give me enough time to put it together and test the weight limit."

A couple years ago, their friend and fellow agent Keith Rossetti had bought a spanking bench from an online retailer, and the thing had collapsed under the weight of a sub who was well under the maximum load limit. Luckily nobody had been injured, but it had taught them to double check those kinds of things.

Jordan slid into the rest of his clothes and washed his face. A quick glance in the mirror made him wince. Though he shaved infrequently and didn't often get a haircut, sometimes those habits made him look more unkempt than he liked. It helped him when he was undercover, but right now, he wasn't on assignment, and he wasn't preparing to go under any time in the foreseeable future. Brandy had approached him about training to become a profiler, and he was seriously considering it.

For the time being, he brushed his hair and put it back in a ponytail. "Haircut," he muttered as he removed his shirt and got out the shaving cream to take care of his face.

Jamie was in the kitchen when he emerged. Bacon and eggs sizzled on the stove, and coffee was already in a mug on the counter. "I didn't put sugar in."

He kissed her cheek as she pulled a slice of bacon from the skillet and set it on a paper towel. "Thanks." Sometimes he wanted sugar, and some days he didn't. Today he didn't.

"You shaved. I like it. You have a cute face." She spooned scrambled eggs onto a plate and added four pieces of bacon. "Eat before you go. If you had time to shave, you have time to humor me."

He really didn't, but he sat down and scarfed Jamie's breakfast. He'd miss having someone to cook for him. Left to his own devices, he usually settled for cereal or instant oatmeal. He wiped his mouth and smooched her cheek one more time. "I'll be back by eleven. I'm taking you to lunch before we go to the airport."

"If you don't get back in time, I'll call a cab."

"I'll be back."

The drive to Wixom didn't take too long since he was going against traffic, and he found Dustin already in the interrogation viewing room when he arrived. His buddy wore a suit, as always. Jordan wore his badge on a string around his neck so that he wouldn't be confused with someone who should be on the other side of the bars.

"Did I miss anything good?"

"Matt Gordon was high when they brought him in last night. He has the shakes now, and he really wants a cigarette and a beer." Dustin pointed to the folder on the table between the officer and the perp. "I asked them to mock him when asking about the graffiti."

That was a good tactic. If it meant a lot to the man, then mocking him would get a rise. If it was nothing but drug-induced idiocy, then the man wouldn't care. "I have cigarettes in my car." Though he wasn't a smoker, Jordan's undercover work sometimes required him to smoke, drink, or snort various substances. He'd found early on that cigarettes were helpful gifts when dealing with a wide range of people.

"I thought we were just watching."

If his gut advised him to step in, he would. "Can't hurt to sit him next to me in the holding tank." There was no smoking inside the building, but sometimes rules needed to be broken.

The speakers crackled, and the tenor of the officer asking the questions changed. "Where was your partner?"

The perp shrugged, and his gaze flicked away. "I was alone."

Jordan crossed his arms. The man was lying. They needed to know why.

"Who was driving the getaway car?"

"I didn't have a car."

"You walked all the way from Redford?" The officer, Dan Birching, made his question sound more like a statement of disbelief.

"I hitchhiked."

"Take us through exactly what happened once again."

The perp exhaled. "Look, man. I admitted I did it. I held up the restaurant. I was high and looking to buy more crack. That's all."

"Where did you get high?"

"At a buddy's house."

"We'll need his name and contact information."

The perp wiped his hand through his hair. He was perhaps twenty-two. His dirty blond hair was streaked with sweat and grime, his teeth were yellow with nicotine stains, and his clothes were overdue as fuel for a funeral pyre. "I don't know his name. We meet up every now and then at parties. He always has a free rock or two for me."

"Was he driving the car?"

"No car. I walked." The perp bounced in his seat, his eyes darting around suspiciously.

"Video surveillance shows you arriving in a car."

"Right. Maybe he drove. I don't remember. Can I have a lawyer?"

Dustin shook his head. "Took him long enough. They went through the story twice already. He has a different story for how he got there every time. He's covering for someone."

"Handler?"

"Or girlfriend."

Jordan's gut screamed handler, so he shook his head. "They didn't ask about the graffiti, and Brandy said he held up a gas station, not a restaurant. I need a fine tipped marker."

Minutes later, the officer left the perp alone in the room. Dustin and Jordan introduced themselves in the hallway. Jordan let Dustin do the talking. "Officer Birching, I'm Agent Dustin Brandt, and this is Agent Jordan Monaghan. Thanks for letting us observe."

Officer Birching eyeballed them distrustfully. "Let me guess: You're taking Gordon off my hands."

"No. We don't want to interfere, but we do have a favor to ask."

"What?"

"Sit Gordon in the holding tank next to Agent Monaghan and leave them alone for five minutes."

"So you can mess up my bust?"

Jordan grinned. "No. I'm going to offer him a cigarette."

"He's invoked his right to a lawyer. You can't question him."

"Noted." Dustin gestured toward the office part of the building. "We need a fine point pen or marker."

Officer Birching turned out to have artistic skills. He drew a small version of the eye symbol found at the scene on the back of Jordan's hand. It looked like a prison tattoo. Then he cleared the other inhabitant out of the holding cell and locked Jordan in there. "You look right at home."

In response, Jordan affected a bored expression. He leaned his head against the cinderblock wall and relaxed on the bench. He didn't have to wait long before Matt Gordon joined him. The tank was small, with room on the benches for four or five to sit comfortably. Jordan had positioned himself in the center against the wall so that no matter where Gordon sat, he was nearby. Officer Birching left them alone. Jordan let the minutes pass. He watched Gordon fidget, and noted how the man's hands shook.

At last, Jordan extracted a pack of cigarettes from his pocket. He poured out a lighter and a stick. Matt Gordon looked around. "Man, you got anymore?"

Jordan gave Matt a long, measured look before tapping out another cigarette. He offered it, stretching out his arm so that his temporary tattoo showed.

Matt Gordon froze as his gaze lingered on the mark, but then he recovered. He lit up and inhaled deeply. "Are you here to kill me? Is this a poison cigarette? Because at this point, I don't care."

Jordan shifted, leaning forward to rest his elbows on his knees as he lit his own.

"I guess not," Gordon said. His hands shook despite the influx of nicotine. "I didn't say anything. You tell him that, okay? I didn't say a word, not to anybody."

Jordan stared. Legally he couldn't ask any questions, but he wasn't obligated to tell the guy to shut up. Silence, as always, worked wonders on a guilty conscience.

"Erikson didn't say anything either. He took off when the cops came, but I don't blame him. I'd have done the same."

Jordan pressed his lips together in disapproval.

"I know it's against protocol, but he got out. He can still serve The Eye. He can still carry out the mission while I'm in prison for armed robbery. I took all the blame on myself, so don't go after him, okay? I am willing to sacrifice for the cause. Just please take care of me in there, okay? You know what I need."

Jordan threw his unsmoked cigarette down and ground it out with his boot heel. He got to his feet as an officer opened the tank to let him out. He met Dustin in the corridor. They walked in silence through checkpoints and stopped where Officer Birching waited near his desk. He grinned. "Clever. You didn't say a word, and he sang soprano on his own. I guess it helps that you're a big son of a bitch who looks like an enforcer."

Cracking a smile, Jordan said, "I am in law enforcement."

Dustin rolled his eyes and offered his hand to the cop. "Officer Birching, thanks for letting us attend your party."

"Are you going to follow up on Erikson?" Birching shook both their hands. "And not tell me anything about what this is really about?"

"We won't be interfering with your collar," Jordan assured the officer. However, if the lead with Erikson panned out or if they found a restaurant that had also been robbed, then they might have to interfere. He handed Birching his card. "If you find out anything else, give me a call."

As they walked to their cars, Dustin asked, "Are you going to headquarters?"

"No. I'm taking Jamie to lunch, and then I'm dropping her at the airport. Tell Lockmeyer I'll be in bright and early tomorrow morning."

Dustin frowned. "You're skipping the part where we analyze what happened and discuss theories."

Jordan took out his cell and dialed Dustin. He walked away as Dustin answered. "I'll put you on my speaker, and I'll be hands-free. We can talk all the way home." He started his car and drove away, noting that Dustin followed him from the lot.

"Erikson was his partner," Dustin began.

"Sounds like they work in pairs," Jordan agreed. "And Gordon didn't seem surprised to see me waiting for him."

"You're thinking corruption at the local level? But why wouldn't his boss pull strings to get him out? I mean, if he can pull strings to have an enforcer waiting in a holding cell, he can probably bribe someone to look the other way while Gordon walks out the back door."

"He thought the cigarette was poisoned."

"Well, it's a lot of poisons. That's what makes them addictive. I don't know how you're not a chain smoker."

"I hate smoking, and so I refuse to do it when it's not part of the job. It stinks. I'm going to grab a shower before I take Jamie out." The expressway was crammed in both directions, but at least traffic was moving. "But I meant that he expects to be killed if he talks. He went out of his way to assure me he'd said nothing and that he was willing to do the time."

"I was watching on the monitors," Dustin said. "He looked proud, and he mentioned a mission. You know what that means."

It meant a coordinated effort by a group of people to accomplish something. "Yep. We need to figure out their objective and stop them."

"We're going to need to question Matt Gordon after we get some more evidence."

"Yeah, but he's a drone. I don't think he knows very much." The sign for the exit he needed warned him to get over. "Besides, I don't want to take him from Birching if we don't have to."

Dustin was quiet for a minute, and Jordan let him have time to think. Finally, he cleared his throat. "Speaking of birching, have you ever tried using a birch switch on a sub?"

Used to sudden shifts in topics, Jordan had no trouble keeping up. "No. I've seen it done, though. It's kind of like caning, but not as harsh. It doesn't sting as much, and the birch doesn't hold up. They're single-use implements. Why? Are you thinking Layla might enjoy it?"

"Don't know. I threatened to use a switch the other day. We went for a walk, and she got mouthy."

Layla was frequently mouthy. Jordan had actually met Layla before he'd encountered Malcolm. She'd been a SAM at a play party he'd attended. As Jordan wasn't much of a sadist, and Layla was thoroughly not his type, they hadn't played together. Jordan chuckled as he pictured Layla's probable reaction to the threat. "Let me guess—she got even mouthier?"

"No, but she did get excited. She said she's always wanted to try it."

His buddy sounded contented, and Jordan was happy for Dustin. "Then you should see where you can get some training."

"You don't know a guy?"

"I know a woman, but you'd have to go to Wisconsin for a lesson. Ask Malcolm. He's more active on the sadism front. Or Keith. He might have some personal experience with it."

"Good idea. I'm going to let you go now. Give Jamie a hug for me, and I'll see you tomorrow."

After a quick shower, Jordan took Jamie out to lunch. At the airport, he hugged her tightly. "I love you, little sister. I'm glad you came for a visit."

She released him and slung her bag over her shoulder. "I am too. Mom was right—you're homesick. You've been here for two years, and though you have made some great friends, it's not home."

The FBI frequently placed agents away from where their friends and family lived because it made undercover work easier. After a time, agents could request to be transferred closer to home. That's how Malcolm and Keith had ended up close to their families. Well, Keith had wanted to be close to Malcolm's family. He treated Mal's parents as his own, and he'd become romantically involved with Mal's sister.

Jordan had grown up in a close family. He missed his five younger siblings and Sunday dinner with his parents. "Two more years, and I can request a transfer." If he became a profiler, it would give him more flexibility in choosing his location, though it might require more travel.

"Or maybe Amy will make this finally feel like home for you." Jamie kissed his cheek and headed toward the machines that would check her bags. This was as far as he could go. He stayed there until she'd progressed far enough that he couldn't see her. Jamie's optimism was infectious. If things went well with Amy, maybe she'd want to move back to Wisconsin with him.

On the way home, he called Amy—not because Jamie had goaded him into it, but because he'd planned to anyway.

"Events by Amy. This is Amy."

Her greeting took him by surprise, but then he realized they'd never communicated by phone before. He had her number because he'd texted her for Darcy when she'd been in the hospital after having Colin. Clearing the sudden frog from his throat, he said, "Hi, Amy. This is Jordan."

It took her a second to respond, long enough for him to wonder how many Jordans she knew, but when she spoke, he heard the smile in her voice. "Oh! Hi, Jordan. How are you? Is your sister still in town?"

"I just dropped her at the airport. I wanted to thank you for talking to her. Where I couldn't get her to listen to me, she heard you loud and clear. Now she's considering living at home through her first year of college. My parents are going to be so relieved."

"Oh, that was no big deal. I didn't do much. She probably would have eventually listened to you and your parents."

Not his stubborn sister. Jordan shook his head even though she couldn't see it. "Not likely. It was you."

He pictured her blushing or shifting under the pleasant weight of his praise. She gave a little laugh as she accepted his gratitude. "Well, then you're welcome."

"I want to properly thank you. Let me take you out to dinner tonight."

"Tonight?" He heard noises in the background, papers shifting and perhaps a laptop closing. "What time? I rolled out of bed and started working, so I never got dressed."

Images of what she might look like naked assailed him. He wanted to ask what she slept in—did she wear something tiny and sexy, or did she wear something that showcased her little side? However he knew better than to rush. Despite Jamie's urging, he knew he had to go slow with Amy so he didn't scare her off. He glanced at his watch and calculated how much time she might need to get ready. "I'll pick you up at six. Wear a pretty dress. Text me your address, okay?"

Amy stared at her phone. Her conversation with Jordan had ended several minutes ago, and she still couldn't believe he'd called or that he wanted to take her to dinner. Then it hit her— this wasn't a date. He was thanking her for sharing her experiences with his sister and influencing her decision-making process. His order to wear a pretty dress just meant he planned to take her somewhere nice, and it reflected his dominant personality. Part of her was relieved, but mostly she was disappointed. And nervous. And excited.

With a start, she jumped out of her seat. She had three events scheduled for this week, and so far she had checked more things off her to-do list than she thought she would. When she'd first started her company, she'd learned the hard way which vendors were reliable and which weren't. Now that she'd been doing it for almost seven years, her checklists and timelines were fairly streamlined.

Rushing to the bathroom, she started the shower and wiggled out of her Hello Kitty pajamas. How embarrassing would it have been if he'd stopped by and seen her in them?

An hour later, she stood in front of her closet wearing only a bra and panties. What had he meant by *a pretty dress*? Without reservations, they weren't going to get into anywhere too dressy. She considered a sundress that had a great slimming effect on her hips, but it had long sleeves and the night was on the humid side. The last thing she needed to do was promote flop sweat conditions. With a sigh, she selected a flower-print frock with a scooped neck that Darcy said made her boobs really pop. If Jordan's gaze lingered for even a second, she'd feel vindicated.

The expected knock came precisely at six. Amy was still in the bathroom trying to put on enough makeup to accent her eyes and cheekbones—her best features—but not cross the line between looking good and trying too hard. She finished blotting the pink lipstick she'd chosen, gathered her confidence, and answered the door. Jordan had cleaned up well, and it transformed his appearance.

Gone was the shaggy, unkempt hair. He'd had it trimmed. Though it was still on the longer side, it was less biker-guy and more metrosexual. The perpetual five-o'clock shadow was missing as well, and she fought the urge to run her fingertips over his jaw to see if it felt as smooth as it looked. Normally Jordan wore loose-fitting jeans that looked like they were one wash away from falling apart. His shirts tended toward plain white or black. Tonight he'd traded his jeans and tee uniform for black dress pants and a white button-down. He'd gone from utterly hot bad boy to utterly hot gentleman.

Amy blinked away her shock. "Come in. I have to grab my purse, and then we can get going."

He smiled, an easy lift of his sensual lips, as he came inside. Keys dangled from one hand, and the other was shoved in his pocket. He looked around the living room of her small bungalow. Sample books lay scattered on her coffee table and sofa, and her latest attempt at a macramé handbag lay over the arm of the chair where she'd left it.

"Sorry about the mess. This is sort of my office." Technically the second bedroom was her office, but she hated being stuck in there. Since she lived alone, she saw no reason not to expand her operation to include the living room and kitchen.

"It's fine. You weren't expecting company, and I gave you short notice."

When she slipped into the kitchen to retrieve her purse, she saw a coloring book she'd left on the table. The steady back-and-forth and application of color helped calm her nerves and improved her concentration, but it was kind of a childish activity, and so she tended to hide evidence of this hobby. She shoved the book and tin of colored pencils into a drawer, and she grabbed her purse.

Jordan had moved to her bookshelf. His fingers traced the spines of several of her favorite titles—Dr. Seuss books she'd loved when she was little and her complete Nancy Drew collection. He crouched down, pulled a well-worn copy of *Chicka Chicka Boom Boom* from a lower shelf, and paged through it.

Amy watched, her anxiety skyrocketing. Most people didn't keep children's books out on a shelf unless they had kids. Nobody looked that closely at her bookshelf, not even Eric, who'd lived with her for two years. He hadn't been a reader.

Jordan glanced up, a huge grin on his face. "I love this book. It was one of my favorites. I read it to every single one of my brothers and sisters until they wouldn't listen anymore."

Tension left Amy. "Darcy and I once made up a routine to it. We made our parents watch us sing and dance to the whole thing."

He replaced the book and stood. "I bet you were cute."

Amy grinned. "I don't know about Darcy, but I was flipping adorable."

She thought he'd laugh, but he merely nodded thoughtfully.

Dropping the smile, she gestured to her dress. "Is this okay? You didn't say where we were going, but given that you look like what Trina says you look like for court, I'm wondering if I should change?"

His gaze traveled down and up, a trip of respectable length that did not make a pit stop at breast level. "You look gorgeous."

The compliment fell flat, mostly because she wondered if she'd sounded like she was fishing. Really she'd wanted to know if she should change into something more dressy. She slung her purse strap over her shoulder. "Then we should get going."

His frown was gone before it was fully there. She felt his magnetism behind her as she headed out. It didn't surprise her that he opened his truck door or helped her inside. No matter what he wore, he'd always been solicitous when interacting with her.

"You don't get motion sickness on boats, do you?"

"Not so far." Because she could do it without seeming too obvious, she looked at him while he drove. "You have a boat?"

"No. There's a restaurant on the river I've been wanting to try. It's called Huron Belle."

Amy had heard of the new place. It boasted elegant surf and turf served as the boat cruised up and down the Huron River. She perked up and clapped her hands together. "Oh, I've heard great things about their cheddar biscuits."

His husky laugh filled the truck's cab. "God, Amy. You're amazing. I love how the little things excite you."

As Amy lived in Ann Arbor, it didn't take long to get to the restaurant located on the edge of the river that wound through the vibrant city. Jordan escorted her up the ramp with his hand on her lower back. His palm was so large it made her feel small—a completely foreign experience. Having a larger frame and being 5'8 meant she was as big or bigger than most men she encountered.

They were seated immediately, and by the time the server brought drinks, the boat was sedately cruising down the Huron River. Amy looked around the upper deck and realized that not every table had a view as good as theirs. The setting was highly romantic. "Did you have a reservation?" She refrained from looking at Jordan as she asked because she wasn't sure she should have asked. Hearing that she'd been a last minute replacement for a planned date wasn't high on her bucket list.

"I know a guy. He owed me a favor."

Now she looked at him, her jaw dropping. "And you cashed it in on me? Oh, Jordan. You shouldn't have wasted this on me. I'm sure some beautiful woman would have loved to be here with you."

He reached across the table, took her hand in his, and captured her gaze in his chocolate pools. "I'm here with a beautiful woman, and I hope you like being here with me."

With the way he was looking at her, she could barely breathe. Heat crawled up her neck, and it wasn't all due to embarrassment.

Some serious chemistry seemed to be arcing between them. "I didn't mean—Of course I like being here with you. I just meant—"

"I know what you meant, and I won't have you diminishing yourself for any reason. If I wanted to be here with someone else, I would be."

Family was of primary importance to him. Amy was well aware of this. She'd heard Malcolm talk about how Jordan was from a close-knit family. To him, this was an appropriate way to thank someone for stopping his sister from making a potentially painful mistake. Amy nodded, and the server putting a basket of bread between them stopped her from having to say anything further on the subject.

Jordan thanked the server and distributed the bread plates. He lifted both dark brows in a dramatic gesture. "It's time to see if the biscuits live up to their reputation. Though if you don't like them, you're kind of stuck here."

Chuckling, she said, "I guess being on a mini-cruise is one way to stop people from leaving if they don't like the food. And nobody is going to get dressed up to jump overboard." She tore a flaky section from her biscuit and popped it into her mouth. Closing her eyes, she savored the way it melted on her tongue. "It definitely lives up to the hype."

She opened her eyes to find him regarding her with a hungry expression, and for the first time, she dared hope he might feel something more than friendship. After all, he didn't seem to be looking at the biscuit.

For the rest of the cruise, they shared stories about themselves. She'd talked with Jordan before about many topics, but they'd always been surrounded by friends and relatives, so they'd never touched on topics that were overly personal. He talked about growing up as the oldest of six and how much he loved undercover work. She told him about how seriously she took the role of big sister until Malcolm had come along. "It's like he took the burden off my shoulders, and now she's one of my best friends instead of someone I have to look out for."

"Who are your other best friends?"

"I'd say Paget. We've been friends since middle school. She moved to Madison for a job a few years ago, so we're not as close as we used to be, but I know she'd be here in a heartbeat if I needed her. And then there's Cori and Mandy. We roomed together in college, and we've remained close. Recently I've become friends with Layla because she hangs out with Darcy so much, and of course Trina. What about you?"

"You know Malcolm, Dustin, and Keith. I'm friends with Brandy, Liam, Jed, Lexee, and Avery as well. Everybody I know here is a fellow agent."

Amy rested her chin on her palm. "What about back home? You didn't know any of those guys until you moved here."

"When I go home, I usually get shit-faced with my buddy Dan. I always catch lunch with Rachel. If Steve or Keith—different Keith—are around, we'll get together. It's hard because we all went our separate ways after college. Most of them went into office jobs, and I went to Quantico."

Amy seized upon the lone female name. "Rachel?"

"She was my first mentor when I began exploring becoming a Dom. She's a Domina who sponsored munches, did demonstrations, and taught seminars in different techniques and philosophies. She still does those things sometimes, but she's in her seventies now and her health isn't what it used to be, so she has passed the torch onto others in the local community."

Knowing they weren't an item made Amy feel better, though she knew there was never a good reason to be jealous about the past, especially over someone with whom she didn't have a future. "I wasn't aware there were different philosophies. It all seems so cut-and-dried, with the Doms throwing out commands and expecting women to follow their orders or be punished for it."

Jordan stared at her thoughtfully as the server cleared away their plates and promised to return with the dessert cart. Once they were alone, he leaned in. "I thought Malcolm and Darcy explained the D/s dynamic to you? That doesn't sound like how Mal would phrase it."

Malcolm had patiently explained many things, and he'd given her a lot of articles to read. They'd answered a lot of questions and set her mind at ease about Darcy's relationship with Malcolm and the one she'd enjoyed with Scott before he'd been killed, but they'd left a lot of stuff in the air. "I know that sometimes women are in charge and the guys are submissive. Or in same-sex relationships, it's whatever fits their personalities. And I know that some people switch. But that doesn't mean I have a complete understanding of it. All the articles explain stuff, but then they end by saying that every relationship is different, which seems to negate most of what they said in the article." She took a breath to gather her rambling thoughts.

The server brought the dessert cart. Jordan looked at the selections. "What would you like, Amy?"

She'd eaten plenty already. "That sundae looks delicious, but I'm stuffed."

Jordan grinned. "A brownie sundae with two spoons." The server left, and Jordan closed his hands over hers on the top of the table. Amy shivered at the accidentally intimate contact. "Cold?"

As dusk had fallen, so had the temperature, but not that much. It was purely a reaction to Jordan's touch. "I'm fine."

"Every relationship is different because they're comprised of different people. There are no hard and fast rules, only common-sense guidelines. If you're not comfortable with something, don't do it. Being dominant doesn't give you a free pass to order anybody around, and being submissive doesn't mean you're obligated to follow orders. All points of authority and submission are negotiated by the people involved, or at least that's how most good relationships operate. I ask you to consider that any worthwhile Dominant who loves his or her submissive worships them and wants nothing more than for them to be happy. What they do and how they do it should always keep the submissive's happiness in mind."

Amy thought about it. "I understand what you mean in theory. And when I look at the people I know in those kinds of relationships, I see that they're happy and very devoted to one another, but all that seems rather vanilla—but not vanilla." She sighed. "I'm not very good at articulating this."

"You can ask me anything." He slid his hands around hers so that he was holding them.

She stared at the way his hands surrounded and engulfed hers. "I don't know what to ask."

"Perhaps when you look at their relationships, you don't quite see a dynamic that appeals to you?"

It was like he'd read her mind. She looked out over the water at the way the lights from buildings lining the shore shimmered on the surface. "I don't want to seem like I'm judging them, because I'm not. They're happy, and I'm happy for them." Looking back at Jordan, she admired the way the lights made his eyes seem infinitely deep. "I guess I don't quite see anything specific that appeals to me, just maybe some small parts, which kind of knocks me out of the kinky world."

He caressed the back of her hand with his thumb. "There's a lot more out there than those flavors. A D/s relationship isn't a one-size-fits-all thing; it's carefully built and nurtured by the people in the relationship. The key is to find someone you want to build a life with, and go from there."

The soft breeze, the great food, and the string quartet combined with his sweet sentiment, and Amy's breath caught. She wanted to say something, but she couldn't quite think while he looked at her with such significance and meaning.

The server brought dessert, and though he tried to set it down and sneak away, the moment broke. Jordan released her hands and gave her a spoon. "Have at least one bite. There's no way I'm going to eat this all."

Later that night, as they stood on Amy's porch gazing into one another's eyes, she yearned for him to kiss her. She waited for it, but he simply unlocked her door, handed over her keys, and said, "Thanks for coming out tonight. I had fun."

Amy watched him get in his truck. He waved before driving off. No kiss. She must have really misread his signals. It wasn't the first time she'd been an idiot. With a sigh, she resolved to not read into anything. He'd treated her to dinner to show gratitude. That's all.

Chapter Five

Attending the rally hadn't been high on Brian's list of things he felt like doing, but then he reasoned that like-minded people probably had more of that high-quality rock he'd enjoyed. As he'd smoked both crystals the man had given him, Brian had nothing else to do.

In a dimly lit basement in a rundown neighborhood not too far from the abandoned house where he was camping out, Brian found the stranger, who he'd decided to call Joe, and seven other people. Four of the men and two of the women looked around nervously. Joe conversed with two men and a woman. He waved at Brian, but he didn't come over. Since Brian wasn't sure of the nature of their relationship—friend? mentor? dealer?—he joined the group milling around the small space.

Pretty soon, one of the guys in Joe's group got louder. "It's these special interest PACs and SuperPACs that own the government. The public is too stupid to realize that every candidate groomed to look good has been bought and paid for." He went on to explain how the wealthy elite had control of the politicians and how the concentration of wealth among the one percent meant no regular people were ever going to get ahead.

Brian didn't care about politics or how overprivileged asswipes spent their money, but the man had a way of speaking that made it impossible to not listen. Plus, he might be a source for more of the free rock.

"They conspire to keep us poor, pay rock-bottom wages, and take away welfare. If we're too busy worrying how we're going to make the rent and feed our families, then we're not paying attention to how they keep all the wealth for themselves."

You want a nice car? Fuck you!

You want a decent house? Fuck you!

You want to not worry about affording a doctor when you get sick? Fuck off and die!

Now he had Brian's interest. It was like he knew exactly what kinds of hardships had slapped Brian around and why he needed a little something to help him get through the day. By the time Joe handed him two more rocks on the way out, Brian knew he'd be back for the next rally.

Chapter Six

"That one." Malcolm pointed to a card with a fancy font. "I like that one."

Darcy looked at him, calculating, Amy knew, whether he'd said that to get out of looking at more invitations. She picked up the one next to it. "What about this one?"

"The *L* looks like a *G*. This one is classy, yet legible. Don't underestimate the importance of being able to accurately read the invitation. Then people know who's involved, where to go, and when to be there." Malcolm slid his choice toward Amy.

Her gift to her sister was to plan her engagement party, which Malcolm insisted be informal, and her wedding, which Darcy insisted be elegant. Though she'd toted over most of her samples, she'd marked the ones she felt Darcy and Malcolm would like best. That way they could speed up the choosing process, which could be overwhelming. Since they only had a month before the big day, time was of the essence.

"Mal, the priest you wanted to use refuses to perform the ceremony. I brought a list of people you can contact. All of them have performed perfectly lovely ceremonies."

He frowned. "I called him last month. He said he'd be happy to do it."

Amy put a sticky note on the font and colors Malcolm had chosen and traded her invitation samples for menus. They already had a venue booked, and so their catering choices were limited. "He thought you were M.J., who apparently goes to church, whereas you do not. Not only that, but Darcy isn't Catholic. He won't marry you unless she converts and you show up for regular services. And he wants you to attend marriage counseling classes."

Malcolm exchanged a look with Darcy who merely arched an eyebrow. Turning back to Amy, he sighed. "Are you calling people on this list, or are we?"

"How much say do you want to have in who performs the ceremony?"

Darcy shook her head. "None. You pick, Amy. You've seen their work, and I trust you to pick someone who will perform a beautiful ceremony."

"Yeah," Malcolm agreed, jerking his thumb in Darcy's direction. "I'll concentrate on getting this one down the aisle, and you make sure romantic and legal things happen when we get to the end. Deal?"

Amy grinned. "Deal. Did you want to do flowers or food next?"

"Food," Darcy said. "I don't give a rip about flowers."

"You like roses." Malcolm looked appalled. "You said you like roses."

Darcy kissed the tip of his nose. "I like when you bring me roses because you always have a thoughtful reason behind how many you bring. Maybe you should handle the flowers."

Amy loved seeing her sister so happy. It was contagious, and Amy couldn't help but beam. The warm, fuzzy feelings brought back pleasant memories from the night before. "Food, then. I had the best cheesy biscuits last night." She spread out the three catering choices on the coffee table. "You probably want beef or pork, and chicken and fish choices. The caterer closest to Mal also offers vegetarian, vegan, and gluten-free options."

Darcy searched all the pictures. "I don't see cheesy biscuits."

"Oh, they aren't offered, though we could probably special-order them from the vegetarian-friendly place. Their bread is decent."

"Is that where you had them?" Mal picked up a glossy flyer that Amy had made herself. She'd found her clients liked to have pictures to go with the descriptions, and the places she liked to use didn't always have nice brochures. Sometimes fantastic caterers spent their time cooking instead of marketing.

"No. Jordan took me to eat on the Huron Belle last night as a way to thank me for talking some sense into his sister. She'd planned to move in with her boyfriend, and I convinced her that she had other options. It's her first year of college. The view and the food were amazing. If you want to go one night, I'd be more than happy to watch Colin."

Darcy and Malcolm exchanged a significant glance. Amy wasn't sure what silent conversation they had, but she figured it had something to do with asking if the other wanted to try the new restaurant.

Picking up a menu, Darcy scanned the descriptions. "Jordan took you to an exclusive, romantic restaurant just to thank you?"

Amy thought about the awkward start to the evening and the mixed signals she seemed to get throughout the night. "Yeah, well, it wasn't too romantic, but I see how it could be with the right person."

Malcolm cleared his throat. "Did you ever get together with Matt? I know you two were talking about a face-to-face."

After she'd indicated an interest in the *B* part of BDSM, her sweet brother-in-law had helped her set up a profile on an internet dating site, and potential dates had to go through him to get to her. "We met for coffee last Thursday."

Darcy smacked Amy's knee. "You didn't say a word! How did it go?"

Amy shrugged. "I don't really find the in-your-face dominance appealing. He made me feel defensive and claustrophobic. I don't think he meant to. He's probably a nice guy under normal circumstances, but he had some definite expectations about me submitting to him that made me uncomfortable."

Malcolm nodded. "Noted. I can see how Matt could come on a little strong, and that would be off-putting if you didn't know him. I'll keep looking."

"You can take a break," Amy said. "With planning your wedding and being in the middle of my busy season, I don't have time for trying to find someone to tie me up. Right now I need you to look at flowers. I think Darcy's picked out the caterer."

Darcy handed over the menu she'd been perusing. "I like the idea of a vegetarian option instead of chicken."

Amy put a sticky note on that choice too. They worked until Colin woke from his nap and Amy had to leave for another appointment.

"I appreciate everything you're doing for us," Malcolm said as he hugged her goodbye. "Darcy was crying last night when she was telling me how lucky she is to have you as a sister."

Darcy hugged her next. "I was crying because I was minutes away from starting my period and my hormones are raging, but you are pretty wonderful."

Jordan called later that evening. "I had a great time last night. You're a wonderful listener."

"Thanks." Amy laughed at how much it sounded like a post-date follow-up call. "So are you."

"I try to be. What are you doing right now?"

"I just had dinner, so I'm contemplating washing the dishes."

"How about skating?"

As it was the middle of summer, she knew he meant roller skating. She was surprisingly good at it, and she'd even spent a season on a roller derby team. The skating part had been fine, but she wasn't aggressive enough to be any good at it. "I'm game."

"Cool. I'll pick you up in five."

"Five?"

"I had a case that brought me into town. I'm five minutes away. Is that a problem?"

"Not at all." She beelined for her bedroom. "I'll see you in five."

Skating in sweats might be comfortable, but the pair she was wearing weren't very flattering. Maybe Jordan didn't want to date her, but that didn't mean she was going to look anything less than her best. She had pride. A nice pair of jeans and a cute yellow top with a big, floppy bow in the back did the trick. She finished changing just as he knocked.

Answering the door revealed the same Jordan she usually saw. The shaggy hair that she rather liked was back, as were his black tee and battered jeans. A pair of dark shades dangled from his grasp. The corners of his mouth turned up with a soft smile. He looked her up and down, and when his gaze didn't linger anywhere specific, she didn't have to hide a sigh. She'd figured out that Jordan wasn't the kind of guy who ogled women, especially not those he respected. Part of her wished he'd respect her a little less and stare at her assets a little more.

"You didn't have to dress up for me."

"You're just supposed to tell me I look great, and then you can ask if I have my own skates."

He laughed, but he didn't comment on her appearance. "Do you have your own skates? I have a saddlebag on my bike."

Amy's mouth worked to form words, but her brain needed a second to catch up. "I've never been on a motorcycle before."

"You'll love it. Grab your things, babe. Open skate started ten minutes ago."

She handed over her skates so he could hold them while she locked up. He didn't need to see her dirty kitchen or the stuff scattered all over her house. "I should warn you that I'm a pretty decent skater."

"Can you go backwards?"

"Yeah."

He stuffed her skates and purse into his saddlebag, and then he put a helmet on her head. Amy waited patiently as he tucked her hair in around her face and snapped things into place. "How does that feel?"

"Fine. My hair is going to look amazing when this comes off."

Flashing a wolfish grin as he adjusted the strap of his helmet, he said, "Just shake it out. That's what I do, and I'm told I look fine."

He looked fine all the time. He'd look fine covered in mud. Or chocolate and whipped cream. Amy shook the image from her head. "We'll see."

He swung his leg over the seat and did that jumping thing that started the engine. Though it was loud, it was quieter than she thought it would be. That explained why she hadn't heard him arrive. "Get on behind me and put your arms around my waist."

That sounded like heaven. Amy did it, but she held him loosely so she didn't press her breasts against his back. He adjusted her hold, forcing her to lean forward so that her girls were pleasantly flattened anyway.

"Relax against me. When I lean, you lean with me. Try not to stiffen up or counterbalance. I'll take care of all that. Got it?"

"Yep."

"It's about trust. Do you trust me?"

"Of course." He'd never given her a reason not to. She snuggled against him because he'd pretty much told her to, and he took off. The bike made louder sounds as it accelerated. He navigated the streets like a pro, driving conservatively, she knew, because it was her first ride.

She'd read about the vibrations of a motorcycle and how they were supposed to simulate masturbation, but she didn't feel anything that intense. Her butt took the brunt of the action, and it went numb after a few minutes. When they got there, he had her dismount first. She handed over her helmet and shook out her hair. "How does it look? And don't lie."

He removed his helmet and set it on the seat as he studied her flattened hairstyle. Wordlessly he ran his fingers through it a few times, fluffing it in some places and smoothing it in others. "It's good."

"Sometimes being a man of a few words doesn't work in your favor. You know I'm going to look in the mirror as soon as we get in there."

He shrugged. "Sexy. How's that?"

Like when he'd called her gorgeous, it wasn't what she'd been fishing for. Instead of letting it make things awkward again, she let the compliment roll off. "That's awesome. I could always use more sex appeal."

Handing her skates over, he shook his head. "I suck at giving compliments. You should know this about me."

She smiled to let him know no harm had been done. "I wasn't looking for a compliment. I was hoping my hair wasn't sticking straight up or weirdly plastered down."

"Then, no. It looks very similar to the way it did when I picked you up. I might have given it a little more body. After all, you have to compete with me, and I have awesome hair."

He did. She ruffled his hair. "Let's go skate. Are you any good?"

"I learned ice hockey when I was three. Played until I went to college."

While they waited in the admissions line, she glanced over and saw her reflection in the mirrored back of the claw machine. He was right. Except for it being a little fluffier, her hair looked exactly the same as it had when she'd left the house. However, the wide-eyed excitement in her expression was new. Riding on the back of a motorcycle had landed pretty high on her list of things she wanted to do again. With those saddlebags, maybe he'd be up for taking her on a longer ride, one where they stopped for a romantic picnic at the halfway point.

They skated for a couple of hours, talking as they zoomed around the rink. He held her hand for the couples skate, and then each of them entered the fun skating contests that had a free game of laser tag for a prize. Since some kids who looked like they spent their entire lives on wheels were there, neither of them won.

During their hot pretzel break, Jordan held up two shiny tickets. She eyed them curiously, reading the neon words on the label. "Laser tag? You didn't have to do that."

He grinned. "You were so disappointed when we didn't win any contests. I can't have that."

"You should know that aiming isn't my strong suit."

"That's okay." He reached across the table and squeezed her hand. "I'm very good."

They headed for the laser tag entrance once they finished eating, and Amy couldn't stop herself from jumping up and down with excitement. She thought she'd have to wait for her nephew to get older before she'd have someone who would enjoy playing these kinds of childish games with her. Yet here she was with a man—friend?—who not only indulged her, but who seemed equally happy to participate.

An employee took their tickets and ushered them to a room where they had to listen to the rules and watch a short video. She stood in front of Jordan, and he rested his hand on her shoulder the whole time. She liked how it felt proprietary and comforting at the same time.

In the next room, he grabbed two red vests. One he put on her, adjusting the straps until it fit better, and the other he donned himself. They greeted other players who had also chosen red, and in the ten seconds before a different employee started talking, they agreed not to shoot one another.

"The object of the game is to find the enemy bases and shoot them. At the same time, you have to keep them from discovering and shooting your base."

Amy leaned closer to Jordan. "Where are the bases?"

He shrugged. "I haven't played here before, but keep one eye on the ceiling. They tend to be overhead."

Her gun buzzed as it went live. "I'm going to get shot a lot."

"Stay close to me. I'll protect you."

The doors opened, and people flooded through. Jordan held her back so they were the last ones inside. "A few will stay close to the entrance, but most will have run to find high ground and look for the bases."

She got shot the moment they entered the room. Illuminated with black lighting, it was enough to make out glowing graffiti that marked the edges of walls and places where the flooring was uneven. Jordan shot quickly, taking out two preteens and a parental figure. He grabbed her hand. "Come on, babe. Let's kick some butt."

They ran up and down ramps and through the maze. Amy quickly adapted to the funky lighting and topography, and she felt that she landed as many shots on her opponents as they landed on her—though that was mainly due to Jordan, who kept shoving her out of the line of fire. She learned to turn around and guard his back against opponents who snuck up from behind.

Once when he did that, their enemy got in a clean shot, and Jordan went down. He slammed into the wall and let his body crumple down in slow motion. With a dramatic gasp, he dragged her closer, not stopping until her mouth was inches from his. She thought he might kiss her, but he only whispered, "Rosebud."

Mouth open, she stared at him, and in the silence, he closed his eyes and let his head loll back. She caught his upper body before it slumped over. "Oh hell, Jordan. I never made it through *Citizen Kane*. I don't know what it means."

His vest vibrated as his life powered back up, and he opened his eyes. "Nobody does, but it's fun to say."

She helped him to his feet. "All right, Rosebud, let's find a base." She tried to run off, but he caught her around the waist.

"That name is not working for me, little one."

With the way he was holding her body against his larger, harder one, she certainly felt little. She squirmed, but he didn't release his hold, and so she stopped. "Would you prefer if I called you Sir?"

Slowly he relaxed his hold. "Not particularly. I'm not a fan of that title."

She wanted to ask what title he preferred—or had she crossed an invisible line and stuck her foot in her mouth yet again?—but he headed off, dragging her behind. They caught up with some red team members and ambushed the green base, which meant they didn't lose as bad as the green team did. However, the blue team won.

When they arrived at her house, he walked her to the door and gave her a hearty hug. "I had a great time. Thanks for skating with me."

She hugged him back. He smelled heavenly, and his body felt good pressed against hers. "Thanks for inviting me."

Once again, he left without attempting a kiss. A few hours later Amy lay in her bed more confused than ever by his mixed signals.

The next morning found Jordan stuck in a small, dark room. The screen he watched flickered, throwing shadows around the place and reflecting asymmetrically from the tinted windows. Turning on the florescent overhead lights only made the details of the screens difficult to discern. It reminded Jordan of his great-grandfather who used to sit alone in a dark room and watch television until he fell asleep. Long after they were supposed to have been asleep, Jordan and his brothers used to dare each other to sneak downstairs and brave the eerie glow. Jordan always accepted the challenge. Not only did it give him street cred with his younger brothers, but Poppa would give him a handful of whatever treat he had nearby. He waited until after Poppa passed away to let his brothers in on the trickery.

But this was not nearly as fun or interesting. Watching local police interrogate suspects in a multitude of armed robberies didn't usually fall within their jurisdiction. However, now that they knew the robberies were related to the rash of crimes that ultimately ended in an assassination, it was their investigation.

Dustin took a hefty bite of his breakfast burrito and slurped his coffee. "I have no fucking clue what I'm looking for."

"Any indication that they committed the robbery because they're part of The Eye."

Dustin crumpled up his wrapper and threw it at Jordan's head. "Thanks. I had no idea."

Easily catching the projectile, Jordan launched it back. "This is definitely the sucky part of investigating."

"Do we have footage of the robberies? Maybe they left behind graffiti like Matt Gordon did."

It was a solid idea, one that had already occurred to Jordan. "Copies and crime scene photos should be here by tomorrow. At least we know what we're doing for the rest of this week."

"Yippee."

"Did you get that bench put together?" Jordan wasn't one for impact play, but he did like the bondage options a spanking bench presented.

"Yeah." Dustin grinned widely. "It was a definite hit."

"Rim shot." Jordan acknowledged the pun dryly.

"You can't say 'rim shot.' You have to actually make the sound."

"My way kicks the mockage up a notch." Jordan stretched his long legs under the table. "So, Layla likes it. You must not have used it for discipline yet."

"I can't discipline her physically. It's a hard limit."

Jordan nodded. He knew enough about Layla's background to understand why that would be a hard limit. "I prefer creative discipline anyway. There's nothing like the sight of a woman standing in the corner with her panties around her ankles. It almost makes you forget what she did to earn it."

"I haven't tried that one yet, but then again, I can't see it working with Layla. She'd probably shake her cute ass at me, and I can't resist her ass."

Jordan sat forward and rewound the video he'd been watching. Something had caught his attention, but he couldn't pinpoint exactly what. Dustin stopped talking. Working so closely for the past year, the pair had learned to read one another perfectly. Dustin stopped the tape he'd been watching and scooted closer to peer at Jordan's.

The door opened, but neither of them turned. The door closed, and whoever it was stepped closer. "Find something?"

Jordan recognized Malcolm's voice. "Don't know. I can't quite figure it out, but something is off." He rewound it again and played the tape. The perp's hands tapped against the table, a steady rhythm that belied a yearning for his next fix.

You were clean for five years. What happened?

I lost my job. My girlfriend moved out. Life went to shit. What do I have to lose?

Your freedom. You've admitted to armed robbery.

The perp shrugged. His gaze sidled around the room. *You got me.*

Jordan paused the tape and peered closer. The image was too grainy to be sure. "Matt Gordon had a similar attitude. He was taking one for the team."

Dustin frowned. "And they're both Jonesing for their next fix. But that's not enough to establish a relationship."

"Jordan's going on instinct again." Malcolm clapped a hand on his shoulder. "Now you have to find an actual link."

Jordan agreed. "Yeah. We need to question this guy."

"We need to finish watching film first," Dustin said. "Going out there armed with information is critical."

Malcolm pulled up a chair. "Speaking of armed with information, I'd like to know what's going on with you and Amy."

Dustin lifted a brow. "You and Amy? I'm crushed. I'm your partner. You're supposed to tell your partner these things. I told you when I went out with Layla."

"I didn't go out with Amy." Talking about it at this point seemed premature. What if it turned out that she wasn't compatible with him after all?

"You took her to dinner on the Huron Belle." Malcolm leaned back, waiting for the story.

Jordan recognized that it was time to come clean, though there really wasn't anything to tell. He didn't want to alienate one of his best friends. "I took her out to thank her for talking sense in to Jamie. Thanks to Amy, my sister isn't going to move in with her boyfriend for at least a year."

Malcolm frowned. "Oh. That's what Amy said."

The comment rubbed Jordan the wrong way. "She wouldn't lie. Amy's a very honest woman."

"True," Malcolm said. "And helpful. She's nothing if not nurturing."

Amy needed to be nurtured. She spent too much time taking care of other people. "And I took her skating last night. We played laser tag too. It was fun."

Dustin perked up. "You think she's a little?"

He had his suspicions. And hopes. "Maybe." He looked at Malcolm. "I'm not going to lie. I find Amy very attractive. I know

~ 58 ~

she's open to exploring the lifestyle, but she doesn't know anything about the Daddy/little dynamic. My plan is to spend time with her and develop a friendship."

"You want to take it slowly." Malcolm narrowed his eyes. "When are you going to tell her about your brand of kink—before or after she falls for you?"

"Before. I don't plan to do anything not on the friend level until I've told her everything. Then, if she wants to explore a relationship, we can. If not, then I've made a new friend. You can never have too many friends."

Mal looked away, thinking, and that worried Jordan. When Dustin had told Malcolm about Layla, Mal's reaction had been immediate. Ditto for Keith and Katrina—though his response to that pairing had been a little on the violent side.

"I won't hurt her. I'm being very careful."

At this, Malcolm nodded. "I can see it now. It explains so much. I wonder why I didn't see it before?"

"Because you're focused on Darcy and Colin." Dustin sipped his coffee. "Which is okay."

"It explains why she hasn't clicked with any of the Doms I've picked out for her."

This was news to Jordan. He scowled. "Why are you picking out Doms for her?"

"Because she asked me to. She signed up on a dating site, and I vet potential candidates. I've approved a few, but so far she hasn't done more than meet with any of them for coffee. If what you suspect is true, then I've been going about this all wrong."

It rankled to know that Amy was actively looking for someone when he was right in front of her face, but at least she was going about it safely. Malcolm would not only interview each man, but he'd run a background check as well. His scowl eased as he reminded himself that she didn't belong to him, and she had every right to go on dates. "Well, you can stop looking until further notice."

"She already asked me to take a break. She wants to focus on the wedding, and I think she's discouraged because she hasn't liked anyone yet." Malcolm got to his feet. "At least there's no chance of her being thrown into this investigation and put into danger like the rest of the women in my life. Jordan, I trust you to treat her well. However, be extra careful. She wears her heart on her sleeve, and that makes it easy to break. If you hurt her, Darcy will never forgive you."

The rest didn't need to be said: If he was in the doghouse with Darcy, it would damage his friendship with Malcolm. Jordan nodded. "Noted."

Dustin clapped his hands together. "It's the way he's looking around the room, as if he thinks someone is watching."

That was it. Jordan's eyes widened. "Yes. That makes sense. Gordon wasn't surprised to see a man on the inside."

"Looks like you're going to need warrants for surveillance and listening devices," Malcolm said. "I'm going to get Dare on this. By the time this gets going, I'll be on my honeymoon."

Liam Adair was gifted with bugs and hacking. Though Jordan hadn't worked directly with Dare before, they sometimes hung out during their off hours. He nodded. "Sounds good."

Malcolm sighed as he headed to the door. "I've been called in for a meeting with the Director. I probably shouldn't be late."

Dustin chuckled because Malcolm was habitually tardy. "What are you in trouble for now?"

"Don't know. I'm not aware of anything I've done lately to piss off the higher-ups. Maybe he has a wedding gift for me." Malcolm flashed a wry smile before closing the door behind him.

Jordan wasn't inclined to comment on his buddy's penchant for playing fast and loose with rules and FBI procedure, so he merely exchanged a look with Dustin that communicated a sincere hope that nothing was amiss.

———

"Agent Legato is here to see you, sir." The unexpectedly smooth baritone floated through the intercom on the phone.

Miguel Lawrence enjoyed a moment of disgust before schooling his features to disguise his true feelings. He hated Malcolm Legato because the man was too good at his job. In the past few years, the exceptional agent had walked on the edge of being too close to The Eye. Taking down Victor Snyder had presented a serious blow to his arm of the organization, and Legato had proven to be relentless when it came to investigating the information gleaned from the hard drive he'd recovered from his fiancée's dishwasher. Reining in his impulse to indulge further in feelings of hatred, he told his assistant to show the agent into his office. "Show him in."

Legato entered the room as if he owned it, exactly the opposite of the attitude Lawrence expected of his subordinates. "Good morning, Director. How are you?" He held his hand out, not offering a handshake, but demanding one.

This was another reason he hated Legato. In fact, he hated almost all the agents under Brandy Lockmeyer. The bitch had a knack for hiring agents of both genders with dominant personalities. Even the women didn't know their place. Lawrence shook hands briefly, controlling the duration, and then he indicated the chair across from his desk. At least the fucker sat when ordered to do so. "Agent Legato, I've called you in as a courtesy. I'm officially closing the book on the Snyder investigation. You've mined as much data from that drive as you're going to get, and your talents are needed elsewhere."

As expected, Legato frowned. "With all due respect, Director, we've linked information on that drive to the Friedman investigation. It helped us crack a nationwide human trafficking ring and saved over one hundred and seventy children who were being exploited. There's more on the drive, but it's encoded."

Lawrence knew all of this. He'd seen the files on the drive—both the encoded and unlocked ones—and he needed his agents to stop digging. If they didn't, then the Detroit operation would go the way of the Chicago cell, and he'd end up in Federal prison. He smiled tightly. "That's precisely the reason I'm sending it to Quantico. They have more resources for this sort of thing."

"Sir, I'm close to cracking the encryption. I just need a little more time." Malcolm's jaw set firmly, and Lawrence recognized the stubborn resolve that led to such a high rate of case closures. That rate wasn't in The Eye's best interest.

Leaning back against the edge of his desk, Lawrence positioned himself to loom over Agent Legato. He sought to diminish the man's power. Judging by the way Legato's dark eyes flashed, he considered his move successful. "Our resources are already stretched thin. I've indulged you in this project for long enough. It's time for you to focus your efforts on your other cases. By my count, you have five open investigations and four recently cold cases. The families of those victims deserve answers, Agent Legato. It's your job to provide them. And I need not remind you of the above-average number of infractions and reprimands recorded in your file already."

Duty meant the world to this agent. It was his Achilles heel. Lawrence watched a war rage behind this agent's eyes, but at last acceptance won the battle. It probably hadn't hurt to remind Legato of the problems in his record that already stood in the way of him ever getting a promotion. "You're sending it to Quantico, then?"

"I already have." And if a powerful magnet happened to erase all that data en route, all the better. "Any information they uncover pertaining to this branch will be sent our way."

"Fair enough." Agent Legato rose in such a way that left no doubt he hadn't surrendered an iota of his personal power. "Thank you, Director. If there's nothing else, I won't take any more of your time."

This time Lawrence extended his hand, but he motioned to the door. "You can go."

As he watched the door close behind the dedicated agent, Lawrence allowed himself to revel in a moment of smug satisfaction. He'd blunted the tip of one thorn, but he had several more to remove. Monaghan and Brandt were next on his list. The men were wading into dangerous territory with their investigation. This would have to be managed carefully. Of course, in a perfect world, these men would become stalwart followers of The Eye. Under his control, they'd become mercenaries. They'd be powerful assets that would pave the way for Lawrence to eventually take over The Eye.

Now he needed to make sure Legato stayed on his leash, and making sure the agent's immediate supervisor kept a close watch was the next item on his agenda. He pushed the button on his intercom. "Get me Brandy Lockmeyer."

———

Amy didn't see Jordan for the next few days, though he called and texted several times. Their interactions were completely innocuous, and that kind of pissed her off. She hated the mixed signals. What if he saw her as a replacement for his sister? She decided on casually digging for the truth via text.

Do you ever get homesick for Wisconsin?

Since it was the middle of the workday, she wasn't surprised when his reply came a few hours later. *Sometimes. Why?*

Just wondering.

That's not an answer.

His dominant tone came through loud and clear with that one. She sighed. *It seems like you miss your sister.*

What makes you say that?

You keep calling and texting me.

I don't see how one thing has to do with the other. Maybe I like you.

Her heart thumped, but she refused to let her immature side *squeee* over that one. He didn't mean anything substantial by it. *Maybe I remind you of one of your sisters.*

You do not remind me of any of my siblings or of home. You're interesting and we have fun together.

A buddy—that's what she was. She was the safe female friend who wouldn't raise eyebrows with any woman he dated. It made sense, and Amy resented being cast in that role. When she didn't reply, he texted again. *Babe—What's wrong?*

Though he'd used the term before as an endearment, she didn't reply. Her bratty side had been riled.

Do you want me to leave you alone?

Did she? *No.*

Are you busy Sunday afternoon?

He knew her schedule was open on Sunday. Amy couldn't bring herself to make up an excuse to not go. What if he really liked her and she blew it by not going? Was indulging her inner brat worth ruining a sort-of/maybe with Jordan? *I should be home by 2.*

At two o'clock Sunday afternoon, he knocked on Amy's door, the contents of their last text exchange playing through his mind. He couldn't pinpoint the cause of her upset, and talking with Malcolm hadn't been helpful. Mal had merely shrugged and said he hadn't talked to Amy about anything but wedding-related topics.

The door opened, and Amy stood before him in a playful sundress. The bodice hugged her breasts and accented her generous curves, and the flowered skirt flowed around her legs. The whole thing was held by two straps on each shoulder. Undressing her would be a simple matter. He struggled not to stare at her shoulders as if he could move those straps by telekinesis, and so he forced his gaze upward because he'd done so well not indulging in his need to stare at her breasts. Staring would lead to touching, and they weren't there yet.

He met her crystal blue gaze. "You look nice."

This time she smiled at his compliment. He'd finally stumbled upon the right thing to say. "Thanks. So do you."

He opened the screen door. "Can I come in?"

"I'm ready," she said as she stepped aside to admit him. "I just need to grab my purse, and we can go."

"I want to talk first."

She twisted a strand of hair around her finger nervously, and he noticed that she'd pinned it back with two barrettes. Her appearance and innocent demeanor combined to make his dick jerk to life. He breathed to maintain control. It wouldn't do to try to talk to her about what was bothering her while he sported a raging hard-on.

He perched on the back of her sofa that delineated the space between the entryway and the living room, and he took the hand that betrayed her nerves between his larger ones. "Amy, tell me what's wrong."

"Nothing's wrong."

"Bullshit. You only get bratty when you're upset. Tell me how asking if I'm homesick turns to you getting upset that I call and text you." Yeah, he'd noticed how her bottom lip turned down in a pout whenever something bothered her, and he'd also noted how she lashed out childishly when she wasn't happy. These were behaviors he'd deal with when she gave him the right.

She tried to take her hand back, but he didn't let her, and that bottom lip sprang into action. "Nothing's wrong. Maybe I had an off day, okay? It's nothing to be concerned about."

"Babe, I know when something is bothering you. You can say anything to me. Let's have it."

She looked away, and he let her gather her thoughts. "Your behavior puzzles me. I get that you took me out to dinner to thank me for helping with your sister, but I don't understand the roller skating and the laser tag. I don't understand why you're suddenly calling and texting. I've known you for almost a year, and before last week, I didn't even have your phone number. You're younger than me, and I'm totally not your type, and none of this makes sense."

It made total sense to him. "I like you, Amy. I always have. If you need to put a label on what's going on between us, I'd go with friendship. Maybe it will develop into something more and maybe it won't. I think it would be a mistake to rush into defining what's still forming."

Her gaze returned to meet his, and he let her search his face for as long as she needed. Finally she nodded. "Friends. But you're hiding something."

Releasing her hand, he stood and headed toward the door. "Just because something hasn't been revealed doesn't mean it's hidden. People take time to get to know."

She grabbed her purse and slung it over her shoulder. It dislodged one of the straps, and immediately his gaze dropped to her breast, but the bodice fit too tightly. It remained in place, and Amy fixed her strap. "You're right about that, but I still think you're not telling me everything."

He opened the door to his truck for her. "In time, little one."

Her putt-putt game was a mess. There was no way in hell he'd ever invite her to play eighteen holes on a real course, not that she'd enjoy it anyway. No matter, this way he could stand behind her and correct her swing. By the tenth hole, she was able to sink the ball in nine strokes. He'd given up keeping score.

"Malcolm told me that he's interviewing Doms for you."

She missed the ball completely. Glancing up, she gave him the evil eye. "He was. I'm taking a break."

"Why?"

She wound up for the swing. He stopped her before she could bat the ball all the way to the next putting green. With one hand on her hip, he corrected her stance yet again. "If you want, I can take you to the batting cages next weekend."

"Don't be an ass," she said. Wiggling her ass, she settled into the wrong stance again. "You're asking things on purpose to distract me and make me miss."

"There's nobody behind us. Stop playing for a minute and answer my question."

"I don't want to answer your question. It's none of your business."

He got out of the way as she swung and missed. "Since we're friends who aren't defining anything yet, it is my business."

She leaned on her putter. "If you must know, I don't like the process. I don't know what Malcolm asks these guys, but whenever I meet one for coffee or lunch, they always want to know my hard limits and fetishes. Since I've never done any of this before, I don't know what those are, and then the last guy—he started in on how I should kneel in his presence and I should like what he tells me to like. He was upset because he'd ordered a bran muffin for me. He didn't even ask what I like, and I don't like bran muffins. That's not going to ever change." She lined up the next shot. "Maybe I'm not submissive. The idea of being tied up appeals to me, but the rest of it—" She pursed her lips in that bratty pout.

A streak of jealousy ran through him, especially when he pictured her on her knees before anybody else, but he forced himself to focus on her concern. "No dominant who is worth anything would expect your submission based on a meeting or ten. It takes time to get to know someone, to understand what makes them tick, and to build trust. After that, you can begin to have conversations about limits and kinks. All that has to happen before you can want to give something so precious as your submission. You're not being unreasonable. Go with your gut. You have good instincts."

She swung, and by sheer chance the ball came very close to her target. She celebrated with a loud *woo-hoo* before turning back to him. "That's right. I forgot you were one of those mentor people like Dustin. I probably should have you vetting prospective dates instead of Malcolm. He means well, but I haven't been impressed by his selections so far."

The idea of her dating anybody else made his blood boil. Maybe they weren't dating, but they were heading in that direction. "Not a snowball's chance, babe, but I'll tell you one thing." He lined up his shot and sank it in one swing. "You are thoroughly submissive."

She eyeballed the distance between her ball and the cup.

"The green is curved. Hook it to the left."

"Thanks." She positioned herself incorrectly. He moved her and helped her line up the shot. She sank it easily. "How do you figure I'm submissive? You've only seen me socially."

A chuckle escaped. "You are one of the most giving, nurturing people I've ever met. Even your business is designed to give you ways to serve others in order to make them happy."

"I don't plan events because I want to serve others. My business is successful because I'm good at what I do."

He fished their balls from the cup and carried them to the next hole. "I'm craving lasagna. What is your first inclination?" He set her ball on the tee.

She shrugged. "I don't know. Make you a lasagna?"

"Really? That's the first thing that came to mind?"

She blushed. "Sort of. I wished I would have known you wanted lasagna, and then I would have made it already so we could have it when we got back from playing golf. I'd have to heat it up, of course, but lasagna takes some time to make if you're going to do it right."

He let her have four shots in a row before he put his ball on the tee. "What if I changed my mind, and now I want steak?"

She frowned. "I don't have any steak. I'd have to go shopping."

"That's submissive, babe. You're a people pleaser, but only for people you care to please. If you're not careful, someone will take advantage of your good nature. A good dominant will protect you, leave you free to be who you are." He aimed for the center hole on the windmill and was rewarded when it spat his ball out in the upper part of the green near the cup.

She exhaled hard. "Do you want steak or lasagna?"

"Ice cream. It's hot out. Take your shot. After this hole, there's an ice cream stand. We'll get double scoops and take a break."

He waited until her pink tongue darted out to lick a drip of ice cream from her cone to ask her about bondage. "So you want to be tied up?"

"In theory. I've never actually tried it." She licked again, and he decided that ice cream wasn't such a good idea. The imagery was almost too much, and the crotch of his jeans suddenly became very snug.

"Would you like to?"

She looked at him, curiosity bursting from her in a shower of unvoiced questions and sputterings.

"Under controlled circumstances and with someone you trust."

"And then what? Bondage for the sake of bondage doesn't seem to have a point."

Oh, it did, but they'd get into that later. He bit into his cone and chased the rest of

the cold vanilla ice cream stuck in the narrow bottom. "Sensory play. I'll blindfold you so that you can focus on what you're feeling."

"I'm not into pain," she said. "I don't want to do anything that will hurt."

"Not a problem."

Her eyebrows drew together in a sharp V that echoed in the crease marring her chin. "Jordan, I don't know. This doesn't seem like the sort of things friends do."

"Friends do things like this all the time."

She stared out over the landscaping dividing this hole from the others. "It just seems so intimate."

"It's very intimate, and many people scene who are just friends. Scenes do not have to—and frequently don't—include sexual elements. It requires trust and an adventurous spirit. Don't you want your first experience to be with someone who simply wants to help you get to know yourself better and who won't put pressure on you to do more than you really want?" He had a huge list of reasons why he was the perfect person to introduce her to this world, but he knew that pushing too hard would be counterproductive. Amy was brave and curious, but she was also facing every fear and insecurity she'd ever harbored about bondage and the lifestyle. He squeezed her hand. "Just think about it. We have nine holes left before you have to make up your mind about what you want to do afterward."

Chapter Seven

Did she want steak or lasagna, or did she want to let Jordan tie her up and do things that belonged to the mysterious Sensory Play category? Amy frowned as she lined up her shot for the sixteenth hole. He was putting no pressure on her at all. After they'd finished their ice cream, he hadn't brought it up. She felt his touch on her hip, pushing it into alignment to improve her aim. Relaxing, she let him correct her stance. "Thanks."

"You're getting better. By the end of the course, you'll have it down."

It had occurred to her that she could continue doing it wrong just so he'd keep touching her, but then, she reasoned, he'd eventually give up, and she'd still be doing it wrong. She hit the ball a little too hard, and it sailed past the cup. "Darn."

"Not bad. Don't be so hard on yourself. You came close, and that's an improvement." He lined up his shot and sank it neatly.

"Would we negotiate everything beforehand? Plan out every detail?"

"No." He didn't pretend to not know she'd changed the topic. "If you had any experience, then yes, we could do that. For this, I'd try a few different things so you could decide what you do and don't like."

She thought about that as she tapped her ball into the cup. "What if I don't like it?"

He retrieved their balls. "You're familiar with the concept of safewords."

She didn't have the sense he'd asked a question, more that he wanted her to explain what she knew. "I know the stoplight system. Red halts everything. Yellow pauses the scene for communication, adjustments, and bathroom breaks." Once she'd come to accept that the BDSM lifestyle wasn't a form of abuse, her sister had opened up about many of nitty-gritty details. And she'd heard the guys talk about being dominant. They took the safety precaution aspects of it very seriously.

"So you'll have safewords. I'll be talking to you a lot so you know you're not alone."

It hadn't occurred to her that he would leave her alone when she was in a vulnerable position. She set her ball on the tee, lined up the shot, and took a swing. It rounded the bank perfectly, bounced twice from the edges of the narrowed curve that linked the two parts of this tricky hole together, avoided the waterfall, and went straight into the cup. Her draw dropped. She looked at Jordan, her eyes so wide she felt they might pop out. "You saw that, right?"

He wore a wide grin. "Your stance was perfect."

Dropping her putter, she clapped her hands over her heart. "A hole in one. I never thought I'd be able to do that."

He hugged her with one arm and pressed a kiss to the top of her head. "You can do anything you set your mind to, little one."

"Yes." She didn't necessarily agree with him, but she was no longer talking about her amazing feat. "I want to try it with you."

"All right. Let's finish this, and then I'll take you to my place."

She'd never been to his place. It made sense that they'd go to his apartment because that's where his equipment would be located. The drive took a little time because he lived two counties away. They mostly chatted about movies and television shows. She figured he wanted to keep the conversation light to put her at ease.

His apartment was exactly like Jamie had described—pristine and sanitary. Amy chalked that up to his modern décor. There was too much shiny metal and not enough color. It could use some fabric and softness to make it homey. Normally she wouldn't judge anybody's home, but this seemed so unlike Jordan. Standing there in a black fitted shirt and worn jeans, his face scruffy from a day's growth, he didn't seem to fit. The lack of color was him, but the sharpness of the furniture reminded her that perhaps she didn't know him all that well.

"What do you think?"

"It's clean." She wasn't going to say anything critical, not to a guy who was planning to tie her up.

He frowned. "You don't like it."

"It's fine. I just pictured your place with more leather, and maybe framed photos of your family on the walls."

He gestured to the sofa. It was the kind with an exposed metal frame and thin cushions for the seat and back. "It's more comfortable than it looks. Take off your dress and sit down."

She hadn't expected him to say that. She looked at her bright yellow sundress, the only spot of real color in the room. "You want me to get undressed? In here?"

"I need to do a few things before we can begin. If you need to freshen up, the bathroom is the down the hall, first door on the left. When I return, I expect to see that you've followed orders."

Orders. His tone had shifted, becoming harder and more commanding. This was definitely his Dom tone. A shiver of anticipation ran up her spine. Finally, being with a Dom seemed right. "Should I call you Sir or something?"

"Let's hold off on titles for now." He disappeared down the hall.

Amy made use of the bathroom. She combed her fingers through her hair and redid her ponytail, and then she checked to make sure she didn't have anything weird going on with the parts of her skin that would be exposed. Standing in front of the mirror wearing only her bra and underwear was a sobering experience. Though she'd worn her prettiest, laciest underthings, there was no way Jordan was interested in her as anything more than a friend. With a sigh, she hung her dress on a hook on the back of the door. He found her a few minutes later perched on the edge of the sofa, which was surprisingly comfortable, without her dress.

He sat down next to her, but he leaned back and stretched his arm along the back. "What's your color?"

She stared at her hands, folded neatly on her lap, and hoped he hadn't meant for her to be completely naked. "Green."

Moving, he slid his leg on the other side of her so that she sat between his legs. He tugged at the band holding her ponytail, taking her hair down. She didn't move, but she did close her eyes when he ran his fingers through her hair and massaged her scalp. A little mew of pleasure escaped as his thumbs moved lower, pressing circles on either side of her spine. She couldn't remember the last time she'd indulged in a massage.

He touched her shoulders and back, alternating caresses with light massages. When he finished, he rested his hands on her thighs, this fingertips feathering barely-there caresses on her skin. "The idea of sensory play is to engage most of your senses. I'm going to put a blindfold on you so that you can focus on what you're feeling."

Without waiting for her response, he tied a silky blindfold around her head. It was wide enough to block all light, and it was soft enough that she didn't mind wearing it.

She felt him move, and now she had the sense he was kneeling in front of her. He tugged at the edges of the blindfold. "Open your eyes. Can you see anything?"

Her eyes had been closed because she didn't see the point to having them open under a blindfold. She opened them now, and she realized she could make out some light through the fabric. "I can see some light, but no shadows."

"Perfect." He stood and tugged at her hands. "Stand up. I'm going to lead you down the hall to the guest room. I've set it up for our scene. Ready?"

He put one arm around her waist and held her hand as he led her down the hall. She sensed the air change as they passed the open door to the bathroom, and she thought about what she looked like without her dress on. Her generous curves were probably a bit too much for a man like Jordan who was made up of solid muscle. "Jordan, you know, you don't have to do this if you don't want to."

"I do know that. Thanks for reminding me. Safewords work both ways, little one. If I want to stop, I'll call red."

She had not known that, but it made sense. There had to be times when the Dom needed or wanted to stop a scene. He turned her to the left and led her into the guest room.

"I'll give you a tour later. I kind of think it'll be a better experience if you don't know what the room looks like. Stand here. Push your feet into the floor to avoid swaying. I'm not going to tie you to anything just yet."

He draped a heavy necklace around the back of her neck, and she realized it was rope. She stood as still as she could while he wrapped it around her torso, looped it around her shoulders and between her legs. He moved around her, pulling, tying and sliding the rope around her body. Though it wasn't too tight and it didn't inhibit her movements, it held her like a firm embrace, and that made her feel safe and calm. She didn't know how long she stood while he did his thing, but when he turned her and took off the blindfold, it seemed like an hour or more had gone by.

She blinked as her eyes adjusted to the light. He'd positioned her in front of a full length mirror, and she couldn't help but slide her gaze away. "What time is it?"

"Why? You got a hot date?"

"No, of course not. I just...I mean...I lost track of time."

He lifted her chin, and she saw his grin. "I know. You went into a light subspace. Pretty amazing for your first time."

"That's not normal?"

"Normal is relative. Some subs chase that feeling for years; others get there quickly. Look in the mirror."

She didn't want to, but his tone didn't leave room for discussion. The first thing she noticed was how her skin seemed to glow. Her eyes shone. Yes—so far, bondage definitely was working for her. She let her gaze wander down, taking in the way he'd tied the rope. A heavy braid separated her breasts and provided an anchor for the rest of the design. White rope wrapped around her torso above and below her breasts, making her lemon yellow bra stand out in sharp relief. The effect continued down her body. Pretty designs spread over her stomach and down her thighs, and the rope he'd threaded between her legs dug into her labia. Though she wore panties, it was visibly parted. She felt a little exposed, but she reasoned that Jordan wasn't looking anyway, so what did it matter?

"It's beautiful. This is bondage?"

"Shibari. The rope is nylon. It's soft and firm at the same time. I have hemp as well, and I can get silk. We can try them out other times to see what you like best." He adjusted the rope that went diagonally over her butt cheek to a knot at her waist.

The touch was an unexpected sensual caress. She shivered.

"Cold?"

"No. This feels incredible."

He smiled. "It looks incredible on you." His gaze moved over her body, perhaps seeing a canvas for more knotty designs. He slipped the blindfold back over her eyes. "Now I'm going to restrict your movement."

He scooped her up as if she weighed nothing. Amy couldn't remember the last time anybody had tried to pick her up. She yelped, the same sound she made when she found an ant in the house, and threw her arms around his neck.

"Relax, little one. I've got you."

Given the effortless way he held her, she believed him. And then there were those nicknames he liked to use. *Little One. Babe.* She had never heard him call anybody else by those terms, so perhaps they weren't generic terms of familiarity. She relaxed her hold, but she didn't let go completely. His strong, broad shoulders felt good under her hands.

He set her on a bed. The mattress was very firm. When he'd removed her blindfold, she'd been too focused on the rope to take in the details of the room, but she had the impression this wasn't really a guest room, and the bed was a convertible futon. The edge of the bed dipped as he sat down. "I'm going to bind your wrists and ankles so you can't move."

She felt the ends of rope brush against her shoulder and arm as he moved, and she had the sense that he was tying it on his own hand or wrist. Her instinct proved correct when he slipped the nylon rope on her wrist. With one tug, he pulled it tight. He shoved his finger between the rope and her wrist, checking the tension.

"Roll your wrist in circles."

She tried with limited success. "I can't really, but it's not too tight or anything."

"You're not supposed to have much movement. I'm looking to make sure it doesn't cut off the flow of blood, even when you move." He lifted her arm above her head, and as he stretched it out, he ran his hand along the skin on the sensitive side of her arm. This intimacy shocked Amy, but she didn't protest. Everything he did made her feel like she belonged to him—and that he cherished her. She really liked that feeling. She barely noticed that he'd tied her to the bed frame.

He repeated this action as he bound her other arm above her head and her ankles to the foot of the bed. Though he didn't ask, when he finished, she tested the give and found none. The nylon rope was a little stretchy, but not enough to matter.

The room was silent. He didn't say anything, and she wondered if he was looking at his handiwork or if he was planning what to do next. Curiously the lack of vision combined with the silence didn't make her nervous or anxious. She trusted him completely, and she felt herself submit even though he'd only asked for her cooperation.

Something tickled over her stomach. She tried to squirm away, but the bondage held up. It went away for a second, but it came back to tease her thigh before migrating to her chest above her bra and continuing up her arm. He tested it all over her body, returning again and again to the places where she seemed the most responsive. Then he added a new toy, something that scratched lightly instead of tickling. He used them together, one after the other, and soon she felt like a quivering, writhing mass.

And she was growing very horny. Every time she moved or breathed deeply, the knots in the rope pressed into her skin and they seemed to stimulate erogenous zones. Did he know what he'd done? Part of her wondered how he could be ignorant, but she wouldn't be surprised if he had no idea. Jordan was, after all, a man, and men were frequently clueless.

It took her a few moments to realize he wasn't doing anything anymore. She expected him to untie her, but next she felt a weird tingling sensation running up her legs. It crossed over her panties and traveled all over her stomach. Amy didn't love her midsection. It was an area she mostly tried to disguise with shirts and dresses that hugged her breasts and floated over her waist and stomach. For the most part, the distraction worked. Laying here in her bra and panties, she was completely exposed, and Jordan didn't seem to think he should avoid her plushy middle. And she was glad. She'd never known her belly was that sensitive, or that it could send pleasant tingles to both her breasts and her pussy.

He worked her over with that toy for a little while. By the time he finished, she was nearly out of her mind with tormented bliss. For the next few minutes, she could still feel the effect of that little wheel rolling over her skin. He rolled her over and retied her legs.

Her hands were tied close together, and the turning didn't seem to affect anything, but he still adjusted the ties at that end.

"How do you feel, little one?"

"Great." She mumbled into the sheet. With tremendous effort, she lifted her head. "Tingly and like I couldn't lift my limbs even if they weren't tied, but not tired." Her words still sounded slurred.

He smoothed his fingers through her hair, moving it away from her face and off her neck. Wordlessly he ran a rough caress all over her back, butt, and the backs of her legs. When he returned, he included her arms. It wasn't as intimate as when he'd touched the underside of her upper arms, but he made up for that with the way he touched her ass. To her recollection, friends didn't feel up each other's asses unless they were friends with benefits. "Your backside is less sensitive than your front side. Remember to use your safeword if you need to, okay? I will only get angry if you don't use your safeword when you should have."

"Okay." She didn't see where he'd do anything that would lead to needing to call caution. It was likely she'd only need to use it if her bladder suddenly woke up.

The next time he touched her, his hands felt funny. It didn't take long to realize his fingertips were pulsing. He started at her shoulders and worked his way down. She recognized the deep pulses from when Layla had shown off Dustin's e-stim machine in their playroom, only these seemed to be attached to Jordan's fingertips. No matter. He cranked up the juice, and it felt like a deep-tissue massage. By the time he made it to her ass, which he didn't skip, her whole body felt like jelly.

She floated. Her mind had taken flight, and the light sting singing over her large muscles groups only kept her there. When her consciousness landed what seemed like hours later, she found herself wrapped in a soft sheet and Jordan's arms. Stretched out on the bed next to her, he'd tucked her against his side with her head using his shoulder as a pillow.

"Welcome back." His voice was soft and soothing, and it pulled her the rest of the way back.

Amy didn't know what to say. How did one go about thanking the man who'd rocked her world without even kissing her? She tried to sit up, but he tightened his grip.

"Don't move yet. You'll get lightheaded if you sit up too quickly." He stroked her hair. "Besides, this is the aftercare part. Never rush the aftercare."

Amy knew what aftercare was, but she thought it was for intense sessions where bruising might happen. She rubbed her wrist. The rope was gone, but the texture had left an imprint in her skin. She lifted it out of the sheet to see. He held her wrist up higher so he could see it as well.

"You have marks like that all over your body. They'll stay for maybe an hour."

"More, probably." She thought about the marks her socks made in her legs. Sometimes the argyle patterns didn't go away until the next morning. "That's okay. I like the way it looks."

He chuckled, but she mostly felt it in the vibration of his body. "You did very well, babe."

She had done nothing but lay there and let him do stuff to her, and so accepting the compliment didn't sit well with her. "You were the awesome one. Thank you for this. Now I know for sure it's what I want, that I was right in the way I've been pursuing a place in this kinky lifestyle."

He tensed for a second, but then he relaxed and released her wrist. "There's a lot more to the lifestyle than what we did tonight."

"I know, and I'm looking forward to learning."

He sat up slowly, taking her with him. She was glad for his assistance because even with it, she felt a little dizzy. He steadied her. "Why don't you get dressed? I'll order a pizza, and we can talk about how you want to go about learning."

Wordlessly she nodded. Was he offering to train her, or did he want to give her advice about what to look for in a potential Dom? Maybe he wanted to relieve Malcolm's burden and take over fielding offers for her? Even though he'd said there wasn't a snowball's chance in hell he'd do that, perhaps he'd changed his mind. Or was he trying to figure out how to tell her this was a one-time deal? If his behavior before was confusing, it was even more so now.

Glancing around the room, she saw that her initial guess had been right. Though he called it a guest room, and it had a bed, it was mostly an office. The bed would convert back to a sofa, and the desk with huge cupboards would once again dominate the space. A number of implements were set out on the desk's surface. The only real concession to this being a bedroom was the mirrored closet.

"Amy?"

Despite agreeing to his suggestion, she hadn't moved. "What did you use on me?"

Jordan glanced at the array of toys on the desk. "Not everything. I wanted choices, and I picked things based on how you reacted to the other things."

Tucking the sheet around her body, she crossed the two feet to the desk and picked up a feather duster. "This?"

"Yeah. You're ticklish."

She hadn't been ticklish in years. "It seems so." Her gaze roved over the rest of the items. Some looked harmless, like a pair of gloves or a silicone bulb. Others were sinister. She picked up a metal rod with a wheel of spikes at one end. "Not this."

"Yes, that. You liked that a lot." He pointed to the silver gloves. "Those are e-stim gloves. They generate an electrical current where I touch, and I can control the intensity. You liked the most intense setting, which is just a light setting on an e-stim machine." Next he picked up a short whip that had metal points on each end. "You liked this too."

Amy took it from him gently, as if the thing might come alive and bite her. "This looks like it would leave scars."

"If you use it as a whip, it probably would." He extracted it from her grip and trailed the falls over her arm. It was the light scratching sensation she had loved. He set it down and picked up an even shorter whip with thin rubber falls. "I used this on you when you were in subspace. It seemed to keep you there. You didn't even start to come out until about ten minutes after I stopped."

"I remember that. It stung, but in a good way." The descriptions Darcy used about how impact play sent her to subspace finally made sense. "Does that mean I'm a masochist?"

"No. Masochists like pain. You like pleasure. Some of the pleasure you like has a light sting to it. If you want, we can explore that avenue further at another time. I'm not a sadist, Amy. I get no pleasure from inflicting pain on a submissive."

Amy looked over the toys he'd set out. "Are you saying you want to do this again? Why? What do you get out of it?"

Jordan took a deep breath and let it out slowly. "I'm hungry. Let me call in an order. Get dressed, and we'll talk about it over dinner."

Twenty minutes later, Amy sat on his minimalist sofa and munched a slice of pizza. She couldn't remember the last time she'd been that hungry. Jordan, by contrast, ate pizza with a fork, and that slowed him down significantly. He'd finished two slices by the time Amy inhaled three and a side salad with ranch dressing.

"I owe you lasagna," she said. "Or steak. Which do you prefer?"

He finished chewing and wiped a napkin over his mouth. "I'm always thankful whenever I get a home cooked meal. I don't care what it is."

That wasn't helpful. Amy indulged in a pout.

Jordan smirked. "Babe, we need to talk about our arrangement."

"What arrangement?" She knew what he was talking about, but they didn't have an arrangement. "You said you'd help me figure out if I wanted to really be in a D/s relationship, and you did. Thank you."

He shook his head. "Very little of what we did was D/s. I topped you, sure, and we engaged in some kinky play, but that's all. There was no submission."

Oh, but she'd submitted completely. She frowned. "I got to subspace."

"Yes, you did. However, submission should be voluntarily and purposely given."

She understood what he meant. "I should have knelt and other submissive stuff?"

He set his crumpled napkin down and nailed her to the spot with the intensity of his stare. "Is that what you want?"

Yeah, she did. "With the right person, I do. Darcy taught me some basic kneeling positions and submissive poses." Some of those poses were definitely sexual, so probably not what Jordan had in mind. "Jordan, are you saying you want to scene with me again? You said there was a lot more, and I trust you more than I've ever trusted anybody."

He just kept looking at her.

She panicked. "Or if I'm totally off base, we can forget all of this happened and go back to being friends like we were this morning."

"You're not off base. I'd like to scene with you, but I'm going to require more from you."

Amy nodded when he paused, her signal that she was listening. It made sense that he'd want more. After all, relationships were a two-way street. She couldn't take from him without giving something in return or else she'd feel like a shitty person.

"Kneeling before a scene is essential. It's symbolic of our relationship, and it shows respect." He sipped his drink. "But most of what I want is outside of a scene."

Now Amy was really confused. Then it dawned on her. "You're talking about training me."

"Yes. I will give you tasks to complete. Some will be daily. Others will be weekly."

Amy twisted her napkin anxiously. "Will we still be friends?"

"Yes. That's my first and most important demand. No matter what happens, no matter where this goes or doesn't go, we'll still be friends. If, at any time, either of us wants to end the D/s aspect of our friendship, we will. There will be no recriminations or reprisals from the other party."

Was he talking about sex? Because she didn't run around sleeping with her friends. Swallowing her nerves, she forged ahead. "Then we're keeping it platonic?"

"For now, yes."

So there was a chance for taking this further. "What if I don't want to do the tasks?"

"We will agree upon suitable consequences."

She thought about him turning her over his knee and spanking her. The image did not appeal to her. She frowned. "I don't think I'm comfortable with discipline."

"Having discipline isn't negotiable. The form it takes, however, is."

"Form? Don't Doms just spank subs whenever they misbehave? I've heard Malcolm go after Darcy." The first time, she'd been horrified, but when Darcy had returned, she'd been both subdued and glowing. Though Amy was curious, she didn't want to wear those shoes.

"That's what they've negotiated, and I've known Mal for a long time. The spanking was Darcy's idea."

Amy didn't like the path they were on. "What are your ideas?"

"It depends on the misbehavior. I'm partial to corner time."

She stared to see if he'd crack a smile and tell her that he was kidding. A minute passed, and his expression remained the same. "You mean, if I fail to complete a task, then I have to stand in a corner?" Her heat beat faster. Nobody had ever suggested such a thing in her life. It seemed like an old-fashioned punishment for a child.

"Yes."

"For how long?"

"Until I tell you it's over. At that point, you'll crawl to me, kneel at my feet, apologize, and ask for forgiveness."

Was it wrong that the image of her doing that made her feel both peaceful and excited? "I'll have to think about that. What kinds of tasks would you give me?"

He leaned forward. "Are you agreeing to my terms, little one? Would you like me to train you?"

She couldn't imagine doing the things she'd done tonight with anybody else. "Yeah. I'm agreeing to your terms, but we still have a lot to negotiate."

"We do. Negotiation is an ongoing process. We will sit down regularly to evaluate where we've been and where we're going." He put another slice of pizza onto his plate. "First task: write a letter to me detailing what submission means to you."

"But I don't completely know what it means to me."

"I know, babe. It's time to start figuring it out." He cut a piece of pizza with his fork and ate it. "I have plans for tomorrow, so I won't see you. I expect the letter Tuesday when I stop by your place. Tomorrow I'll text you with your task for the day."

Chapter Eight

Brian's skin crawled, but the nightmares were a thousand times worse. It began with a few robberies—after all, where was The Eye going to get the funding it needed to take down all these crooked politicians? Voters were too stupid to stop electing politicians that had been bought and paid for by big money. Things needed to change, and the democratic process wasn't getting it done. But then it progressed from smash-and-grab to armed holdups.

And every time he successfully completed a mission, Joe rewarded him with that wondrous, high-grade crack. It made a difference. *He* was making a difference. Finally his military training was coming in handy, and he was fighting for the ideals that had led him to serve his country in the first place. His legacy wouldn't be a bad one.

In the past month or so, he'd progressed from camping out in a series of abandoned houses—he'd accidentally burned one down trying to get a fire going on a cold night—to sharing a room with Maher Erikson. Maher had been with The Eye for about six months longer than Brian, and he acted as a mentor of sorts. The duo spent most of their time high, and when they came down, Joe frequently had a job for them to do. Maher had taught Brian how to break into places, what kinds of things to steal, and where to cash in their haul.

The room they shared was in the basement of a church. It turned out that Joe was a preacher. Religion had never meant much to Brian, and it didn't now, but he liked listening to Joe's sermons. They were all about brotherhood and sticking together, about making sure every man had what he needed to be happy. For Brian, that was a clean, heated room with a high window that could be cracked on really hot nights and a steady supply of drugs. As a bonus, it came with three meals and an endless supply of wine. It might have been meant for the church, but Joe never said anything about how much disappeared. Brian figured he was funding his habits just fine with the almost nightly break-ins.

At the last holdup, the clerk hadn't cooperated. He'd reached under the counter, probably for the silent alarm or a gun. Fear of failure made Brian's trigger finger twitchy, and he'd shot the teen dead center in the chest. Sick to his stomach, Brian could only stare at the dark, spreading stain. Maher, Brian's accomplice, had his wits about him. He'd grabbed the money and Brian. They'd narrowly escaped.

Because he was such a great buddy—and probably because he hadn't wanted to take the chance that Joe would withhold those precious rocks—Maher had spun the story to make Brian look like a dedicated disciple of The Eye who would do whatever it took to accomplish his mission. Brian wasn't sure how much of the story Joe bought, but there was no denying reports of a dead teen on the news. He'd been some district attorney's step-kid.

Maher happened to hear the report first. At the next meeting, he lauded Brian as a True Believer. And now Joe wanted Brian to prove this wasn't a coincidence, and he wanted Maher to make sure Brian was a good little soldier.

"There's a judge who always sides with big business and special interests." Joe looked deep into Brian's eyes. "He put my son away for life on a trumped-up charge. A rich kid did the crime, and they pinned it on my boy."

Brian nodded and hoped that Joe couldn't tell he was scared shitless. This was just like going into battle. Some high-ranking blowhard gave a rousing speech about why they had to do what they were about to do, but Brian was the one putting his life on the line. He'd hated it then, and he hated it now.

"You're going to kill that judge."

Brian shook his head. "You got it wrong—I didn't mean to kill that kid. It was a mistake. I thought he wasn't going to give up the money."

A coldly firm frost settled over Joe's features. Brian knew he was fucked. Forget not having a roof over his head or a steady supply of drugs. He hadn't realized just how deeply he was involved in this organization.

"You're in too deep." Joe stepped closer, his eyes bright with preacher fever. "you belong to us now. You're going to kill that judge, or you will wish you were dead."

————

Dustin's house was in an older neighborhood full of mature trees and immaculate landscaping. Though many of the homes still belonged to retirees, a good number had turned over, and the sounds of children once again echoed from the brick and siding. Jordan rang the bell and waited patiently for someone to answer. He was early, and that meant his timing could be off. In that case, Jordan would politely wait for Layla and Dustin to compose themselves before answering the door.

This evening, Layla answered the door. She was a slight woman, small and petite, but her attitude and personality made up for the lack. Pleasure lit her face as she stepped back to let him in. "Hey, Jordan. Did you have dinner? Dustin said you liked omelets, so I made you one."

Intending to hit a drive-thru with Dustin, he'd skipped dinner. "I'd be a fool to turn down a free meal."

"Then you're in for a treat. I may not cook as well as Amy, but I'm no slouch in the kitchen."

Dustin came down the stairs in time to hear Layla's boasting. He caught her around the waist and kissed her neck. "You're good in every room, Angel."

Though her cheeks reddened, Layla's smile only grew.

Jordan had only eaten Amy's cooking a couple of times. It was her baking that tempted his palate more. They followed Layla through the hall to the kitchen. "You told her about Amy?"

Dustin shrugged. "There's nothing to tell, right? I only mentioned that you liked her, and that you were trying to figure out if she was harboring an undiscovered little." In the kitchen, Dustin motioned for him to sit. Layla had already set the table, and a plate with a third of a humongous omelet and a pile of hash browns waited for each of them.

"Looks and smells great. Thanks for doing this, Layla."

Layla sat down and dug in. "I don't know any littles, so I can't help you with Amy. Have you tried asking her?"

Being direct in this case might be deceptively easy, and the easy path wasn't always the right one. "She's just started trying to figure out where she belongs on the D/s spectrum. I don't want to confuse her by throwing something she's never heard of at her."

"You might be surprised." Layla slurped her orange juice. "Amy's smarter than you think."

"She's highly intelligent. But she needs to do this at her pace, not mine. I've taken her under my wing, and I'm training her. As part of the process, I'm having her think about, research, and explore different aspects of the lifestyle so she can reconcile them with her wants and needs. We've only been at it for a week."

Dustin and Layla both stared. Finally Dustin shook his head. "Sometimes you're too analytical."

Jordan looked from Dustin to Layla and back again. "Seems to me patience paid off for you."

Dustin conceded the point.

After dinner, Jordan and Dustin headed to the office. Dare had called with some breaking news, which was why they were on the night shift. They found him in his lab sitting before seven monitors. He sat in a rolling chair, coasting up and down the long curved desk, fingers flying over keyboards as he controlled the flow of information. Liam Adair had first come on the FBI's radar when he'd hacked into their database at age fifteen. Ten years later, he was one of their most brilliant minds. The CIA occasionally tried to poach him, but Dare's mother lived in Livonia, and she refused to leave the area for any reason. Therefore Dare wouldn't move either. He liked his job, and sometimes he hacked into the CIA for fun.

He glanced up when the door opened, scowling. "I have a virus."

Jordan paused in the doorway. "Is it contagious?"

"Not that kind." Dare waved them closer. "I have something you might find interesting." He pulled up several windows on one of the monitors, each emails to or from a perp arrested for robbery and suspected of having ties to The Eye.

Jordan skimmed the text before going back for a closer read. "Looks like someone planned the robbery in exchange for a place to crash and some crack." Nothing specific was said, but code words and allusions were used to refer to drugs.

"As an added bonus, I traced the IP to an address." He punched some keys. "Which I just texted to both of you."

"Layla hates when I go to work in these kinds of clothes."

Jordan took his eyes from the road to glance over at his buddy. For this surveillance assignment, they had to dress to blend in with the people who were generally found in that area. T-shirt casual was Jordan's normal uniform. Unless he had a court appearance scheduled or an important date, he stuck to jeans. Brandy Lockmeyer, his chief and friend, never bothered him about not adhering to the dress code. People in the McNamara Building that housed the DOJ and FBI headquarters were used to his look. "Why?"

"Because she knows I'm doing something that could be dangerous."

"You're a Federal agent. Every day has the potential for danger. That's why you like your job." They were all adrenaline junkies.

Dustin chugged the rest of his coffee. "Yeah, but I'm not going to tell her that. She'd probably start showing up to try to save my ass. I'd rather she pictured me doing mountains of paperwork and sifting through boxes of evidence for clues."

After what she'd done to help break their last case, Jordan didn't doubt it. "Keith keeps extra clothes in the trunk. You could always change after you leave. But then you're being extra deceptive, and maybe you don't want to open that can of worms. Layla is a strong woman. She knew what she was getting into with you."

They arrived at their destination, a multi-level apartment building where a nearby corporation kept an apartment for when they temporarily shifted employees around to different states. Just now it was vacant. The neighborhood, a mixture of homes and apartments occupied by young professionals and businesses, housed three active churches in five blocks. Dare had traced emails sent by one of the robbers they believed connected with The Eye to an IP address across the street from the apartment building.

Jordan grabbed a backpack from the trunk, and Dustin took the travel bag full of surveillance technology. The pair didn't speak as they went into the building. Dustin took the elevator, and Jordan climbed the stairs. Both visually swept for bugs or anything suspicious. They met up again at the apartment.

"Tigers are up by three." Dustin fell into their sports-based code talk as he opened the door. "Last I checked." That meant he'd encountered several people in the elevator, but none had looked out of place.

"I was hoping for a no-hitter." Jordan hadn't seen a soul. Apparently no one used the stairs for fitness. They went inside, keeping up the sports chatter—most of it meaningless—as they swept the place. Once they were satisfied that everything was as it should be, they set up their equipment. They didn't have a warrant, so they could only keep watch. Any listening devices would require judicial approval.

"I think someone inside is involved," Dustin said, voicing something they'd both thought but neither wanted to say in mixed company. The investigation in Chicago had been flawless, yet their brethren hadn't been able to close the case. At best, the whole thing had a suspicious stench.

"Hopefully we'll find a lead today." Leads tended to be the result of careful research and vigilant observation. Jordan's instincts screamed that this stakeout would be fruitful. They just didn't supply a timetable.

Dustin grunted at his premature prediction. "Great. Now we won't find anything."

"Maybe not tonight," Jordan conceded, "But eventually."

The evening was eventful, but only for the people on the street. Folks got home from work and chatted on the sidewalks. Couples and friends went for coffee, drinks, or dinner. The economy was good in this Motor City suburb. Activity dropped off around nine-thirty, and the place was dead by eleven. When the next shift replaced them at midnight, they had nothing to report.

Six days later, nothing significant or out-of-the-ordinary had happened, and Jordan was growing impatient. He flipped through the notes from the other agents sharing this detail.

"If you scowl any harder, your face will freeze like that and Amy may decide you're not that handsome after all."

Jordan pointed his scowl at Dustin. "Amy isn't shallow. She doesn't care what I look like." She did, however, respond very well to smiles and softly spoken praise. She liked cuddling and physical displays of affection. In the past two weeks, she'd blossomed as she got in touch with her submissive side and started to accept that aspect of herself.

"She told Darcy she thought you were hot."

Darcy had likely told Layla, who had relayed that information to Dustin. "Does Layla tell you everything her girlfriends tell her?"

"Pretty much, but especially when it's juicy gossip concerning you or Amy. Have you decided when you're going to make your move?" Though Dustin wasn't looking at him, he knew he was paying careful attention to both the conversation and his job.

"After the wedding." Amy had too much on her mind right now. When he sat her down to talk to her about being a Daddy Dom, he wanted her undivided attention. "I told her that she has to take the day off Monday."

"How do you think she'll take it?"

People who were ignorant of this part of the lifestyle tended to be full of disturbing misconceptions. He had every confidence that Amy would listen with an open mind. "I think she'll be fine with it. I've been having her mostly focus on herself and her journey, and I know she's very curious about me. I've shared some things, but she knows there's a big part I haven't revealed."

Dustin nodded, but he was frowning out the window. "I think that guy was on one of the surveillance tapes from the robbery in Wixom. He was another shopper in the store who left before Matt Gordon came in."

They were thirty miles from the scene of the crime. It was too much of a coincidence. Of course, the man could simply look familiar because they'd been watching the neighborhood for six days. "I'll pull up the videos."

Dustin came over to the laptop after a few minutes. "He went inside the church. I think they run an unlicensed homeless shelter out of the basement."

Jordan had looked out the window at the man. "He doesn't seem homeless." The man had an air of authority about him, like life had done the opposite of beating him down, but he wasn't officially affiliated with the church. The building housing the church had formerly been a Mexican restaurant. Though it had large windows, curtains blocked the lower two-thirds of each window to give worshippers privacy while still letting in light. In addition to weekly services, it looked like they ran meetings or support groups for addicts, many of whom seemed to crash in the basement on a regular basis. "Maybe he owns the building?"

"We ran a records check." Dustin dug out another secure laptop. "I'll see if we have a picture of a person, but I'm pretty sure it's a corporation."

The church hadn't raised any kinds of red flags. Though the ones that sprang up quickly tended to be shady, they were usually committing tax-related crimes that didn't interest them. That's what the IRS was for. Jordan kept an eye on the church as he scrolled through footage they'd already analyzed. It was protocol to rule out bystanders, and so those people had already undergone cursory scrutiny. He paused on the image of the man they'd just seen. "Here he is." They traded places so he could keep an eye on the street while Dustin looked over the footage.

"We're going to have to look through tapes at the other places as well." Dustin sighed.

"Going back five days," Jordan added. They were going to need to request more footage from store owners. "Get Rossetti on it. He has a great eye. Ask Lockmeyer to get him some help because we may need warrants. Did you find the owner?"

"It's a corporation with no red flags on it. They seem to own a series of churches, restaurants, and other kinds of real estate. I bet Dare can dig into it." His eyes gleamed with excitement. After so many days of nothing, even something this small was an event. Dustin got on the phone. At the same time, he opened another video file to peruse.

The church was quiet. Jordan wished it wasn't a church so he could go sniffing around the exterior or maybe even pop inside. He swept his gaze up and down the block, noting the things that were always there. Then he closed his eyes and hit the figurative reset button on his brain so he could take fresh look.

No robberies fitting the M.O. of The Eye crimes in either Detroit or Chicago had been reported in the last week. Did they know they were being watched? Jordan looked back through the other agents' surveillance notes. "This guy came around yesterday at eleven in the morning and three days ago at around six in the evening." Dustin and Jordan hadn't been on surveillance at those times, so this was their first opportunity to see the man.

"I really want to know who he is." Dustin tapped the keyboard. "I found him at the site of a robbery in Warren three days before it happened."

"He's leaving now. Let's go for coffee. Maybe we'll run into him." Two fast food places and a coffee bar were down the street in the direction their mystery man had vanished. Even if he turned onto a side street, there were more restaurants.

Dustin logged off both laptops. "Sounds like a plan. Are we buddies or a couple?" In this neighborhood, either cover worked, but they needed to select one that would fly under their target's radar and allow them to get close enough to find out anything relevant, or maybe pick up a phone the guy "accidentally" misplaced.

Despite Dustin's best efforts to appear otherwise, he looked like he could be heading out for a night on the town. "Buddies. It's Friday night, so we're grabbing a bite before heading to clubs."

The pair tailed the target around the corner and down the block. They strode along with the casual air of two friends looking forward to tearing it up. Though this street was largely residential with local businesses mixed in, a few streets over, nightclubs catered to the singles in the younger, upwardly mobile crowd.

Jordan and Dustin kept up a steady stream of innocuous chatter and tried to outdo each other with bad puns.

"It's not that the man didn't know how to juggle; it's that he didn't have the balls to do it." Dustin ended with a grin instead of a rim shot.

Jordan started with a soft one. "A gun-shaped eraser was confiscated from an algebra student because it's a weapon of math destruction."

That was a groaner. Dustin easily bested that one. "A chicken crossing the road is poultry in motion."

"I'd tell you a chemistry joke, but I know it wouldn't get a reaction."

"I wondered why the baseball was getting bigger. Then it hit me."

"A dog gave birth to puppies near the side of a road and was cited for littering."

Thankfully their guy stopped at a fast food restaurant and ordered a milkshake before they ran out of material. Behind him in line, Jordan and Dustin debated the merits of coffee versus chocolate shakes.

"Chocolate has a little bit of caffeine in it," Jordan said. "And a lot of sugar. That'll keep you going."

"It's not real chocolate, so no caffeine. It's mostly soy, isn't it?" Dustin frowned. The man was an authority on chocolate.

"Still need a pick-me-up." Jordan mumbled. "We'll go see Matt. Gordo always comes through with some sweet rock."

They got their target's attention. He tilted his head to better listen to their conversation.

Dustin played along. Someone had supplied these junkies. Each had been freshly high, and they'd all crashed in custody. "No fucking way. Your guy got arrested last week. Didn't Jody tell you?"

"Crap." Jordan washed his hand over his face. "Christine is supposed to be there tonight. She's horny when she's had a little something extra, and she doesn't care if people can see us."

"You can find another slut. You'll just have to buy her a few drinks first."

"But now I'll have to try. This was a done deal." His turn came next. He ordered two coffees and noted how closely their target listened to their exchange.

They followed the man, wandering down the street toward the clubs. They watched him go into a nightclub. Dustin shook his head. "He didn't bite."

"Nope." But he had been interested in their discussion of drugs. "Let's hang for a bit, see if he comes out."

Dustin leaned against the brick building behind him and stared at the venue well-known for catering to gay clientele. If they followed him inside, then he'd know they were onto him. "We should have been a couple."

Jordan grunted. "Or at least talked about guys who were easy lays. We need to practice using androgynous names and avoiding gendered pronouns."

Chapter Nine

Jordan stretched out on his sofa and unfolded the letter Amy had written two short weeks ago. She'd handwritten it because she'd said it was easier to organize her thoughts that way.

> *I don't know exactly what submission is supposed to be. I've read about people who feel a desire to serve. Serving sounds so demeaning, like I have no self-esteem at all, which isn't the case. That doesn't resonate with me unless it maybe describes how I feel a deep need to do things for the people I love. I want to give them my time and energy. I want to make them happy, but in return, I want to be loved and appreciated. Nobody in my life takes advantage of my good nature, and I'd hate it if that happened.*
>
> *So, what does submission mean to me? I picture it as a safe place, a refuge where I can be myself without fear of being judged. It's where I can be close to someone who understands what makes me tick and maybe even likes those things about me. For that person alone, I'd gladly and devotedly serve him.*

Jordan liked that she'd written it out in neat script, like the final draft of an important paper. She'd penned it on scented stationery that had decorative flowers dancing across the bottom. It was playful and whimsical, much like Amy herself. He read and reread the lines where she talked about wanting to be herself without fear of being judged. Though he'd been working with her for two weeks, she hadn't yet shared anything that would undeniably reveal her inner little. No doubt she'd been ridiculed by someone before, and now she went through great pains to hide the evidence.

He sniffed the paper, but it had spent so much time in his wallet that it only smelled like leather. Carefully he folded the note and put it away. Then he grabbed his cell and dialed her number.

"Hey. I thought you'd be busy with groomsmen stuff." Her tone was tight, evidence that she was stressed.

"Mal is planning to stay home with Colin because he'll miss him when they go away for a week." Keith had wanted to throw a bachelor party, but Malcolm had vetoed the idea. Instead they'd planned a play party and collaring ceremony for next month. In the BDSM community, the ceremony where a Dom and a sub proclaimed their commitment often meant more than legal vows.

"Yeah, Darcy is staying home too. That's good, though. It gives me time to double check reservations and orders."

"I thought you already did that?" Jordan was amazed by the sheer volume of work Amy had done in the past fourteen days. Through it all, she'd maintained the childish glee of anticipation. But Darcy was right about the fact that Amy worked too hard and needed to have fun.

"I did, but you can never be too careful. If you do it right, you only get one wedding."

"True. Seeing as how you've already worked your ass off and everything is set, how about I come over and help take your mind off things?" They'd scened twice, not including the time after mini-golfing, and she'd responded well. He wasn't sure if she was up for a scene tonight, but some submission would do her a world of good.

"I think I'll be too tired," she said, confirming his suspicion. "After I call the caterer, I was going to see if Darcy needed anything. And then I was going to maybe watch a movie and fall asleep in front of the TV."

"Darcy is fine." He used his Dom tone, which was a little deeper and slower than his normal voice. "I just talked to

Malcolm. And the caterer is fine. You have a very efficient checklist, so stop second-guessing it. I'll be over in an hour."

"I don't have steak or lasagna." That was her way of saying she didn't feel prepared to serve him.

"That's fine. I'll bring you some takeout, and we can watch your movie together."

An hour later, she answered the door wearing a lavender shirt and matching plaid lounge pants. She smiled widely and gave him a heartfelt hug. He returned the gesture, embracing her tightly and holding her soft body against his for a little longer than was polite.

"You don't have to do this, you know."

He set a canvas bag down next to the entryway. After closing and locking her front door, he headed back to the kitchen with a bag of food. "Do what?"

"Entertain me so I don't spend all night worrying. I'm a big girl. I can take care of myself." She wrung her hands and shifted her weight uncertainly.

Jordan smiled gently, seeking to ease her mind. "There's nowhere else I'd rather be." He extracted two plastic containers he'd picked up from one of his favorite diners. "I brought fried chicken and mashed potatoes for dinner. And these for dessert." He held up the last surprise he'd packed into the bag—a huge box of Sno-Caps. She'd mentioned a few days ago that they were one of her favorite treats to have with a movie.

She clapped her hands together and beamed a smile into his heart. "I love those."

"I know." He let himself bask in her adoration for a few moments. "I'm going to change into sweats, and then you and I can camp out on the sofa in front of a movie, eat until we're full, and then we can share dessert."

"Okay."

He heard the hesitation in her voice. Pausing in the doorway, he turned to face her. "What's wrong?"

"Nothing. It's just I don't think I have a movie you'd enjoy. I can run out and rent one. What haven't you seen recently?" She picked at her cuticle.

He knew that she needed to watch a movie that would help her relax. In the hour it had taken him to get from his place to hers, she had likely hidden any evidence she'd been engaged in childish activities that would help relieve her stress. "Let's watch whatever you originally planned on seeing."

A hint of a blush traveled up her neck, and she averted her gaze.

Returning to her side, he took her hands in his. "Little one, tell me what's wrong. Are you afraid I won't want to watch your movie? I assure you that I like a lot of different kinds of movies—even chick flicks and kid movies."

She slid the tip of her toe in circles on the floor. "I was going to watch Finding Nemo. It's childish, I know, but I find it relaxing."

Pleased that she'd opened up a little more, he rewarded her with a smile and a hug. "I like it too. Go get it set up while I change." His grin stayed put as he thought about the fact they'd be watching a movie about a Daddy searching for his little one who was stuck in a prison that society deemed an acceptable way to live life. How fitting.

When he returned, he found her placing glasses of grape juice on the coffee table where she'd already set out the food. She'd put it on plates. Forks on folded paper napkins lay next to each setting. She looked him up and down. "You look ready for bed."

"So do you." Except she was wearing a bra. If she was his, he'd make her take it off so that she could really relax and so that he'd have easier access to her breasts. She had delectable breasts, and he couldn't wait until he had the right to play with them whenever he wanted. He parked himself on the sofa and patted the cushion. "Sit. Let's eat."

She followed his order, but her lower lip stuck out in a bratty pout. "Are you here as a friend or as my trainer?"

"Both. I can't help but top you, little one. That's not a part of my personality that goes away, especially not since you've given me permission to dominate you." He picked up his plate and set it on his lap. "I'm starved. Go ahead and start the movie."

They watched and ate, saying very little for the next hour. When the food was gone, he pulled her so that she cuddled against his side, and he covered her with the light throw blanket she kept over the back of the sofa. She rested her head and hand on his chest, and once when he laughed, she looked up at him, her lips parted in surprise. He wanted so badly to kiss her, and he barely refrained. *One more day.*

Amy woke quickly, the excitement of the day to come bursting in her like fireworks. Two months of planning was culminating this afternoon. Her little sister, the one she'd worried about for years, was getting married. And Amy had planned every detail according to Darcy's wishes. Well, Malcolm's too. He had definite opinions on most things, including the flower arrangements.

Last night had been strangely perfect. Never before had she let someone over while she indulged in one of her secret guilty pleasures. The last time she'd tried to get one of her boyfriends to watch Finding Nemo with her, it hadn't gone too well. Eric had always managed to leave her alone when she watched a movie he didn't want to see, which ended up being most times. If he chose the movie, she stayed whether she liked it or not.

Jordan had not only accepted it without comment, but he seemed to really enjoy the movie. Thinking of the way he snuggled her as they watched, her smile grew. He liked her as more than a friend. He had to. Friends didn't snuggle like that. They didn't share intimate moments without there being more to their relationship. He'd said they were going to see where things would naturally go, and Amy felt they were almost there. When he'd hugged her goodbye, he'd held her for a long, long time, and it had felt right.

She showered, snagged her beauty supplies, and headed to Darcy's house where all the bridesmaids were gathering to get ready. The place was mass chaos with women running around half-dressed as they took turns with the hair stylist and makeup specialist that Amy had hired.

Clad in a wispy slip that didn't hide the angry welts decorating her backside and upper thighs, Darcy hugged Amy tightly. "Do you have something to tell me?"

Amy hugged her back, but she frowned as she racked her brain for a detail she'd forgotten to relay. "No?"

"Are you sure? You look very happy today. You're glowing."

In fact, the opposite was true. If anybody was glowing, it was the bride—from both ends. The welts had most likely been an early wedding gift from Malcolm to help Darcy deal with her nerves. Despite having to do it all the time, Darcy was still anxious about speaking in front of a group of people for any reason, and getting married definitely qualified as public speaking. "You're the one glowing. It's probably reflected glow. I'm so happy for you."

Darcy laughed. "So, nothing has happened with Jordan?"

Though she'd confided to Darcy that Jordan was training her, she'd also issued assurances that it was strictly D/s with no romantic or sexual elements. Amy shrugged. "Same story as last time. Mixed signals. He came over last night. We snuggled on the couch and watched a movie. He brought Sno-Caps."

Cupping Amy's face, Darcy pressed their foreheads together. "Promise you'll call me if something happens?"

"Don't hold your breath. Just enjoy your honeymoon and know that I'll be helping Mom and Dad watch Colin until Malcolm's parents take over." Their parents were scheduled to stay with Colin for three days, and then Malcolm's parents were going to watch him for the rest of the week. The Markeviches loved their grandson, but they didn't like babies all that much. They were planning to head out Tuesday in their RV to continue exploring the nation via campgrounds and RV parks full of retirees. The Legatos, on the other hand, were made to be grandparents. They were chomping at the bit to take their grandson for a few days of uninterrupted spoiling.

The architecture of the nondenominational chapel was classy and clean, a blank canvas for a decorator. Flowers burst all over the place. Malcolm had insisted on chrysanthemums and roses—with the thorns still on—as the décor. Amy had made sure the mums made it to the places where children could reach, and so they decorated the pews. The thorns were special for Darcy.

As she was the maid-of-honor and Keith was the best man, he walked her down the aisle. They were the last pair to make the trek before the bride, and Amy's gaze was drawn to the altar where Jordan stood off to the side next to Dustin and Malcolm's brother, MJ. Taller, bigger, and more handsome than any man there, he definitely stood out. His cheeks and chin were smooth, and his dark hair was once again neatly trimmed. The ends curled gently against his broad shoulders. She hadn't been allowed to touch it yet, but she had imagined what it would be like to shave his face and brush his hair. It would be soft, and...

She stumbled. It was a little thing, with her ankle buckling on the unfamiliar high heel. Keith caught her easily, saving her from an embarrassing spill. He'd been aware enough to sling his arm around her waist before she twisted or sprained anything. To onlookers, it would look like a friendly embrace or show of emotional support instead of the result of inattention or klutziness. She smiled gratefully.

He leaned down. "Are you okay?"

"Yeah. Thanks." She could walk just fine if she paid attention to what she was doing and not how handsome and alluring Jordan looked in a tuxedo.

She joined Layla, Trina, and Jennifer, MJ's wife, in the place where the bridesmaids stood. The flower girl, Keith and Trina's adopted daughter, Angie, came next. The tiny four-year-old in a frilly white dress sprinkled red and white rose petals carefully on the white fabric runner that marked the bride's path. Right behind her, Alex and Andrew, MJ and Jennifer's sons, shared ring-bearer duties.

Trina beamed as she regarded her child. "She's been practicing for a week," she whispered proudly.

"She'd doing great," Amy whispered back. She meant to watch Angie and the boys, but her gaze was pulled to Jordan, where she found him staring at her with a fierce expression. She smiled with the hope he'd lighten up and return the gesture. He did.

During the vows, Amy cried at the sheer beauty and meaning of this momentous occasion. Since it was a summer wedding, she didn't have sleeves in which to tuck a tissue, but she did her best to wipe the tears away with her fingers before they completely ruined her makeup. Darcy's voice shook, and Amy knew her sister was barely holding it together as well, but she had Malcolm right there to give her strength. Her voice grew stronger as she spoke, and that only made Amy cry harder.

On the return trip down the aisle, Amy found Jordan had replaced Keith as her escort. He stuffed his linen handkerchief in her hand so she could wipe her eyes, and he steadied her on the walk. Once they exited the church, Amy intended to join the line that led to the newly married couple, but Jordan pulled her aside.

"Did you twist your ankle?"

"No. It's fine. Keith caught me before I could do any damage." Heat crept up Amy's neck, evidence of latent embarrassment. She didn't think anybody but Keith had noticed her stumble.

Jordan took the handkerchief she'd balled in her fist. "Look up." He gently wiped under her eyes, fixing her makeup so she wouldn't look like a raccoon.

"Where did you learn to do that?"

"I have sisters, remember?"

"Yeah." She sniffled.

He handed over the handkerchief. "It's fixed as long as you don't cry again. Now blow your nose."

She regarded the cloth uncertainly. "In that?"

"That's what it's for."

Her first inclination was to protest, but the look he gave her quelled that impulse. She made use of it, but then she refused to give it back. Jordan got that Dom look, and his lips parted to give an order.

"Amy, it was a lovely wedding. You did a fantastic job putting this together on such short notice." The voice arrested the command Jordan had been preparing to issue.

She turned to find Aunt Stephanie and Uncle Darren standing nearby. Uncle Darren was her mother's brother. She preened under her aunt's praise. Aunt Stephanie had always been Amy's favorite. She and Uncle Darren were those people who were always positive and upbeat. Too bad they'd moved to Madison, Wisconsin two decades ago for better jobs. "Thank you. It was nothing."

Stephanie snorted. She leaned in for a hug. "Honey, I know what it takes to pull off a wedding. I have four daughters with two recent weddings under my belt. It's hell, and you pulled off a miracle." Stephanie turned to Jordan. "Hello there, young man. I'm the aunt of the bride. I'm Stephanie, and this is my husband, Darren."

"Oh, sorry." Amy blushed anew. "This is Jordan Monaghan. He's Malcolm's friend."

Jordan shook hands and initiated a short, polite conversation until the photographer shouted for the wedding party to assemble on the steps for posed photographs.

"I won't fall," she assured him as he slung an arm around her shoulders to help her into position.

"I know you won't." He didn't let go, but he did manage to wrest the used handkerchief away from her and stuff it in his pocket.

At the reception, Amy greeted her parents. "Dad, you look so handsome, and Mom, you're just gorgeous. I love that dress."

Her mother, Francine, looked her up and down as if seeing her for the first time that day. "Thank you, Amy. You look amazing as well. Are you wearing Spanx?"

Amy exhaled slowly. She'd struggled with her weight all her life. Though she wasn't all that large, she was carrying about thirty extra pounds according to medical charts and indexes. It was just like her mother to bring that up now, when she'd been feeling pretty good about herself. She was, in fact, wearing undergarments that supplied extra support. Rather than respond, she said, "I didn't see you at Darcy's this morning. Is everything okay?"

"We had some trouble parking the RV in her neighborhood. It appears there is an ordinance against having one around for more than three days. And then your sister's house was a wreck, so there was no point in staying there anyway. We ended up going to Uncle Darren's hotel room and getting ready. It was far more civilized, and the hotel welcomes campers. But we did stop by."

Oh, but Amy had not missed her parents or the emotional complications they brought. Darcy had rejoiced when they'd moved away, but she had never been forced to bear the brunt of their mother's constant disapproval. Blessed with a fuck-off attitude Amy envied, Darcy had literally flipped off their parents when they'd come out against Scott, telling them all—Amy included—that they could either accept the relationship she had with him or get out of their lives. Amy, on the other hand, had thirsted for her parents' approval. Without bothering to listen to Darcy's explanations, she'd sided with their parents in labeling him an abuser.

Of all the things she'd done in her life, that filled her with the most shame and regret. Scott had been a good man who'd loved Darcy with his whole heart. His sudden and violent death had broken Darcy. But now she had Malcolm, and she was once again happy and in love. At least Amy hadn't made the same mistake with him that she had with Scott.

She managed a weak, polite smile at her mother's disapproval of the pre-wedding turmoil. "I didn't know you stopped by."

"Darcy said you were on the phone dealing with the caterer." Her mother arched a brow, challenging her to reveal Darcy's lie.

Amy nodded, thankful for Darcy's quick thinking. It had been nice to not see her parents until now. "Several last-minute things cropped up." Across the room, she saw Jordan laugh at something Keith was saying. His whole face lit up, and she was transfixed.

"Your behavior during the ceremony was deplorable," her father, Paul, said. He'd followed her line of sight to Jordan. "Flirting with a groomsman where everybody can see."

"He's out of your league," her mother continued. "Not your type at all—far too young and fit to be interested in you. Now, Jason Hammond is here. He's the son of your father's former business partner. He runs a successful investment company, and he's single. I'll introduce you."

"We've met." Years ago, but it would suffice. Neither of them had been overly impressed with the other. "And I'm not looking to be set up right now. Jordan is a good friend of mine, and we were not flirting. I stumbled coming down the aisle. He's a nice guy, and he was merely concerned for my wellbeing."

Darcy floated up to them. She hugged her parents and kissed Amy on each cheek. "Amy, I need you. Maid-of-honor stuff."

Their mother looked affronted. "She's done enough for you today. Let her be."

Unaffected, Darcy merely smiled blandly. Once again, Amy envied her sister's aplomb. "Mom, I have to go to the bathroom, and I need Amy to help get my train out of the way, unless you want to do it for her?"

Francine drew back. "I'll excuse the two of you. Your father and I are going to visit with family we haven't seen in a while. We'll see you later."

They hurried off.

Darcy slung her arm around Amy and hugged her close as they headed in the direction of the restrooms. "What were they saying?"

"Mom said I looked good, so I must be wearing Spanx, and Dad said I flirted inappropriately with Jordan during the ceremony. Apparently I'm a fat slut."

"Ignore them. They don't know what the hell they're talking about. You're beautiful, and I would hope you'd flirt with Jordan, but when I looked over at you, you were crying and watching the ceremony."

Amy sighed. "I wish I had your armor."

"Having Malcolm to support and guide me gives me the strength to deal with anything life might throw at me."

"You've always been immune."

"Not immune, but I've learned to find their disapproval funny instead of letting it skewer me through the heart. Mom told me I looked pretty considering I hadn't lost all the baby weight. Dad frowned at the mention of me having a baby before I got married. I smiled and assured them that there was no point in losing the weight just to gain it back. Malcolm chimed in and said he wanted another one before the year was out."

Amy knew for a fact that Darcy had been working out every day to slim down, and that she and Malcolm wanted to wait a few years before having another child. In the past six months, Darcy had managed to lose all the weight and then some. She looked incredible.

"He's going to request *Baby Got Back* later tonight, and he's been pinching the welts on my ass at regular intervals. He's so wonderful."

After dinner the DJ called for the bride and groom to kick off the dancing. Amy had arranged a dance solo to a salsa number that Malcolm had selected. He'd said it was the first song to which they'd danced on their first date. Watching from the sidelines, Amy's heart melted at the way Darcy gazed softly into Malcolm's eyes.

Jordan pressed a handkerchief into her hand. "It's fresh."

She dabbed at her eyes. "I don't know why I'm crying."

"Because love that strong and pure is a beautiful thing, and you're the kind of woman who cries when she sees beauty."

It had annoyed more than one former boyfriend. "I'm sorry."

"Don't be. It's one of the things that makes you who you are. Never apologize for that." The DJ called for other dancers to join the bride and groom, which was the cue for the bridesmaids and groomsmen to get out there. Jordan swept Amy into his arms and led her in one of those slow dances designed for people who don't know how to dance. Amy didn't mind because Jordan held her close and gazed meaningfully into her eyes.

The night seemed steeped in magic. After the dance, she spun around the floor with various friends and relatives. Malcolm and

Darcy left at nine to catch their plane, and the party began to wind down. She had many glasses of bubbly, giggling every time it tickled her nose. Through most of the night, Jordan remained by her side.

"Those in law enforcement will be the last to leave," Jordan said. "We take advantage of every opportunity to blow off steam."

Amy smiled indulgently. "The bar closed fifteen minutes ago. This shindig will be a ghost town in a half hour, and then I'll be able to go home."

Jordan looked around the room with that critical air he often affected. "I wanted to talk to you."

Responding to his serious tone, she gave her undivided attention. "Okay."

"Alone." He led her to a deserted hall. They passed the bustling kitchen where servers worked to clean up after the feast. He paused where it was quiet and there was some semblance of privacy. When he gazed at her with those heavy-lidded bedroom eyes and began to lean down, she knew the moment she'd waited for had come. She sprang to her toes to meet him halfway. Their lips met, a brief brush, and he jerked away, his eyes wide with the oh-shit expression

The dreamlike quality created by the music and the mood shattered, shards on the floor that would cut her soles. He hadn't meant to kiss her. He'd been leaning in to make sure they weren't overheard. Her parents had been right, and she'd made a huge mistake. "Damn. I'm such an idiot."

She fled, running down the hall toward the service entrance. Out there, hidden in the shadows the streetlights didn't reach, nobody would witness her shame.

Chapter Ten

Amy burst out the service entrance and onto a concrete landing surrounded by an iron railing. Hesitating only a second, she bounced down the stairs. Jordan would come after her out a sense of duty. Though she wasn't even close to being his girlfriend, they were friends, and he was her Not-Master. He took those last two roles seriously. Well, she didn't want him to follow. She wanted to be left alone to lick her wounds and deal with the humiliation. Then she'd return to the reception with her head held high and pretend it had never happened. Denial would work wonders to solve this problem.

She rounded the side of the building, and that's when she heard firecrackers. They were loud, echoing up and down the deserted street before dying away. Normally the sound would startle her, but she was too preoccupied with her emotional plight to do more than note the noise. She glanced behind her to make sure Jordan hadn't been able to track her, and that's when she tripped.

For the second time that evening, her inattention due to Jordan caused her pain. She landed hard, catching herself on her hands and knees. Rocks and other debris dug into her palms, and strong arms lifted her from the ground. She kicked out. "Let go of me!"

"Shut the fuck up."

Immediately she stilled. That voice didn't belong to Jordan—he would never speak to her like that—and the arms holding her immobile were unfamiliar. Fear spiked through her, and she finally became aware of her surroundings. A man's inert form lay prone on the ground at her feet. In the dim light, she recognized the dark stain spreading over his shirt on his right side.

She'd tripped over a body.

That noise hadn't come from a firecracker.

And that was the barrel of a gun pressed against her temple.

"Please," she breathed. "Let me go. I didn't see anything. I didn't even notice you until you picked me up." She tried to get a look at him by moving only her eyes and not her head. On second thought, the man wasn't much bigger than her. He had a medium build, and his wire-rimmed glasses and receding hairline made him look like someone's dad.

"FBI, motherfucker. Hands in the air."

She tore her gaze from the body to see Jordan standing a few feet away with his gun trained on the man using her as a shield. Now the way he'd grabbed her made more sense. He'd seen Jordan before she had.

"I don't want trouble," the guy said. He backed up two steps, dragging Amy with him. They were near the side of the building. Perhaps the man meant to run.

"Let her go." Jordan followed them, stepping carefully over the body that had tripped her up. "Get on your knees. Put the gun down and your hands in the air."

Suddenly, the man pushed her hard. She stumbled, and Jordan caught her as she knocked into him. He steadied her. "Are you hurt?"

"I'm fine." She knew he needed to give chase. "Go. I'll get whoever is left inside."

He ran off, and she hurried into the hall. Brandy Lockmeyer, the special agent in charge who she'd met only once, was the first person she ran into. She had gathered her things to leave, and her date whispered something in her ear. She laughed, a husky sound that rustled through the air.

"Chief Lockmeyer, Jordan ran off after a guy with a gun who shot another guy out back."

The Chief's demeanor changed, immediately transforming into the formidable woman who effectively managed a large group of agents. She turned and called across the room. "Rossetti! Adair!"

They responded to their boss's tone and hurried across the room. Keith made it first, and Liam came up behind. "Brandy? What's wrong?"

"Monaghan is in pursuit of an armed man believed to have already killed." She turned to Amy. "Do you have a description?"

"My height, probably around my weight, wire-rimmed glasses, maybe in his forties. He has a gun, and there's a dead guy out back." She rubbed her hands together, which reminded her of the rocks sticking into her palms. Gesturing to the southeast, she said, "They went that way."

Chief Lockmeyer nodded at Keith and Liam, and they took off. Brandy whipped out her phone and started talking in FBI jargon to the person on the other end. She walked toward the back of the building, and Amy watched, feeling scared and alone. Though she knew this was Jordan's job, he mostly talked about research and desk work. Even with the stories her sister and Layla had related, she hadn't imagined him ever actually being in danger.

Warm hands on her shoulders pushed her onto a chair. Amy looked up to find Trina leaning over her. "Honey, you're white as a sheet. Talk to me."

Amy had first met Trina a year ago, and the pair had become friendly, though they really only saw one another when they were at Darcy's. She was a sweet woman, warm-hearted and caring. Suddenly aware she hadn't been breathing, she inhaled sharply. "I tripped over a body. Jordan went after the shooter, and then Chief Lockmeyer had Keith and Liam go after them." She held up her hands to see places where the gravel had cut into her skin.

Trina examined them with a frown. "Let's get you washed up."

Her first attempt at standing didn't go so well. Amy crashed back onto the chair. "My knees feel like jelly."

"Okay." Trina flagged down a server. "Can I get a clean wet cloth? She's cut herself."

"Sure thing." The server, a girl Amy had worked with many times but whose name she couldn't quite recall, rushed off. She returned quickly. "Ms. Markevich, are you okay?"

"I'll be fine," she assured the girl. Veronica—her name was Veronica. "Thanks, Veronica. I fell down outside, but I'm fine now."

Trina cleaned up her hands, and the blood turned out not to be Amy's. "They'll get him, and they'll be back soon."

"He held a gun to my head." The tears started then, big fat ones rolling down her cheeks. Unlike her earlier waterworks, these were full of terror and relief, and then more terror at the thought of Jordan, Keith, and Liam out there facing off against an armed murderer.

Trina wrapped her arms around Amy and pushed Amy's head onto her shoulder. "Go ahead and let it all out. You're safe now."

"It's my fault. I shouldn't have gone out there."

A short, ironic laugh escaped from Trina. "Honey, we all saw him drag you out of here. Jordan's going to be kicking himself for putting you in danger even though nobody could have predicted you'd stumble onto a shooting."

Amy shook her head and sobbed harder. "I ran away from him. It was my fault. He didn't take me outside."

"Amy? I'm going to need to ask you some questions." Chief Lockmeyer had returned.

Trina let Amy sit up, but she kept her arm around Amy's shoulders. "Brandy, can't those wait until tomorrow?"

"I'm afraid not." Lockmeyer's expression managed to be both firm and bland. "Walk me through what happened."

The last thing she wanted to share with anybody was the humiliation she'd endured. Her mouth opened and closed several times as she tried to think of a way to gloss over her stupidity. "I— I got upset with Jordan and ran out the service entrance. I didn't want him to find me, so I ran around the corner, and that's when I tripped. I didn't realize it was a body until I got up. I mean, I didn't get up. The shooter guy picked me up and put his gun against my head. He used me as a shield because Jordan was there, and he was pointing his gun at the guy who was holding onto me. Then the guy shoved me at Jordan and ran off. Jordan went after him, and I came inside to tell you what was going on."

Trina watched Lockmeyer closely, and she frowned at the lack of apparent reaction. "It seems pretty straightforward. What's not adding up?"

"You said a man had been shot?"

"Yes." Amy sniffled. She indicated her back on the lower right side. "His shirt was bloody. Trina washed blood off my hands that wasn't mine."

Chief Lockmeyer's mouth turned down and a line crinkled between her eyebrows. "There's no body that's been shot. We found Judge Caldwell out there, but he hasn't been shot, and his wound isn't where Amy is indicating."

Amy blinked. "I don't understand."

"She might be in shock." Trina spoke gently. "Is Jordan back? He can probably give you a clearer picture of what happened."

Amy frowned. Maybe she hadn't made complete sense, but a body didn't just get up and walk away. "I'm not wrong. I know what I saw. I know who Judge Caldwell is. Herman Caldwell was on the guest list. I seated him and his wife at table five with a lawyer and another judge. They're from Malcolm's guest list." The fog was beginning to clear, and her tears dried up. "He wasn't there. The guy on the ground was a stranger. He was wearing a light dress shirt, not white, and pants, but not a tux. Judge Caldwell was wearing a tuxedo with a clip-on bow tie."

Lockmeyer's frown lines eased. "That's true, and we did find trace amounts of what could be blood on the cement. We'll need forensics to confirm that it doesn't belong to Caldwell. Okay, we have a missing body on the loose." She got back on the phone and ordered a BOLO for area emergency rooms.

The guests who had lingered to find out about the drama cleared out quickly. Amy wanted to leave as well, but she knew she couldn't go until she'd been officially dismissed. They'd want a statement. Someone turned on the brighter lights in the reception hall, and people with FBI jackets swarmed the place.

Trina stayed by her side through the process. "A judge is involved, so it's automatically a Federal case. We're going to be here a while."

"You can leave." Amy turned to Trina. "You didn't see anything, and I'm sure Keith will understand if you want to go home."

"He will," Trina agreed. "But I'm not leaving you alone. You've had one hell of a night." She stood. "You know what? I'm going to take you home. They know where you live, and they can get your statement tomorrow."

Before Amy could say anything, Trina went off to find Lockmeyer.

Amy rested her head on the table. Exhaustion was close to winning out. She barely opened her eyes when she felt a hand on her arm. Jordan's large form bent over her and blotted out most of the light. "Babe? Come on. I'm going to take you home. Tomorrow I'll take you downtown to give your official statement."

She sat up. "Trina's going to take me home."

The lines around his mouth tightened ever so slightly. "Keith is taking her home. I'm taking you home. Let's get your purse and whatever bags you've brought with you."

"My car is in the lot. I can drive myself home." She stood and extracted her arm from his hold. Her purse was across the room, and the two bags full of backup plans she'd brought in case something went wrong were in the coat check room. The room was empty, and so her things were easily acquired.

Jordan followed her, though she did her best to ignore him. He snagged her bags and held out his hand, palm up. "This is not open for discussion. Hand over your car keys. I'm driving."

When he used that tone, she knew better than to disobey. Gracelessly she dumped her keys in his hand. She didn't say a word on the way home.

"Amy, we need to talk."

Streetlights cast stripes over her body as he navigated the side streets that led to her place. "I'm tired. I just want to go to sleep." She closed her eyes to block out the recurring sense of humiliation that came back when she looked at him. He was younger and sexy and so incredibly handsome. What had she been thinking? Of course he wasn't interested in her. He'd been clear that training her was a friend thing, something he was doing because he was a nice guy who wanted to help her navigate her way through a world with which he was intimately familiar. The whole idea of it possibly turning into something more had been something Jordan had consistently pushed aside.

He rested his hand over hers, but she pulled away. "Amy—"

"Don't, Jordan. I'm exhausted, and I've had one hell of a day."

Though he didn't respond and she didn't look over at him, she knew he was scowling. He hated not being in complete control of a situation.

He said nothing as he walked her to the door and unlocked it. He came inside without being invited and set her bags on the floor behind the sofa. "Thanks," she said. "Did you want to borrow my car to get home? I won't need it tomorrow. My parents are coming over with Colin. We planned to spend the day together."

How pathetic was it that she preferred to spend the day with her parents in order to avoid Jordan?

"You'll have to give your statement tomorrow."

"You don't need it first thing in the morning." She washed her hand over her face and stared at the black streaks of makeup on her fingers. "Bring my car back in the afternoon, and I'll drive you to Detroit so I can give my statement. It shouldn't take long because you were there too, and your statement probably carries more weight than mine would. And then I'm sure one of your buddies can give you a ride home."

He closed her front door and twisted the deadbolt. "I'm not leaving you alone tonight. As you said, you've been through a lot."

Too tired to argue, she nodded. "I'll make up the sofa for you. There's no bed in the guest room anymore." She'd converted it to storage space for her business.

In the last twenty-four hours, everything had gone sideways. Jordan lay on the sofa, thinking about the fact that last night, he'd been there too. Only she'd been with him, her warm, curvy body molded to his harder planes. She'd been relaxed and content, willingly submitting to his embrace. Even a few hours ago, she'd been giggling from the effect of too much alcohol and laughing at him as he danced with her and sang along badly with the song. He lived to make her happy. Her genuine smile was a gift for which he'd do just about anything.

Right now the house was silent. He'd conducted a perimeter check, making sure the windows and doors were secure. Since he'd run down the gunman, overpowered him with little effort, and arrested the bastard—who had also assaulted a Federal judge—he knew she was safe.

She was asleep in her bed, a place he desperately wanted to be. He'd planned the reveal perfectly, only he'd thrown caution to the wind. She was in an excellent mood and attuned to him even though she was unaware of it. He'd meant to talk to her, to explain about his unusual kink. He'd been hoping for immediate acceptance. Why wait until the next morning to tell her the secret he'd been keeping?

The way she'd looked at him—soft and vulnerable, and utterly trusting—had combined with the headiness of the night to rob him of his better sense. He'd jumped the gun. He'd been about to kiss her. He knew she would welcome it, and she had. Only he'd remembered the promise he'd made to himself to be completely candid so she could make an informed, unemotional decision. He'd spent a lot of time finding out who he was, and she was just beginning her journey. If he'd told her about his Daddy side from the beginning, she would have spent the last month trying to mold herself to fit what he wanted instead of trying to figure out what she wanted.

He'd halted the kiss a second too late, and she'd been severely hurt. The image of her face then, and again when the gunman held a gun to her head, haunted him. He wouldn't be sleeping anytime soon.

A sound from her room had him on his feet. It had been a tiny, distressed noise. He crept down the hall, listening to see if it happened again. It did, but louder this time. He paused outside her closed door. "Amy? Are you okay?"

She didn't answer. Pushing open the door, he tiptoed into her room. It was dark, but his eyes had adjusted, and he had no problem making out her form in the middle of the bed. She shifted, flinging her arm above her head and mumbling. "No. Let me go."

It was a nightmare. He slid into bed and took her in his arms. "Shhh, little one. I'm here. You're safe."

She curled into him without waking, her fingers grasping desperately at his chest. He shifted them both until she was comfortable enough to calm down. A lump of covers under him pressed uncomfortably into his lower back. Lifting up, he grabbed the wad to smooth it out, and he found a stuffed animal. He set it carefully on the chair next to her bed. Before long, he fell asleep with the woman of his dreams snuggled peacefully in his arms.

In the morning, he woke first. Amy was still curled against his side. Though he was tempted to remain in her bed, he reasoned that she wouldn't want him there just yet. He gently eased his arm out from under her and shifted her head to a pillow. She frowned briefly, and then her face smoothed out as she fell back into a deeper sleep.

His stomach growled, so he headed to the kitchen to make breakfast. His little one was going to need her strength today. Before long, he heard the bathroom door close. She entered the kitchen just as he finished browning the French toast.

"Good morning, babe. I hope you're hungry because I made a lot. I used up the last of the strawberries to make a strawberry topping." He glanced over his shoulder in time to catch her frown.

"Why are you still here? I said you could borrow my car."

"Thanks. I will." He plated two pieces of French toast, added the topping, and put a whipped cream smiley face on each of them. Then he added two sausage links. "Sit. You need to eat."

"I'm fine." She sat anyway.

"You're grouchy. You'll feel better with some warm food in your tummy." He joined her at the table, and they ate in silence. He hoped to improve her mood, but she seemed to go from irritated to sad. He squeezed her hand. "It's normal to feel out of sorts after an experience like that."

She stared at his hand. "I'm fine. It's over. You caught the guy, and he's in jail. You don't need to be here." She slid her hand out from under his and set it in her lap.

They seriously needed to talk, and she needed to be reined in. "Amy, you've had a decent night's sleep, and now you've eaten a proper breakfast. I can only overlook brattiness for so long. You're coming very close to earning a punishment."

That got her attention. She blinked at him in shock. "We—We haven't discussed punishment."

"Not really, which is why I gave you a warning."

She pushed her plate away with her food only half-eaten. "I'm full."

"No you're not. Finish breakfast, or I'll tie you up and feed you."

Her bottom lip quivered. "My parents are coming over in a half hour. I need to shower."

He slid her plate back to her. "Then you'd better eat. I'm sure you're not ready for your parents to see you tied to a chair while I feed you breakfast." The image of her in that state made his cock stir. He half hoped she'd disobey. The doors were locked, and he could have her untied quickly enough to avoid a situation she'd find humiliating.

Though she continued to pout, she finished her food and drank her orange juice. If he wasn't mistaken, his display of dominance had also helped her find some inner peace. When she was finished, she turned to him. "I don't want my parents to know about last night. They have enough to worry about, so please don't mention it."

For a second, he thought she meant the almost-kiss, but then he got his head back in the game. "Do you really think you should keep something like that from them?"

"They'll find a way to blame me for what happened. I know it's my fault, but I don't need them to rub my nose in it. I feel bad enough already." She rubbed her hands together under the table. Her shoulders hunched under the weight of the blame she assumed.

Jordan frowned. "How is any of that your fault?"

She shrugged, and he knew she was thinking of the way she'd run away after he'd stopped the kiss.

Lifting her chin with one finger, he forced her to look at him. Her bright blue eyes shone with unshed tears. "Babe, that guy assaulted a Federal judge and shot another man. You are not at fault for any of that. In fact, if you hadn't stumbled upon the crime, I wouldn't have caught the bad guy. You saved a life, perhaps two. I give you permission to take the blame for that, but nothing else. Got it?"

Though she nodded, he wasn't sure his message penetrated. "I need to get in the shower and get dressed."

They seriously needed to have the talk he'd been putting off until the wedding was over. He'd wanted to talk to her today, when her schedule was clear and she had nothing weighty on her mind. That was before he'd known that she'd promised her free time to her parents. He couldn't intrude on her family time, and so he would wait until after she made her statement to force the issue. He exhaled. "Go. I need to check in with Brandy. I'll see what time someone can take your statement."

She all but fled from the room, and he stared after her until he heard water running in the shower. Who would have thought she'd turn out to be a runner? The sage advice she often gave was full of stories of when she'd faced her problems, not examples of when she'd run from conflict. Once she felt comfortable enough to let her inner little run free, he'd finally get to know the complex woman for whom he'd fallen. With a sigh, he rinsed their plates and put them in the dishwasher. At least she hadn't broken off their D/s relationship and thrown him out of her house. So far her running was physical, not emotional.

A knock sounded at the front door as he finished cleaning up from breakfast, so he answered it. The look on Fran Markevich's face reminded him that he wore only a pair of sweats. She looked him up and down disapprovingly while Paul scowled.

"Good morning, Fran. Paul." He shook Paul's hand, and although Amy's father reciprocated with obvious reluctance, his grip was firm and steady, communicating a silent warning to the strange, half-naked man in his daughter's house. Jordan pasted on his friendliest smile. "Amy's in the shower. Come on in and make yourself at home."

"Well, you certainly have." Fran brushed past him with Colin in her arms. The five-month-old pumped his legs and squealed at Jordan. Since he looked like he was about to leap out of Fran's hold, Jordan took his buddy's son from his grandmother.

"Hey there, big guy. You've grown a lot in a week."

Paul grabbed four bags full of baby stuff from the porch and came inside. "He's grown since last night. I swear, when he woke us up at the crack of dawn, he was bigger." He dropped the bags next to the sofa and sat down heavily. "I don't remember kids being so much work."

"That's because you went to work, and I took care of the kids. Now you don't have an excuse to get out of it." Fran took Colin back. She'd spread a blanket on the floor where she set Colin on his stomach with an array of toys to keep him occupied. Fran settled on the sofa next to her husband. "Jordan, would you mind telling Amy that we're here?"

He glanced down the hall uncertainly. "I'm sure she can hear you. She knew you were coming over."

"And she decided to have her half-dressed lover answer the door?" She turned to Paul. "She's throwing this in our faces, you know. This is your fault."

Jordan held up a hand. "Whoa. Hold on. Amy hasn't thrown anything at anyone. I needed a place to crash last night, and she graciously offered her couch. I'm not wearing a shirt because I could only find a pair of sweats to sleep in. Once she's out of the bathroom, I'll get dressed. I have to be at work soon."

Fran and Paul seemed to accept his explanation. Colin squealed loudly and flapped his limbs so hard that he turned over. He'd spied his favorite aunt before the adults had.

"There's my handsome man!" Amy sat cross-legged on the floor and picked up her nephew. In his excitement, Colin grabbed her hair, yanked hard, and pitched forward to bite her nose. Amy giggled. "I missed you too." She kissed every inch of his face before setting him down and distracting him with a colorful toy. "Hi, Mom and Dad. How is babysitting duty going so far?"

Jordan left them as they chattered about the baby. He washed his face and donned his shirt and pants from the night before. In his truck were a pair of jeans and a clean shirt. He missed his truck. In deference to his usual look, he left off the bow tie and cummerbund, and he didn't button the shirt up all the way. Was it wrong that he could only think about the fact that she didn't mind having her hair pulled?

On the way out, he pulled Amy aside. "I'll be back at around two or three to pick you up. Are you going to be okay?"

"I'm fine." Her answer was too quick. She wanted to get rid of him.

"Thanks for letting me borrow your car." He kissed her forehead and left, reasoning it was his turn to flee the scene.

Chapter Eleven

Herman Caldwell had been a judge longer than Jordan had been alive. The venerable man was known for running a tight ship, and he had an unflagging sense of justice. Just now, he felt he'd been gravely wronged, and he had.

Jordan arrived at his floor of the McNamara building to find the thin, wrinkled man with his fist raised and his voice thundering through the reception area. His red face highlighted the whiteness of his wispy hair, and he wore the same tuxedo he'd worn at the wedding. "That son of a bitch grabbed me when I went to get my car. Why wasn't there a valet service?"

"Because agents are paid a crap salary." Keith Rossetti, well-rested and impeccably attired, leaned against the receptionist's desk with his arms crossed. "Pay us better, and I'll have valet service at my wedding."

Jordan lifted a brow. "Did Trina finally say she'd marry you?"

Keith scowled. "She hasn't said she wouldn't, just that she wants a more romantic proposal."

"That's not the point, young man." Caldwell threw a quelling glare at them both. "The point is that I was accosted, knocked out, and tied up. They argued about whether to kidnap or kill me."

Keith clapped a hand on the judge's shoulder and steered him down the hall. "Judge Caldwell, let's discuss this in my office."

Though Caldwell allowed Keith to lead him away from the public area, he huffed. "I gave my statement already. Unlike the two of you, I was here first thing in the morning."

Over the judge's head, Keith shot Jordan a sardonic grin. They'd been out late taking care of the arrest, and they'd both made it to the office before ten. Jordan opened the door to Keith's office and went inside. "Sorry about that. We don't like to get in too early on our day off."

Re/Defined

"It's Monday morning, not the weekend. You take weekends off, not weekdays."

Sometimes it was useless explaining that they were always on call, that their nights and weekends were frequently spent working. They scheduled time off whenever their overtime threatened to break the department's budget. "I was with the other witness," Jordan supplied. "I know you made a statement, and we'll read it later, but right now, we'd like to hear the details from you."

Inaccuracies in memory tended to be exposed with repeated retellings. He and Keith would analyze all versions of the story from everybody involved.

Slightly mollified, Caldwell seated himself on one of the chairs facing Keith's desk. Jordan took the place next to him. He pressed his fingertips together thoughtfully. "Walk us through what happened, Your Honor. What time did you leave the reception?"

Herman Caldwell exhaled, and some of his dudgeon deflated. "Margie was getting tired. She had her hip replaced last year, and it looks like we're going to have to get the other one replaced soon. I went to get the car so she wouldn't have to walk all the way around the building and then across the parking lot. It was about ten o'clock, and some idiot closed the bar an hour before the reception was supposed to end."

Jordan refrained from chuckling. Amy had said people would leave once the bar was closed. He hadn't doubted her, but he liked this confirmation of the depth of her understanding of human nature. He shifted, spreading his hands wide to encourage their witness. "So you left the building right after the bar closed?"

"I'd finished my drink an hour beforehand. Margie finished her drink right after they closed the bar. I think I left to get the car at about quarter after. She stayed behind to freshen up and was to meet me out front in ten minutes. Did she raise the alarm when I didn't come? Is that why you were out looking for me?"

They knew better than to answer questions while a witness or victim was giving their account. Keith cleared his throat. "What route did you take to the parking lot?"

"I turned left out of the front door. I walked around the side of the building, and when I got to the dark part just before the parking lot, that's when they grabbed me."

Jordan frowned, making a mental note to check out the lights in the parking lot. Having a well-lit parking lot seemed like something Amy would insist on before choosing a venue. Also, they'd only arrested one individual. It looked like the man who'd been shot was one of the assailants. "Can you show me how you were grabbed?" He stood, intending to play the part of the bad guy.

Keith came around the desk to play the part of the guy who got shot.

Caldwell walked them through a reenactment that included an assessment of the body odor and breath of the perp. "He didn't smell like alcohol, but he also hadn't bathed or washed his clothes in a while." He positioned Keith a few feet away. "I didn't see you until after the guy grabbed me. He had his arm around my throat and a gun pointed at my head. The other guy came out of the shadows. He said, 'Good job, now kill him.' The guy holding me refused. He shook his head and said, 'I don't want to do this. Don't make me do this.' I was hoping to play on that, so I told him to resist the devil."

Jordan eased his hold on the judge. He didn't want to set off a fear reaction that might derail the retelling. "What did he do next?"

"The guy holding me threw me behind the trash bin. I hit my head against the brick on the building. I spent the night in the hospital getting x-rays and a CAT scan. I have a mild concussion."

Jordan didn't follow through with throwing the judge against a wall. He let go and faced Keith. "What happened between the two guys?"

Judge Caldwell sat back down. Though he tried to hide it, the man was shaking. "They argued, but my hearing aid had been knocked out, so I couldn't make out what they said. And that bump on my head left me fuzzy. I heard the shots, though. I was trying to sneak away behind the trash bins, and I froze. I didn't know what had happened. I didn't see that the other guy had a gun. I closed my eyes and prayed. The next thing I knew, Chief Lockmeyer was there. The paramedics showed up a few minutes later. Margie can't drive, you know. She rode to the hospital with me. My daughter picked us up at five in the morning. They wanted me to stay for observation, but I refused."

Mentally Jordan filled in the cracks. Amy had caused a distraction when she'd stumbled into the fracas, and neither of them had seen the judge cowering in the shadows behind the trash bins. He handed Caldwell his card. "Thanks for coming down this morning, Your Honor. We appreciate it. If you think of anything else, call me."

They walked the judge to reception where his daughter was waiting. Dark circles under her eyes told the story of her night. She wore sweats and an old shirt, and her blonde hair had been hastily thrown into a ponytail. She rose when she saw them.

Caldwell patted her shoulder. "Heidi, I'd like you to meet Agents Rossetti and Monaghan. They'll be handling the case."

She smiled tightly, an expression of worry and exhaustion. She shook Keith's hand first, and then she focused on Jordan. "Chief Lockmeyer said you'd already caught the gunman."

"I did, but there was another person involved who had not bee located." He handed a card to Heidi as well. "This has my cell number on it. Take your father home, and both of you get some rest."

As they headed back down the hall, Dustin joined them. "And here you thought you'd have the day off. I take it you and Amy didn't have an enlightening conversation?"

Keith chuckled. "Probably not. Kat said Amy ran away from Jordan. She wasn't able to get details, though. One wonders what you said to make her leave like that? 'Call me Daddy' doesn't sound all that threatening."

Jordan narrowed his eyes at Keith's mirth. "I didn't get a chance to say anything. I messed up, and she ran away. When I went after her to explain, that's when it all went to shit. Then she wouldn't talk to me last night, and this morning, her parents came over."

Keith wrinkled his nose. "They can be unpleasant. I've heard stories."

"They jumped to conclusions because I answered the door shirtless." If he had his way, they would soon be the right conclusions. Nevertheless, he didn't blame her parents for being upset. If that had happened with his daughter, he could imagine being less than polite. "But they were fine after I explained that I crashed on the sofa." The pillow and blanket there helped corroborate his story even though it wasn't technically true.

Dustin shook his head. "Man, you need to talk to her."

Jordan agreed. "First I need to see the file on and question Brian Gartrell. I'll straighten things out with Amy later today."

Keith clapped a hand on his shoulder, and Dustin made a similar move on the other side. Dustin shook his head. "Buddy, you can watch. You can even talk into our earpieces. But you cannot go in there. If you kill the only person we have who can describe our other perp, we've got nothing. That parking lot isn't under video surveillance. Nothing in the area is."

"I won't kill him."

Keith chuckled. "Right. Because he didn't put his hands on your woman and hold a gun to her head."

Cold rage, the kind that had boiled in his veins last night, coursed through him. He hadn't harmed the suspect last night, but then again, Keith and Liam had arrived soon after he'd caught up with the man.

"Thought so." Dustin gave him a shove toward the room where the feed from the interrogation rooms went.

Liam Adair was inside tweaking the controls. He grinned and jerked his thumb to the chair behind his. "I saved you a seat."

Brandy Lockmeyer looked up from the file she was reading. "Gartrell has been sitting in there for three hours. He has a severe headache and diarrhea."

Those were symptoms of cocaine withdrawal. Gartrell was probably feeling like he had a really bad flu. Rossetti and Brandt would play upon his discomfort during questioning. He took the seat on the other side of Brandy and opened the file she gave him.

She touched his forearm gently. "Jordan, it was my order to keep you out of there. I know how emotional you dominant types get over your women, and we can't afford any missteps with this. A Federal judge was assaulted last night. Caldwell is a highly respected and influential person."

"I know. I get it. I'm calm." At her snort, he looked up from the file he hadn't yet started reading. He scowled at the shrewd knowledge in those green eyes. They'd been through a lot together, and she knew him better than most of his friends. When she didn't let up, he sighed and let the tension drain from his shoulders. "I'm fine."

"After Rossetti and Brandt wrap this up, I want you to take the rest of the day off."

"Can't. I have to go get Amy and bring her here to give her statement."

Brandy tucked a lock of hair behind her ear. "We have your statement, Judge Caldwell's statement, and now we're getting

Gartrell's. Amy's statement can wait until tomorrow. She probably saw less than you did."

Amy wasn't trained to assess a situation the way he was. She'd likely focused on the immediate danger to herself, and then when that had passed, she'd focused on his needs. Without needing to be told, she'd assured him that she was all right, and then she'd headed into the reception hall to alert the other agents. "Fine. I'll let her know."

Keith and Dustin entered the interrogation room while Jordan watched on the monitor. The pair had a presence that, even on camera, made them seem larger and more prominent than the sweating man sitting with his head in his hands.

Dustin set a water bottle and a small paper cup on the table as he took his seat next to Keith. "Headache? I brought some extra-strength Tylenol."

"They already gave me some." Gartrell rocked back and forth. "I'm a dead man anyway. The pain doesn't matter. I feel like I'm gonna throw up again."

Keith maintained the stoic expression for which he was known. "Why are you a dead man?"

Gartrell squeezed his head between his hands, and then he reversed direction, pulling what remained of his hair. "I messed up. They're not going to let this go. I'm dead. The judge is dead. The girl in the dress is dead. And the guy who arrested me is dead."

Dustin leaned forward, frowning doubtfully. "Are you making threats?"

Gartrell rocked again, and this time he shook his head violently. "All for some rocks. I could have gone out and looked for a new job. I wouldn't have lost my wife or my kid, and I wouldn't be here now. Why? Why? All for some fucking crack!"

"Brian, walk us through what happened. We may be able to help." Dustin pushed the water and Tylenol closer. "Drink some water. You have to keep hydrated. It'll help with the detox symptoms."

Gartrell downed the pills with a long swig of water. This was the first time he looked up so the camera could see his face. "I don't deserve this." He set the half empty bottle down. "I don't deserve to live. I deserve what's coming to me. But that judge don't. That poor woman don't, and that cop don't."

Keith nodded thoughtfully. "What were you doing at that reception hall in the first place?"

Jordan started as he remembered Gartrell's face. He grabbed the microphone from Dare. "Dustin, Gartrell is one of the homeless guys who has been crashing in that Mexican restaurant church."

Though Brandt didn't openly acknowledge Jordan, his blue eyes flashed with recognition.

But Gartrell was talking. "They said I had to do it. At first it was just robbing a few places, and then that kid died. I never shot no one who was innocent before, and I didn't like it. It was an accident, and I was sorry, and I didn't want to do it. I didn't want him to die, but he did, and now they want more. I didn't want to do it, but they got me. They own my ass. I was going to give myself up, but they know where my ex-wife and daughter are. They're going to kill my daughter. I done enough to her with being a shitty dad. All I got left is protecting her, and I'm going to do it."

Dustin let silence fill the room after Gartrell stopped to take a breath and drain the rest of the water. Then he clasped his hands together. "What is your affiliation with the New Day Church?"

Gartrell blinked. "It ain't a fucking church. It's where they get you by the balls and make you their bitch." He looked around, and then he started trembling. He put his head in his hands and rocked back and forth. "Dead. We're all dead. Joe don't like no one seeing his face."

"Joe who?" Keith frowned, a severe expression that struck fear into the hearts of many, but Gartrell wasn't paying attention.

"Don't know his name. I call him Joe because he don't tell us his name. I had to shoot him because he was going to kill the judge. He tried to take the gun. I wish I'd let him have it. He'd-a shot the judge and me, and we'd both be dead, and I wouldn't be here waiting to die." Suddenly he shot forward, trying to leap across the table, but the handcuffs only let him move so far. He crashed to the table, falling flat on his face. "Make sure he don't kill my wife and daughter. They ain't done nothing bad but give me a chance."

Keith and Dustin stared. They'd both shot to their feet when Gartrell had leaped. Keith grabbed Gartrell by the collar and lifted him. The man flopped around, dead weight. "He passed out." He shook Gartrell and slapped his cheek lightly. "Wake up, Brian. It's not nap time yet."

Gartrell, however, didn't respond.

Keith pried open Gartrell's eyelid and checked for signs of other problems. "He's completely out of it."

"I guess we're done for now." Dustin headed for the door. "Leave him here. Nobody's going to carry him to the holding tank."

As his fellow agents exited the interview room, Jordan turned to Liam and Brandy in the monitoring room. "That was Tylenol, right?"

Dare shrugged, more an indication of not caring than not knowing.

Frown lines creased Brandy's chin. "As far as I know." She went to the door and called out. "Rossetti, Brandt, get in here."

Keith and Dustin entered wearing matching frowns. "Has he been awake all night?"

Re/Defined

Dare pulled up a digital log of Gartell's activities since he'd arrived late last night. "He spent the night curled up on his cot. He may or may not have slept."

Dustin motioned toward the file in Jordan's hand. "Double check the drug test. Maybe he's on more than just cocaine."

"His pupils weren't dilated, and they were responsive to light." Keith looked at the slumbering man on the monitor. "Run his blood work and another drug test."

Jordan looked over the test that had already been done. "Just cocaine. No alcohol or anything else. You're sure that was Tylenol?"

"I took it from the break room." Dustin rushed out the door as he said it. Cocaine withdrawal shouldn't have induced the kind of reaction Gartrell was having.

Brandy shot orders at each of them. "Monaghan, call the paramedics, and see if anybody else has taken anything from that bottle. Rossetti, get forensics and run every test you can think of in that room and in his cell. Adair, check all the surveillance footage in this building for the last forty-eight hours." She continued as she ran down the hall after Dustin. "Forsythe, I want tests run on everything in that room. Hardy, seal off the break room. Brandt, get everybody into the briefing room—now."

The break room would be the best place to carry out his task. He rushed there and called the group to order to ask his questions, though he didn't think there was anything wrong with the Tylenol. Not enough time had passed between Gartrell taking the pill and him passing out for there to be a connection. Once he ascertained that the agents were fine, he surveyed the support staff. Two administrative assistants had taken pills, so he sent them with medics for testing.

While the hustle and bustle was happening, Jordan slipped into the interrogation room. He found Sydney and Jack from forensics. "Where is the prisoner?"

Sydney waved him away. "Medics took him in a body bag."

Jordan got out before they could rail at him for breathing on their possible crime scene. He intercepted Keith coming down the hall. "Where is Gartrell?"

"He died. The coroner is suiting up right now for the autopsy."

Jordan stared at Keith, a thousand possibilities running through his mind. He had to find Dustin. "Where's Brandt?"

"Lockmeyer pulled him from the investigation until he's cleared. He's in her office." Keith grabbed him before he could storm into Brandy's office. "Do this by the book, Monaghan."

"Fine. I'll help Dare go through the surveillance footage."

Keith nodded. "That's where I'm headed now."

When an intern came by for their dinner order, Jordan realized he hadn't called Amy. He excused himself. "Hey, babe. Something came up, and I'm not going to make it back to get you today. Lockmeyer rescheduled you for tomorrow." His eyeballs felt like glue from staring at monitors, searching for something to clear one of his closest friends.

"That's okay." Amy's neutral tone raised a red flag. "I don't need my car until the morning anyway."

"I'll have someone bring it back by seven."

"Okay. Thanks. Have a good night."

"Amy?"

"Yeah?"

"We're going to discuss this."

"There's nothing to talk about. Listen, my parents are still here. We're about to have dinner. I'll see you tomorrow."

Jordan stared at his phone. She'd been polite and considerate. He could understand if she'd been angry or disappointed—she had every right to both emotions. The lack of reaction bothered him, but he couldn't dwell on it now. When he returned to Dare's computer lab, he found both Keith and Liam on the phone.

"I'll be home in an hour, Kitty Kat. I love you." Keith pocketed his phone and regarded Jordan solemnly. "Dustin went home a few hours ago."

"I know. I'm going to call him after I talk to Brandy."

Liam ended his call as well. "That was our wonderful and talented coroner. It seems that Brian Gartrell's food was laced with aconitum, also known as monkshood or wolf's bane. It manifests in symptoms similar to cocaine withdrawal. I wonder if he's a fan of Greek mythology or Dexter? Ah, well. It's out there, a pretty flower that can kill you with one touch. Time to check footage from the cafeteria."

Jordan sat down in front of a monitor. "Start from the time he got it and work backward. I'll pull up the duty roster to see who was on this morning." He glanced at Keith who took his spot in front of yet another monitor. "Go home. We got this."

Keith shook his head and sent a text. "We're close. Kat will understand."

Jordan shrugged. Those who loved agents knew what they signed on for. "I'm going to call Dustin and let him know."

He pulled into Amy's driveway at one-thirty in the morning. It had been one hell of a day. It hadn't taken long to backtrack the food's path. The guard on duty had tried to hide his actions, but the McNamara building had eyes everywhere. Though the guard had shielded his actions from one camera, another hidden camera had caught him adding the poison to the runny eggs. Prison food was bad enough to cover the taste.

The call to Dustin had been a relief to make, even if he found out that Brandy had called first. Of course she had—she took care of her agents. Her team always came first.

Amy's house was dark. She hadn't left the porch light on because she had no idea he'd planned to come over. He'd sent her car back with a rookie agent who lived in the area. Jordan navigated the steps using a flashlight because the flowers and bushes surrounding her porch blocked the streetlights. She hadn't given him a key, but he knew she kept a spare key hidden in a fake rock jammed behind a well-established rose bush. He retrieved it with minimal injury.

Tonight he planned to sleep on her sofa. If she had another nightmare, he'd be there to soothe her fears.

Chapter Twelve

The unsettling dream of being chased and captured at gunpoint came and went faster this time, but the second dream was far worse. The gunman was on top of her, his weight pressing her against the soft forest floor. Though rocks didn't press painfully into her flesh, the pine scent threatened to suffocate her—or was that his bulky body restricting the ability of her lungs to expand? The long skirt of her bridesmaid dress worked with him to inhibit her movements. She struggled against him and to surface from the terrifying dream.

She woke screaming, shoving at the weight holding her down as she rolled ungracefully from the bed to land on the floor. Her hip caught the brunt of the action, and her side throbbed with pain.

Jordan leaped from bed, fists at the ready, and blinked sleep from his eyes. "What? What's going on?"

Amy got to her feet slowly, trying to ignore the sight of almost six-and-a-half feet of pure male perfection. He wore only a pair of blue shorts that did nothing to hide the bulge of his endowment. His chest, which she'd been forced to face yesterday morning as she tried to eat breakfast, was a mass of corded muscle and smooth flesh. A dark swatch of hair began just below his sternum and spread a little wider as it blazed a trail into his underwear. He had powerful thighs and legs that went on forever. If Amy hadn't been so pissed at him, she might have tackled him back into bed where something that scrumptious belonged.

She grabbed the top blanket and used it to cover herself. Thinking she was alone just because nobody was there, she'd slept in her favorite My Little Pony nightgown. "What the hell are you doing in my bed? How did you get into my house?"

He sat on the edge of the bed with his back to her and washed his hands over his face. "This is not my favorite way to wake up."

Amy smacked him across the back with a pillow. "Being crushed and suffocated by a strange man in my bed isn't my favorite way to wake up, either. How did you get into my house?"

Twisting to face her, he nailed her with a fierce scowl. "I'm not a strange man, I didn't crush or suffocate you, and you keep a spare key behind your rosebush out front."

She hadn't known he knew about that, but it didn't make a difference. "That's not an invitation to break into my house and sleep in my bed." *While she was wearing My Little Pony pajamas.* If she'd known he was going to be there, she would have put on something a little more flattering and made for an adult. She hitched the blanket higher.

Jordan narrowed his eyes, which made him appear more dangerous than when he wore just a scowl. "Amy, I've seen you wearing less than that."

"Yes, but it was during a scene. That doesn't count." And she'd been wearing lingerie—lacy bras and panties.

With a sigh, he once again turned his back to her. He grabbed a pair of jeans from where he'd slung them across the chair next to her bed and slid into them. "You had a nightmare the night before last, and so I didn't want to leave you alone last night in case you had another one, which you did. I didn't sleep on the couch two nights ago, babe. I came in here when you cried out, and I soothed you back to sleep. I slept here, but you didn't notice because I woke up before you did. Last night, I fully intended to sleep on the couch, but you cried out again, so I stayed in here again. That's all."

So many emotions zinged through Amy that she had trouble grasping at them. He'd been in her bed twice now, and she'd slept through it. She didn't know whether to be angry that he'd be so forward, happy that he cared so much, or frustrated that she hadn't been awake to enjoy it. Finally she settled in neutral territory. "Fine. I understand that you had good intentions, but please understand that I can take care of myself. I've had nightmares before."

He donned his shirt, covering up that distracting expanse of tantalizing flesh, and regarded her with a firmly patient gaze. "You've never been held at gunpoint before, Amy. It's normal to have nightmares. It's normal to be upset afterward, and it's easier if you have someone with you to help you deal with the emotional upheaval."

"I'm okay," she said, though her heart beat faster just because he was talking about it and forcing her to remember it. "You saved me. Your job is done."

He closed his eyes briefly, and a shadow passed over his features. "No, babe. I'm nowhere close to being done with you."

She wished he meant it in a different way, but as her stupid actions at Darcy's wedding proved, he didn't. He felt a responsibility toward her because he was her Dom. He was training her, and he took that duty seriously because that's who he was. That was one of the reasons she liked him so much. Casting her gaze down the way he'd taught her, she reined in her regret. "Thank you for what you've done for me. I'm okay, though, so you don't need to sleep here anymore. I'm sure you miss sleeping in your own bed. I mean, you barely fit on mine. It's a queen size, and you're much too large to fit comfortably."

"I fit just fine." And then to prove it, he took off his jeans and flopped down on her bed. Then he snagged the blanket she'd wrapped around her body and covered himself up. "And I'm going back to sleep."

His eyes were closed and he looked like he wasn't going anywhere, so she gathered her clothes and left the room. As she showered, she thought about the mixed signals he was still sending, and it made her a little mad. While she ate breakfast, she thought about the protective and proprietary way he treated her, and her level of emotional discontent ratcheted up a couple of notches. Yes, she was angry, but she couldn't figure out if she was angry with him or with herself. He'd been very clear about who he was and what he wanted, and he'd been transparent about his intention to help her figure out who she was and what she wanted. After all, that tended to be the point of her daily tasks—writing letters about submission, setting goals, and doing things that made her life easier, like putting her daily schedule onto a calendar. Once he'd made her dust and polish her furniture, which she'd been meaning to do for a couple of months.

Well, she knew what she wanted. She wanted a man who was protective and proprietary and who was attracted to her. She did not want a Dom who was a friend to train her. It had been a very nice introduction to the lifestyle, but it wasn't working out as a long-term plan. When Malcolm got back from his honeymoon, she was going to talk to him about the kind of Dom she wanted. He'd be able to find someone suitable now that she was more in touch with what kind of submissive she was.

She spread her schedule book, task lists, and relevant samples on the table and set to work planning her next two events and confirming reservations and orders for the events scheduled for this week. Jordan wandered into the kitchen a few hours later. He'd showered and dressed in different clothes, evidence that he'd planned to stay the night this time. Hopefully he'd get his things together and leave soon. He was already very late for work.

But, no, he helped himself to the pot of coffee she'd made. "Where's the sugar?"

Wordlessly, she got up and retrieved the container from the cupboard. She set it on the counter and turned to walk away, but she found herself caged between his arms.

"Little one, let me start by clearing up a few of your misconceptions."

She froze. Usually he called her *babe*. At first, the nickname had grated on her, but after she realized he meant it as a term of endearment and he only used it for her, she'd come to like it. He rarely used *little one* outside of a scene, though for some reason she liked it better. Somehow it made her feel even more protected. This was unfair warfare.

He turned her to face him, and then he tilted her chin up, forcing her to meet his mesmerizing gaze. "First, I very much wanted to kiss you back. I've dreamed of kissing you, Amy. I've fantasized about it." He trailed off, his gaze flickering from her eyes to her lips. She suddenly couldn't breathe, and when he brushed his thumb over her lower lip, she didn't care if she never took another breath.

His fingers spread through her hair as he gripped her head, positioning it just the way he wanted. Then his lips met hers, a gentle slide that turned ravenous as she melted. His free hand moved, wandering over her back until his touch became urgent, and then he crushed her to him. This was the kiss she'd wanted when he'd led her down the service hallway at the reception. This was the one she'd been prepared to meet halfway. It took some time, but she gathered her wits and kissed him back. He groaned, a sound of desperate joy, and broke the kiss.

"Damn it, Amy." He squeezed the hand in her hair to a fist, pulling harder than perhaps he intended. Amy gasped. Nobody had ever pulled her hair before, and she was finding it quite arousing. "I'm sorry. There are things I promised to tell you first. I want you to know everything before you make a decision about us. That's why I didn't kiss you—not because I didn't want to, but because I want to do right by you."

He released her slowly, easing his grip on her hair and ass. She'd been so caught up in the kiss that she hadn't realized he had a grip on half of her butt. Big hands, for sure. "I don't understand," she said, her voice breathy and husky. "I know you're a Dom. You've been training me. Who did you make this promise to?"

"To myself, and to Malcolm." Stepping back carefully, he gave her space. "You should sit for this."

Now she was worried. What horrible thing did he want to tell her? Was he into blood play and wanted to cut her? She frequently couldn't handle the sight of blood, and she didn't want to be cut, so that wouldn't work for her. Or maybe he wanted to try out impact play, more than the little bit he'd already done. She'd said it was a hard limit, but she might be willing to try if he really wanted to, only the idea made her cringe. She sat back down at the table and closed her laptop. "I'm listening."

He took the seat opposite her and sipped his coffee. "I'm a particular kind of Dom known as a Daddy Dom. You may have noticed that I won't let you call me Sir or Master." At her nod, he continued. "I prefer to be called Daddy."

He paused, she knew, to let that sink in. It had a hell of a time penetrating, so it just stayed there, floating on the surface. Lots of half-formed thoughts zoomed beneath the surface, but she didn't delve deeper because they promised to be unpleasant. Hoping he'd explain, Amy didn't say anything.

"A Daddy is attracted to women who have an underlying innocence and a childish spirit. She's open and giving, a generous woman who wears her heart on her sleeve. A Daddy is driven to protect and nurture her, to help her find and nourish the child that lives inside." He watched her, his expression heavy with meaning.

Amy thought about the time they spent together. Sometimes he took her out to eat, but mostly he geared their outings toward childish activities. In addition to mini-golfing and skating, he'd taken her to the zoo and the Hands-On Museum. They'd gone for ice cream and to an arcade. She'd enjoyed it all. However, the whole concept sounded not right. He was attracted to childlike women? That wasn't her. She owned and ran a successful event planning business. A child—even an immature adult—couldn't successfully do what she did.

Okay, maybe she had My Little Pony and Hello Kitty pajamas, and she liked to watch movies aimed at kids, but that didn't make her childlike or innocent. She sucked her lips in to keep from saying something harsh or judgmental.

"It's not age play." Jordan continued when she didn't say anything. "That's the most common misunderstanding people make when they first hear about the Daddy/little dynamic. I'm not attracted to children or to women who dress like children. I'd never want you to dress up like a kid during a scene or pretend to be one."

She let out the breath she'd been holding. "Thank goodness. You had me worried for a minute."

"I know. You're very easy to read, babe."

"Because I wear my heart on my sleeve?"

"Partly, yes. You don't tend to hide your feelings."

No, she didn't, sometimes to her detriment. "So that makes you think I'm a little?"

"No. There's a lot more. You're strong and passionate, and you frequently speak before you think. You're open and honest. You have an inner joy that bursts through and draws me in. From the first moment I met you, I was entranced by your vivacity and your love of life. I love the joy you seem to find in the everyday and the way little things make you happy."

Nobody had ever described her quite that way before. She'd been called on the carpet for shooting off her mouth and not sugar-coating things she said. She'd been criticized for not tempering her emotions enough and for getting excited about stupid stuff like butterflies and rainbows. It would be nice to be with someone who liked those fundamental aspects of her personality.

"And then there are the other things that you try to hide from me. Those things are more definitive."

Shame washed over her when she thought about the fact that he'd slept in her bed. For the past two nights, she'd curled up with her favorite stuffed animal, a green tree frog she had purchased years ago. Heat rose up her neck.

"Don't be ashamed, Amy. Never be ashamed of your little side." He grabbed her hand where it lay on the table and held her with the intensity of his gaze. "You like to wear bows and flowers in your hair, and you prefer your clothes the same way. You have coloring books and crayons hidden in your kitchen drawers, stuffed animals in your bedroom, and though you tried to hide it, I saw your pajamas. It's okay, babe. I don't want you hiding those things from me."

It was too much, too personal, and besides, she didn't always color, wear My Little Pony pajamas, or sleep with a stuffed animal. She only did those things when she really needed to. It was a way of comforting herself. She'd recently read an article about how adults who color were better able to tap into their creativity. In her job, she needed to be creative. Amy withdrew her hand from his. "This is a lot to spring on a person."

"Yeah, it is. I didn't mean to spring it on you. I wanted to talk yesterday, but your parents were here. I've been moving slowly, trying to figure out if you were a little, but at the end of the day, that's an identity you have to accept on your own. It's not one I can assign to you. I've spent a lot of time finding myself and figuring out what kind of Dom I am. I'm not rushing you, babe. Take all the time you need. But I want you to know who I am before you make a decision about whether or not you want more than friendship with me."

She wanted to be alone. She wanted to hole up in a stack of pillows and color until her head cleared. But she couldn't. That would be selfish. Jordan had just disclosed something deeply personal, and she couldn't leave him hanging. "Is there anything else?"

"I'd like you to research Daddies and littles." He sat back and drank deeply from his cooled coffee. "And you should probably know that I have a deep and abiding fascination with breasts." When she reflexively looked down to check on hers, he chuckled. "You have a fantastic set, babe. I've already spent a lot of time checking them out."

He'd been nothing but a gentleman, even when she'd worn outfits designed to show them off. She scoffed. "I've never seen you look."

Flashing a cocky grin, he winked. "I'm that good."

Amy watched as he poured a bowl of cereal. "I have to work today."

"I figured as much. I'll be back at noon to take you to lunch and then downtown to get your statement." He ate standing at the counter.

She glanced at the clock and thought of all the errands she needed to run. "It's quarter to eleven."

"Hmm." He munched another spoonful. "I guess I'm sticking around. You'd better get to work."

"How long will it take? I have to be at the florists at three, and I'm meeting with the caterer at four."

"It might be close, but you'll make it. I'll drive."

The next few hours unfolded with the disconnectedness of a dream. Amy found herself setting aside items from her to-do list that could wait a day or two so she could look up information about Daddies and littles. Some of the things she stumbled upon brought a frown to her face, and so she spent most of her time reading blogs written by littles who explained what being a little meant to them.

Jordan glanced uneasily at the woman in the passenger seat of his truck. Oblivious to him and everything else, she stared at her phone as she had been doing for most of the day. He knew what she was doing—exactly what he'd told her to do. However, things weren't progressing as he'd anticipated. She frowned, bit her lip, and furrowed her brow as she read, but she didn't say anything.

"How's it going?"

"Huh?" She didn't look up from the screen on her cell.

"How is it going? The research." He'd hovered in the background as she'd very politely haggled with the florist and talked the caterer into serving exactly what the client wanted instead of what the caterer wanted to make. Amy was a complex woman, and the more he came to know her, the more he fell for her. Now he wanted to accompany her on this new journey—if it was an adventure she wanted to undertake.

"Fine."

"Do you have any questions yet? I've seen you frown quite a bit."

She gazed at him, surprised. "You want me to ask questions? I thought you wanted me to research it on my own."

"You can do both. As with any D/s dynamic, every relationship is unique. What you find online can only educate you in broad strokes."

She put down her phone. It slid between her thighs, a place where Jordan had fantasized about putting his face. He shook the thought away because now wasn't the time.

"Well," she paused, sucking her lip. "I think you're right. I think I'm a little. I'm trying to figure out what age, though. Some of the descriptions of a little seem to fit me, and some of the descriptions of a middle do as well."

Jordan hadn't considered that Amy might identify as being a pre-teen. "You don't have to pick an age. Many littles don't. You can just be who you feel like being, and that might change depending on the circumstances." At this point, it was more important for her to come to terms with being a little. "What makes you think you're a little?"

"Why are you asking me? You're the one who brought it up in the first place."

He glanced over to confirm the bratty sparkle in her eyes, but he could tell from her tone that she was playing around. Still, it was a good question that deserved a serious answer. "Just because I suspect something doesn't make it true. Last week I followed a suspect and chose straight cover. He headed into a gay bar."

"Maybe he was meeting a friend or he knew you were following him."

Now why hadn't he considered that? "Good points. But Amy, I've already told you why I think you're a little. I'd like to know *your* reasoning."

She took a breath to gather her thoughts. "Though I've learned to hide it, I've always enjoyed childish things, and when I'm stressed or overwhelmed, doing those activities helped me calm down. The stress melts away, and I'm free to just be happy for a little while. Reading these blogs—there's one that talks about needing a lot of attention and affection, and another that talks about needing unconditional love and support, and another that talks about needing discipline, protection, and mentorship—I see so many of my internal conflicts articulated. I've always wanted these things, but I've been taught that it's weak to expect them, or that I'm too needy. I'm not a weak person, and I've taken great pains to not be childish. But I hate telling myself I can't buy the headband with the big daisies on it because I'm too old for it."

It boiled his blood that she felt she had to deny a vital part of who she was. "Where did you see the headband with the daisies?"

"An accessories store in the mall." She waved it away. "You have a child-like spirit as well, Jordan. You have enjoyed taking me mini-golfing and to the zoo."

"Absolutely. Indulging you often means indulging myself. It's a huge draw, for sure." He slowed to accommodate the traffic of two merging freeways at rush hour. "But I like spoiling you. I want to give you all the things you said you wanted. I *need* to give you those things. It's what makes me who I am."

"But outside of the discipline, it doesn't sound dominant. This is where I always get confused. If you're the dominant one, then why would my wants and needs call the shots in the relationship?"

Another great question. He loved the way her mind worked. "Your wants don't dictate a thing, babe; your needs do. You might want to stay up late, but you need to go to bed early because you have a morning meeting. I'd give you a bedtime, and if you didn't follow it, you would be punished."

"What if you're not there to know?"

"You'd tell me." He had every confidence in her honesty.

"I would." She sighed. "I totally would. What kind of punishment?"

"We'd negotiate that as we would with all punishments. I believe the punishment should fit the crime. I'd likely take away a privilege or assign corner time." The image of her standing in the corner, serving time for excessive brattiness, made him have to shift his sitting position.

She gazed at him uneasily. "You've mentioned standing in a corner before, but I haven't misbehaved yet. You'd really make me stand in the corner?"

"Yes. With your panties around your ankles, and depending on how much you hate it, I might make you suck your thumb." Other variations included kneeling or having to wear a ginger root butt plug. He might have to restrain her for that one.

She inhaled sharply. "Whatever happened to spanking?"

"It's a hard limit right now, so it's off the table. If it wasn't, I would definitely spank you. You never know—that might be something you like." Spanking could be very erotic if she were in the right frame of mind.

She dug around in her purse and came up with a sucker. It was an avoidance technique he allowed her. "Want one?"

"Sure."

She unwrapped it before handing it over. "Guess the flavor."

It wasn't difficult. "Cherry."

"Mine is root beer. It's my favorite." She sucked on it for a moment before popping it out. "I might like to try an erotic spanking with you. Darcy says they're incredible, but she's a painslut and I'm not."

"You don't have to like pain to like an erotic spanking, but we'll table that for now. What other questions do you have?"

Again, she released the sucker with a popping sound that had him wondering if she enjoyed giving blowjobs as much as she liked playing with that sucker. "The virgin thing. Several of the blogs written by Daddy Doms mention deflowering their little over and over. What's with that?"

He exited the freeway and came to a stop sign. As he looked for a break in traffic, he addressed her question. "Daddy Doms are attracted to the innocence and apparent naiveté of their little. And right or wrong, men feel proprietary about being the first one there. I'm pleased as hell to be the first person to tie you up and introduce you to the pleasure of sensory play. Every time we've played, even when I'm doing the exact same thing to you, you react as if you've never experienced it before. That's part of your openness and innocence. It's not different with sex. I'll never expect you to be the aggressor."

Her face flamed.

"Babe, don't be embarrassed. I know you're not a virgin. I don't expect you to be."

"It's not that." She looked out the window, hiding her face from him. He didn't like that.

"What, then?" He bit the head off his sucker and crunched on the sugar shards.

"The other night—you were turned off because I kissed you."

One of the shards went down the wrong way, and he coughed. Thankfully he was at a red light. "I was not turned off because you kissed me. I liked it, and I welcome your kisses and any other sign of affection you want to give. I meant that I'm comfortable with you taking a submissive sexual role and a submissive approach to sex. Maybe you dress in a sexy nightgown, but you wait for me to make the first move. Like that."

She nursed her root beer sucker the rest of the way home with a furrowed brow. When he pulled up in her driveway, she turned to him. "Jordan, are you sure about this? You already know what kind of a Dom you are and what you want out of a relationship, and I'm really just beginning to figure it out."

He put his hand over hers. "We can figure it out together."

"But what if it turns out that I'm not a little and I can't be what you want? Or what if it turns out that you're not what I need? We're friends, and I'd hate to lose that." Distress turned her eyes a darker shade of blue.

Because no words could adequately address her concern, he kissed her. "There are no guarantees in life. What if we're exactly what we need, and we never take the chance to find out?"

She nodded slowly, momentous thoughts manifesting in her brilliant blue eyes. "You're right. I want to find out."

"Then it's settled, babe. We're going to find out—together."

Chapter Thirteen

"Sounds like fun. Thanks for hanging out with me yesterday. Have a great trip." Amy ended the call and tossed her phone to the coffee table. "My parents are officially gone. They called to tell me what a nice job I did with the wedding and what a cute baby Colin is."

"That's nice." Jordan lounged on the sofa, his long arms resting along the high side and back. "You seem relieved that they're gone."

Amy shrugged. "They're sometimes a bit much to take. My mom is hypercritical about a lot of things, and my dad fills in the gaps with everything else. Darcy and I were both happy when they moved to Florida. They pretty much called me a fat slut at the wedding because I was apparently flirting with you during the ceremony."

Jordan scowled, his expression morphing instantaneously. "What the hell? You weren't flirting at all, not until later when you'd had a few drinks. And they have no right to comment on your build. You're voluptuous, not fat."

She giggled. "That's a nice euphemism."

He pointed to the floor near his thigh. "Kneel here."

Amy obeyed. Their scenes always started with her in kneeling position. Now that they were in a relationship, he'd made it clear that he expected her submission whenever they were alone. She knelt demurely, with her knees spread, her head held high, and her gaze lowered. After a few moments, she felt his finger under her chin, guiding her gaze to meet his, which was firm and somber.

"I know you grew up in a house where those who were supposed to love and accept you made judgments and comments on your weight. Listen to me, little one: There's nothing wrong with your body. It's sexy, babe, sexy as hell. When we've done scenes, half the reason I blindfolded you is so you couldn't see how hard it made me to look at you and touch you. You're healthy and active, and your diet is better than most people's. You're beautiful, inside and out, and there's nothing about your appearance I'd change. I've listened to you make disparaging remarks about yourself, and that stops now. It's going to be difficult to accept, but you're going to work on it, and I'm going to help you."

A tear slipped down her cheek. Nobody had ever said those things to her before. Eric, who'd loved her and wanted to marry her, had frequently invited her to go to the gym with him so they could both get in shape.

Jordan caught her tear, wiping it away with his thumb. "Babe, I need you not to slip into little space because I really want to scene with you right now. I've waited a long time for this."

Having read about "little space," Amy knew that some littles slipped in and out of a mode where they essentially functioned as children. When she was like that, she knew Jordan wouldn't touch her. He'd nurture and coddle her, but he wouldn't cross a sexual line. "I'm not. I'm just a bit overwhelmed. I've heard about men who like bigger women, but I've never met one."

He smiled. "That was fate saving you for me. And seriously, you're not big. I can lift you with one hand, babe. That's small in my universe."

She liked his universe, and all she could do was smile.

"Come sit on my lap."

She scrambled up and was rewarded with a kiss that enveloped her senses. Jordan kissed with his whole body. He kissed like he was drowning in bliss, and he dragged her down with him. His hand, which had been supporting her back, traveled around and went straight for her breasts. He'd warned her about his fascination, but she thought he might take his time in getting there. He cupped and squeezed, kneading in time to the thrust of his tongue in her mouth.

And then he tilted her back until she was lying on the sofa. He covered her body with his, nudging her legs apart so he could settle between them. Since she wore a skirt, that meant only her panties and his jeans separated them. When he finally broke the kiss, they both gasped for air. Jordan watched her with heavy-lidded bedroom eyes that promised this was just the beginning. His hand hadn't left her breast. Through the layers of her bra and shirt, he pinched her pebbled nipple.

"I can get quite rough, babe. If it's too much, use your safeword, okay? I'm learning your body, and I can't do that accurately if you don't tell me what you like and don't like. This is not the time to be shy."

"Oh. Okay." She didn't think they were in a scene. This just seemed like making out on the couch, something she'd done with her dates since high school. "When did we start a scene?"

"The moment you knelt before me."

"Are you going to tie me up?"

He lifted a brow. "Eventually. I'm going to do a lot of naughty things to you first, though, if that's okay with you." Though his words seemed like he was giving her a choice, his tone pretty much told her that she wasn't going to get a say in what happened and when.

She expected no less, but this was the first time the element of sex had entered their scenes, and it was the first time he didn't discuss what might happen beforehand. "Jordan, don't you think we should talk about what's going to happen in the scene first?"

He pressed his pelvis between her legs, rubbing his hardness against her pussy. "You're going to lay back and do as you're told. If you're a very good girl, you'll be rewarded with several orgasms. As for the rest, you're going to have to trust me."

Trust him? Of course. That didn't mean she wasn't nervous. This was her first time having sex with a Dom. "Okay."

"Okay, what?"

"I trust you."

He stopped pressing against her. "I'd like you to use my title, babe. It's going to feel weird at first, but the more you use it, the more natural it will feel."

"Daddy." She pressed her lips together to keep from giggling. It was weird, though if she'd been asked to call him Master or Sir, that would have been just as funny.

With a sigh, he shook his head. "We'll work on that. When you giggle, it makes me want to tickle you more." Instead of giving in to that inclination, he captured her mouth and held it prisoner as he took what he wanted. Sensations rioted through her body, all of them driven by the power of his kiss. When he finally released her and moved his lips down her neck, she gasped and arched. "Oh, God, you're good at that."

She'd worn a low-cut top with her skirt. It showed off her cleavage, and now she was glad she hadn't given up on trying to impress him with her 'girls.' He shoved the fabric down to expose her right boob. "Babe, I'm not God. If my title isn't working for you quite yet, then use my name."

She caressed his cheek. "Jordan, you're a very good kisser."

With a superior half-smile, he rolled her nipple between his thumb and forefinger. What began gently increased in pressure as he rolled. Amy's breath caught.

"Breathe through it, babe. Let me know when it's too much."

Her nipples had never been all that sensitive. He squeezed harder and harder, and the only thing that happened was that her pussy got wetter as tingles zipped on an invisible line directly from her nipple. She gasped and ground her pussy against his bulge. It was almost enough to get her there. "Harder, Jordan— please."

He eased his grip. "Damn. I think you can handle clamps. Next time. I brought some equipment today, but not those." With that, he closed his hot mouth over her areola and sucked with short, hard bursts.

Amy cried out and clamped her hands on his head to hold him in place. She ground against him harder. Somehow he made her feel things through her breasts that she'd never felt before.

His hand came between them, separating their bodies and robbing her of a source of friction. He held her down with pressure on her thigh, and his finger eased beneath her panties. He dragged it through her wetness, circling the pulsing bundle of nerves that made up her swollen clit, and then he pinched it to the same rhythm with which he sucked her nipple.

She writhed and squeezed a fistful of his long, dark hair to keep him from stopping. "Jordan," she breathed. "Oh, please don't stop."

He increased the pace of his sucking and pinching, and she climaxed. It was a small one, and as she came down, she slowly released the death grip she had on his hair. "Manners, babe. I just gave you an orgasm. What do you say?"

She looked up into his fathomless brown eyes. "Thank you, Daddy."

His smile made her heart stutter. "I love hearing that word from you."

And she liked the way he looked at her when she used it. The title was representative of his relationship to her, and so she didn't mind it, though she suspected it would be clunky and awkward for some time. He was the one who would love and protect her, guide and cherish her, and he was the one who would rock her world with his kisses, his touch, his ropes, and his toys. She traced a caress down the side of his face, and when she got to his cheek, he turned his face to kiss her palm. "When we've scened before, you always called me little one. I liked it a lot."

He shifted them both, pulling her up to sit as he knelt up on the cushion. "I wondered if you picked up on that." She tried to move her leg so that she wasn't sitting spread-eagled in front of him, but he stopped her with a firm hand on her thigh. "Little one, when I open your legs, never close them without permission." He brushed his knuckle along her wet slit that her panties no longer covered. "I'm far from finished with this pretty pussy. I'm going to shave it, and then I'm going to have my way with you all night long."

The "all night long" part was clearly a boast—no mortal man could last that long without drugs—but the shaving thing was what had her sputtering. "Shave it? You? Shouldn't that be something you ask me to do?"

He stood, looming over her with a patient, cocky grin. "Ask? No. You're mine, little one." Taking her hands, he lifted her to her feet, and then he grabbed her ass. "This ass is mine." He palmed her breasts. "These tits are mine." And then he cupped her pussy. "And this sweet little pussy is mine. When it's mine, I don't ask."

She still couldn't wrap her mind around having him shave between her legs. "But shaving—that's so personal."

"Sure. It's my personal property to shave, eat, fuck, and play with. When you gave yourself to me, you gave up that kind of control. It's what you wanted, little one. Tell me I'm wrong."

A thrill of excitement raced through her. This was what she'd wanted. Somehow, she didn't think the thoughtful, sensitive, and caring friend standing before her would actually turn out to be a real Dom. Sure, he'd tied her up and he'd been commanding and generally bossy, but that air of authority seemed like it just came with the territory of being an FBI agent. Right now, for the first time, she realized his power as a dominant—her Daddy Dom. She lowered her gaze, submitting to his wishes. "It's what I want, but that doesn't make it not weird."

"Unfamiliar," he corrected, and she conceded to his word choice. In time, it probably would become familiar. He followed her into the bathroom where he spread towels in the counter. "It's not an ideal setup, but we'll make it work. Take off your skirt and panties, and then hop up."

While she did that, he rooted around in her cabinet until he found a fresh razor.

"Don't worry, little one. Though you wouldn't guess it to look at my face, I'm quite skilled at shaving. Lean back against the mirror and let me take care of you."

She cooperated, holding her leg up and out of the way so that he had enough light to see what he was doing. The pose and the activity combined to make this the single most intimate experience she'd ever shared with another human being. Exposing herself and allowing him to denude her woman parts with a sharp razor—that was trust and submission. Lovers had certainly seen her naked before, but none had ever taken the time to look at her, to study her, like Jordan. He shaved her slowly, using generous amounts of shaving cream and feeling the area with gentle strokes of his fingertips. She found that highly erotic.

It didn't take all that long. When he finished, he washed her off with a warm cloth and patted her dry. "Stand up. Move around and tell me how it feels."

Weird. Different. Yet, it also made her much more aware of her labia. Just the kiss of air felt sensual. She hadn't thought her pussy capable of this level of sensitivity.

"Little one, tell me what you're thinking. Don't keep it inside. Never censor your thoughts from me."

"Sensitive." She cleared her throat. "Very aware of even the slightest breeze."

He knelt down and blew gently across her pussy lips. She gasped, and he licked the edge of her labia. His tongue felt hot, much warmer than she remembered a tongue feeling. "I'm going to tie you up. I'm going to lick and suck you until you beg me to fuck you. I'm going to show you a couple of new positions tonight, little one. Learn them well because you're going to find yourself in them quite often." Moving up her body, he kissed her soundly. "I'll give you a few minutes to compose yourself, and then I want you to undress, go into the bedroom, and lay down on the bed with your hands above you and your legs spread."

Amy watched him go, and she was glad he closed the door behind him. It allowed her some privacy, and given what she'd just shared, she needed that time to gather her wits. She supposed it was part of his grand scheme—to knock her out of her comfort zone so she had no choice but to give over everything to him. Well, he was very successful. She'd never felt so unsure about what was going to happen, and yet so peaceful and calm in the face of the unknown.

Most men would have fucked her by now. When given the green light, even if bondage or submission were involved, most men would have plowed this pasture right away. Not Jordan. First he'd patiently waited while she talked on the phone with her mother. Then he'd made out with her on the sofa until she came. Even now, as she finished undressing and arranging herself on the bed, his first order of business was to lick her pussy. He hadn't removed one stitch of clothing. His shoes were next to the front door, but his pants were still on his ass.

Of course, if she were a virgin and he was the experienced one, then it made sense for him to ease her into it with a smaller orgasm and gentle dominance.

She didn't know how long she waited in the position he'd indicated. At least he'd chosen something comfortable and easy to maintain. Darcy and Layla had both regaled her with punishing poses they'd been forced to hold until their muscles burned and screamed for relief. Curiously, Trina had only smiled mysteriously and said that Keith was too impatient to keep his hands off her for long when she was in a submissive pose.

"You're exactly how I wanted you. Good girl." Jordan patted her thigh, and she started. Her mind had certainly drifted, which was incredible considering that she was lying in her bed naked with her legs spread wide open and her newly shorn lady bits exposed. "This is a relaxed presentation pose, one I'll put you in when I expect you to lay there for a while. Bend your knees and grab your ankles."

Amy did as he asked, though in order to grab her ankles, she had to lift her head and shoulders. Jordan slid a pillow underneath her shoulders so she could relax.

He sat on the edge of the bed and balanced himself by placing one hand on the other side of her body. He'd shaved his face, and the fresh scent of soap and something uniquely Jordan wafted down to tease her senses. "I'm going to give you some stretches to do so that you can eventually lie flat and be comfortable. Until then, I'll use cuffs on your wrists and ankles to span the distance. Anticipating that you might swing my way, I've ordered some equipment just for you, but it hasn't come in yet, so I didn't bring it."

"That sure, were you?"

He drew his fingertip down the center of her chest. "I was right, wasn't I?" His attention drifted to her breasts. Licking his lips, he stared at them as if they were a plate of lasagna. "Damn, little one. You are so tempting and delectable. I may have to take a detour from my original plan. Go back to the relaxed presentation pose. I'm going to tie you up and do kinky things to your boobs."

In no time flat, he had her wrists secured to the headboard. Since it was a solid piece, he had to route the rope under the mattress. He did the same thing to secure her ankles. Though he hadn't brought cuffs, he'd brought plenty of rope and some other things in his bag of tricks. As he moved around the bed, tying and testing his rope work, he paused frequently to kiss her mouth and fondle her breasts.

Then he took off his shirt, and Amy forgot how to breathe. Just that morning, he'd been in her bed without a shirt, yet now that she had permission to look, to appreciate, and to drool over his body, everything had changed. "Am I ever going to get to touch you?"

He chuckled as he shucked his jeans. "Yes, little one, you will. I'll even insist on it. But right now, having your gorgeous body at my mercy is enough stimulation. I'm barely holding it together."

Looking closer, she noticed the fevered heat in his eyes. She didn't need to look closer to see his erection. He was a big man, tall and broad-shouldered, and so was his cock. He slowed his movements, drawing out the reveal as long as he could. Then, when he was naked, he stood there and let her drink him in. The trail of hair she'd spied that morning widened even more below the waistband of his shorts, fanning out in a terrific nest of dark hair from which sprang a magnificent cock. Amy had seen her share, and Jordan put them all to shame. It wasn't that he was larger or wider than some of the models in the porn pictures online, and he wasn't so unbelievably huge that she wanted to close her legs and deny entry. No, it was more that he was Jordan, and that alone made him perfect. The fact that his cock was a good size—not too long or short; not too skinny or wide—only underscored the fact that she loved his body. Her pussy wept in anticipation.

He took something from his bag and knelt on the bed straddling her stomach. "I'm going to fuck your breasts, little one. Your choice if you want a blindfold this first time."

Put on a blindfold or watch him climax? There was no contest. "I don't want one. Maybe if you tell me when you're close, I can open my mouth. It'll be like skee-ball."

She must have shocked him because he stared at her in stunned silence. After a few long seconds, he scratched his eyebrow. "I don't know. I guess we'll see." The thing he'd taken from his bag turned out to be a bottle of lube. He drizzled it over her breasts, and then he rubbed it around before coating his cock with the excess. Then he wiped his hands on a towel he'd put on the bed that she hadn't noticed. "This shouldn't hurt, but if it does, use your safeword."

"Yes, Jordan." She flashed a smartass grin, and he responded by tweaking her nipple. Since he'd slicked it up, the gesture lacked bite.

He squished his cock between her boobs, and as he moved his hips, she wished he'd left her hands untied. She would love to hold them together so he could get off. When he began to squeeze her breasts and play with her nipples, she understood that just fucking wouldn't be enough. He wanted the full tactile experience, and he never closed his eyes, not even when they grew heavy as he got close.

"You are so sexy right now."

His rhythm slowed, and he gazed at her in astonishment.

"You said I shouldn't censor my thoughts." Right now, her thoughts were very dirty. There was something about having a handsome man straddling her body and getting off with her breasts that made naughty thoughts scroll through her mind.

"Never," he agreed. "And I'll gag you if I don't want you to talk."

In that case, there was no sense in holding back. "You have incredible thighs. I've fantasized about surprising you by rubbing against one of them until I came. I want to leave a wet spot on your jeans and send you off to work that way."

His expression grew heavy-lidded. "You'd shake your tits until I buried my face in them."

"Then I'd suck your cock. I want you to cum on me, Daddy." Yeah, she knew how using his title drove him crazy. He pinched her nipple and increased his pace. "I want to feel you and taste you. I want to rub your essence into my skin and leave it there for always."

"Now. Open." He barely grunted the order in time for her to comply. One thrust later, his milky stream spurted over her chest and neck, and some of it made it into her mouth. She licked her lips in search of more.

"Thank you, Daddy. You taste good."

He dragged the tip of his cock through the line of semen, and then he pressed it against her lips. She eagerly licked it clean, and when he didn't immediately pull away, she kept at it, sucking the sensitive tip to drive him crazy. He rewarded her with a small moan, and he let her have it for a little longer. She kept the pressure of her tongue gentle because she figured he would be super sensitive right now, and she didn't stop a small whine from escaping when he pulled away.

He dragged his finger through the cum drying on her chest, scooping up a dollop. Then he traced her lips with it. Amy stayed still as long as she could, which wasn't long. She lifted her head suddenly and took his finger into her mouth, sucking it harder than she'd sucked his tip. She scraped her teeth and nipped at the pad of his finger, and he rewarded her by fucking it deeper into her mouth. She made unspoken promises this way, showing him the ways she wanted to please him.

With a reluctant chuckle, he extracted his finger from her hot mouth. "I'll show you how to suck my cock another time. You like to swallow?"

"Yes. And I like when..." She trailed off, censoring herself—even after he'd proven that he didn't want her to do that—because she didn't want to sound like a hussy.

He situated himself between her legs, but he held his weight over her, and he kissed her thoroughly. When he broke away, he forced her to meet his gaze. "You like when what? Tell me, babe. I want to know."

"I...um...I like when you hold my head and maybe make me take a little more than I can fit comfortably." No guy had ever done that to her before. At least, not on purpose. She'd been with one man who used to get carried away, but he always caught himself after a few thrusts and apologized when she'd wished he'd continue. "I just wish I didn't actually choke. I don't want to vomit or anything."

Jordan chuckled. "Deep throat, huh? We can do that. I'll help you learn how not to gag. It'll take practice, but I'm willing to donate my services." Then his expression turned dreamy, and he kissed her tenderly. "I like you so much. I've wanted you under me for so long, and now I have you. It's a dream come true. I'm so very lucky, little one. And now I'm going to take my time. I'm going to show you what it means to belong to me."

He wandered leisurely down her body, exploring with his lips and hands, and rubbing his face over her skin. By the time he made it to her pussy, she was a trembling mass of need. He pushed her legs even farther apart and licked her bare pussy lips. He feasted slowly, devouring her by centimeters. She came once, delicate waves of pleasure lapping through her arteries, and he took her there again when he added his fingers.

As she panted and tried to return from the climactic voyage, she felt his finger push into her anus, and that brought her around. An involuntary yelp escaped.

"Are you a virgin here, little one?"

"Yes." She wasn't shocked that he would want her there because she'd listened to her sister expound on the ecstasy of anal sex for years. It seemed this was something Doms liked to do.

"Mmm. Tragedy. I'll have to rectify that. But first, I want this pussy." He tugged on the rope around her ankle, and it came free. Then he untied her wrists. "Now you get to touch me, and I'm going to make love to you."

He covered her body with his as he took her in his arms, and he kissed her as if that act was vital to his continued existence. Amy felt surrounded, protected, and cherished. He touched her everywhere, his hands roaming without apparent purpose or direction, yet he made every cell of her body vibrate with anticipation.

She touched him as well, exploring his arms and shoulders, caressing his chest and hips. She slid her legs up and down his, and she pumped her hand along his cock. She didn't know how long they rolled across the bed, kissing and touching, moaning and sighing as they learned one another's bodies. True to his word, he didn't rush, and he worshipped her with his caresses. By the time he donned a condom and positioned his cock at her entrance, she was a mass of quaking need.

He brushed a tear from her cheek as he thrust deep, but it didn't seem to bother him that she couldn't control her emotions. "God, Amy. You're so fucking tight. You feel incredible." He hiked one of her legs higher so he could slide deeper.

Though she wanted to respond, to tell him how wonderful he felt inside her, she couldn't form words. With the tender expression on his face, he let her know that he was in control and he didn't expect her to have her emotions under control. He drove her up the cliff slowly, holding and supporting her the whole way. Faster and faster, he drove the rhythm until it was a frenzy, and she sensed that neither of them was in control. She grasped desperately, and he only held her tighter. For the first time in her life, she had an orgasm so large that her mind took flight. Vaguely and from a distance, she heard his moans crescendo, and then he buried himself to the hilt and collapsed on top of her.

When she became aware again, she was comfortably cocooned in his arms and their legs were tangled together. "That was amazing," she mumbled into his chest.

He kissed her forehead. "Yes."

"Was that a deflowering?"

"In a manner of speaking." His voice rumbled through his chest and came out a little hoarse. "After I feed you dinner and get you hydrated, we'll play some more."

At the mention of food, she stirred. She hadn't eaten since they'd left the house to go give her statement and run errands. "I have leftover chicken cordon bleu from last night. It's not as good the next day, but it should do the trick. If not, I can make something else. My mom brought over a bunch of food from Darcy's house so it wouldn't go bad."

Yep, her mother liked to comment on her weight even as she foisted a bunch of food off on her. As Jordan had ordered her to do, she pushed away the negative thought. No doubts lingered about how much he liked her body. That was all she needed.

He tucked himself into his boxers. "Leftovers are fine. I like the idea of something quick because then I'll have you back in here faster."

She reached for her shirt, but he stilled her by placing his hand over hers.

"No clothes for you. Get used to being naked around me. I'm a visual creature, and I love looking at you."

Never in her life had she walked around without clothes. Still she dropped the shirt without comment. When she started retaining water and her boobs hurt unless she wore a bra, then she'd bring it up. Until then, there was no need.

"Of course, I can't have you near a hot stove without some kind of protection, so you can wear an apron."

Amy rolled her eyes at that one, and she found herself facing Jordan with a scary look of disapproval on his face. "What?"

"Little one, rolling your eyes at me is disrespectful. This is your only warning. If you do it again, you will be punished."

She lowered her gaze. "I'm sorry, Daddy."

At her use of his title, his expression transformed, and that made her feel pleased and powerful. Did that mean using his title was as much a manipulation as it was a show of respect? He slung his arm around her, which made her forget that line of thought, and herded her toward the kitchen.

After a meal of salad and cordon bleu, which they ended up making together, Amy snuggled on Jordan's lap as he sipped coffee.

"Won't that keep you up tonight?"

He chuckled. "Maybe. That's okay. I plan to spend most of the night in bed, but I don't plan to sleep." He set the cup on the table and ran a caress along her thigh. "I love the marks the ropes leave on your skin. Later I'll tie you up and we'll do some sensory play. This time I'll be able to include your breasts and pussy in my plan. One of the ways I challenged myself when we've played before was that I tried to see how wet I could get you." He kissed from her temple to her jaw. "I love the smell of your arousal. It was very difficult not to rip your panties off and lick away all your cream."

Amy shivered because when she'd been bound and blindfolded, she'd often wished he would do exactly that. "And now you can do whatever you want to me whenever you want."

"Yes. And no. You've given me the gift of your submission, Amy, but you haven't ceded your right to say no to something. That's what your safeword is for. I expect you to use it when you need it."

"But that's only if you go too far or if I'm hurt or have to use the bathroom."

He sighed. "During a scene, yes. But now that we're together, I'm always going to be your Dominant. When I want something from you, I'll take it. I'm a kinky son of a bitch. I might tie you up and strap a vibrator to your clit and force you to have orgasms until it hurts. No scene is required. If I stop by in the middle of the day, I might order you to bend over so I can fuck you. Your safeword is the only means you have of stopping me. Excuses or protesting won't have an effect."

She lifted a brow and played the Ultimate Female Card. "What if I'm on my period?"

"That's what old towels and showers are for. Just warn me if you're wearing a tampon because if I'm in a hurry, then I'll probably just fuck your ass." He wore a smug grin as he shredded her card.

Stunned, she said, "That's kind of gross."

He shrugged. "Tomato, tuh-mah-to. And there's always your tits. Have I told you what a gorgeous rack you have?"

"You might have mentioned it." The conversation made her uneasy. Apparently she'd given him an all-access pass. "Does this mean you view me as a sex toy?"

"Not at all." He urged her to stand and took her hand. Then he led her into the living room, where he'd thoughtfully closed the drapes, and unzipped his bag of tricks. After rooting around, he extracted a brand new dildo still in the package. "This is a toy. You're my girlfriend, my submissive, my friend, my lover, my little. The toy gets used; I will never seek to make you feel used. Sex is a part of our relationship. Our relationship isn't sex. I like you, Amy. I like your personality as well as your luscious body."

Heat bloomed across her chest and cheeks at his vehement and heartfelt declarations. "Good. I haven't suddenly started seeing you as a stud who belongs only in my bed, though you do look really good there."

He petted and squeezed her ass as he pressed her front to his. "Your feelings about having me in your bed have certainly changed in twelve hours."

The way he held her knocked her off balance, so she clung to his shoulders. "I was only against having you in my bed when I thought you didn't want to be there. I don't want you to regret this. I'm older than you, and I really had a hard time believing I was your type. Now that I know I'm exactly your type, I feel much better about taking advantage of your luscious body."

He bent down and kissed her softly, but sparks exploded, and the kiss turned ravenous. The kiss went on and on, turning her into a creature that existed symbiotically with him. When he broke it off suddenly, she felt severed and adrift. "Do you remember the presentation pose I showed you earlier?" At her nod, he continued. "You're going to try another one for me. I want you face down on the bed, your knees under you spread as wide apart as you can get them and still balance, and your ass in the air. Instead of holding your ankles, your hands should be above your head. Understand?"

"Yeah. Can I turn my head to the side so I can breathe?"

"Yes." He swatted her lightly on the butt. "Go. Now."

The position wasn't hard to figure out, but it was a bit ignominious. All of her private parts were out in the open and lifted in the air. It would be the first thing he saw when he came into the room. It didn't matter how much he liked pussy, this couldn't be at all attractive. Had he meant for her to be humiliated? While she didn't feel exactly shameful, she was uncomfortable with being this exposed.

She heard him in the bathroom. Water ran for a long time before he came to the bedroom. He set a rolled towel on the chair next to her bed, and then he grabbed her hips and turned her so that her privates faced the side of the bed. "Sorry," she said.

"That's okay, little one. It's your first time. In the future, position yourself so that I have easy access. I should be able to reach your pussy from the side of the bed. Here and at my place, the footboard gets in the way if you're pointing that way." He unrolled the towel on the bed next to her, and she saw that he'd washed some toys. There was a very skinny and short dildo, a skinny and longer dildo, one that was wider, and a bottle of lubricant.

"Those are interesting dildos."

"They're butt plugs. We need to stretch you out before I can fuck your ass. I don't want to take the chance of hurting you, and if we rush this, it can hurt. Some people like the pain, but you, my princess, aren't one of them. If I make you scream, it'll be with ecstasy." He caressed her ass and thighs, and she felt the weight of his gaze. It made her pussy swell and weep with anticipation.

"I trust you," she said. "I know you won't hurt me."

He traced a finger through her wetness, and then he gathered her moisture, spreading it all the way to her back entrance. "Nothing that goes in your ass should ever go in your pussy, though that's not true in reverse. I will always wash my hands, little one. I won't take a chance with your health." Then he drizzled cool gel from the bottle of lube between her ass cheeks.

His care and concern were unexpectedly sexy. All these months meeting potential Doms, and the perfect man had been right in front of her face. Amy smiled even though he'd inserted a finger in her anus and was wiggling it around.

"Tell me how this feels."

"Not like much of anything, but a little odd."

Through the corners of her eyes, she saw his arm move as he rotated and massaged her sphincter muscles into submission. Once she let go of the unusualness of the experience, she found that she liked his touch there. Then he selected the shortest, skinniest butt plug. It disappeared behind her, and as she waited for him to shove it in, she tensed.

"Relax, babe. Take a deep breath. Now let it out." The moment she exhaled, he pushed it in. It didn't hurt at all, just a little pressure and now a fullness where she didn't expect to feel full. "How does that feel?"

"Like I have a butt plug in my ass."

"Hmm. Being a smartass again, I see."

She heard the rustle of fabric and the rip of a wrapper, and then she felt his cock slide into her pussy. With the plug taking up some of the room, she wondered if his cock was being squished. If she thought it felt full down there before, it was nothing compared to now. She could only manage a gasp.

"How does it feel now?"

"Full. It feels really, really full. And tight. Too tight. I don't want it to hurt you."

He chuckled. "Babe, I'm fine. This feels fantastic, and I never pass up a fantastic opportunity." With that he withdrew halfway and plunged back inside. He did this a few times, thrusting harder and harder. The front of his thighs smacked against the back of hers with loud slaps. He tilted her hips, angling her ass higher and causing her to arch her back even more, and he increased his pace.

The sensations in her pussy were indescribable. If she thought he'd sent her to unimaginable heights before, this blew that airplane out of the water. A loud *Oh-Oh-Oh* sound echoed from the walls. He pushed the noise from her with every violent slam of his cock. And then he grabbed a fistful of her hair. Using it as reins, he yanked to the rhythm of his thrusts. Hot sparks showered through her head, down her arms and chest, and exploded in her pussy.

It was too much and not enough at the same time. She clenched the bedcovers in her fists and arched her back even more, rocking her ass back to meet every thrust. Her pussy contracted, convulsing around his cock, and he kept going. She bucked against him, but he slapped her flank, and though it hadn't hurt, it shocked her into halting her half-hearted protest. She relaxed, subsumed her will, and submitted to him. "Jordan," she murmured. "Oh, Jordan, yes."

Her body lengthened, becoming a space shuttle trying to reenter the atmosphere. She quivered and shook, her body coming apart because the trajectory was impossible. Fear and excitement gave way to the intense feelings that now defined her soul. He grasped her hips harder, pumping into her wildly. Her brain stalled, and she was obliterated by an explosion the likes of which she didn't think she could survive.

But she did. When she opened her eyes, she was in Jordan's arms, shaking and sobbing. "I'm sorry." She clutched at him even though she knew she should excuse herself and get her emotions under control. "I'm so sorry."

"Shh, little one. No apologies for crying. I love that I drove you to this point. You're even more lovely when you come apart. I'm going to do this to you regularly. You're mine, and you gave me everything. Thank you. That's a priceless gift." He stroked her hair away from her face and feathered caresses down her back.

"I don't mean to cry over nothing. You didn't hurt me. Not at all. It was surprising, what you did, but I really liked having my hair pulled." She didn't so much love the fact that he'd slapped her ass. That, she knew, had been discipline.

"Good to know. I liked pulling your hair."

Aftershocks still rumbled through her body. "It was wondrous. Momentous. I should shut up."

"No, you shouldn't. I always want you to share your thoughts and feelings with me. Communication is key to making this work." He kissed her forehead, his lips both soft and firm, and the gesture was calming. "It was wondrous and momentous. I came so hard I almost fell on you."

"Jordan?"

His fingers made a few more treks through her tresses. "Yeah, little one?"

"Are you really going to have sex with me all night?"

"No. Probably just for another couple hours. You have to work tomorrow, so you're going to need some sleep. If I'm not mistaken, you have an event in the afternoon?"

He'd memorized the schedule she'd posted on the refrigerator, and as he said he would do, he was making sure she got what she needed. She snuggled closer and nodded. For the first time in a relationship, she didn't think of anything at all. She didn't analyze how long he'd want to hold her or try to guess if he might be hungry. If Jordan wanted something, he'd tell her, and she would jump to make it happen.

Chapter Fourteen

Jordan woke, smiling with remembered bliss, to the feel of the mattress shifting. She'd been a trooper, not protesting even when he woke her at three for another round of sex. Tonight he wanted to take her to his place where he'd introduce her to his set of breast pumps and maybe he'd set up the swing. She'd like that.

Her groan pulled him from his musings. "You okay?"

She'd perched on the edge of the bed. "Does your dick hurt?" It could have been a neutral question, but her tone verged on annoyance. She shouldn't wake up cranky the day after a night of hot loving.

"No. Why? Do you kick in your sleep? If so, thankfully, you missed my package."

"My lady parts are sore."

He chuckled and pulled her into his arms. She didn't squirm away, but she also didn't soften into his embrace. He kissed the top of her head. "I guess that means no morning sex."

"Even if I wasn't sore, I'd want to shower and brush my teeth first."

"Noted. How about you jump in the shower, and I'll make breakfast?"

Her whole body finally relaxed. "Okay. I'm not picky about what you make as long as it's accompanied by coffee."

"Coffee. That's probably why you're a little surly in the morning. You're not a morning person, are you?"

She turned to glare. "Morning people are annoying."

Laughing, he sprang from bed and grabbed his jeans. "I won't take that personally, not unless you repeat it after you've been caffeinated."

Moving gingerly, she scooted out of bed and gathered her clothes. He wanted to order her to remain naked, but that would have been a selfish order. She had to work, and he would be a dickhead if he interfered. He snagged her panties from her pile of clothes. "No underwear today." Then he took her bra. "You can do without this until it's time to leave the house."

She chewed the bottom corner of her lip as she stared at the lingerie he'd taken. "Should I keep my pussy shaved?"

His dick jerked. "Yes."

She sighed. "I'll wait until you're gone for a few days on assignment before I wax. I'd rather not have to shave another thing every day."

Blood finished rushing to his cock. "If you don't go get in the shower now, I'm not going to care if you're sore."

Her gaze turned openly appreciative as it wandered down his chest and came to rest on the bulge in his pants. "My breasts aren't sore, and I give pretty good blowjobs."

He closed his eyes and thought about his responsibility to feed her and get some coffee into her system. While he was picturing making waffles, he felt her tentative touch at his zipper. His eyes flew open, and he watched her slowly unfasten his fly and lower his jeans. She didn't do it to be seductive; she did it because she was shy, and that turned him on even more. She lifted his cock and licked the tip, her tongue lightly flicking around the crown. Amy, his little, on her knees was the sweetest early morning image he'd ever witnessed.

She took her time getting to know the topography of his cock, and then she sucked one of his balls between her lush lips. He hissed with pleasure. Her hair fell forward, blocking his view, and so he smoothed it back. She perked up as he petted her. Her touch became more confident, and when she closed her mouth over his cock again, she moaned. He let her get used to having his dick in her mouth, and then he gripped her head and fucked her mouth. With her hand wrapped around his base, she controlled how deep he went, and he let her keep that control for now. As she acclimated to his pace, she moved her hand down his shaft to take more.

Her eyes watered with the strain, and he noted her challenge point. She'd asked him to teach her to take all of him, and there was plenty of time to get around to that. He whispered her name, a warning that he was about to come, and tightened his grip on her hair. She moaned and gripped his ass. He thrust once more and cried out his climax.

Her throat convulsed as she swallowed repeatedly to keep up with his ejaculation. She sucked gently once he stopped, and she let him go with a soft *pop*. In one swift movement, he lifted her into his embrace. Her feet dangled above the floor, and she threw her arms around him. He held her closely and panted against her neck. "You're right. You give a pretty good blowjob."

From the tops of her breasts to the tips of her ears, she flushed red. Even her scalp brightened. He set her down, and she fanned her face. "Hot flashes are coming on a couple decades early."

Breakfast was a quiet affair. Mostly Amy stared into the middle distance with a dreamy look in her eyes. Jordan wanted to know what she was thinking, but he was loathe to say or do anything that might chase away the mood. And so he indulged himself by watching her. She was deeply beautiful, and he finally had the right to look at every part of her for as long as he wanted.

After they ate, he assisted in the cleanup. Once the kitchen was in shape, he checked her schedule once again, mentally adding his items to it. If he was going to take her ass tonight as he planned, he needed to introduce her to a larger plug.

"Lift your skirt and bend over the table."

In the midst of drying her hands on a dishtowel, she stared at him in shock. "Jordan, I have work to do."

He replied with a look that conveyed how he expected her to obey without question. Seconds later, she lifted her skirt and bent over the table, carefully positioning her backside so that nobody passing the house would get an unexpected show. "Good girl. Stay there." His sack of supplies was in the bedroom. He retrieved the lube and a larger plug than the one he'd used the night before. She'd been very responsive while wearing it, climaxing faster and harder than she had without it.

He drizzled lube over her anus and rubbed it over the plug. "Exhale, babe." A little pressure, and it slid in easily. "How does that feel?"

"Full. Very full. How long do I have to wear it?"

"Until it's time to get ready for your party." He helped her stand. "Go ahead and work. I won't bother you." As she walked away, waddling to avoid pressing her legs too closely together, his phone rang. "Monaghan."

"How is domestic bliss treating you?" Keith's smooth tones glided over the airwaves. "Please tell me you closed the deal."

"I did. Everything is copacetic here. How are you doing?" Jordan watched for Amy to return, but she didn't. He crept down the hall to find where she'd gone, and he found her in the second bedroom, which was packed with carefully labeled boxes of event supplies. Pausing with a handful of what looked like paper tablecloths, she questioned him with the lift of one eyebrow. He winked and closed the door so she wouldn't overhear the conversation.

"Not so great. We can't get warrants for the New Day Church, but we've stepped up surveillance, and we've arrested some of the people using it as a home. Brandt and I questioned three of them, and we didn't get much. They're all addicts, and none of them will admit to ever seeing the man Gartrell referred to as 'Joe.' Also, no emergency rooms reported a GSW. Our guy is MIA."

Jordan moved a chair in the living room so that he could see down the hall. Amy didn't need to overhear any of this. "He probably has private access to medical care. Look for medics or doctors with a history of drug use, especially those who've lost their license."

"Dare is already on it. Brandt is working surveillance on the church, and I need you to come in. You and I are going to question Gartrell's ex-wife. I've located her, and she's expecting us in an hour."

Running a hand through his hair, Jordan exhaled. "I can't leave Amy alone. She doesn't know about Gartrell's threat. Or that he's dead."

Keith made a sympathetic noise. "There's a lot you can't tell her, but it's your call whether to tell her that she has agents watching her. I sent Kinsley and Hardy to tail her, and I gave them the itinerary you sent."

Jed Kinsley and Lexee Hardy were good agents, more than capable of keeping an eye on Amy without her knowing. Besides, this light level of protection was probably overkill. 'Joe' didn't know Amy's name or location, and he was probably laid up somewhere recovering from his injury. It was a long shot to think he'd actually go after her. If she weren't the sister-in-law of an agent, then she wouldn't have rated even this much protection. "Fine," Jordan said gracelessly. "Text me the address. I'll meet you there in an hour."

Amy looked up when he came back. Though she was on her knees, she didn't lean back to rest her ass on her heels. "You have to go to work?"

Surprised she'd be so perceptive, he asked, "How did you know?"

"You've been off four of the last five days. Agents never get that much time off unless they prearrange it, which you haven't. I know you're good friends with Chief Lockmeyer, but she's not a pushover. If you don't do your job, she will hunt you down and taser your balls. Or at least that's the threat she uses with Mal." She set her clipboard on the floor and slowly got to her feet. "I guess that means you're going to take this thing out of my butt now." She bent over a stack of plastic storage bins and hiked her skirt to her waist.

Jordan stared at the smooth expanse of flesh facing him and noted that her pussy was very moist. He stood behind her, crowding her with his presence, and caressed her ass. "Does wearing this make you horny, babe?"

She cleared her throat. "Pretty much everything you do makes me horny—the way you look at me, the way you stand in the doorway like you own the room and everything in it, that tone or that look you get that warns me not to argue with you. Wearing this thing is a constant reminder that I'm yours, and I really, really like the way that makes me feel."

He planted a kiss on her right butt cheek. "I wish I had time to make you come, but I had to leave about ten minutes ago. Exhale, babe." He extracted the plug. "Go wash up, and then meet me in the living room in five minutes so you can properly say goodbye."

Five minutes later, she threw her arms around his neck. "I'm going to miss you, but I'm working today anyway, and that's not the kind of quality time I want to spend with you. Go catch a bad guy and make the world a safer place."

"Anything for you." He kissed her, drowning in her flavor and the softness of her lips against his. She melted into him, and he was in heaven. Kissing Amy was pure bliss. He could do this for hours.

She broke away suddenly. "Daddy, you said you had to go. As much as I want you to stay, I'm not going to be one of those greedy, manipulative littles who use their wiles to get their way."

"I like how you're getting more comfortable with those titles."

A hint of color rose in her cheeks. "It's still odd, but I'm trying. The hard part is thinking of you when I say it. I'm not going to lie—I still find it unfamiliar that you want me to call you Daddy. However, if we keep this up, I may eventually forget your given name. Won't that be funny if we have dinner with my parents? For once, it'll be me who shocks them instead of it always being Darcy's job to give them fake heart attacks." She smoothed her hands over his shirt.

"If it helps, I can reward you when you use my title, and then it'll have a positive association." He planted another kiss on her lips.

"Mmmm. I like that idea. Can I pick the reward? Because I've always wondered what you'd look like with a braid and ribbons in your hair."

With a laugh, he shook his head. "That's not going to happen." He loved her sense of humor, and that she sent him off with bright, happy thoughts. When he met Keith outside of Deanna Gartrell's apartment, he was still smiling.

Wearing a dark suit and dark sunglasses, Keith exuded the aura of a badass FBI agent. Most new recruits were afraid of him. Even years later, they treaded lightly around Agent Rossetti. Jordan had been wary of Agent Rossetti when they'd first met, but as he got to know Keith as an agent and a Dom, his opinion had changed. He'd felt sorry for the man who didn't let anybody get emotionally close to him. Since he'd been with Katrina, all that had changed. He'd even begun smiling and laughing regularly.

"What the hell are you staring at?" The corner of Keith's mouth turned up in a sneer.

Jordan hadn't shaved. He was wearing the same jeans as the day before, and the black cotton shirt he'd chosen was a twin to the other twenty he owned. They were a mismatched pair of agents. He kind of wished Dustin was there instead. Somehow Dustin's good looks and magnetic personality put people at ease. Once their guard was down, Jordan could slide in with a few innocuous questions. They tended to get what they needed from a witness relatively quickly.

Jordan folded his sunglasses and hung them from the collar of his shirt in front. "You, hot stuff. It's ninety degrees out, and here you are looking sharp in your designer suit."

"For fuck's sake, Monaghan. At least buy me a drink first." A year ago, Keith wouldn't have responded to Jordan's joke. He would have ignored it and issued procedural instructions. The pair shook hands and pounded each other on the back. "Congratulations, by the way. Malcolm called a few minutes ago. He was asking about you and Amy. Darcy wants to know."

"Amy wants to wait until they get back. She doesn't want to interrupt their honeymoon."

Keith nodded. "I didn't say anything about Gartrell's threat-slash-warning."

"I'd rather figure out if it's baseless first. No sense in worrying everybody for nothing." Jordan clenched his jaw. He didn't like that Amy was involved at all, but realistically, the chance that anybody was gunning for her was basically nil. However, he'd feel better when they confirmed that fact.

Keith motioned to the apartment building. "Deanna Gartrell filed for divorce about six months ago. It was never finalized, so she's a widow, not an ex-wife."

Jordan pressed the buzzer, and a woman in her mid-forties answered the door. With her short hair dyed blonde and nondescript clothing, she looked like anybody's mother. Her eyes were red from crying. He flashed his badge. "Mrs. Gartrell, I'm Agent Monaghan from the Detroit Bureau, and this is Agent Rossetti. You spoke to him on the phone earlier today."

She looked from Jordan to Keith and back again, and she wiped her hands on a dishtowel. "Yes, I remember. I lost my husband, not my mind. Come on in." The door opened into the living room. She indicated the sofa. "Please, sit down. Can I get you something to drink?"

"Water, if you don't mind." Keith removed his sunglasses and smiled, showcasing the one asset he owned—an unexpected charm. Whether or not he was thirsty, her absence would give them a chance to sweep for bugs and get a general feel for the kind of person she was.

"Nothing for me." Jordan flashed a friendly grin calculated to put her at ease. "Thanks."

The room was full of knickknacks and other places someone could squirrel a listening device, and so they didn't get to do a thorough sweep before she returned. Deanna sat on a chair opposite the sofa where she expected them to sit, which meant she wasn't all that comfortable in their presence. "You have questions for me?"

"Yes, if you don't mind." Keith sipped the water. "Your late husband was in trouble with some people. Do you know anything about them?"

Deanna shook her head. "I wanted nothing to do with that side of his life. He was clean when we met, and he fell off the wagon about ten years ago. I threatened to divorce him if he didn't get his act together. He got help, saw a counselor, and things had been going well for almost seven years. Then he lost his job and immediately went out to score some crack. I told him we were through, and I didn't let him see our daughter when he was high. When he did, it was always in a public place, and I was nearby. She's only fifteen."

Gartrell had mentioned that Joe knew about his wife and daughter. Jordan brought up an image on his phone. It was a surveillance photo of the man they suspected as being Joe. He handed the phone to Deanna. "Does this man look familiar?"

She studied the picture for a few moments, a frown marring her chin. "No. I'm sorry. Was Brian mixed up with drug dealers? Usually he just used. He wasn't a criminal. He wasn't the kind of man who would rob a bank or do something that would hurt someone else. When he was sober, he was a great father and a loving husband."

Drug addicts were ruled by their addiction, not their sober morality, but Jordan didn't say that to the grieving widow. He wasn't there to shatter her illusion or educate her on the evils in the world. She'd been through enough.

Keith pressed his fingertips together. "What makes you think this man is a drug dealer?"

She shrugged. "Why else would the FBI be showing me a picture? Did Brian die of an overdose? They won't release a death certificate. I can't collect his life insurance without it."

Life insurance? Dare had conducted a thorough background check, and Brian Gartrell didn't have a policy. "Mrs. Gartrell, we might be able to help. Do you have a copy of the policy?"

"Yes. I got it in the mail a few months ago, which I thought was weird. I mean, his only thought is about scoring more crack, and he takes the time to buy a prepaid policy? But then, Brian was a good man. He always said he wanted to take care of us." Her filing cabinet was in a desk in the far corner of the room. She found the policy quickly. "As you can see, it's for almost fifty thousand dollars. That would really help us out."

Keith perused the policy because she handed it to him, so Jordan kept the conversation going. "We believe the man in the photo I showed you might have caused Brian's death. Your husband was murdered."

Color drained from her face. She pressed her hands to her chest. "Is that guy an addict too? Brian knew better than to bring his druggie friends around us. He knew I would cut off all contact with our daughter." She broke off, sniffling. "The last time I saw him was over six weeks ago. We're supposed to meet every Wednesday evening at a fast food restaurant, but I wasn't surprised when he didn't show. The last time I saw him, he looked like shit. Not just like he was using, but like he was being hunted.

He was paranoid. I thought maybe he'd started using other drugs. He said an eye was watching him. He kept repeating that I wasn't to trust an eye. He freaked us out, and we left early. Do you think this guy killed him for crack?"

"It's possible." Keith set the policy on the table and took out his phone. "Do you mind if I take pictures of this? It might be useful in tracing Brian's steps. If we can find where he's been, then we'll have a better idea of what he's been doing."

"Go ahead." Deanna Gartrell's eyes remained wide with shock. "I never thought anybody would want to kill Brian. Even high, he wasn't the kind of person who rubbed people the wrong way."

He'd held Amy at gunpoint, and that rubbed Jordan the wrong way. Squelching that thought, he focused on Deanna. "Did he say anything else about eyes, being watched, or The Eye?"

She shook her head. "Mostly he talked about missing us, missing being home. He said he didn't like living the way he was. I thought maybe he'd hit bottom again and was going to sober up. Our marriage was over, but it would have been nice if he could have been part of Caitlyn's life."

Keith handed his card to Mrs. Gartrell. "If you think of anything else Brian said or did that was out of character or suspicious, please let us know."

She walked them to the door. "Do you know when the death certificate will be released? I can't collect until it is."

"Probably not until we close the investigation." Jordan affected a sympathetic tone. "It could be a few weeks."

She sighed. "I'm never going to see that money."

Amy arrived home much later than expected. The party, a corporate event, had gone very well, and they'd wanted to negotiate six more dates for themed parties. When she'd texted Jordan the reason she'd be late, he'd been very supportive. He'd merely instructed her to be at his house by eight. That gave her an hour to freshen up. She'd stopped by the mall and purchased a bustier top that accented her boobs and made her midsection look sexy. The matching skirt was so short that her butt cheeks showed. And she'd bought the headband with the oversized daisies that she'd loved. Hopefully Jordan would like her in that as well, though she didn't plan to wear it with the sexy lingerie.

As she opened her front door, her neighbor ran up, waving frantically and calling Amy's name. Peggy Johansen's only concession to turning eighty was to start wearing lighter highlights in her deep brown hair. She had an immaculate flower garden, the best on the street, and she regularly helped Amy improve hers.

Amy threw her purse and bags into the house and went toward her neighbor. "Peg, is everything okay?"

"Yes and no. I saw the young man you've had over a lot recently, and I meant to say congratulations. You bagged yourself a handsome devil. My first husband rode a motorcycle. It was very exciting." She took a breath. "But Chicklet has gotten out of the house and run away. Can you help me find him?" Peggy's hound dog mix was a fan of hide-and-seek, and he did not come when called.

"Of course." Amy tucked her keys into her bra—she'd waited until she changed for the party to put one on—and scanned the yards along the street. "Which direction did he go?"

Peggy pointed, and the two of them started out, calling for Chicklet. Within five minutes, two more neighbors, the Slingerlands, joined the search, and Sandra suggested luring him with food. They waited on the sidewalk in front of Peggy's house while she retrieved Chicklet's favorite treats.

April and Melvin, their neighbors from across the street, joined the hunting party, bringing their total to six. "Hi, Amy," Melvin called. "How was your sister's wedding?"

"Fabulous. Beautiful. She's on her honeymoon now." Amy beamed as she remembered the ceremony. When Darcy got back in four days, they were going to both have a lot of great stories to share. After they found Chicklet, she'd send Darcy a quick text to let her know that she'd hooked up with Jordan. The rest could wait.

"Do you have pictures?" April grabbed her wrist. The college student had stars in her eyes. "I love weddings. When I get married, I'm going to have you as my planner."

Melvin rolled his eyes. He'd probably heard quite a bit about her love of weddings already, and his four older daughters were already married. "Not for at least ten years. Maybe thirty. I'm not ready for my baby girl to even think about getting married."

April opened her mouth to deliver a cute or scathing retort, but a boom sounded. The world stuttered and tipped sideways. Amy found herself laying on the grassy expanse between the sidewalk and the street. Mouth opened as if she was shouting, Peggy rushed toward her, but Amy heard only a ringing. She lifted her head to look around, and saw her four neighbors who had been standing with her also on the ground. Debris rained from the sky. She sat up, and looked toward her house to see smoke and flames billowing from the windows.

Pieces of glass glittered everywhere. The huge picture window that faced front was broken. Her front door wavered drunkenly from the lower hinges. Chunks of items that resembled furniture littered the lawn. A lamp had skewered her car through the front windshield. A single daisy from her brand new headband floated down to land on the grass next to her.

My house blew up.

Two people knelt over her, their mouths moving as they said things Amy couldn't hear. A moment passed before Amy recognized them, but even then, she didn't respond. Lexee Hardy and Jed Kinsley were FBI agents. Giving up, Lexee helped Amy to her feet. Jed was on the phone, hopefully calling the fire department. Flames billowed from the gaping hole where her living room window had once been.

Chapter Fifteen

Blood left Jordan's extremities. The familiar office took on a garish glow. Keith peered at him from across the table, alarm replacing the normally stoic expression. "What's wrong?"

Jordan shook his head because everything seemed surreal. The words coming through his phone from Jed Kinsley couldn't be real. "What hospital?" He forced himself to focus on Jed's words, but they came through a long tunnel.

"U of M. We'll meet you in the ER."

"Thanks." Jordan shoved his cell in his pocket and ran for the parking garage. After interviewing Mrs. Gartrell, the pair had returned to the McNamara building in Detroit and holed up in Keith's office to plan their next move. They suspected that Brian Gartrell's fear of eyes was connected to The Eye, and that meant this case was connected to the string of robberies. The escalation to assassination—they'd meant to kill Judge Cantrell—meant this case had become priority one. And Amy was on the assassination list.

Keith ran with him. "Jordan, who is in the hospital?"

"Amy. They planted a bomb in her house. Lexee took her to the hospital. Jed stayed behind to work the scene." For fuck's sake, his girlfriend's house was now a crime scene for a known domestic terrorist organization.

"I'll ride with you." Keith slid into the passenger seat and began making calls. By the time they arrived at the emergency room more than forty miles away, the bomb squad had cleared the scene and the forensics crew was combing through the rubble for evidence.

Jordan flashed his badge at the front desk, and they led him to Amy's private room where Lexee stood guard. With her dark hair pulled back in a severe bun and her tailored suit, Lexee exuded the air of someone that wouldn't take shit from anyone. She moved to let Jordan pass.

Amy sat on the edge of her bed, and she looked like she was trying to stand up. He rushed the four steps across the room and stopped her. "Little one, stay in bed." He searched her body for signs of injury, while she glared.

Her clothes were dirty and singed in some places. She had a tear in her shirt at the shoulder, and her hair was a mess. Clean patches on her skin marked the places where she had small cuts. Overall, she didn't look too bad, all things considered.

"Are you hurt?"

She continued to glare. Then she huffed. "I can't hear anything you're saying, but I know you can hear me. I'm pissed at you, Jordan. How could you have FBI agents following me and not tell me? You knew I was in danger, and you said not one word."

He attributed her loud volume to the fact that she couldn't hear. "Lexee!"

Agent Hardy came into the room. "Yes?"

"Has a doctor seen her yet?"

Lexee pursed her lips. "Just the medic in the ambulance. Her injuries were less severe than some of the others. She arrived home at seventeen hundred hours and fifty-seven minutes where she threw three shopping bags and her purse inside the front door. Her neighbor, Peggy Johansen, asked her to help find her dog. Four neighbors joined the search: Sandra and Joe Slingerland, and April and Melvin Desjardin. Mrs. Johansen went into her home at eighteen hundred hours and fourteen minutes. Amy and the four neighbors continued talking outside, at which time the explosion occurred. Amy, April, and Melvin sustained mild cuts and contusions and temporary hearing loss. April and Melvin were treated on site and released home. Sandra required seventeen stitches on her back and arm, and Joe is in surgery where they're trying to relieve the swelling on his brain. I brought

Amy here to get her away from the scene. I would have told you that outside, but you were in a hurry."

While Lexee spoke, Amy again tried to get up. Jordan grabbed her arm, and she pushed him away. "I have to go to the bathroom. I can walk fine. I just can't hear."

Jordan narrowed his eyes at her tone and the lack of enthusiasm in her greeting. "Maybe if you shouted louder?"

She swiped a pad and paper from the tray and shoved it at him. "I. Can't. Hear. You. Asshole." With that, she left the room.

"I'll tail her. The restroom is across the hall." Lexee went after her.

Keith smirked. "She's pissed, all right. You didn't tell her about the threat?"

"No. We didn't know if it was credible. Why would I needlessly worry her?" Jordan scribbled words on the pad.

"She needs a spanking."

"She does not." Jordan growled. If he spanked her for the first time as discipline, it would damage their relationship. She wasn't cut out for that kind of treatment. "She just went through a traumatic experience."

"Littles are hard to keep in line. They need a firm hand."

Jordan looked up to see the merriment sparkling in Keith's eyes. Trina had forbidden physical discipline. She insisted they talk through their differences, and Keith was learning a different kind of dominance. "You son of a bitch. You're enjoying this."

"Oh, yes. For years subs have held you up as the epitome of the perfect Dom. So loving and gentle, indulgent and understanding, and now you have to learn to administer tough love." Keith laughed so hard he had to sit on the bed. "This is priceless."

Jordan added more to his note. "I need to be patient and understanding. She's feeling betrayed. I kept something from her, and she was caught unaware. She lost her home. You can't understate the significance of what she's going through."

Keith stopped laughing and regarded him somberly. "Buddy, going soft is the wrong tactic. More than anything, right now she needs your strength. Once that anger wears off, she's going to fall apart, and if she's still mad at you, she's not going to let you put her back together. You'll lose her."

While he agreed that Amy would shut him out if he didn't handle this right, he didn't think that being harsh was the right course of action. Amy needed him to protect her from the big, bad world, and he'd failed miserably. He glanced at what he'd written, tore off the top sheet, and threw it in the trash.

Amy returned as he scribbled something else on the pad. Jordan eyed Lexee and Keith. "Can you wait outside?"

"Okay," Keith said, "but just so you know, we'll be able to hear her replies."

Lexee rolled her eyes. "We'll be right outside, and yes, we'll frisk anybody before letting them inside—even the doctor."

Amy avoided eye contact as she trudged toward the bed. Jordan planted himself in her way, and when she tried to go around him, he took her in his arms. Though she held herself stiffly, she didn't push him away. "I'm so sorry, little one." He whispered even though she couldn't hear. "I'm going to catch the bastard that did this. I promise."

He helped her onto the bed, and then he conducted his own inspection. He cleaned away the smudges of grime from her skin to check her arms and legs. On the paper, he wrote two things: *I'm sorry* and *Where are you hurt?*

She read them both, and when she met his gaze, her eyes glittered with unshed tears. "I'm not hurt. I just can't hear, but I think it's starting to come back."

Since she wasn't speaking as loudly as before, he figured she was right. He wrote: *I will explain what I can later.*

She nodded and looked away. He began writing more, but she spoke, her voice small and tremulous. "I bought the headband with the daisies, and I got a really great outfit for tonight." Leaning back on the pillows, she closed her eyes. Tears leaked out to trail down her temples. "Maybe this is a sign. I made a mistake."

He shook her, forcing her to open her eyes and face him. "No." He shook his head. "This isn't a sign, and you didn't make a mistake."

Even if she could hear him, he didn't know if his denial would have penetrated. Her gaze sidled away once again. "I hope Peggy found Chicklet. That dog getting out saved my life. I would have been in there, getting ready to come see you, and I would be dead now."

He gave silent thanks for the dog that ran away. He perched on the edge of the bed and took her hands in his. Because she couldn't hear—and words would ring hollow anyway—he kissed her fingers, and then he peppered her forehead and cheeks with more kisses and caresses. She needed affection and reassurance, and he had so much of that to give her.

The door opened, and he turned to find Brandy Lockmeyer with her lips pressed together. He could count the number of times he'd seen her feathers ruffled on one hand. She was cool under pressure, and this display of temper put him on edge. "I received an email an hour ago. The Eye takes responsibility for the bombing. Hardy, Brandt, Rossetti, get in here and close the door."

She conducted a visual sweep of the room, something Jordan had been too distraught to think to do.

"I swept three times, Chief." Lexee stood at attention, her hands clasped in front of her in ready position. "It's clean."

"Fine." Brandy finished her inspection. "According to Agent Adair, the email originated on our secure server. Either we have a mole, or The Eye has hacked our system. I will not countenance sabotage and terrorism in my state and in my FBI. This ends now.

We're taking down The Eye. Listen carefully. This is how we're going to play this. The Eye thinks they achieved their goal. Therefore Amy Markevich died in that bombing. She'll go into protective custody and remain hidden until we have acquired our target. Judge Caldwell is already at a safe house. That leaves Jordan as the only witness they have left to erase, and therefore Agent Monaghan is the bait."

Jordan moved between Brandy and Amy, blocking her with his body just in case she could read lips. "Brandy, they killed a man in our custody. If they've infiltrated the FBI, it's just a matter of time before they figure out Amy is alive." Even putting her in a safe house wasn't enough. They'd find her eventually.

"I know. That's why I'm trusting just the people in this room." She took a deep breath. "The email said they'd clean house, kill anybody who got in their way. They threatened me and referenced a covert operation I took part in years ago. It's someone from inside with access to classified documents. They knew things they shouldn't know."

He knew what covert operation they'd referenced. Brandy hadn't spent a lot of time in Special Forces, and the look she gave him communicated what her words didn't. Venezuela had been a mess. Though Jordan had saved Brandy's ass that night, he still didn't have the clearance to know exactly what had happened. Their survival had been a combination of luck and skill, heavy on the luck part.

"I have a cabin up north." Dustin rubbed his hands together. "I can take Amy there. Malcolm is due in two days. We can make it seem like he's extended his vacation, and put him on babysitting duty."

Keith nodded, liking the plan. "He'll want to bring Darcy, which Amy will appreciate, and his parents can keep Colin for a little longer. It's not ideal, but it'll work."

"Yeah. Sure." Jordan crossed his arms and let the sarcasm loose. "Darcy's reaction to her sister's death is definitely going to be an extension of her honeymoon. These guys are morons, but I don't think they're stupid."

Brandy scowled. "You have a better idea?"

Fuck, yeah, he had a better idea. He'd underestimated these motherfucking terrorists before, and Amy had paid the price. "They weren't watching Amy's house to make sure their plan was successful. They scoped her out beforehand, probably broke into her house and saw the schedule she keeps on the fridge. Maybe I was there with her when it blew up. That was the original plan. Put out a press release saying I died in the bombing with her. Write a fucking amazing obituary. I'll take Amy into hiding at Dustin's cottage. The person who did this will come to our funerals. Watch the crowd. I'll disguise myself and come as one of my brothers. We'll set them up and take them out."

Brandy exhaled hard and rubbed her chin as she thought.

Keith shook his head. "It's good except for the part where you disguise yourself and come to your funeral. That's not going to fly. If they identify you, then the whole op is blown. Stay with Amy and keep her safe."

"I agree with Keith," Lexee said. "I know it's hard to sit back and let us do the heavy work, but you're going to have to."

Dustin eyed him silently. They'd been partners for years, and they'd come through more than a few close calls together. Dustin knew Jordan better than most people did. "If we plan this op without Jordan, he'll show up and throw a wrench into our plan. This is personal. He needs to take down this guy."

"It's true." Jordan spread his hands wide. "Jed and Lexee can watch Amy when we run the op."

Lexee glared at him. "I can't miss your funeral. I'm already mourning your loss."

Brandy lifted a hand to silence them. "I'll take care of Amy. I have some friends in private security who owe me."

As Jordan had worked alongside some of those friends of Brandy's, he knew Amy would be in good hands. "Then it's settled. I'll take Amy into hiding until Saturday." Jordan felt behind him for Amy's hand to hold. She had to be feeling left out, and he wanted to reassure her that she wasn't alone.

"Saturday?" Keith scratched his chin. "I'm thinking it'll take a little longer to close the investigation and release your remains. Let's say Amy's funeral is Monday, and yours is Tuesday. We're not shipping your ass back to Wisconsin, either."

That worked for Jordan. Amy needed him now, and this way he'd be able to take care of her and have a hand in rectifying the situation. "I'll need supplies and a vehicle. Get us out of here ASAP."

Brandy handed out orders. "Brandt, see to transportation and supplies. Have it ready in an hour. Hardy, coordinate the paperwork for a death certificate and a press release with Adair, and then arrange an exit for these two. Rossetti, head back to Markevich's residence and make sure that crime scene is wrapped up the way we need it to be for this to work. I'll run interference so the hospital staff doesn't know what the hell's going on."

Amy watched their lips move, and she judged from their expressions that her fate was being decided. While she couldn't make out what they were saying, she was beginning to catch garbled sounds. When Jordan sought to hold her hand, she figured that things weren't going the way he wanted. So many thoughts and emotions zinged through her brain, and she desperately wanted to curl up on her sofa under a blanket and lose herself in a movie—one where Hollywood guaranteed everything would turn out all right.

Because right now her life didn't look like it was heading toward a happily ever after. One day of bliss with Jordan, and everything had been ripped from her. And she'd called him an asshole. There was no way he was going to let that pass. He might not be saying anything right now, but that was because she couldn't hear. She was sure she'd hear about it later, once things calmed down. He'd mentioned punishing her by making her stand in a corner. Though she wasn't looking forward to the punishment, she could do with some absolution.

The doctor came in, all business and frowns. She examined Amy's cuts and bruises, and she looked in her ears. Jordan remained in the room for the exam, and so the doctor's questions were all directed to him. Discharge instructions were given to him as well, and Amy found this highly irregular. He wasn't even a relative.

She cooperated when Agent Hardy smuggled them out of the delivery entrance and into a strange car with darkly tinted windows. It was late, and when Jordan got on the freeway, she surmised that he was taking her to his house. At least she had a place to crash. If Darcy had been home, she probably would have asked to stay in the guest room. Though Darcy and Malcolm probably wouldn't mind if she wanted to stay in their house now. She had a key. Well, she used to have a key. Who knew if it survived the fire? It hadn't been on the key ring she'd tucked into her bra.

Glancing at Jordan, she realized he wouldn't let her stay alone, and that was okay. She didn't want to be alone. Every time she closed her eyes, she felt the force of the blast knocking her to the ground and saw the flames billowing from her living room. Miles disappeared beneath the tires, and she realized they were heading too far north and not at all east. They weren't going to Jordan's apartment either.

"Jordan, where are we going?" She tried to modulate her volume because she suspected she'd been shouting earlier.

He looked over, flashed a brief smile that didn't reach his eyes, and squeezed her knee reassuringly. She waited for a response, but he said nothing, and she wondered if it was because she hadn't used his title.

"Daddy?"

This time, he took her hand in his. "Try to get some sleep. We'll be on the road a while."

She stared at him blankly. Her hearing had improved remarkably, but he hadn't exactly answered her question. After a minute, she realized he wasn't going to say more. Yes, she was exhausted, but she couldn't sleep. She stared out the window and watched shadows of trees in the moonlight. Jordan turned the radio on and flipped through stations.

The next thing she knew, Jordan was talking to her. "I'm so sorry this happened, little one. I promise I'll catch the bastards who did this. We have a plan in place, but until then, you and I need to disappear for a little while."

She opened her eyes to find that he'd reclined her seat. Fatigue must have combined with the monotony of the ride to lull her to sleep. Though it was still dark, the sky was lighter, a hint at the coming dawn. Jordan sat in the driver's seat of the sedan, his left hand resting at the top of the steering wheel, but the car wasn't moving. She sat up and looked around. They were parked near a cottage in the middle of a clearing. Beyond that was a heavily treed area.

"Where are we?"

"Dustin's cabin. I helped him remodel it. We're going to stay here for a few days while we're laying low."

There was nothing wrong with her hearing. It had all come back. "Why are we laying low?"

"Because the people who planted a bomb in your house want us both dead. The FBI is going to act as if we were both killed in the blast in the hope of drawing out the suspects. We're thinking they'll come to either your funeral or mine to make sure they achieved their objective." He rubbed his eye. "How is your hearing? Are your ears still ringing?"

"A little, but I can hear you." She blinked away the sleepy disconnectedness that made everything seem unreal. "Why didn't they just stick around to make sure the bomb went off and killed me? Can you even be sure they think I'm dead?"

"They sent an email to Brandy bragging about it. As for why they didn't stick around, they probably knew the FBI was following you. If they'd hung around, Lexee and Jed would have spotted them. We've run background on all your neighbors and know their schedules. Anybody new would have stood out." He yawned and rested his head back.

Amy hadn't known she was being followed, and as she thought about it, another disturbing thought came to her. "All this time you've spent with me over the past couple of days—you were working, weren't you? I was your assignment."

"We were still trying to figure out if it was a credible threat or the ravings of a drug addict. I didn't tell you because I didn't want you to worry needlessly. I was planning to be around anyway, so I insisted I be primary on your security detail."

And she'd all but insisted he leave and go to work. She'd been afraid he'd get in trouble, and she'd shooed him out the door. It had also been easier to get her work done without him underfoot. No matter how unobtrusive he tried to be, having him around was distracting. He was handsome and sexy and hers.

He opened his door, and light flooded the interior. "I'm going to sweep the house, and then I'll bring in our bags."

"I don't have any bags." Except for the clothes on her back, she had nothing.

"I had Dustin pick up a few things for you." He got out of the car. "Stay here. I'll only be a minute."

Amy watched lights come on in the cabin. As cabins went, this one was large and nicely kept up. The exterior had light yellow vinyl siding and a wide front porch with four rocking chairs arranged side by side. The inside, which she got to see moments later, consisted of a long living room that ran all the way to the kitchen in the back. A large dining table defined the dining room as a divide between the living room and kitchen. A combination bathroom and laundry room was off the kitchen. To the left, a hallway led to three bedrooms and another bathroom. It was cozy and homey, but some décor choices didn't make sense.

"What are all the hooks for in the ceiling?"

"Bondage. They're screwed into the rafters, so it'll work for suspension. One of the bedrooms is set up as a dungeon with a St. Andrew's cross, two different bondage tables, a spanking bench, and a pleasure-torture chair." He didn't grin lasciviously or get a twinkle in his eye, so she figured that room was off-limits to anybody but Dustin and Layla. "We'll take the front bedroom. It's the guest room. Give me a second to get the rest of the bags from the car, and then I'll make up the bed."

"I can help."

"No. You've been through enough. Sit down and take it easy."

Amy stood in the middle of the large room, staring after him. She wished he'd give her a task, something to make her feel useful, but he seemed intent on coddling her. Sinking down on the sofa, she folded her hands and waited while Jordan made two more trips in and out. Then she followed him into the bedroom. When he spread the fitted sheet over the mattress, she went around to the other side and tucked it in.

"You don't have to do that. You've had a tough night, little one. Let me take care of you."

His command would have worked better if he didn't look so exhausted himself. "I slept in the car, and you've been up all night. Let me help, and then we can both go to bed. I'll even sleep naked because I have no clothes that aren't stained and torn." She tried for a cheeky smile, but it came out tired and sad. "I'm the submissive, remember? I need to take care of you."

He fluffed the top sheet in the air and let it float down to cover the bed. "You can wear one of my shirts to sleep. I told Dustin to get you some clothes, but I don't know if he had time to get everything. He only had an hour to get supplies and the car for us."

The idea of Dustin picking out her clothing did not appeal to Amy at all. Besides, there was no way he knew her size. Layla's tiny frame couldn't be more than a size four, where Amy bounced between fourteen and eighteen. Men were notoriously bad at guestimating that kind of thing.

Jordan set a travel bag at the foot of the bed and opened it up. Amy recognized it as having been shoved behind the seat in his truck. She expected him to pull out the shirts, jeans, boxers, and socks she knew he kept in there, but instead he extracted women's clothing. Two shirts and two pairs of yoga pants looked to be about her size. She was pleasantly surprised. He threw a plastic-wrapped package of six panties on the pile, and then he added two bras. One was an underwire, and the other was a sports bra. It was all her size.

"Wow. I think it will fit. I'm impressed. Wait, this means you told Dustin my size."

Jordan frowned. "I didn't even think to tell him your size. I should have. Lucky for us, Dustin is good with women's clothing. He says it's a gift and a curse. I can't see the downside of getting it right, though."

There was a downside to people knowing her size. That was information she didn't share. The only way Jordan would find out was if he looked at the tags in her clothes. Still, she wasn't about to get upset that Dustin had bought clothes that would fit her. Upon closer inspection, he'd also chosen styles she liked. "I'll thank Dustin when I see him next."

The rest of the clothes in the bag were Jordan's. He grabbed a pair of sweats and a shirt, and he tossed a shirt to Amy. "He forgot pajamas for you, so wear my shirt. Come on. Let's take a shower before we go to bed. You'll feel better once you're clean."

She followed him to the bathroom and waited patiently while he got the water going. This would be their first time showering together, so she had high expectations.

And she was doomed to disappointment. He washed and conditioned her hair carefully, and then he gently cleaned away all evidence of her ordeal from her skin. She expected that since they were both wet and naked, he'd want to get frisky, but he didn't make a move. She chalked it up to fatigue. He'd worked all day and night. In bed, he curved his body around hers and held her securely in his arms. She fell asleep in seconds and stayed asleep until he woke her by easing his arms away.

"You don't have to get up yet, babe. I'm starving, though, so I was going to make lunch."

Bright light filtered around the blinds. Amy sat up. "I'm hungry too. Is there any food in the house or do we need to run to the store?"

"I brought food. Just relax. I'll take care of everything."

Amy watched him leave the room, and a heaviness settled over her heart. He felt guilty about what happened, and that was killing the fragile relationship they'd just begun to build.

Chapter Sixteen

Two nights with Amy should have been heaven, but it wasn't. No matter how well Jordan took care of her, she only became more withdrawn. He'd surprised her with a coloring book and colored pencils, and she had yet to touch them. Mostly she wandered around the house aimlessly or read from the novels she found in the master bedroom. They were in hiding, and that meant they needed to stay inside and out of sight. Though Dustin's cabin was in the woods, the main road wasn't far, and it was the height of tourist season.

The morning of the second day, Friday, he was startled to hear pounding on the door. Amy was in the bedroom, reading or sleeping, and he'd just finished cleaning up the breakfast dishes. He grabbed his gun and hurried to the front of the cabin. Amy hovered at the mouth of the hall, and he motioned her to get out of sight.

"Who is it?"

"FBI. Your ass is grass, Monaghan."

He recognized Malcolm's voice and his impatience. Opening the door a crack, he found both Malcolm and Darcy on the porch. "What are you doing here?"

Malcolm pushed the door wider, and Jordan stepped back to let him in. "Visiting my dead sister-in-law. I tell you, it's wonderful to be on my honeymoon and get news like that over the television."

Darcy rushed in, her eyes darting around the room. "Where's Amy? Is she okay?"

Amy came out from the hallway, rushing at her sister with arms wide open. "I'm okay, and I'm sorry I worried you."

The women embraced tightly, and Jordan was struck by their physical similarities. They were definitely sisters. "We drove by your house on our way here." Darcy's voice was muffled because her face was buried in Amy's shoulder. "I'm so glad you weren't inside. It's a shell. Keith said they had propane tanks wired to your alarm system so that when you opened the door, a timer started. I didn't even know you had an alarm system."

"I didn't know it worked." Amy came up for air, so her words were clearer. "I thought it was disconnected."

"It was," Malcolm said. "Whoever did this knew what they were doing. Propane tanks were hidden in the front closet, under the kitchen sink, and in the hall closet. The crews working the scene are trying to save what they can." Darcy reluctantly released Amy, and Malcolm took her place. He squeezed her tightly. "I can't tell you how good it is to see you safe and sound."

Darcy grabbed a bag from the porch. "We can't stay long. We're part of the sting operation to get those fucking bastards. But I brought you some of my clothes. Dustin said he sent two outfits for six days. That's not enough." She pulled Amy toward the bedroom. "Let's go in here where we can be alone and those two can have their FBI powwow."

Jordan motioned toward the kitchen. "I have a fresh pot of coffee brewing."

"I've had enough coffee. Darcy made us leave at four in the morning. She's been beside herself with worry, and seeing Amy in person was the only thing that would calm her down." Malcolm took a seat at the table. "On the plus side, if the sister of the corpse is a mess, it makes the funeral more believable. On the negative side, we had to tell her parents that Amy is a really dead. They're liable to not show up to the funeral otherwise."

"They're interesting people." Jordan poured himself a cup of coffee, his second of the day, and joined Malcolm. "Are my parents and brothers and sisters planning to attend?"

"Jamie and your parents are already at your apartment. Your mom plans to pack up your things and take them back to Wisconsin. Dustin is storing your sex toys and rope at his place.

No sense in giving your mom a heart attack." Malcolm grinned, but it was more grim than happy. "The rest of your family is flying in today. We're not telling them you're alive. The fewer people who know, the better."

Though Jordan didn't want them to have to go through the heartbreak, he recognized the need for secrecy. "If I survive this, they may kill me."

"Maybe. Let's focus on the positives, though." Malcolm got up and opened the fridge. He lifted a carton of milk. "Is there any cereal in this place?"

Jordan pointed to a cupboard. "What positives? Amy has lost everything, and now my family thinks I'm dead. Bowls are to the left."

Malcolm found the right cupboards. He poured milk over his cereal. "You and Amy are together. Though, now that you mention it, she doesn't look like a well-loved woman. Does she blame you?"

"No. She was mad at first because I didn't tell her about the threat or that we had her under protective surveillance, but she got over it. Right now, she's depressed, but that's to be expected. She lost everything—her home, her business, all her possessions. That's a harsh thing to bear." Sadness settled in his heart as he thought of the enormity of her loss.

Malcolm scowled as he chowed down on a granola-based cereal. "Keith said you were being an idiot. Please tell me you're not coddling her and letting her bask in depression."

"She's mourning the life she's spent a lot of time building."

"A life she still has."

"Everything of her business is gone. Her computer, her files, sample books, contacts, client lists, and all the supplies she's amassed—everything was destroyed." She'd been crying over it earlier that morning.

Malcolm waved dismissively. "She can rebuild her business. It's probably not going to be as difficult as she thinks. This case is all over the news, and you can't get better advertising than that."

His buddy had lost his mind. Jordan's expression soured. "She didn't ask for any of this, and it's all my fault anyway. She never would have stumbled over that body if I hadn't not kissed her at your wedding."

With a snort, Mal pushed away his empty bowl and took Jordan's coffee. "Let me know when you decide to get down off that cross. Dustin is in the market for a St. Andrew's for his dungeon at home, and he could use the wood to build one."

Jordan snatched his cup back before Malcolm could take a drink. "Get your own. There's a whole pot. Or better yet, leave. I can do without you riding me. I'm the one who knows how to handle a little, not you."

This time, Malcolm sighed. "You've got it bad, not that I expected less. It might take you forever to move on a woman, but when you do, you're all in. That's probably why all your exes still send you Christmas cards." He put his hands on the table. "Look, I'm not denying that Amy has been through a lot, and I'm not minimizing it. But she's a strong woman. Don't treat her like she's fragile just because she's also a little. She's resilient and smart, and I can't help but think that you're letting her down."

"Did Keith put you up to this?" Jordan clenched his fists. Being younger than the rest of them, he was often treated like a kid brother. As the oldest of six, he chaffed under such handling. "She's my little, my girlfriend. I know what's best for her." Except that he'd expected her to retreat into a different headspace to deal with what happened, yet she hadn't.

Malcolm nodded. "I'm going to tell you what I know about Amy, and a lot of it is stuff you probably already know as well. She's generous and kind. She has a deep and abiding need to take care of the people in her life. She's inquisitive and industrious. Sitting here doing nothing will kill her spirit. She's had her world turned upside down, the figurative rug yanked from underneath. She needs your guidance and a firm hand. If you're not going to be the pillar of strength she needs, then you have no business being in her life. Now, I can see that you love her, but you're letting the guilt override your better sense. You're an excellent Daddy Dom, and she needs you to be at the top of your game."

Love her? Jordan hadn't considered that he'd fallen head over heels, but as Malcolm spoke, the realization hit him like a fist in the gut. He wanted to fall asleep with her in his arms, wake up next to her warm body, make love to her often, and fill her life with happiness. He couldn't imagine an existence without Amy by his side. He tucked his injured pride away with his guilt and nodded at Malcolm. "Noted. Now tell me what you know about the op. What's changed?"

Malcolm's frown didn't disappear, but it did ease. "Nothing, as far as I know. We're gathering intel and putting the pieces in place. They raided the New Day Church yesterday. Lockmeyer said they found where the bomb was assembled and a list of robbery targets. The propane tanks they used were small, only five pounds, but there was enough to do the job. Dare is going through the computers we seized, and I'll be giving him a hand when I get back. Avery and Lexee found addresses for property owned by the New Day Church. They're getting warrants this morning."

Darcy threw some bags on the bed and hugged Amy again. "Please don't die again. I can't lose you."

With a small, uncomfortable laugh, Amy squeezed Darcy tighter. She was so glad that her sister had come for a visit. Jordan was wonderful, but she needed more. "I'll try not to."

"Okay, I'm done crying." Darcy wiped a tear from her cheek. "I'm going to focus on the positives, as Mal keeps telling me to do. Check out what's in the bags."

Amy dumped the nearest bag on the bed. It contained lingerie. She held a deep red bustier up to her body and looked in the mirror. "Interesting choice. You know, I was late getting home because I stopped at the mall and picked up a cute bustier and skirt combination. It's probably dust right now."

Darcy bit her lip as she eyed the lingerie. "I'm not sure about that one. It looks fabulous on me, but somehow it doesn't seem right on you. It's too harsh. You need a soft pink or purple. I looked up this Daddy/little thing while I was on vacation. It seems a lot like you."

Not ready for the change in direction, Amy took a second to respond. "You knew Jordan was planning to talk to me?"

"Yeah. Jordan told Malcolm to lay off looking for a Dom for you. Mal said that Jordan was the kind of guy who thought through something from every angle before making a move. He certainly took long enough." She grinned, and her blue eyes sparkled.

Warmth traveled up Amy's neck as she thought of exactly how thorough Jordan could be. "Well, you were right about sleeping with a Dom. They are very attuned to their partner's pleasure."

Darcy dived onto the bed and rested her chin in her hands. "Tell me everything. Start with when I left the reception. I saw the way he was looking at you, and he didn't let you far from his side the whole night."

Amy perched on the mattress next to her sister and let loose with the details. By the time she finished, she felt as if a huge weight had lifted from her shoulders. She'd done nothing wrong, and none of this mess was her fault. It wasn't Jordan's, either.

Silence fell over the room as she finished speaking, and Darcy waited for more. "Amy, you're stuck in a cabin with your Daddy for six uninterrupted days. Why are you so miserable?"

"Besides the fact that my house and business blew up? Besides the fact that I have to restart my business from scratch and find somewhere else to live?"

Darcy nodded. Her sister knew her too well to think she'd throw in the towel because of a setback like that.

Amy sighed. "Jordan hasn't been at all dominant since it happened. At the hospital, I called him an asshole. I thought he'd punish me, but since we've been here, he's done everything for me. He won't even let me cook or do dishes. He caught me folding the clothes and putting them in drawers, and he made me stop. He finished it. I just wish he'd give me a chore or a task, like he did before we started going out, when he was just my Dom and not my Daddy or my boyfriend."

Darcy sat up and cupped Amy's face in her hands. "Honey, have you told him any of this?"

"No."

"He's not a mind-reader, and your relationship is new. If your Daddy isn't meeting your needs, it's not because he doesn't want to. It's because he doesn't know what they are. If you want this to work, you're going to have to talk to him. No matter how uncomfortable the topic may be, you have to bring it up. Communication is the key, but the lock is sometimes really rusty and resistant."

A tear rolled down Amy's cheek. She wiped it away, and Darcy hugged her. They stayed that way for a little while.

The door opened, and Malcolm hovered at the door. "Ladies, I'm sorry to be the bearer of bad news, but we have to get going. I have work to do, and Darcy needs to pick Colin up from my parents this afternoon."

Darcy didn't beg for more time, and Amy didn't take it personally. Now that she knew Amy was safe, her sister likely wanted to see the son she'd been away from all week. Darcy hugged Amy one last time. "I'll see you in a few days. Stay strong."

At the front door, Malcolm hugged her as well. "Be patient with Jordan. He's young, you know."

"I'm right here." Jordan glared at Malcolm.

Amy made sure she stood between them. "Mal was kidding. He has a dry sense of humor that many people understandably fail to appreciate."

Jordan pulled her closer and slung his arm around her shoulders. "When he's funny, I laugh. When he needs his ass kicked, I indulge him there too."

Darcy hopped up on her tiptoes, and Jordan bent his head so she could kiss his cheek. "I'm trusting you to take care of my sister. I expect her back in one piece. Or blissfully broken."

He smiled until they left, at which point, Amy said, "I have to tell you something."

The smile faded like yesterday's sunset. He steeled himself. "I'm listening."

"Okay, so the past couple of days have been a little hard for me, but not because I lost my house and all the stuff from my business. It's been hard because you're not being you. I mean, yeah, having my house blow up and not knowing if Chicklet is okay has been difficult. He's a sweetheart, always wagging his tail and putting his head under my hand so I'll pet him, but he's got a wanderlust streak a mile wide." She was getting off track, so she tried to shove her hands in her pockets, but yoga pants don't have pockets. Darn. She stared at the floor, tracing her toe over the smooth wood surface. "Anyway, before we started a romantic relationship, you used to be firm with me and give me chores and tasks to do. I liked that a lot. It made me feel like I had a direction, a purpose—even if I didn't particularly want to do the task. It made it easier to concentrate and get all the other stuff done that I needed to do." She gathered her courage and looked at him. "I need my Daddy."

He took her in his arms, holding her tightly and gripping her hair at the nape. "I'm right here, little one. I've been lost for the past few days, but I'm back now." The hand at her nape pulled, tilting her face up, and he took her mouth in an utterly dominant kiss that curled her toes.

Soft moans came from the back of her throat, and he thrust his tongue into her mouth, claiming that territory as well. He lifted her against him, kneading her ass as he pressed his pelvis into her stomach.

Abruptly he broke away and rested his forehead against hers. "I keep thinking you need a safe place so you can get into little headspace to deal with the stress."

She'd read about that in her research. It was where littles regressed into their child persona to deal with stress. Amy shook her head. "I tend to do that to unwind, not to avoid dealing with a problem."

"Like when you wanted to watch Finding Nemo?"

"Yeah, like that. It was thoughtful of you to get a coloring book, but I like to color pictures after a long day or to relax on a day off. It clears the clutter from my head and lets me really loosen up. With things uncertain between you and me, I can't relax. No amount of coloring or watching movies is going to change that."

He released her from his embrace. "I'm sorry you thought things were uncertain between us. Let me clear that up. Amy, I love you. I don't know how long I've been in love with you because I don't remember falling. I just know that somewhere along the way, you became a vital piece of me that I can't imagine functioning without. I mishandled this situation. I see that now. I'd say I'll do better next time, but I'm not really planning for a bomb in your house again."

She laughed. "I hope not. And I love you too. And I'm sorry I called you an asshole. I had a tough day, but that was no reason to treat you disrespectfully. I accept any punishment you want to give me for that."

"How about we call it even? We both messed up. Let's forgive and move forward."

That sounded good to her. "I like that idea."

"Great. I have more ideas."

She waited for him to continue, but he merely regarded her with an arrogant half-smile. He was devilishly handsome with that sardonic lift of one corner of his mouth, and she guessed at the caliber of the thoughts percolating through his brain. Though he didn't tell her to, she got to her knees and assumed the first submissive pose he'd taught her. She was rewarded when he ran his fingers through her hair. "Darcy brought some things you might like to see."

"Yeah? Like what?"

"Sexy clothes. There's a bustier in there that's almost like the one I bought to wear to your place after that party on Wednesday. Only the one Darcy brought is red, and the one I bought was pink with white ribbons. It was really pretty, and it had a matching skirt."

He tilted her head back and stepped forward so that she had to lean against him to remain upright. It was unexpectedly intimate. "I'll wait to see you in a bustier until we can buy that outfit again. It's definitely on my list of Amy fantasies. Right now, I just want you in the bedroom, naked and on your back, presentation position."

Amy took her time undressing. Jordan had headed into the dungeon for supplies. She barely made it into position when he came in with a familiar bag slung over his shoulder. A vague memory of him bringing it into the house that first night flitted through her mind. She'd been more out of it than she'd realized if she had seen that bag and hadn't automatically started creaming in her panties.

She couldn't hold her ankles and lay flat on her back, so she held onto her shins, her pussy exposed to his view, and waited. He dropped the bag down and looked at her, his visual inspection as powerful as his caresses. Her pussy responded to the heat of his gaze by swelling, and she knew it glistened with juices.

"Good girl," he said. "I like how you've changed the placement of your hands to be truer to the pose. And your pussy is dripping, babe. You're so fucking hot." He dragged a finger through her wetness and circled her clit. "Mine. All mine." He knelt on the floor and lowered his mouth to her pussy. Amy gasped as he took her clit between his lips and sucked hard. He licked, tasting her all over, and then he sat back on his heels. "You're going to earn this."

Shocked that he'd stopped before he got going, she lifted her head. "What? How?"

He stood, and the expression on his face brooked no questions. His dark brown eyes glittered hard with equal parts possessiveness and lust. She was going to satisfy her man before he gave her anything, and she was more than okay with that. He lifted his shirt over his head and tossed it to the floor. Amy let herself enjoy the sight of his magnificent chest the way he'd indulged himself in looking at her body. Next he unbuttoned his pants and slowly unzipped his fly. Briefly she glanced at his face to find that he was basking in her attention. He stripped with excruciating lassitude, and when he was naked, he stayed there for a minute, letting her appreciate his perfection. He had scars scratched across one thigh and starburst from what looked like a healed bullet wound in his left shoulder. Freckles decorated the tops of his shoulders, and his cock jutted from an untamed nest of black curls.

"You're a very sexy man," she said. "Don't ever let anybody tell you differently."

"Funny." He didn't crack a smile. "You're the only one who gets to stare at me like that, and nobody else's opinion matters anyway. Scoot up. Lay so that your head is hanging off the other side of the bed. You can put your legs down, but keep them spread."

Scooting across a bed was never going to be a graceful move, so Amy did it as quickly as possible. She let her head dangle off the side. Her legs were spread, but she didn't have anything to do with her hands, so she folded them across her stomach. Jordan lifted one of her legs, exposing her even more. Then he drizzled lubricant over her sphincter. He held up a dildo, this one nearly as big around as his cock, and rolled a condom over it. "Exhale, little one. Let me know if this pinches or hurts."

She cooperated, and it pinched a little. The sensation was momentary and over quickly, and it left behind a generally pleasurable pulsing. "It pinched a little, but I liked it, so please don't stop."

He came around to the other side of the bed and kissed her lips. "You're doing very well. I'm proud of you."

She felt herself bloom and preen from his praise.

"Remember when you said you wanted to learn to deep throat my cock?"

"Yeah."

"Lesson one is right now. I'm going to give you a red ball to hold. When it's too much, drop the ball. Since your mouth will be occupied, that'll be your safe signal. Got it?"

"Yes, Daddy."

"I'm not going to come in your mouth, so don't get pouty when I pull out."

She felt a little slighted, but she reasoned that she would get to blow him until he erupted later. She meant to reply, but he pushed his thumb into her mouth, fucking it in and out teasingly. Next he used his fingers, and she was confused by their position. It would be much easier to suck his cock if she was on her knees. He answered her unasked question by tracing the wet tip of his cock along her lips. His body blocked her view, and the only things she could see were his balls and his powerful thighs. She opened her mouth and explored his crown with her tongue. Jordan let her wet his cock this way, working his length deeper into her mouth. Once he made it as far as she'd taken him the other morning, he pulled out.

Lifting his cock, he set his scrotum on her lips. "Lick my balls, babe. Suck them gently."

She did, finding pleasure in the low moans she elicited from him.

But he took them away too soon. "Open your mouth. I'm going to go deeper this time, babe. Swallow when I get to the back of your throat."

He eased inside slowly, and when he got to the back of her throat, she swallowed, trying to draw him in farther. He pulled out and thrust forward again and again. Amy's eyes watered, but her gag reflex thankfully didn't kick in. She learned to take a breath when he pulled out. He pushed in once again and stayed there.

"That's everything, babe. You did it. I'm not going to fuck your mouth today, but I will soon. Remember what this feels like because, babe, your mouth feels incredible on my dick." Slowly he eased out.

Amy basked in his praise and the way he'd kept his promise. This position, with her head tilted back, allowed her to take all of him. She wasn't sure it would work if she was on her knees, but at least she was on her way to mastering the skill.

"Stand next to the bed."

She scrambled to obey as he rooted around in the bag again, muttering to himself. "Ah, there it is. I want to use twisted cotton on you so it'll leave behind a gorgeous design once I take it off." He extracted several coils of rope and threw all but one on the bed. "First I'm going to tie a corselet harness on you. It'll frame your breasts and provide a way for me to tether you to the hooks in the ceiling above the bed. It's both aesthetically pleasing and functional."

Amy looked up. She hadn't noticed the steel rings placed at intervals in the ceiling. "Is this whole cabin set up for bondage?"

"Every room but the kitchen."

"You could have bondage parties here, or whatever you'd call a D/s party. I guess people shouldn't be restricted to just one kink." She giggled when she said *restricted*. It wasn't quite a pun, but it would do.

Jordan nodded thoughtfully. "That's a great idea." He folded the rope in half, lining up the fluffy ends. Then he held the middle loop against her stomach and wrapped the dual line around behind. He threaded the two lines through the loop and adjusted the rope to make sure the lines didn't overlap. Then he routed the lines around her the other way, and he secured that pass by looping it through the topmost lines. Back and forth, he wrapped her torso until the corset covered her from waist to just below her breasts. Each pass drew her deeper into a calm headspace where the pleasure of belonging to him was the only available thought.

He paused to make sure all the lines were exactly how he wanted them. "How does it feel?"

"Comfortable. The rope is soft, and it's tight, but not too tight." She looked down at the white expanse of rope wrapped around her body. "We should get a yellow rope."

For a second, he frowned, and then his smile turned dreamy. "You do look fantastic in yellow. I loved you in that yellow sundress. I had a hell of a time trying to keep from staring at your chest, though that's really an everyday occurrence." He bent down and buried his face between her breasts, rubbing his cheeks and lips over her tender skin. When he tired of that, he cupped her breasts and tongued her left nipple until it was a pebble.

Amy wasn't sure if she was supposed to keep her hands at her sides, but she couldn't help herself. She grasped his head and sighed as the sensations traveled a path to her core.

He let go with a *pop*. "These are mine."

"Yeah, I got that memo."

"Smartass. We'll see how smart your mouth is when you're all tied up and I'm fucking your mouth."

She giggled. "Smart enough to make you come so hard you see stars."

With an easy smile, he tied a complicated knot about eight inches above where he'd left off with the corselet wrap. "This is a double coin knot. It's going to leave a very sexy little design right below your throat."

He brought the lines up, separated them, and draped them over her shoulders. The knot rested at the top of her sternum. She looked down, and he was right—it was a very sexy design. He turned her so that her back was to him. She couldn't see what he was doing, but it felt like he was tying a knot.

"It's another double coin. You'll have matching marks on your front and back." Next, he brought the lines under her arms and threaded them through the double line leading from the corselet to the double coin in front. He pulled the lines apart, creating a diamond that curved along the tops of her breasts. Then he redirected the lines behind her and made another knot. "All done. Now I'm going to tie dragonfly sleeves. This will bind your arms behind you and force you to thrust out your boobs."

He stayed behind her for this. She felt him caress her bare shoulders. Gradually his touch became firmer, and he massaged her neck and shoulders around the lines from the corselet.

"I'm going to need you to drop your shoulders back and hold your arms behind you." He corrected her posture until she had her arms in parallel lines behind her. He wove the rope between her arms, binding them securely together. Then he threaded the two lines of rope between her legs. It pressed into her labia and held her pussy lips wide apart.

Ever since he'd shaved her there, she'd been extra sensitive. Sometimes the way her panties shifted brought pleasurable sensations. She gasped, and he chuckled.

"You're so wet, babe. I'm glad this is as much a turn on for you as it is for me." He threaded each line through the first loop around her shoulders, and then he tied it off with knots on either side that he slid down until they were over the corselet. "We're done. That wasn't so bad, was it?"

"It was wonderful." Her torso was bound, like a constant, cottony hug, and her arms were immobilized. She was completely at his mercy. She giggled again, and she was so grateful that he wasn't turned off by her girlish laugh. He was the first man with whom she didn't subvert her personality or her inclinations, and it was incredibly freeing. She felt bubbly, like she was floating away in a sea of bliss.

He tilted his head as he watched her. "Babe, where is your head?"

"Right here, silly." She tried to point to her head, but her arms were tied. It made her laugh even harder.

"Look at me. Focus on me." He used The Voice That Could Not Be Denied.

When she did, the floaty feeling diminished. She stopped giggling. "What's wrong?"

"You're heading into subspace, and I need you to stay here with me. I'll let you go later, but right now, that's not the plan."

Amy blinked. He'd taken her to subspace before, but it had taken a long time to get her there. It must have taken longer to tie the ropes than she thought. As she breathed, awareness returned. "I'm sorry."

He kissed her forehead. "No need to apologize. It just means I did an extraordinary job and that you respond very well to bondage. We'll definitely do a lot more of this in the future. Lift your leg and step into this." Somehow he'd procured a flat device with two loops as leg holes. Amy recognized a butterfly vibrator. Once he'd put it in place, he said, "Kneel on the center of the bed facing the headboard."

Walking on her knees with her arms bound behind her back challenged her sense of balance, but she made it. If she was going to keep up with Jordan and this kind of acrobatic sex, she might have to start stretching. Or maybe she'd take a yoga class. That was supposed to help with all kinds of things, and it could be adapted for any ability level.

He hopped up to stand behind her. The bed dipped under his weight, but she was more concerned with the way he hooked the corselet to a chain he looped through the hook in the ceiling. She heard clicks and recognized the snap of a carabiner. She wiggled and found she had a little play. He let her test the boundaries for a few moments, and then he knelt in front of her.

She ran her gaze over him, hoping he read the high levels of lust she envisioned were blazing from her eyes. He threaded his fingers through her hair, taking control of her head, and devoured her with his kiss. It went on and on, and she moaned encouragingly when she felt him press the butterfly firmly against her pussy. He pushed a button, and the thing came to life. She moaned even louder.

He ended the kiss and faced her with an evil grin. "You're not allowed to have an orgasm with the butterfly." Getting to his feet, he stood before her with his hard cock pointed at her lips. "Open up, babe. I'm going to fuck that gorgeous little smart mouth."

Like before, he started slowly, letting her wet his length. Once he could slip in and out, he gripped her head and took over. Amy relaxed her jaw and did her best to accommodate his pace. He played with her, going fast for a bunch of shallow thrusts only to slow down for a few deeper ones.

She tried to ignore the vibration of the butterfly against her clit, but it felt so good that she couldn't. And when Jordan cried out with a soft exhale and came, she no longer had that to distract her. She hoped he would either remove the butterfly or let her come, but he merely collapsed on the bed with a satisfied smile and stared up at her.

"Jordan, I—"

"No."

"Daddy, I'm so very close to coming."

"Toughen up, babe. Breathe through the urge."

A ticking started in her core, and that meant she was close to losing control. "Oh, Jordan, please!"

Still sporting that devilish grin, he reached up and tweaked her nipple. It hurt, but it took her mind off the pleasure spiraling hotter and hotter.

"Oh, Daddy, please! Please say I can come." She twisted and writhed, dangling helplessly from the rope. The vibrations stopped. Amy panted as the urgency receded. She was sad to see it go, but happy that she wasn't going to disappoint her Daddy.

"No, babe, you can't come yet." He sat up, bent over the edge of the bed, and fished something else from his bag. Two cylinders, each with a pink twisty thing at the top that looked like it would turn on a hose, lay on his palm. "Do you know what these are?"

She shook her head.

"Suction cups. I have much larger ones at home that I will eventually use on your boobs. These will only fit your nipples." Without waiting for her to react, he sucked one nipple to wet it and slipped the cylinder over it. Then he twisted the pink thing. "Tell me when it's too much."

Amy watched the cylinder suck her nipple into it, distending it and forcing it to fit the shape of the device. She felt the suction differently from when he used his mouth. It pulled deeper, tugging lines in the backs of her breast clear to her pussy and even down through her legs. It didn't hurt, and yet it hurt. Amy had never felt anything like it, and the sensations overwhelmed her. "Oh, God."

Jordan chuckled as he pushed a strand of hair away from her eye.

She writhed, but her movements were limited by the bindings holding her in place. Her mouth opened and closed because she couldn't string any more words together. He dialed it back a quarter turn, and the sensation settled on pleasurable. "Right there. That's perfect."

He chuckled. "Looks like I know what to do when you get mouthy. One more. Breathe, babe. I can't have you passing out on me."

She forced herself to inhale and exhale, and some of the feeling in her nipple dimmed. But that was okay because he cranked the other suction cylinder, and that invisible cord tingled all the way to her crotch. She exhaled in short puffs. "There. Right there, Daddy."

He stopped and surveyed his work. "Some people prefer clamps, but I like these. When I take them off, your nipples will stay dark and swollen for a few hours. And when I play with them, they'll be extra sensitive."

This time when he slid off the bed, he put his bag on it. She couldn't see what toy he selected next, but it didn't matter. He was going to tease and torment her until he wanted to see her climax, and because he'd just come, he didn't feel the same urgency she did.

It was the pinwheel. He rolled it across the fleshy parts of her ass and down the backs of her thighs, over her calves, and across the bottom of her feet. It tickled, and she laughed, which jiggled her breasts and made the suction cylinders pull on her poor nipples. He changed sides, treating her other leg and foot to the same pleasure. Back and forth he went, making her laugh even though it caused her to groan at the spikes of pain that tugged at her nipples.

Just when she thought she'd go out of her mind, he changed devices. She recognized the feather and the flogger with the metal tips that scratched across her skin. He alternated devices as he played all over her body, spending time on her legs, her arms and torso between the ropes, and her breasts. Her head began to spin and float, the way it eventually did whenever he engaged in sensory play.

She barely noticed him removing the cylinders. Needlelike pain registered in her nipples, but it came from a distance. She closed her eyes for a second, and when she opened them, he had the deerskin flogger, and he was carefully whipping her breasts. The falls flashed in front of her and caressed her tenderized skin. Her nipples felt like twin points of fire in a sea of heat. She focused on them, and that drew her out of subspace and back to Jordan.

When he stopped, the heady feelings surfed on the roar of blood rushing through her body. Amy could feel every inch of every nerve ending dance on the electrified sea. He said something, but it was like after the bomb went off—she could only see his lips move, and his volume was no match for the white noise flooding her ears. She stared blankly; her vocal cords and facial muscles seemed to be paralyzed.

He moved out of her field of vision, and she felt the bed dip behind her. The knots at her sides loosened as he tugged, and soon the dragonfly sleeve that had bound her arms fell away. He rubbed her shoulders, finding the tight places and massaging them with an expert touch. By the time he finished, Amy's faculties had mostly returned. She felt him unhook the carabiner from the back of her corselet, and when he reached for the knot to undo it, she put her hand over his.

"Please leave it, Daddy. My shoulders are happy for the relief, but the corselet is comfortable, and it makes me feel extra sensual."

He hugged her from behind, and Amy let her head fall against his chest as she luxuriated in his embrace. He held her for a moment, and then he guided her face to look up at him. His strong fingers gripped her jaw, and he kissed her hungrily. "I need to be inside you."

She gave him her best come-hither smile. "I'd really like that."

"Presentation pose, face-down. I'll be right back."

Amy assumed the position gingerly. Trying to extend her arms above her head revealed that her shoulder joints were sore. It felt a lot better if she held them in a diamond shape around her head.

Jordan returned quickly. "That's not quite the pose, babe."

"I know. My shoulders are sore from being bound, and this doesn't hurt."

"Sore? Did the sleeve hurt? I could have modified the position of your arms. Why didn't you call yellow?"

He was upset. Though she couldn't see his face, she heard it in his voice. He'd told her repeatedly that he wouldn't be mad at her for safewording, but he would be angry if she needed to safeword and didn't. "It just started hurting. It'll be okay in a little while. I think I'll start doing yoga or something if you're going to keep tying me up like this. Please tell me that you're going to keep tying me up like this?"

She felt his hands on her shoulders. He gripped the fleshy part as he tested the movement of her arm. "Tying you up, yes, but maybe we'll dial it back and work up to this. Later today, I'm going to give you some stretching exercises and make it a daily task."

"Thank you. I promise to do them."

He released her shoulder. "You're not injured, but we have to be careful. Keep your arms like you had them or put them down at your sides."

She kept them how she had them. He ran his hands over her arms and down her back, and she felt a tug at her back entrance. She'd utterly forgotten about the butt plug. It was gone quickly, and he wiped away the lube with a moist towelette. She heard foil rip, and her entire body relaxed. At long last, he was going to fuck her.

And then she felt something hard and plastic nudge her vaginal opening. She was so wet that it didn't need additional lubrication to slide in. The thing came to life, and she identified a vibrator. Why would he say he needed to be inside her, and then use a vibrator? The answer hit her a second before she felt his cock at her back entrance.

"Don't move, babe. This shouldn't hurt, but it may feel uncomfortable until you get used to it. Take a deep breath, and now let it out slowly."

As she exhaled, he pushed past the tight muscle guarding her anus. It didn't hurt at all, and it wasn't uncomfortable. A cold heat started at the base of her spine, splintering in all directions as it traveled upward. The vibrator in her pussy suddenly felt bigger.

"I'm all the way in. Tell me your color."

"Green. I'm so fucking green I could explode."

He chuckled. "Great. You have permission to climax as many times as you can. I want to hear you, babe. Got it?"

"Yes, Daddy."

He withdrew almost all the way and plunged back inside. The cold heat turned molten, and it was suddenly everywhere. She cried out, but the sound never made it past her lips. He fucked her hard and fast, and it was so much more intense than when he'd fucked her pussy with this much urgency.

Her hands became claws that gripped and tore at the bedding, and she buried her face in the covers because she couldn't halt the shrieks of pleasure ripping from her core. Even that first time with Jordan, she hadn't been this loud. The first orgasm—the one that had been hovering at the edge for so long—rocked her system. As he buried himself in her over and over, the orgasm lengthened and grew. It went on and on, robbing her of sanity and awareness.

She had no idea when it stopped, but she woke up with her limbs entangled with his and his face nestled against her breasts. The vibrator lay on the bed next to them. "That was incredible."

"Yep. No doubt about it. I'm a highly skilled lover." Except to hug her tighter, he didn't move. "You're fucking amazing, babe. I want to marry you."

Joking or not, his statement shocked the post-coital languor out of her body. "What?"

This time he lifted his head and opened his eyes to meet her gaze. "I want the world to know that you're mine."

"Jordan, this is moving a little fast."

The corners of his mouth turned down. "We've spent the last year getting to know each other and developing a close friendship. And now we know we're compatible on all other levels as well. I love you, Amy. I want to spend the rest of my life making you the happiest little subbie alive."

Cupping his face with her hands, she regarded him somberly. "I love you too, but we've been together for less than a week. It's too fast for me."

He studied her for the longest time, and then he kissed her palm. "What's too fast, marriage or collaring?"

Amy wasn't stupid. To many in the BDSM community, collaring was more significant than a wedding. "Besides the legal issues, what's the difference?"

"None."

Right now, he needed reassurances, and she didn't know why. "I'm not going anywhere. You're my Daddy, and I'm your little one."

"We can parking lot the issue for now, little one, but it's not going away. You're a forever kind of woman, and I'm a forever kind of man. I've known since I met you that you were it for me. Maybe I've taken my time making a move, but that doesn't change the fact that we're soul mates."

For some reason, she felt like crying. Nobody had ever said anything so beautiful to her before, and she knew he meant it. Jordan Monaghan was anything but impulsive. He was deliberate and methodical. And he kissed her tenderly, conveying with his actions what he felt in his heart.

"How long have you known?" She wiped away her tear from where it had wet his cheek.

"Known that you were my soul mate or that I wanted to marry you?"

"Both. Either."

"It hit me the first time I saw you. I think that's why I took so much time getting to know you, and dating you without actually dating you. My dominant side knew you were a submissive, but it took some time before I was convinced you were a little. Even then, I had to figure out if the signs were real, or if I was seeing things that way because it's what I wanted to believe." He smoothed her hair away from her face. "Amy, I haven't looked at or touched another woman since we met, and I sure as hell haven't been on a date. But I understand that you haven't been thinking along these lines as long as I have. Your naiveté is one of the things I love about you. I'll give you as much time as you need."

That was a good thing because she was not ready to make that kind of commitment. Part of her was still waiting for the other shoe to drop.

Chapter Seventeen

Hiding in the bushes and watching a cabin in the middle of Nowhere, Michigan was not Miguel's idea of a great night, but at least it would be a productive one. He could not afford to let this mistake fester.

The mercenary he'd hired to take out the couple had failed. Though he didn't necessarily enjoy it, wetwork didn't bother him. It was just so messy. Miguel liked things neat and orderly, and he did not like mistakes. His counterpart in Chicago had fucked up The Eye's operation there. He'd become arrogant and overconfident, and that had made him sloppy. The Feds had noticed, and The Eye had been forced to severely scale back that operation.

Detroit was a starter town. It had all the graft and corruption of a big city, but nobody paid attention to it. Miguel had grown up here, and that's why he'd been trusted to take over the Motor City. They'd originally chosen Victor Snyder for the job, but he'd been snagged for murder-one by one of Lawrence's own agents who'd been on a case that shouldn't have been related.

Lawrence wanted bigger fish. Most of the operations he'd nurtured had been fruitful. His agents had even taken down the Friedman brothers, a pair who had been a thorn in his side. He was fine with sex workers and trafficking, but that business about using underage girls had rubbed him the wrong way. He was old-school that way, but he firmly believed that sex workers should be the legal age of consent.

Proving himself here would give his superiors confidence in his abilities, and then maybe he'd go to Chicago to show them how it was done.

One fly in his ointment, one egregious error in judgment, and it threatened to take him down. It wasn't going to happen. He was going to win, and that was that. Brian Gartrell had been trained as a marksman in the Army. He'd assassinated several high-profile targets before breaking. He'd changed his name and built a new life, but the addiction never went away. Miguel knew how to make life deliver another beat down to Brian that would put him in a position to become The Eye's killing machine.

But then that fucking addict, Brian Gartrell had balked at killing the judge. Almost as if he was an unseasoned soldier, Brian had shot Gary, the intermediary and handler the addicts referred to as "Joe." He hadn't even fatally wounded the man. Miguel had been forced to finish off the ineffective handler himself.

Brian wasn't supposed to be unpredictable. His profile hadn't indicated that he would refuse to follow orders. In fact, it had implied that they'd be able to use his addiction to make him do just about anything short of murdering a little girl. He had a daughter, so that created a conflict there. His profiler had fucked up, and that meant he'd have to liquidate this one and find someone new.

So it fell to Miguel to clean up this mess, fall back for a little while, and then reassert The Eye's muscle. At first, he'd thought the cleanup mission he'd contracted out had been successful, but then he'd learned his mistake. That fucking cunt, Brandy Lockmeyer, had hatched a covert plan that she'd kept off the books. She'd gone behind his back with this little operation, circumventing the procedure that would make her get his permission before undertaking such a complicated—and brilliant—plan. If she wasn't so dedicated to law enforcement and doing her patriotic duty, then he'd try to lure her away to work for The Eye. She was exceptionally competent.

It was total chance that he'd found out that Markevich and Monaghan were alive. If he hadn't been combing through her emails, he wouldn't have caught her oblique reference to the covert affair. After he was finished taking care of this part of the mess, he was going to make Brandy pay for her subterfuge. The email he'd sent had been carefully designed to push her fear buttons, alluding as it did to the massacre in Venezuela she'd narrowly escaped and threatening that something like that would happen again, but this time to the agents in her care. She'd do anything in her power to keep them safe, and that would lead to her downfall.

The kitchen window had no curtains. Miguel had to watch from a tree stand someone had erected long ago and wait for his moment. The pair of lovers behaved as if they were on a honeymoon—not two people hiding out while their families grieved for their passing. He watched as Amy stood in front of Jordan, who was seated on the sofa, and lifted her dress. She touched her pussy until he lunged forward and buried his face between her legs. When he'd eaten his fill, she climbed onto his lap and rode him while he played with her breasts.

Miguel knew that Jordan Monaghan was a Dom, and that meant Amy Markevich was his slutty little sub. Perhaps Miguel would keep her around for a little while, see how well she served a master who was much more serious and sadistic. Lost in the fantasy, he missed the action, and so he focused on using his observations to formulate a plan. Agent Monaghan would be a formidable opponent, and though Miguel could at one time have given him a run for his money, he was no longer in his physical prime.

He scrolled through the images on his phone once again. Rather than risk a digital copy of Monaghan's file that might be traced, he'd taken pictures of it. Reading the stats made Miguel think that he'd be better off incapacitating Monaghan before taking him to the kill spot. He looked through his binoculars again to see the couple in the midst of a bad dancing routine that had them both laughing. He clambered down from his post. He'd be back later with the correct supplies.

Chapter Eighteen

Amy lay stomach-down on the hardwood floor and groaned.

"What's wrong, babe?" Jordan stood in front of her, eating a breakfast burrito as a late-night snack. "Need help?"

For the past three days, she'd been regularly running through a stretching routine that seriously tested her limits. Though it was slightly easier today, the routine was more strenuous than she imagined stretching exercises could be. "I'm going to fail at yoga."

"No, you're not. Start slowly. You're still getting used to moving your body in different ways. There's no rush and no pressure. I promise that your lack of flexibility will not impact my libido. Just looking at you laying on the floor at my feet is getting me hard."

She snorted and rolled over. "You're too easy."

"I'm making up for the past year."

"In one long weekend."

He shrugged. "I can't help it if you're that tempting. That's all you. I'm just a helpless victim of your luscious curves."

Giggling, she got to her feet. When she looked at herself through his eyes, she no longer saw her voluptuous figure as a problem. The perfect man found her sexy and alluring. It was the self-esteem boost she sorely needed. Over the past few days, he'd made love to her countless times, and he'd been supportive and snuggly when she needed to bask in her inner littleness. He'd also been firm when she pushed boundaries too hard.

Like yesterday when she'd snapped at him because she didn't want to hold a stretch for as long as he'd dictated. He'd said something encouraging, and she'd told him to go fuck himself. She'd spent five minutes staring at a corner with her pants and panties around her ankles. He'd sat on the sofa and watched. Under those circumstances, five minutes was a hell of a long time. After she'd served her time, she'd apologized, and he'd made her continue the exercise. There were no recriminations and no lingering hostilities, and that was the part that solidified Amy's feelings of emotional safety with Jordan.

"I'm finished, but my butt and thighs are sore."

"Go run a bath. Put some Epsom salts in it. I'll join you in about twenty minutes."

With a grin, she ran off to do as he'd said. Knowing him, he was probably measuring out rope and lining up condoms. They'd gone through so many already. Once this was all over, she'd see about getting an IUD.

He came into the bathroom twenty minutes later, but he merely perched on the side of the tub and checked her out. Reclining against the backrest put her shoulders mostly in the water, but her breasts peeked above the waterline.

"What are you thinking?" *As if she didn't know.*

"How incredibly lucky I am to have you." He knelt next to the tub. "Have you washed yet?"

She shook her head. She'd showered that morning, and the purpose of this bath was to soak in warmth.

"Good. I'm going to do it for you." He bypassed the soft cloth and used his hands, soaping them up before running them along every inch of her body. By the time he finished, her lady parts were screaming for his touch. He pulled the plug on the drain, but he set a restraining hand on her stomach. "I'm not finished." He only let half the water out before replacing the plug, and then he grabbed a disposable razor.

Amy knew better than to protest. Being shaved, especially in her pussy area, was very intimate, but she was becoming used to his lack of boundaries where she was concerned. Jordan took his role as a Daddy Dom very seriously.

First he shaved her pussy, which didn't have much growth because she'd shaved that morning. Then he tended to her legs and underarms. Afterward, he ran his palms over her skin, checking out his work. "Stand up." He let the rest of the water run out as he rinsed her body, and then he carefully dried her with a soft towel.

"This weekend has been bittersweet, little one. On one hand, I've had four uninterrupted days with you. On the other hand, our families are bearing unimaginable sorrow. Tomorrow, my job will pull me away from you."

Shocked, she stared at him. "I thought we were going back Tuesday."

"I'm leaving tomorrow. They moved up my funeral. I'll be replaced by two people from a private security firm who will guard you with their lives. One is an old friend of mine, and Brandy knows the other one really well. I trust them to keep you safe." He caressed her cheek and pushed her hair back. "I just got off the phone with Brandy. There's a lot of prep work that goes into an operation like this, so I'll be leaving very early in the morning."

Hot tears pricked behind her eyes, but she blinked them back. "Is it selfish of me to not want you to go?"

"No, but it would be selfish to expect me to stay. I'm a Federal agent. This is what I do. There will be many more cases that take me away from you. Depending on the assignment, there will be days or weeks that I won't be able to see you. I want you to know that moments like this etch themselves on my soul. This is what will get me through long and tough days. This is what I'm fighting for." He wrapped the towel around her body and lifted her from the tub.

Amy caressed his face, rough because he liked to shave her legs instead of his cheeks, and stared into his dark, liquid eyes as he carried her to the bedroom and laid her on the bed. "I love you, Daddy. Heart and soul. You asked me a question a couple of days ago, and I want to tell you that I've made my decision—yes, but it comes with a condition."

He covered her body with his, pinning her with his weight. "Yes to which part?"

"Yes, I will wear your collar, and yes, I will marry you." This was the third time Amy had been asked for her hand, but it was the first time she'd consented. The other times, it just hadn't seemed right. Now she knew why—it hadn't been Jordan asking.

"And the condition?"

"I want a long engagement—one year. I get where you're coming from and why you asked so quickly. You're thoughtful and sure about me because you've been thinking about this for a long time, but this is still new, and I want more time. I need to explore being a little, and I need more time with you to grow our relationship and work out the kinks. Literally and figuratively."

"Anything you need, babe. I'm a patient man, and you're worth the wait." He kissed her, communicating a wealth of emotion with that simple act, and then he made love to her. No rope or toys, just the two of them coming together.

———————

The light in the bedroom remained on long after Miguel estimated the sleeping pills he'd ground up and put into their wine had taken effect. This operation was made complicated by the fact that Monaghan made regular sweeps of the house and grounds. Thankfully, the suddenness of the man's departure from the hospital hadn't given him a chance to make sure he had high-powered binoculars or night vision equipment. Monaghan had been forced to make do with his eyes and ears—which were no match for the long-range, military grade binoculars Miguel was using to spy on them from a safe distance.

Due to the number of trees, the site lines weren't exactly clear, and so the infrared sensors that went with the spy equipment were coming in handy. And after a few days of nothing happening—Monaghan was under the impression that nobody outside his trusted circle knew where he was—the man's guard had relaxed. It could also have something to do with having a horny piece of ass within arm's reach. Markevich was proving to be quite the distraction. Still, he'd been watching them for the better part of two days, and he hadn't been able to figure out how to set his plan in motion. He'd decided on sleeping pills because there was no way he could take down that big son of a bitch when he was at full strength.

Sure, he could shoot them, but by the time he got close enough to make the shot, Monaghan would be able to return fire. Miguel needed to get them out of the cabin without leaving a trace. They would simply disappear without a trace.

The opportunity had presented itself somewhat unexpectedly. While setting the table for dinner, Monaghan's phone had rang. He'd gone into the bedroom to talk, and Amy had followed him after a few minutes. Either she didn't like being excluded from the conversation, or he'd called her in for a quickie since he was in the bedroom anyway. They were in the nauseatingly cute phase of their relationship, but that wouldn't last long. Miguel didn't give them until morning.

He chuckled at his macabre joke.

Careful to move silently, he crept to the cottage and peeked in the bedroom window. They had both fallen asleep with the light on, which meant the pills had worked. He toyed with cutting the main, but if the cottage was without power, the agents who showed up would know something wasn't right.

The locks were easy to break, and they hadn't activated the security system before drifting into dreamland. Miguel hoisted the woman first, reasoning that she'd be easier to move. He groaned as her full weight hit his shoulder. Monaghan had picked her up and slung her around like she weighed nothing. It just underscored the reason hand-to-hand combat with Monaghan wouldn't be a good idea.

Grunting with the effort, he finally made it to the unmarked car in which they'd arrived. His own car was hidden a few miles away. Miguel had walked the distance, and after he disposed of the bodies, he'd abandon the car at a private airport. A bus line ran down a nearby highway. He'd just get off at the nearest stop and backtrack to his car. He had exactly six hours to get this done.

He threw Markevich in the back seat, wincing as the sound of her head hitting the edge of the door echoed through the small clearing. He eyed her, and frowned. She was naked. People didn't often travel naked in cars. He brought out a large T-shirt and wrestled it onto her.

Monaghan was next. In the spirit of fairness, he put the man's boxer shorts on him. In the midst of doing so, Monaghan stirred. Miguel froze. The dose he'd given the man should have kept him in a deep slumber for a lot longer. Combined with the wine, this should have been a slam dunk—unless Monaghan had built up a tolerance for opiates. Given his record, it was possible he had experience taking many different kinds of illicit drugs.

Miguel frowned, briefly considering killing Monaghan before putting him in the car. If possible, he'd rather kill him elsewhere. That way no evidence would be left behind.

Jordan jerked somewhat conscious suddenly with the feeling that something was very wrong. His instincts had never led him astray. Someone was in his room, and it wasn't Amy. Last night had been unexpectedly exhausting for both of them. Amy had fallen asleep seconds after they'd finished making love, and his eyes had closed before he could think of ways to tease her about it. He hadn't even turned out the lights or set the alarm, two very uncharacteristic moves.

Cotton coated his mouth, and he couldn't quite wake up. Part of him wondered if this was a lucid dream—or nightmare. The rest of him knew it was real, and Amy's life hung in the balance. He had to wake up. Dimly, he realized he'd been drugged. He didn't know with what or when, but he knew that he could fight it. Whoever had done this wouldn't expect him to come out of it so quickly. That was one of Jordan's superpowers: Drugs often had a limited affect on his physiology. It sucked when he needed antibiotics or had a headache, but it was a bonus when he'd been drugged. And some pervert was trying to undress him.

Jordan came up swinging. His fist connected with a satisfying *crunch*, so he guessed he'd hit a nose. Because his eyes wouldn't open, he couldn't be sure. The man swore and backed away, so Jordan seized the opportunity. Launching himself off the bed, he aimed his shoulder at where he estimated the man's midsection to be. They hit the floor hard. The activity helped Jordan shake off some of the effects. He opened his eyes to see a familiar face— Director Lawrence. The man was so high up in the FBI administration that he was almost never found below the top floor. Frequently he was at Quantico for some reason or another. He was a phantom figurehead, someone who almost never crossed their minds unless they needed information that only someone with a higher level of clearance could get.

All of this information flitted through Jordan's mind as he thumped his fist into the man's midsection. Then something hit his head hard, and blackness closed in.

Bent in half, Miguel groaned. He snagged a shirt from the floor to staunch the flow of blood from his nose. Who would have thought Monaghan would have been aware enough to not only know something wasn't right, but to fight so hard? Luckily his movements had been sluggish, and his hits weren't as lethal as they could have been. Good thing this kinky motherfucker was into bondage. Miguel used the rope neatly coiled on the dresser to bind Monaghan's arms and legs. There was enough left to wrap it around his body, binding his arms to his torso.

He grabbed the blanket from the bed and rolled Monaghan up in it. This bundle was easier to drag to the car, and it didn't leave a telltale path. He heaved the man into the back, not caring what end was up or where he landed. With that taken care of, he returned to the cottage, packed their things, and closed up the house. He remembered to set the alarm system. Even when running off with his girlfriend, Monaghan wouldn't leave his buddy's property unprotected.

He'd kept out one bundle of rope, and he used that to tie the woman's wrists together. She was soft and out of shape. While she had a lovely plus-sized figure, she was not athletic, and there was no way she'd be able to mount an effective defense. Besides, she'd obviously had the larger dose of the sleeping medication. It was unlikely she'd wake up before he killed her. That suited him just fine. Wetwork was hard enough without having to deal with someone fighting for their life.

———

Road noise and the jolt of a car rattling over a pothole woke Amy. Lethargy made it difficult to come fully awake, and so it took her a few seconds to realize that she was in the backseat of a car. Outside, moonlight bounced from tall trees, throwing sinister shadows across the road. Shifting her arm, she realized her wrists were tied, and so she froze. Jordan would never tie her up while she was asleep and put her in a car. Plus, her wrists were bound one on top of the other, which meant the rope pressed against the inside of her left wrist. That was not safe, and Jordan would never practice unsafe bondage. Adrenaline rushed through her system, banishing the effects of sleep.

Without giving away her change in consciousness, Amy turned to assess the situation. A heavy bundle took up most of the space in the back, and a heavy lump pressed against her shin. In the faint light from the moon, she saw that whoever was driving hadn't bound her very well. Though he'd tied several knots, they were one on top of the next and easily undone if she could reach them. Moving right now would alert the driver, and she couldn't risk it. She'd wait for the opportunity to use her teeth.

The lump pressing into her leg was beginning to feel more and more like a head, and she realized it was a body wrapped in a blanket. Out of the other end, propped up against the opposite door, Jordan's bare feet stuck out, as did the rope binding them together. Her heart stuttered. Jordan was in there, bound and unconscious. How had this man taken them unaware? Not only was Jordan a trained agent, but he'd spent time working top secret missions for the military. Someone had to be very good or very devious to overpower him.

They'd been drugged, she decided. She didn't know when or how, but they'd been given something to render them unconscious. Otherwise they'd be in the cottage right now, likely standing over a badly beaten body. There was no way Jordan would countenance this bullshit.

She used the momentum of the next turn to slump forward. That way she could reach down and make sure the blanket didn't suffocate Jordan. Aware the driver had turned to check the movement, she made sure to stay relaxed and still. As soon as she thought it was safe, she stuck her hand down the blanket to give him air space. Satisfied that he was breathing, she worked on untying the knots on her wrists. Then she loosened the ropes around her wrists and retied the knots, reasoning that this man needed to think she was still immobilized.

The car turned, and the terrain became bumpy. Soon the car stopped, and the driver got out. He went to the trunk, and she used the opportunity to untie Jordan's ankles. The kidnapper had used the same sloppy knots, so it only took a second. On the positive side, their kidnapper seemed inept when it came to what kinds of knots could and couldn't be easily undone. On the minus side, he'd been clever enough to drug and kidnap them.

Amy chose to stick with the good news. This glass had to be half full.

She'd just returned to her slumped-forward position when her door opened. He slid his hands under her arms and clumsily dragged her from the car. It took all her willpower not to tense up as he knocked her head against the frame of the car. Her ankle, pinned between Jordan and the seat, twisted painfully. A whimper escaped, and the kidnapper froze.

"Shhh." His voice was low and his tone was meant to soothe, but when someone most likely had planned to engineer a bad ending to a person's life, a quiet volume and tone was more creepy than calming.

She chose to not broadcast that fact.

He set her down gently on the ground. "I'll put him in first, that way you won't get crushed by that big son of a bitch. Though I'm not sure it matters. I'd show mercy and slit your throat or something, but I can't chance leaving a blood trail."

She heard the crunch of his boots on the forest floor as he walked away, and she peeked at her surroundings. They were in the woods, so the moonlight didn't penetrate the canopy very well, but he'd left the headlights on. Though they were pointed at an angle to where she lay, she was able to make out the bags of clothes and personal items they'd brought to the cottage. They were stacked at her head. Surrounding the miniscule clearing, red pines towered above them, ensuring seclusion. Next to her, the ground dropped away. The mound of dirt told her that he'd dug a pit.

A grave. He'd dug a single grave for her and Jordan.

While she eventually hoped to be buried next to him, that was a long-term goal, not something she wanted to accomplish until she was at least ninety.

Re/Defined

The kidnapper dragged Jordan toward the hole. From the way he gripped him, Amy realized the kidnapper was holding Jordan by the ankles. Her poor Daddy was being bounced and knocked around mercilessly. Because she liked to look at the positive side of things, she realized the blanket was coming unraveled, as was the rope the man had looped around Jordan's torso.

She did not laugh at the man's idiocy. Instead she took a deep breath, and when the kidnapper got close to the side of the grave, she hefted her legs and kicked at the back of his knees. They buckled, and the man went down, tumbling over the edge and into the chasm. Amy didn't know how deep it was, but she figured that if the man had dug it, he could probably climb out.

Loosening her bonds with one tug, she attacked the ropes around Jordan. "Jordan, wake up. Someone is trying to kill us, and I'd rather not die today."

Nothing. He didn't even stir.

"Fucking bitch. I will put you in first." The kidnapper's head appeared above the rim of the grave. His hands scrambled for something to hold onto that would help him out, and he grabbed Jordan.

Amy pounded him with her fists, shrieking bloody murder. Maybe the noise would rouse Jordan, which would be great because she could really use his help right now. With her hits proving ineffectual, she shot to her feet and kicked him, heedless of the fact she was wearing a T-shirt and no underwear or anything else. Having gone to bed naked, she did not question how she'd come to be wearing a shirt—but she was thankful.

Balancing on one foot, she used her heel to deliver kicks directly to the bad man's face. Yelling, she heard, would make her kick pack more power, so she let loose with a primal scream that turned into a joyful whoop as blood spurted from the man's nose and he slid back into the hole.

Immediately, she dropped to her knees and continued untying Jordan. "It's very inconvenient for you not to be awake. I'm a lover, not a fighter. Though, if I had a golf club or a bat, I think I'd be in business."

The man's head appeared again on the other side of the grave. Amy rushed around it, grateful the villain hadn't turned off the car's headlights, and kicked his head again. Coming from the side, she got him in the ear or temple—she couldn't tell which.

"You fucking bitch! I'm going to kill you slowly. You're going to die screaming—your throat will fill with dirt. Nobody will hear you as you suffocate under a pile of dirt."

A terrific growl distracted her, and her third kick didn't pack the same power the first two had. Jordan leaped across the dark expanse that marked the top of the grave, landing on the kidnapper and would-be killer's back. He wound one arm around the bad man's neck and pounded the villain's head with his fist.

Relieved that he was awake, she immediately started worrying about Jordan. He was still suffering the effects of the drug, and he might not have his wits completely about him. The headlights didn't illuminate what was going on in the hole, and the shadows of fists flying was the only thing she could make out. Torn, she looked toward the car, wondering if she should see if there was a tire iron in the open trunk. Fuck it—Jordan wouldn't expect her to stand there and do nothing. She covered the distance quickly. Tearing back the carpet in the floor of the trunk, she found a short tire iron. It was smaller and thinner than she'd expected, but it would have to do. She grabbed it and ran back to the edge of the abyss.

The pair had sunk to the bottom of the pit, and so she couldn't see them anymore. "Jordan, please tell me you're beating the hell out of that man." Though he didn't respond, she heard some horrific crunching noises. Another shot of adrenaline raced through her system because she didn't know who was on the receiving end of those deadly sounds.

The next head that poked up was Jordan's, and owing to his height, he could easily reach out of the pit. Relieved, Amy grabbed his hand and fell on her ass to provide leverage to help him out.

Tears of relief welled in her eyes. "Oh, Daddy. I'm so happy you're not dead."

On his hands and knees at the edge of the pit, Jordan coughed and wheezed. He put a hand to the back of his head, and it came away coated with a dark substance.

Amy gasped. "You're bleeding!"

"A little." He struggled to stand, and Amy had to catch him so he wouldn't fall. "I woke up when he was taking us. We fought, but I was too drugged. He hit me over the head with something. The next thing I know, you're shouting like you're acting in a bad karate movie—and kicking ass. Or face. Babe, you did good. I'm proud of you."

His words were slurred. She wound his arm around her shoulders. "Lean on me, Jordan. I think you have a concussion."

He put his hand to the back of his head again. "Probably. Motherfucker hit me hard enough to knock me out. I returned the favor. He won't be waking up anytime soon."

Amy didn't care about the bad man—not now that he'd been neutralized. She cared about her Daddy, and he needed medical attention. "Let's get you in the car, and then I'll grab the bags. He brought our luggage to bury with us."

They were on the side of the grave nearest the car. Jordan glared at her suggestion, but his eyes were glazed and unfocused, so it didn't have the intended effect on her. He hefted all three bags in one hand. "*I* take care of *you*, little one. You will never carry bags when I'm around. That's a rule."

"More rules," she said drily. If she wanted to get him in the car and away from the dangerous man in the grave, she needed to humor him. "Yippee. At least let me drive you to the hospital. You're hurt, and you sound like a drunk."

His eyes darted around, not focusing on anything in particular. "We were both drugged. I think he snuck in when we were occupied and slipped something into the wine we had with dinner. That's why we both fell asleep so early. I fucked up, Amy. I should have been more vigilant."

This was not the time to play the blame game, otherwise she might have pointed out her role in distracting him from always looking out the cabin's windows.

He dug through each bag before slinging them into the backseat. "He didn't bring our phones, which makes sense. They have GPS, and if he buried them with us, then we'd be findable."

She opened the passenger side door and tried not to think about how close they'd come to being buried alive. He needed her to be strong. "I'm going to have to insist. I'll drive. We need to get you to a hospital."

"Are you saying I need my head examined?"

"Yes, but only because it might be cracked open, and not because you're crazy." She inclined her head toward the opening. "Get in."

From the gingerly way he moved, she figured he might need more than just his head examined. It was only when white-hot pain shot up her left leg that she realized she also needed medical attention.

Amazingly, Jordan had noticed. When she got in the car, he put a hand on her thigh. "You're hurt."

"My ankle, but it's way better than being buried alive in an unmarked grave, so I'm going to call this a win for the good guys." Their kidnapper had mentioned shooting her not being an option, but that didn't mean he'd been unarmed. She checked the glove box, but it was empty, so she felt around on the floor under the seat.

He chuckled, a dumbfounded sound, and shook his head. "Christ. How are you so upbeat right now? Most people would be shaken up and freaking out."

Though she tried to keep her tone positive, the dried tracks of tears crinkled on the skin of her cheeks. "I don't know. I guess I'm glad to be alive, and I am crying. I'm just not breaking down. Stuff like this is outside my everyday experience. Maybe I'll fall apart later, and then I'll need you to snuggle me until I feel better." Her search for a firearm had come up empty, so she figured the gun must be in the grave with the bad guy. They needed to get out of there quickly. She started the car and headed toward the main road. The faster they were out of there, the better. "Did you kill him?"

Jordan let his head fall against the headrest. "No. I beat the crap out of him. He's going to need his jaw wired, and he might have some other broken bones. Definitely multiple contusions, and if I hit him hard enough, internal bleeding. I'm still a little out of it, and many of my thoughts don't quite make sense to me, so I'm not entirely sure. He's not going anywhere without an ambulance. I need my phone."

Amy frowned. "He probably left them back in the cabin. Why would he think he could make it look like we disappeared?"

It took a second, but he responded. "If people think we ran off, they tend not to look too hard. Fuck. I shouldn't have left the scene. Take me back, and then go back to the cabin for the phone. Call Brandy. She'll bring the cavalry."

She scoffed, and not just at the idea of going back to where a would-be murderer had dug a premature grave for them. If he'd been in his right mind, there was no way he would have allowed her to herd him into the car. She wanted to put as much physical distance between them and the threat to their lives. "First of all, we couldn't run off. And secondly, our friends and family would look for us. I can't see Dustin, Malcolm, Keith, or Brandy throwing up their hands and saying, 'Oh, well. I guess they wanted to start new lives.' That's not realistic."

"I know that, but he didn't. Director Lawrence doesn't know the close connections you and I have with the people in our lives. According to my file, I'm a loner from Wisconsin who is good at blending in and building cases that lead to convictions. I have many acquaintances but no friends."

Amy started. That wasn't the man she knew. "You have lots of friends, and one smoking-hot girlfriend who can kick face."

He climbed over the seat and into the back. A couple of manly grunts of pain accompanied his journey, and Amy decided to head straight to the hospital. Jordan was one of those macho guys who ignored pain. "When I first began suspecting this was an internal matter, I had Brandy plant false information in my file. We knew that no matter how secret we made this operation, a mole would have access to the information. We honestly didn't think the mole was the director of the Detroit Bureau."

"That guy is your boss's boss?" She worried that he might make her turn the car around. His voice wasn't nearly as slurred, and coherence had returned.

"Yep. It explains the access he's had to prisoners and evidence, and why we haven't been able to discover much so far in the investigation. Hey, you passed the road that will take us back to the cottage."

Amy snorted. She glanced in the rearview mirror to see him moving around like he was putting on clothes. It reminded her that she was wearing only a shirt. "Yeah. I think it's more important to take you to a hospital. I'm heading to the freeway. There has to be something somewhere. I plan to speed like a demon so we'll pick up a cop and get an escort."

"Babe, head to the cottage. I'll call this in, and Brandy will take care of all that."

Miffed that he'd rather rely on his boss—and that he was taking control of the situation, she executed a U-turn with maximum centripetal force. Jordan wasn't thrown far, but he was leaning against the backseat, whereas before he was not. She muttered, "Maybe Brandy will take care of other things for you."

"Don't be bratty, little one. This is a bigger deal than you know, and the fewer people who know about any of this, the better."

"I want to get you to the hospital." Her voice sounded way too tremulous for her liking. "You're hurt, Daddy." The turn off to the cottage didn't take long to find. The villain hadn't taken them all that far down the road. She stopped in the driveway.

"We're both hurt, but we can't compromise this mission. Lawrence needs to be brought to justice, and we don't have time to waste." Jordan got out of the car with minimal help, which was good because her ankle really hurt now.

She limped to the house, and he stopped her before she opened the door. "I need to secure it first. Stay close."

He went in, and she followed him silently, the tire iron still in her hand. She hadn't put it down even while driving. Their movements reminded her of when they'd played laser tag. She stuck to his six, keeping an eye out for anyone who might come at them from that direction. The cabin wasn't large, so it didn't take long to clear.

He found his phone on the dresser, and he dialed a number. "Security six-nine-delta-seven. Thanks." He escorted her to the sofa, and she sank onto the soft cushions. He talked, but not to her. "Lockmeyer, we've been compromised. Director Lawrence just tried to kill Amy and me. We're okay, but Amy might have a broken ankle."

His words were less slurred, but it didn't sound quite normal. "And you have a concussion." She said it loud enough for Brandy to hear.

He shot her a dirty look, but said nothing as he listened to his boss give detailed instructions. Jordan set the bags next to her, and as he continued talking with Brandy, he fished out yoga pants and handed them to her.

Amy eased into the pants, but she watched Jordan. Though his long hair disguised it, a trail of blood trickled onto the collar of his shirt, and the stain was spreading down his back.

Chapter Nineteen

Jordan filmed Amy's injuries. She hadn't noticed the rope burn on her wrist or the huge goose egg near her temple until he pointed them out. Then there were the smaller bruises and cuts from being dragged across the ground and dumped next to a grave, and her heel hurt from repeatedly kicking face. Even when he was woozy from a concussion, he still noticed everything. When she took the cell from him to document his injuries, he protested.

"I'm fine."

She snorted. "Indulge me, Daddy. I need to do this."

He caved, and she wasn't sure if it was the power of his title or the way her voice came out a little too thin and tremulous. With a graceless sigh, he let her film the gash on the side of his head, the blood matting his hair, and the bruises, cuts, and scrapes scattered over his body. When she'd recorded everything, she hit the stop button, but she didn't tell him.

"Flex your butt muscle."

"No."

"Link your hands behind your head, twist around, and give me those smoldering bedroom eyes. You know, like a supermodel does."

He took the cell away and studied it to make sure she hadn't recorded that part. Then he helped her from the sofa. "Let's get cleaned up. Once everybody gets here, the place is going to be a madhouse."

She knew he wanted to go back to the grave site, but Lockmeyer had forbidden him from doing that without backup. Amy seconded the motion, and she was trying to keep him distracted. Malcolm, she knew would have ignored orders and gone back by now. Thankfully, Jordan wasn't the type of man who disregarded orders.

Like before, they showered together. Only this time they said very little, and Jordan sat on the ledge so that Amy could clean the blood from his hair. His pallor had her worried, and the tight set of his jaw belied his attempts to appear as if he wasn't in pain. Amy didn't call him on it. She just made sure to be gentle and careful.

"You need stitches."

"Can you do them?"

Nobody had ever asked her that question before, but then again, her life to this point hadn't included bombings, kidnapping, attempted murder, or villains. "I can sew clothes. I guess this wouldn't be different. But I don't have anesthesia or a sewing kit."

"Dustin's first aid box will have stuff for field stitching."

"Are you sure about this? I've never sewn a person's head before."

"I trust you. And I don't need anesthesia. I'll be fine."

After they were dressed—with Jordan wearing his holster for the first time in days, he got the first aid supplies and helped her find the materials she needed. Then he sat on the bathroom floor so she could sit on the edge of the bathtub. Putting any weight on her ankle was proving to be very painful.

Sewing skin wasn't significantly different from basting together thicker materials. She was careful, and she made the stitches as even and small as she could. In all, he ended up with seventeen. Not once did he flinch or make a noise.

"It's okay if you're in pain. I don't expect you to pretend like you're okay when you're not."

"I'm okay. This isn't my first rodeo." He had the scars to prove it.

She laid her hand on his shoulder. "I can tell. But I'm saying you can let down your guard with me. I don't expect you to be Superman all the time."

He squeezed her hand. "Good, because I'm not." A knock sounded at the door. "That'll be Frankie and Jesse." He scooped her up and deposited her on the sofa in the living room with her legs stretched across the cushions. He propped her hurt ankle on a pillow. Then he answered the door.

"Well, hello there, Monaghan." A woman who had to be almost six feet tall, sauntered past Jordan, her shoulder brushing his chest. Her black hair was cut short, but that only emphasized her lively brown eyes. Her skin was a beautiful mix of cinnamon and brown sugar, and it sort of made Amy crave snickerdoodles. The woman paused a few feet into the room and scoped out the premises.

The man who followed her through the door shook hands with Jordan. "Jesse Foraker. We haven't met, but Brandy has told me a lot about you." He was about the same height as the woman, perhaps an inch or so taller, and he wore his light brown hair shorn close to his head. As he looked around the room, assessing it with the critical eye of a trained operative, his piercing pale blue gaze fell on Amy. It seemed to see more than what was there, and she shifted uncomfortably.

Frankie came over to Amy. "You must be Amy. Brandy told me that you lost your home. I'm sorry to hear that. We'll keep you safe while Agents Lockmeyer and Monaghan close the noose on that psychopath." She perched on the coffee table, her expression serious. "I'm Francesca Sikara—Frankie to my friends. You can call me Frankie."

She was a rush of forceful energy who looked like she could kick serious ass and break hearts. Amy didn't want to be left alone with Frankie and Jesse, but not because she doubted their abilities or their intentions. She didn't want Jordan to leave—and so she forgot to reply. The moment stretched into an awkward silence.

Frankie lifted her brows. "It looks like you hurt your ankle. Sprain?"

"I'm not sure." Jordan came to stand at the foot of the sofa. "She'll need x-rays once this is all over."

"What happened?" Frankie faced Jordan with a flirty glint in her eyes. "Did she run away when you offered to show her your ropes?"

Jordan didn't seem to notice that Frankie was both flirting and teasing. His face remained impassive as he responded. "Amy and I were kidnapped tonight and almost murdered. We managed to get away, and I know who the perp is."

Frankie stared as if she was waiting for the punch line. "Somebody got the drop on you? *You?*"

"We were drugged," Amy supplied. She didn't understand the tension between Frankie and Jordan, but she wasn't about to sit idly by while some woman criticized her Daddy. "But Jordan managed to wake up and fight the guy."

The look he threw her was the opposite of indulgent. It bordered on impatient. Whether he didn't want her defending him or he didn't want her to reveal too many details to these non-agents, she didn't know. It rankled her that he was treating her this way. After all, she'd helped fight off Lawrence.

Jesse cleared his throat. "Jordan, why don't you give me a tour of this place, and Frankie can take a look at Amy's ankle? She is still one hell of a doctor."

"Fine. We'll start with the perimeter." With that, the two of them went outside.

"If you had to lose your house and hide out, at least you got locked in with that gorgeous hunk of man flesh." Frankie scooted down the table and peeled the leg of Amy's pants back. "I'm going to touch it. Let me know what spots hurt." She probed the foot, ankle, and leg.

When she poked an area that really hurt, Amy hissed, and Frankie had her describe and rate the pain. "I think it's twisted because it happened when the guy yanked me out of the car. My leg was wedged between the seat and Jordan's head."

"I think it's most likely a sprain as well. I'm going to splint it." She glanced around for materials to use.

"The first aid kit is in the bathroom. I sewed the gash in Jordan's head."

Frankie looked impressed, but she didn't remark. A few seconds later, she rummaged through the kit, which was huge and contained items one would expect to find in a medic's bag, not a household first aid kit. "So, tell me. Is tall, silent, and deadly still single?"

"No." Amy wondered how this woman knew Jordan. Had they served together, or had they once been romantically involved? "He's not."

With a wistful sigh, Frankie closed her eyes. "I didn't think so. He's too yummy and family-oriented to avoid that trap. I bet his girlfriend is hot. And sweet. He always went for the super nice ones."

"You'll have to ask him." Amy pressed her lips together to avoid saying something not nice to the woman who was going to be guarding her for the next day or so, and who was currently wrapping her ankle.

"Tell me if this is too tight. It needs to be firm, but it shouldn't hurt. And I'm going to get you some ice. It's swollen, and Jordan is right about it needing x-rays." Frankie wound the bandage around her foot and moved up her leg. "What about you? Do you have a boyfriend or husband who thinks you're dead right now?"

Her long-term fiancé most certainly did not think she was dead. "Only my parents and friends think I'm dead. Everybody else knows."

Frankie hesitated. "That's right. Your sister is married to Jordan's agent friend. I hear he's a hottie too."

Malcolm was very good looking, but he was nothing compared to Jordan. Amy opted for a neutral response. "My sister thinks so."

Studying the bandage, Frankie drew her eyebrows together. "Is it okay where I tucked it under? There's no other way to secure the wrap. There's no Velcro."

"It's fine." It was tucked under the top layer, and it didn't rub against her skin. "Thanks."

Frankie opened the freezer and took out the ice bin. "I bet you're getting homesick. Don't worry. This'll all be over tomorrow. Jordan always gets his man or woman. He's relentless like that." She threw a towel over Amy's wrapped ankle and set an ice-filled baggie on top of that. "This will help with the swelling."

The front door opened, and Jordan returned with Jesse. Before he closed the door, they heard cars approach. Jordan and the two security specialists drew their weapons. Amy looked to Jordan, and she relaxed when he holstered his weapon. "It's Brandy, Dustin, and Malcolm."

The trio wasted no time in piling into the cabin. Malcolm man-hugged Jordan, but then he came immediately to the sofa and hugged Amy. "What the hell happened to you? Was this a bondage mishap? Damn it, Monaghan, you know better than to try advanced positions with a beginner." He turned his fury to Jordan. "I'm supposed to let Darcy know that Amy is all right. I thought it was a foregone conclusion because she was safe with you. What the fuck is going on?"

Jordan looked to Brandy, silently asking for instructions.

Brandy, her hair pulled back in a severe ponytail, frowned. "Jesse, Frankie, can you give us a moment?"

"Nope." Frankie crossed her arms and faced Brandy. "We need to know everything if we're going to do our job effectively." Jesse took his position next to her, a united front.

"Fine. You can stay. This is all confidential."

"Of course," Jesse said. "Unlike a governmental agency, SAFE Security always keeps its client's secrets."

It was a dig that Brandy ignored. She turned to Jordan. "Agent Monaghan?"

"Director Lawrence drugged us. It might have been the wine we had with dinner. Amy had poured it, and then we got...distracted and left the room before finishing it off. After dinner, we were both very tired, and we fell asleep quickly. I awoke to Lawrence trying to drag me out of bed. Amy was already gone. Though I was groggy, I fought him. I manage to break his nose and land a few good hits, but I was too out of it. He hit me over the head with a spreader bar."

Heat rushed up Amy's neck. They'd played with the spreader bar the morning before. Both Dustin and Malcolm sidled glances in her direction.

"When I came to again, Lawrence was in a hole—I think it was some kind of grave he'd dug for Amy and me—and Amy was kicking him in the face to prevent him from getting out. Amy had loosened the knots on my hands, so I got out of the ropes, leaped across the hole, landed on Lawrence, and incapacitated him. He should still be there. He may or may not be alive."

Brandy's brows drew together. "You don't know?"

"I'd been drugged and hit over the head. I wasn't exactly thinking as clearly then as I am now. If I had been, I would have frisked the body for a weapon, and I wouldn't have let Amy drag me away from there until you'd arrived. I would have sent her back to the cabin to call it in." He sighed and ran his hand through his hair, the frown on his face showing how displeased he was with the way things had played out.

Malcolm pointed at Amy's leg. "How did she get injured?"

Amy grabbed Malcolm's hand, and he squeezed back reassuringly. "Mal, I'm okay. My foot got caught between the seat and Jordan's head when Lawrence pulled me out of the car. I was playing like I was still passed out while I was trying to figure out what to do next. Jordan was unconscious, tied up, and wrapped in a blanket. Dustin, I'll get you a new bedspread, and the bad guy knows your alarm code."

"I'll change it," Dustin said. "And don't worry about the blanket. I'm just glad you're all right."

"I'm wondering how you got Monaghan untied and Lawrence in the pit?" Jesse looked and sounded impressed.

"When he dropped Jordan down next to me, I kicked the backs of his knees. He lost his balance and fell in the pit. Then I untied Jordan. He really didn't do a good job with the knots, so they were pretty easy to undo. Lawrence couldn't lift Jordan, so he had dragged him from the car, and the blanket had come loose. I tried to wake Jordan up, but he was completely out. Lawrence tried to climb out, and I didn't know what to do, so I kicked him in the nose really hard with my heel. He screamed and fell down, which gave me time to finish untying Jordan." She took a breath. "And then he tried climbing out the other side, so I went around and kicked at him to stay in the pit. Luckily, Jordan finally woke up because I think Lawrence was close to grabbing me and dragging me in with him. I'm pretty sure that Jordan has a concussion, and I put seventeen stitches in his head."

Brandy frowned in Jordan's direction.

Dustin high-fived Amy. "Nice. If you want, I can teach you kickboxing."

"I can teach her kickboxing," Jordan scowled.

"Jesus, not now, you two." Brandy growled. "Stow the dominant crap for later. Right now we need to get out there. Director Lawrence may need medical attention if he's not dead, and I'd like a full confession. If he's involved with The Eye, then he's high up, and we can get better intelligence from him. Brandt, Legato, Monaghan—get in the car. Sikara and Foraker, guard Amy."

Jordan dropped a kiss on Amy's lips and admonished her to behave, and then the place cleared out. Frankie and Jesse had a silent conversation, after which, Jesse took a post by the front window. The curtains were drawn, and from his position, he could see the only point of entry from the woods.

"Lawrence walked here," Amy said. "Probably through the woods. He had to have come in from the back door. Jordan and I were in the front bedroom. We would have seen or heard a car."

Frankie smiled triumphantly. "So, you've managed to snag the elusive Jordan Monaghan. You naughty little minx. Why didn't you say anything? I would have totally toned it down out of respect for your relationship." She wandered to the back of the kitchen to take up her post there. "While we're stuck here for hell-knows-how-long, why don't you dish? I'd love to know your secret."

"You were fine," Amy said. "I wasn't offended. And I didn't do anything. He pursued me. I certainly never thought I had a chance with a guy like him."

Jesse frowned, but he didn't say anything.

"You're very pretty, and you seem sweet." Frankie made the rounds, looking out every window on the living room/kitchen side of the cottage. "So I was right about that." She turned her attention to Amy. "I could never go for a guy who couldn't take me."

"Well, Jordan would never take a woman without her consent and cooperation. He's dominant, not a jerk. Didn't you two date? You should know that." Okay, Amy was fishing for information, but she didn't think she was out of line. After all, Frankie was openly fishing as well.

Frankie wrinkled her nose. "Date? No. He's a gorgeous example of man candy, but he's not my type."

"You want a submissive?"

Jesse disappeared down the hall, mostly likely checking that side of the house.

Frankie shrugged. "I've been looking for years. I only know what I don't want."

Somehow that admission made Amy feel sad for Frankie. Not too long ago, Amy hadn't known what she wanted, but she'd had a support system, and then Jordan had opened a door to a new world that felt so right.

———

Jordan peered down into the narrow chasm. The morning sunlight provided some light, and Dustin and Malcolm's flashlights provided the rest. "I don't understand. I beat the fuck out of him. Where is he?"

"There's blood," Malcolm said, moving his flashlight over the bottom and up the far side. "A good amount, but not a fatal amount. We'll have forensics test it."

"Whose blood is on this blanket?" Brandy held it up in one latex-gloved hand.

"Mine, most likely. That's the blanket I was rolled up in after Lawrence hit me over the head."

"With your own spreader bar," Malcolm added.

"And tied you up with your own bondage ropes." Dustin snickered.

"Fuck off, you two." He knew they were ribbing him as stress relief. Not only were they standing on the edge of what had been meant as a grave for him and his little, but Lawrence had escaped. He pointed to a spot of blood a few feet away from the site. "Here. This is heading away from the car, so it's not mine."

Brandy picked up the trail. She pointed to a piece of fabric. "He snagged his clothes here. My guess is that he's lost blood and reeling after the fight. He can't have gone far." She continued walking, slowly making her way along an invisible path.

"Chief? I didn't know you had tracking skills." Malcolm sounded impressed.

"There are a lot of things you don't know about me, Agent Legato." Brandy stopped, studying a patch of dead leaves and the low plants typically found on a forest floor. "See the way the St. John's wort is crushed? He fell here." She put a yellow marker next to the crushed flowers.

"How do you know an animal didn't use this spot for a nap?" Malcolm asked.

"The blood." She pointed to bright red spots on the leaves and darker spots where it had soaked the soil. "He's not trying to cover his tracks. He knows he's been outed."

"Did you notify the Bureau?" Dustin asked. "He's a wanted man now, right?"

"Yes. I took care of that as soon as I got off the phone with Agent Monaghan."

"I just can't believe it," Dustin continued. "I've consulted with Miguel Lawrence on a few cases. He was always honest and above-board. All this time, and it was a cover. What does The Eye hope to accomplish by robbing convenience stores and trying to assassinate judges?"

"Power," Malcolm supplied. He'd spent the past several days catching up on the intel Dare had uncovered. "He wants power. Lawrence was passed over three times for promotions that would have taken him to Quantico and put him in charge of large-scale operations. He's not content to be the director of the Detroit field office. To a man who wants power and glory, it's small potatoes."

Dustin snorted. "I've turned down offers to transfer to Quantico. The higher you move up the FBI food chain, the more it takes over your life. I like knowing that I'm not going to miss my mom's birthday and that I get to come home to the same wonderful woman every night. I'm not saying we have it easy, just that if you let it, this job can take over your life."

"Is that your way of asking not to be assigned to long-term undercover operations, Agent Brandt?" Brandy shook her head as she asked. "The hours are long and hard no matter what case you're working."

Long and hard hours—Amy would have giggled at that. Jordan smiled as he thought about her laugh. It was refreshingly unguarded and honest. He loved to hear her laugh.

"I don't know that I'm cut out for that anymore," Dustin said. "I plan to be married soon, and I want to start a family. I don't want to be an absentee father. I'd change careers first, maybe go into consulting."

Jordan thought about what Dustin had just said. Malcolm was also finished with long-term undercover work, though Mal usually focused on white collar crimes and online scams. Those jobs were often a matter of gaining access and hacking. At the most, the undercover aspect only took up parts of a day. Jordan wasn't ready to give up working undercover, and he didn't know how Amy would feel about that. But how could he maintain his little if he was gone more than he was home?

Then he shook the thought away. Amy had thrived just fine on her own. She wasn't the type of woman to become completely dependent on him, and he wasn't the type of man who would force her to rely solely on him. He admired her strength and independence, and he loved her little side that she'd shared only with him.

"It's hard, being gone a lot," Malcolm added. "Darcy has complained more than once about feeling like a single parent. Luckily we have a great support network of family and friends."

Jordan's family lived in another state, and Amy's family was no support network. And he hadn't met her friends. He'd heard plenty about Paget, Cori, and Mandy, but he hadn't met them.

Malcolm clapped him on the back. "What are you frowning at? I've been looking at the same patch of ground as you, and I'm not seeing any crushed plants or drops of blood."

"I've never met Amy's friends."

"Oh. Well, Cori and Mandy are nice. They've been over a few times. Neither have files, and background checks found nothing out of the ordinary. Cori is a project manager for an automotive engineering company, and Mandy is a blogger for an online political magazine. She writes a lot about gay rights, but I don't think she's a lesbian. Neither are married."

"What about Paget? She talks to her on the phone several times a week."

"Never met her, and Darcy hasn't said anything substantive. She lives in Wisconsin, near your brother, Harvey. You might ask him to do some recon. Other than the basics, I can't find a thing. She has a great credit score."

"If you two are finished trading gossip and planning for your future outside of the agency, we have an investigation to run." Brandy's tone warned that she was close to losing her temper. Most of the agents thought she was just a hardass dedicated to catching criminals, but Jordan knew the truth. Brandy avoided forging close personal ties with those in her command. Venezuela had left her with so many scars. Yet she hadn't managed to avoid caring deeply for her agents.

Jordan threw her one of his gentle smiles. She rolled her eyes and continued tracking the trail.

"Here," Dustin said. "Tire tracks in the mud. My guess is that he left a getaway car here. It's not far from the intended dump site."

They gathered around the area, careful not to disturb the evidence that Brandy recorded with her phone. "Looks like blood here." She placed another yellow marker and zoomed in for a close up. "Let's call in forensics."

Dawn streaked the sky, and Miguel Lawrence was in bad shape. The problem with northern Michigan was that it had too much open space and not enough towns. He needed medical

Re/Defined

attention. That motherfucker Monaghan had dislocated his jaw, at least one rib, and probably his wrist. And that bitch Markevich had kicked his face so hard that she'd broken his nose where Monaghan had failed that first time. Then she'd kept kicking him in the same spot. When he got his hands on her, he was going to enjoy her death. No more mercy. He'd originally planned to kill her quickly, but she'd ruined it all.

Brandy Lockmeyer. Miguel had recruited that cunt six years ago after she'd tanked an assignment for the CIA. An FBI field office wouldn't be nearly as stressful, he'd said. All she had to do was follow instructions—take the cases he told her to take and handle them in the manner he recommended.

It had worked so far. She hadn't asked questions. She hadn't delved beneath the surface. Just as he'd wanted, she'd been his minion. Unwitting minion. She hadn't been aware of the repercussions of half of what he'd instructed her to do. Ignoring some cases had meant The Eye's operations had remained secret. Taking other cases had smoked out The Eye's competition.

And then Judge Caldwell got in the way. His rulings became more liberal, more humanitarian—as he called them—in his efforts to actually rehabilitate criminals. Fucker had cost him several million dollars already. He had to go, and The Eye had the perfect person waiting to take his place. She was coldly efficient—and Lawrence had failed in his mission to get her in place yet again.

He'd meant for Gartrell to make the Judge's death look like a robbery. That would deflect suspicion, and the FBI would decline the case. Local cops would easily find the mugger dead from a heroin overdose, evidence from the robbery in plain sight.

The plan had been foolproof. Until Gartrell had refused, Markevich had stumbled over Gary's body, and Monaghan had caught Gartrell. And then Brandy hadn't let it go.

He found a twenty-four hour walk-in clinic in a small strip of businesses in some hick town—he didn't know where he was. Blood loss was making him woozy. The receptionist on duty had that tired look about her that said she'd stayed up all night too many times. Miguel pointed his gun at her. "Where is the doctor?"

The woman stared at the gun, frozen in fear. He did not have the time to deal with half-wits, so he put a bullet in the middle of her forehead. That ruined the expression of blazing stupidity on her face. The sound brought the doctor running. An Indian woman in a white lab coat faced him, eyes wide, but the look passed quickly. She felt for a pulse in the receptionist's neck. "You killed her."

"And you're next if you don't do exactly as I say. Hands up, step back." Due to the pain in his jaw, his spoke in a strange growl that suited the situation. The clinic had none of the sophisticated safety features one would find in more populated areas. "Lock the front door and put up the Closed sign."

She followed his instructions with quick, efficient movements.

Miguel scoped out the security and found the place had none. No alarm system, no panic button, and no surveillance cameras. Lady Luck had finally smiled upon him. This was a sign. He could fix this. He'd made mistakes, but they were still contained. If he rectified them before they got out, then it would be like they'd never happened. "Open the door to the back. You're going to fix me up and give me a transfusion."

"We don't stock blood."

"Bullshit. There's an ambulance bay in the back. I know you have emergency supplies. Don't fuck with me, or I will kill you." He was going to kill her anyway, but he'd rather she patched him up first.

She was a good doctor—he'd give her that. Not only did she cast his arm and wrap his chest to immobilize his broken rib, but she managed to put his jaw back in place. X-rays showed that it had been dislocated, not broken. While this was going on, she hooked up an IV and gave him a transfusion that had him feeling a whole lot better. "Do you want me to set your nose?" she asked. "It's going to hurt a lot."

Moving his jaw had hurt a lot. The nose was nothing. "Sure."

She did, and she bandaged it too. "What now?"

"Now I'd like to thank you for fixing me up, Doctor Mehra. You did a fantastic job under the circumstances."

She disconnected the IV. "You should follow up with your physician as soon as possible. Your jaw has two hairline fractures that should be watched."

Miguel smiled. "Oh, honey, I'd take you with me if I could. You have a great bedside manner, all things considered. However, I have to travel solo. It's the nature of the beast." Without altering his expression, he shot her in the chest. She had a pretty face, dark eyelashes framing dark eyes, generous lips, and smooth skin, so he wanted to preserve that part for her family. It was best they remembered her beauty and brains. The receptionist had been an ugly hag. They were better off having a closed casket.

If he had time, he'd come back for Doctor Mehra's funeral. Her death was a real tragedy, another fuck up to lay at Brandy Lockmeyer's feet.

He rummaged through the purses in the break room and took a fresh set of car keys. If Brandy was onto him, then she'd likely put a BOLO on his car. He'd figure out how to pin this neatly on her, but first he had a judge to kill. If he'd learned one thing, it was not to send an intermediary to do an important job. Killing Herman Caldwell was something he should have done himself.

Chapter Twenty

"He'll need medical attention," Dustin said when they reached the cottage. "Let's get local police to check in on all clinics and emergency rooms in a thirty-mile radius, any place he could find a doctor."

Brandy nodded, her mind lost in thought. "Get on that."

"The funerals are off, right?" Jordan asked. "I'm going to call my parents and let them know I'm alive. They've been through enough. Amy's parents should be notified as well."

"Darcy already took care of that," Malcolm said as he climbed out of the passenger seat. "She thought our plan was crappy, something only dickheaded cops would think to do, and so she told her parents that Amy was alive, but that they had to pretend otherwise. Then she told your family. They're still hanging at your house, waiting until you get home."

That made Jordan feel better. As wonderful as this time with Amy had been, it had been tainted by the fact that the people he loved most were going through a personal hell. He glanced at Brandy. "Did you know?"

She glared at Malcolm. "Agent Legato, you were instructed not to reveal to anyone that Amy and Jordan weren't dead, and that included your wife."

Malcolm didn't bother looking guilty. "I promised Darcy that I'd never lie to her again. Not telling her something like this would have qualified as a lie. If it makes you feel better, she forfeited a month of spankings."

Darcy was a painslut, and a spanking was a daily treat she very much enjoyed. Not having one was a punishment. Brandy didn't appear impressed. "We'll talk about this later, after I decide what kind of disciplinary action to pursue."

Malcolm and Dustin went into the cottage ahead of them, and Jordan held Brandy back with an insistent hand on her arm.

"If it didn't harm our case, do you really need to discipline him?" Malcolm was already on thin ice for not following procedure a number of times. "He could lose his job. He's a good agent, Brandy."

"I know." She sighed. "But he leaves me no choice. I can't look the other way while he flouts the law and plays fast and loose with procedure. We're lucky Darcy didn't post Amy's status on social media. She makes no secret about her attitude toward law enforcement."

The police had put Darcy through hell when her fiancé had disappeared. She still harbored a deep distrust of cops, agents, and the government in general. Jordan had worked hard over the past eighteen months to earn her trust. He slung his arm around Brandy's shoulder in a short hug. "I know you'll do the right thing."

She snorted derisively, but she didn't shake off his hug. "The right thing might not be what you want it to be."

They went inside. Jordan was anxious to see Amy. He found Malcolm perched on the coffee table across from her, talking. Amy beamed at whatever he was saying. "Hey, there, little one. Did Malcolm tell you that your parents know you're alive?"

"Yes. Also that Darcy kept them in the dark for two hours while she forced them to say nice things about me." The sparkle in Amy's blue eyes made his chest ache. He was torn between loving that she was happy and hating the cause of her happiness. His parents had always been positive, encouraging, and supportive—and that's what he would be to Amy. She deserved more from people who were supposed to love her.

He couldn't summon a smile. "We're going to be here for a little while longer. Lawrence wasn't in that hole, and we'll be using this as a base to coordinate the manhunt. I'm going to send you home with Frankie and Jesse."

Amy's bottom lip quivered, and her gaze dropped to her lap. "I don't have a home anymore."

Malcolm held her hand. "You can stay with us for as long as you need. *Mi casa es su casa.*"

Though his knee-jerk reaction was to say that Amy would live with him, he used his head. Throwing her into a situation where she was surrounded by his family probably wasn't for the best. Though they were wonderful, she'd only met Jamie once. Amy would do better if she was with Darcy. He stroked her hair. "Spend a couple days with Darcy. When I come home, you can move in with me, at least until your house is rebuilt." He lifted a brow at Malcolm. "Unlike Keith, I sealed the deal."

Mal looked from Amy to Jordan, a slow smile spreading across his features. "You're engaged? That's wonderful." He hugged Amy again. "I won't tell Darcy so you can surprise her."

"What's that? You're engaged?" Dustin shouted from the kitchen. He came closer and clapped Jordan on the back. "Congratulations. The twins will be so disappointed. They may stop coming altogether."

Dustin and Jordan ran a regular munch, a group that met once each month to discuss BDSM. It attracted many new to the lifestyle. He and Dustin often provided information and advice to the newbies. "The Twins" was a nickname they'd given to a pair of women who came together each time. They mostly giggled as they ogled Jordan and Dustin. They'd stopped making comments about their availability after Dustin had informed them that the Doms who ran the munch had a policy of not dating or playing with any of the group members.

Jordan didn't really care if they stopped coming. He didn't think they honestly wanted to get involved in the lifestyle, and he mostly ignored them. Maybe he'd start taking Amy to the munches. They needed a responsible submissive who could give advice from the other side of the equation.

"We've got bodies," Brandy announced. "Twenty-three miles south of this location at a twenty-four hour walk-in clinic. Two women. The local PD have unofficially identified them as a doctor and a receptionist. Let's go."

Jordan kissed Amy's forehead. "Be good for Frankie and Jesse. I'll come see you as soon as I get home. I love you, babe."

She pressed her lips to his. "I love you too. Be safe, and come home in one piece."

Amy watched Jordan go with mixed feelings. She supposed it was going to be like this always. He'd been clear about the demands of his job and the ways in which it would interfere with their time together. She shifted, gingerly moving her foot to the floor so she could stand up.

"What are you doing?" Jesse rushed to her side and scooped her up. "You can't put weight on that ankle."

"I have to visit the bathroom, and then I thought I'd unpack some things for Jordan. He'll need a change of clothes." Amazed that yet another person felt free to pick her up, she regarded him with amazed curiosity. He hadn't said much the entire time he'd been there.

Frankie let loose with a dramatic sigh. "He's one of them, Amy. Don't even think about arguing." She gestured for Jesse to come closer. "I'll help her walk to the bathroom. Women are funny about strange men watching them pee, something guys will never understand."

Ten minutes later, they were on their way to Darcy's house. Amy lay down in the backseat of the large SUV and tried to sleep. The darkly tinted windows helped, and soon she found herself drifting off. The feel of the vehicle stopping woke her suddenly.

"What happened?" She sat up to see that they'd arrived at her sister's place.

Darcy flew down the walk. Her father brought up the rear. Frankie climbed out of the driver's seat and held up a hand. "Take it easy. She's a little banged up, but she'll be fine."

Jesse helped her from the back. She balanced on one foot and smiled at her father and sister. "Hey. How was your honeymoon?"

Her father, Paul, looked her up and down. "Seriously? That's what you choose to ask about? Not how are your parents, who thought they'd lost their oldest daughter? Not how are your neighbors, who think you died in a freak accident?"

"Dad, shush," Darcy waved her hand, dismissing him. "Can I hug you?"

"Yeah. It's just my ankle." Amy held her arms open, and her little sister embraced her tightly. When Darcy finally released her, she held her arms out to her father. "I know Darcy told you almost immediately. How about a hug for your oldest daughter, who you did not lose?"

He shook as he held her. "Maybe we knew you weren't dead, but we knew you were in danger, that some lunatic was trying to kill you. At least now they've caught him, and you're safe."

"Oh, they didn't catch him." Jesse grabbed her bags from the cargo area. "That's why we're here. Frankie and I will be keeping Amy safe until he's caught."

"They didn't catch him?" Darcy clapped her hands over her mouth. "Malcolm said you were coming home, and that the funeral operation was off. I assumed that meant they caught him."

"Let's take this inside." Frankie scanned the neighborhood, looking for whatever it was that security people looked for. Hidden dangers, probably.

Amy threw one arm around Darcy's shoulders and the other around her father's. They helped her up the steps to the porch. "Where's mom?"

"She took Colin grocery shopping. We didn't expect you home for another hour." Paul opened the door and turned sideways so they'd all fit through the opening.

"Speed limits are a suggestion," Frankie explained. "We made good time."

Jesse came inside last. He dropped the load of bags to the right of the front door. "Mrs. Legato, I'm going to need to look around your house. Do you mind?"

Darcy frowned. "I'll accompany you. I don't trust cops farther than I can throw them."

"We're not cops. We're private security."

Paul frowned. "You're mercenaries?"

"Not today, sir," Jesse replied. "Today we're a personal protection detail for Ms. Markevich."

"But don't fret, sir." Frankie grinned wickedly. "If things get dangerous, we're prepared to do whatever is necessary to protect your daughter."

Amy couldn't tell if her father was outraged, shocked, reassured, or if his acid reflux was acting up. She opted to redirect the conversation. "How about putting me on that really comfortable couch in the family room?"

Darcy must have been worried, because she didn't call Amy a traitor or make a crack about the black leather sofa that Malcolm had brought with him when he'd moved in. She'd been on a mission to get rid of it for over a year.

Her mother, Fran, arrived with Colin a little later. The tears in her mother eyes spoke volumes, and she hugged Amy for a long, long time. Even after she released her, she sat on the floor next to the sofa and held Amy's hand. Their parents had never been good at expressing their feelings, and that simple act made Amy feel very loved.

Around dinner time, Jordan's family descended on them, which sent Frankie and Jesse into a tizzy. Jesse blocked the front door with his massive presence. "I'm sorry," he said. "But I have orders that no one else comes inside."

Amy heard Darcy at the door. One did not mess with Darcy, and nobody but Malcolm told her what she could or couldn't do. "For fuck's sake, Jesse. They're obviously Jordan's family. They look just like him. Their little boy is out there, risking his life to catch a criminal, and they want to meet his girlfriend." Though Amy couldn't see it, she imagined Darcy shoving Jesse aside, throwing the door open, and welcoming them inside.

Silence reigned while she and her parents exchanged puzzled glances. Frankie sipped coffee. "The more people inside, the more difficult it is to watch and secure everybody. They'll have to consent to being searched."

Fran narrowed her eyes at Amy. "Did she say you were Jordan's girlfriend? So there *was* something going on when we came over and he was walking around your house half naked."

"No, there wasn't. That was before we decided to change our relationship. And he was only missing his shirt." Though she was telling the truth, she couldn't stop the blush that traveled up her neck.

They must have agreed to a search because the next thing Amy knew, she was being picked up and passed from one person to the next like a new baby. All of them were tall and athletic. They each had dark hair and the same sharp features that Jordan sported. The last huggers sandwiched her between them. "Amy, it's so good to finally meet you. Jordan and Jamie have told us so much about you. It's like you're already family."

"Okay, give her space." Jamie pried her from between the people Amy assumed were Jordan's parents. "Can't you tell she's been hurt?" She threw her arm around Amy and helped her back to the sofa. Then she made the introductions. "These are my parents, Paul and Paulette Monaghan. Not kidding about that.

And these are my sisters, Lela and Della, and my brothers, Harvey and Cliff."

Amy greeted them all, and she made some introductions of her own. "You've met my sister, Darcy. These are my parents, Paul and Fran Markevich. The 'Paul' part should be easy to remember."

Frankie snorted, but she didn't look at Amy. Her attention was focused on the outside.

"Oh, and this is Frankie. You met Jesse at the door. They're my bodyguards until Jordan gets back."

Darcy sat cross-legged on the floor next to the blanket where Colin was practicing sitting upright. She grinned at the group and winked at Jesse. "You should all stay for dinner. We can have pizza delivered and watch Jesse search the delivery boy."

Blood spatter coated the wall behind the receptionist, and the exam room where the doctor's body was found was even worse. The grisly scene etched itself in Jordan's mind. "He's lost it."

"Completely." Dustin had faced some seriously fucked up crime scenes, and Jordan had never seen him so shaken before. "I can't believe the man who trained me as a field agent did this. That sick fuck needs to be stopped."

Jordan pushed the emotional horror out of his mind to deal with the facts. "He shot the receptionist in the face. That signifies rage. Most shooters aim for the chest or gut."

"He shot the doctor in the chest," Malcolm said. "And arranged her body on the exam table, arms crossed over the hole in her chest. Where did the rage go?"

"She fixed him up," Dustin answered. "Lawrence likes people who show they care about him. Doctor Shamila Mehra must have impressed him."

Gesturing to one of the local officers who was guarding the perimeter, Jordan said, "According to local PD, she was an effective doctor with a great bedside manner. No matter what the complaint, she was sympathetic. It's likely she tried to make Lawrence as comfortable as possible, and this is how he showed his appreciation."

Brandy breezed down the hallway in their direction. "I just got off the phone with the West Bloomfield police. They found the body of Gary Nelson buried in Miguel Lawrence's backyard. I'm waiting on the blood work, but the description of the wound in Nelson's stomach matches Agent Monaghan's description of the man behind the reception hall last week. The coroner estimated the time of death as early the next morning. I've sent our crime scene people to check it out. In addition to the stomach wound, Nelson was shot in the back of the head. I had them send pictures to Agent Adair, who will use facial recognition software to confirm that he's the man scoping out the places that were robbed by The Eye."

Jordan drummed his fingers on his thigh as he tried to fit together all the pieces of the profile. "Gartrell and Nelson are dead. He's escalating, and he's trying to clean up the mess his subordinates have made."

Brandy agreed. "I've ordered the detail around Judge Cantrell to be doubled. He has refused to stay in protective custody, so he's at home now."

"Amy," Jordan said. "Amy and I are still loose ends. He's failed to take care of us twice. He's going to go after her next."

"I disagree." Malcolm frowned. "He's badly wounded. He's going to need someplace to lay up and recover."

Dustin shook his head. "He knows how we work, and he isn't going to waste time. The faster he kills Cantrell, Amy, and you, the faster he takes care of business."

This didn't make sense. "We have too much evidence against him," Jordan said. "He's never going to get back to where he was—in charge of both the Detroit FBI and a crime syndicate. We've got this motherfucker."

"Not yet." The determined light in Brandy's eyes energized them all. "But we will. Let's wrap this up and head to where we think Lawrence will be. He's going after either Cantrell or Markevich next. Legato, I'm putting you and Rossetti on Cantrell. Brandt and Monaghan, you're on Markevich."

"All due respect, Chief, but Amy is at my house with my wife and son." Malcolm's jaw set obstinately, and his eyes glittered with a hard light. "I'll join Monaghan. Put Brandt with Rossetti."

Hand on hips, Brandy didn't back down. "You'll do as I say, Agent Legato, if you want to keep your job. You're too hot-headed when you're emotionally involved, and decisions you've made in the past have almost lost cases. Trust that Monaghan and Brandt will keep them safe. Don't forget, Frankie and Jesse are there as well."

While Brandy sought to mollify Malcolm's fears, she didn't understand that Malcolm wasn't asking. Jordan would have intervened on his behalf, but Brandy wouldn't countenance his interference, and if he openly challenge her authority, she'd eviscerate him in so many ways. He grabbed Malcolm by the tie and dragged him out the back way. Dustin followed, making sure Mal didn't get away.

Once sunlight hit them, Malcolm ripped loose and turned his venom on Jordan. "Listen carefully, you fucking ass-kisser: I'm going to Ann Arbor. I'm going to make sure my family is safe, and I'm going to kill the bastard if he comes near my home."

"This is why the Chief put you in West Bloomfield." Dustin growled, and he pushed Malcolm away from Jordan. "We need Lawrence alive. He's not the head of this organization. While the Chicago branch of The Eye was imploding, Lawrence was heading operations here. If we can get him to give us names, we can bust this nationwide. If you kill him, we can't do that."

"Brandy's not going to change her mind, Mal." Jordan tried reason, but he was fast losing patience. Amy's life was on the line.

He understood Malcolm's feelings, but there was nothing he could do. "Right now, you're barely keeping your temper in check. You're already up for disciplinary action for telling Darcy about Amy and me being alive. Don't push it, Mal. You're close to losing your job. Amy means the world to me. I won't let anything happen to her or those she loves. Dustin and I will protect Darcy and Colin as if they're ours. We love them too."

Malcolm tried to brush past him—likely to grab a car and head home—but Jordan seized him by the jacket and pushed him against the cinderblock wall of the clinic. He waited while Mal combated internal rage.

When the tension solidified at a lower level, Jordan made Malcolm meet his eyes. "If you fly off the handle, one of them could end up hurt. You've never forgiven yourself for getting Darcy hurt on the Snyder case. If something happens now, guilt would eat you alive, and it will destroy your marriage."

"We've got your back, buddy," Dustin added. "You have to trust us."

Slowly, Jordan released Mal and took a step back to give him space. Malcolm smoothed out his jacket, and then he nailed Jordan and Dustin with twin glares of contempt. "What would you do in my position?"

Both of them looked away guiltily.

"That's what I thought." Malcolm headed toward the car. "Lockmeyer can fuck off. The FBI can go screw itself. My family comes first."

"All right," Jordan said as they piled into the car. "After this is over, I'm going to say I told you so."

Brandy joined them, but she spent much of the time on the phone coordinating pieces of the plan. As the sun set, they approached the turnoff that would take them to Ann Arbor or Detroit, and she faced Malcolm. "I know you aren't pleased about my decision, but it's for the best. Miguel Lawrence has never liked you. He's wanted to fire you since the third time he met you, but I've successfully argued him down. No matter how you think this will play out, if you're with your family, then you're at his mercy. He'd like nothing better than to see you suffer, and hurting your family would do that. If you're not there, he won't piece that information together. Don't do something stupid, Mal. Don't give him this."

For the first time, Malcolm appeared conflicted. "Won't the same thing happen if you send Jordan in there? He knows Jordan and Amy are together."

"Jordan is bait." Brandy exhaled hard, and her gaze sidled to him, seeking his approval. It was a bad idea to use unwary bait.

"I knew that." Jordan sought to reassure her. "It's a good plan. But Brandy, if I'm bait, and I'm in Malcolm's house, then Lawrence will know something is up when he gets there and Malcolm isn't there."

"That's a great point," Dustin said. "Plus, I think he'll go for Amy and Jordan next. He's pissed because they got away. That's where his rage is currently pointed. He'll return to the idea of killing Caldwell afterward."

Brandy thought about that for a minute. "He's riding high on having completed two easy kills. He needs this to validate his position. Okay, I'll agree. But Malcolm, keep tight reins on your temper. If you ruin this, I will fire you."

Jordan turned toward Ann Arbor. "If you've doubled the guard on Caldwell, perhaps you should have Brandt and Rossetti working on the outside here?"

"Agent Rossetti is running the Caldwell operation. I can't pull him. He's using Hardy and Kinsley. I can give you Forsythe." Brandy made the call. "We'll meet her in the parking lot of that supermarket around the corner from your place in fifteen minutes."

Jordan hadn't called, and Amy tried not to let the demons of worry take over. She shifted in bed, seeking a more comforting position.

"Can't sleep?" Darcy's voice proved that she hadn't been sleeping either.

With their parents occupying the guest room and Jordan's parents camped out in the family room downstairs, Darcy's bed was the only space left to sleep. When they were little, Darcy used to crawl in bed with Amy all the time. She'd nursed a fear of the dark that left Amy free not to reveal that she'd suffered the same malady.

"I hope Jordan's brothers and sisters got home safely." They'd promised to text their parents when they arrived, but Amy had gone to bed before their plane was due to land. Paul and Paulette had opted to stay in Michigan until Jordan returned home. They needed to see with their own eyes that he was safe.

"I'm sure they did." Darcy groped for her hand and squeezed it. "But that's not what's making you toss and turn."

Amy sighed. "Does it get easier?"

"Sleeping soundly while the man you love is out trying to stop dangerous criminals?"

"Yeah."

"No. I think you just learn to sleep through the anxiety, especially when you know you can't do anything and that you've got a baby who will be up at the crack of dawn." Darcy laughed, but Amy heard the helplessness. "I thought I was falling in love with a tech geek, and he turns out to be a Federal agent."

Amy knew what she was getting from the start. "I fell in love with a Federal agent. I thought I knew what I was getting into."

"That was before someone tried to kill you. Twice. Even if Jordan wasn't a factor, what you've been through would give me nightmares."

She thought about the nightmares, and the way Jordan held her until she felt better. "It does. Jordan helps. Even before, when we were just friends, he broke into my house just so he could be there in case I needed him."

Darcy laughed. "That's such a Dom thing to do. He'll take good care of you. I have to admit, I didn't know much about the Daddy Dom/little dynamic until Malcolm explained it to me. I used to think it was kind of warped, but so many of my assumptions turned out to be wrong. I can see where you'd be happy in that kind of relationship."

"I am. I'm just worried that something bad will happen to him."

"Focus on the positives. When I can't sleep because Malcolm is gone, I try to think of all the ways he calms my nerves and relaxes me."

Her sister's voice had taken on a dreamlike quality, and Amy snorted. "You channel the memory of being spanked?"

"Or whipped. Or tied up. Or held in his arms during aftercare. Or of the look of love and pride on his face when he sees Colin. There's a lot, and he's usually here by the time I wake up." A wistful sigh escaped Darcy. "So, what's Jordan's kink? I mean, besides being called Daddy instead of Master."

Amy thought about that for a few seconds. "Well, he likes boobs a hell of a lot. He's very tactile about it, always brushing against my chest or outright parking his hand on one of my girls. He likes when I don't wear a bra. He's into bondage, both functional and shibari." Though she'd kept her voice low out of habit, she dropped her volume even more. "He likes to tie me up and fuck my breasts. It's kind of hot to watch."

A foghorn of laughter burst from Darcy, but she had the sense to clap her hand over her mouth. When the flow of laughter slowed to a trickle, she said, "I never would have predicted those words would come out of your mouth. Goddamn. This is so fantastic. We can finally talk about all these wonderfully kinky things together. Malcolm is all about the bondage."

Amy had frequently seen Darcy wearing an intricate design of ropes on her body.

"He even made a rope bra when I complained that I was retaining water and my boobs hurt. Surprisingly, it helped make the soreness go away."

"Jordan gives me daily tasks and chores to do. I didn't do them today, but I think he didn't expect me to. With my ankle like this, I'm not sure I can do many of the stretches he's assigned."

"I'll help you tomorrow." Darcy yawned midway through her offer. "I think I know what a lot of them are. Mal has me stretching regularly so that he can tie me up in different ways."

"Go to sleep," Amy said. "I'm exhausted too."

The house was dark when they pulled into the driveway. Jordan visually swept the area. Satisfied that nothing was suspicious, he called Frankie. "We're in the driveway."

"Did nobody ever teach you to start a conversation with a greeting?"

Frankie had been an excellent operative, and Jordan had learned a lot from her—some of it had even saved his ass. She'd been his superior, and it was difficult to shake the mentality that had been drilled into him. The flippant attitude marked the way she dealt with most people, but with him, she'd been nothing but business. Where she'd flirted with other members of the unit—male and female—she'd never treated Jordan as anything but a subordinate. He was still acclimating to the fact that she was treating him as an equal.

He unbuckled his seatbelt. "We're coming in."

"By all means, join the party. I can't wait."

He ended the call. "Let's go."

The front door opened, and Frankie waved. "What are you doing here so late? It's the middle of the night."

"I'm tired," Malcolm said. "And looking forward to sleeping in my own bed."

"That might be a little difficult." Frankie closed the door and locked up. "Who's doing surveillance down the street?"

"Brandt and Avery Forsythe. How did you spot them?" Malcolm sounded impressed. They were in the driveway of an empty home with a For Sale sign in the yard. The landscaping was kept up by a service, and the older gentleman living there had left his furniture behind when he'd moved out. It didn't look abandoned.

"Because I'm amazing." She smiled at the pair. "Status report: Everybody is asleep. The Monaghans are in the family room, and the Markevichs are in the guest bedroom. Colin is in his crib, which we moved to the master bedroom. Darcy and Amy are asleep in the master bedroom."

Malcolm blinked, probably shocked that Darcy had anybody but him in her bed. "Amy's sleeping in my room?"

Jordan wasn't surprised. She needed as much comfort as she could get, and her sister was one of her best friends. "Let's leave them be. We can grab some blankets and sack out on the floor of Colin's room."

"I don't want to sleep with you." Malcolm headed up the stairs. "I love you like a brother, but you're no substitute for my wife."

That was true, but Amy had to be exhausted. She'd been through enough. When they got to the top of the stairs, Jordan meant to talk some sense into Malcolm, but he didn't have to. Amy was waiting in the hallway. She wore Darcy's pajamas, and she held the wall for balance. She smiled. "Hey. I thought I heard you two." She inclined her head toward Darcy's bedroom door. "She's asleep, but she won't be upset if you wake her up."

"The loveseat in Colin's room folds into a bed. It's small, but you can make it work. Sheets and blankets are in the hall closet." Malcolm kissed Amy's cheek as he brushed past. "Sweet dreams."

Jordan scooped her up and carried her into the baby's room. The teal loveseat sank under his weight. He snuggled her against his body, and she curled up in his lap. "I'm so happy to see you, Daddy. I haven't been able to get to sleep yet."

He kissed the top of her head. "Sleep now, little one. I'm here."

Chapter Twenty-One

The security around the Legato house was as tight as a nun's vagina, which was exactly what Miguel had expected. They thought he'd fixate on Markevich and Monaghan because they'd eluded capture. He wasn't a psychopathic serial killer devolving into frenzy because his ritual had been disturbed. Miguel didn't need to kill anyone in order to feel contentment.

But he didn't mind killing them. He was even finding a grim satisfaction in the successful completion of an act. If people listened to the inspirational memes found all over social media, then they'd be living life to the fullest already. Killing them wasn't such a tragedy if they'd already seized the day.

The killing he needed to do was purely functional. He had to clean up some messes that were only growing more muddled by the minute. He couldn't take out Lockmeyer's entire unit, but he could add Lockmeyer to his list. The email he'd sent from a dummy account that referenced that tragic operation in Venezuela should have been enough to make her abandon the line of investigation he didn't want her to follow. In the past, any reference to that fatal operation had made her freeze up and fall in line. He hadn't counted on her getting over it. For not listening and for being a cunt in general, she deserved to die.

Being in charge of a branch of a multi-million dollar operation like The Eye meant that Miguel didn't need to go home to regroup. His wife had probably let the FBI into the house to search. Unless they were morons, they'd found Gary's body where he'd hastily buried it near the tall privacy fence. Nope, home was not a place he'd visit again. However he did have cash and credit cards in alternate names stashed all around the state. The Eye also had several safe houses. After the agents had discovered the New Day Church, he'd moved resources away from there.

Down the street, he'd invested in a nightclub that catered to the gays. It was pulling in a pretty hefty profit. Those gays certainly liked their alcohol and techno music. Whatever. Gary had done a nice job moving his assets, so that's where Miguel went first. Since it was a bright, sunny Monday morning, the street was deserted. He accessed the back entrance easily. This particular place had a panic room built into what had been intended as a bomb shelter when the original establishment had been erected in the Sixties. He stayed there, resting and letting his wounds heal, until the next morning. When he finally left, dawn was breaking on a new day, and he had a new van and a rocket launcher.

He headed for Herman Caldwell's house. Though it would be guarded, they'd expect him to sneak in and attack from a close range. The shoulder-fired missile he intended to use would be very accurate from a distance of three-hundred meters, though he'd still hit the house if he had to set up farther away. Caldwell lived in an area where the houses were set on one acre, and every lawn was manicured to within an inch of its life. The landscaping was lush and pampered, much like the people who lived there. And a golf course wound through the community and provided all the access he needed.

Miguel set up a quarter of a mile away, at the crest of a hill that overlooked the eleventh hole. He had a view of Caldwell's house, and a strategically placed natural area supplied cover. Thank goodness for ponds, cattails, and willow trees. This nasty hazard had eaten more than a few of his balls. Until a few months ago, he'd thought Caldwell was a friend, and he'd debated bringing him into The Eye as a true believer. That was before the fucker had taken a hard line on several cases that messed up critical operations.

Oh, well. Friendship, like life, was fragile and fleeting. He had a far better candidate for the position of judge.

He drove the van onto the course, which was largely abandoned. The people in this golfing community were having breakfast and preparing for work, and maintenance would be easy to avoid. Peak tee times began at eleven, when the more daring broke for an early lunch and a few holes. He parked the van and peered through binoculars to find his target. The judge and his wife were having breakfast in the nook that overlooked the back patio and the impressive sixteenth hole. Agents were posted inside the house, and though he didn't spot agents posted outside, he knew they were there. Lockmeyer was annoying, but she wasn't inept. He readied the equipment, opened the back of the van, and fired the missile. The whole event took seconds, and he drove away with a hopeful smile after the explosion rocked the sleepy neighborhood.

Jordan woke to the sound of the door opening slowly. Darcy tiptoed into the darkened room, heading straight for the changing table where she grabbed several diapers and a box of wipes. In this dim light, Jordan was struck by how much the sisters resembled one another. He'd thought Darcy was cute when he'd met her, but Amy was the one who'd swept him off his feet.

Darcy glanced over, a contented smile curving her lips, and gasped softly. "Sorry. I didn't mean to wake you. Though, if you want, my parents are up, so you can use the guest room. That bed is much more comfortable than being crunched on a loveseat."

He'd slept in places far less comfortable, but that didn't mean he was going to turn down a perfectly good mattress. Shifting Amy, he cradled her against his body so that she wouldn't wake up. He followed Darcy to the guest room, where the bed was neatly made.

Darcy turned down the covers and whispered, "Fresh sheets."

He put Amy down, and then he took off his shirt and jeans and crashed next to her. The next time he woke, he found his mother standing over him, shaking his shoulder. "Jordie, honey, wake up. I want to see you for a little while before we have to leave."

"Leave?" He sat up. "Where are you going?"

"Home. We've been here for almost a week, and it hasn't exactly been a vacation. Though, I suppose it could have been worse. Thank goodness Darcy came over and told us the truth." Her voice caught, and she threw her arms around him. "I'm so happy you're alive."

Next to him, Amy shifted. While still holding his mother, he put a restraining hand on Amy's shoulder. "You can sleep some more."

"Her parents are leaving too. We'd love for us all to have lunch together."

Jordan glanced at the digital clock across the room. It was past noon. "Okay. Let us get showered and changed." He assumed Amy had the rest of his clothes. She'd thoughtfully left a complete change for him at the cottage.

Lunch was an interesting affair. Amy's parents seemed relieved that they were an item, which was an about-face from the suspicious way they'd treated him last time. Though, if he thought about it from a parent's perspective, he wouldn't be pleased to find a half-naked man at his daughter's house either. Once he announced their engagement, their entire demeanor brightened.

Her mother eyed her warily. "Are you pregnant?"

"No," Amy said.

Fran clapped her hands together. "Then that's fabulous news. It's a little fast, but wonderful nonetheless. Both of my girls will finally be married. I'm so happy for all of you."

Her father nailed him with a firm look. "As long as you make my little girl happy, I won't have a problem with you."

His parents were ecstatic. His mother hugged him and kissed Amy's cheeks. "You're going to make beautiful babies together."

Amy's eyebrows shot into her hairline. They hadn't discussed children. Jordan was on the fence about them. Right now, he didn't have room in his life, but maybe in ten or so years, he might be ready to commit to something like that. He squeezed her knee under the table.

His father congratulated him and hugged Amy. "Welcome to the family."

Though her parents seemed surprised, his didn't, and he chalked that up to the fact that he'd begun mentioning her over a year ago. The last time he'd visited home, his mother had grilled him about when he intended to make a move on Amy. *Good women don't stay single forever.* And Jamie had no doubt regaled them with every detail of her interactions with Amy.

Darcy beamed in Amy's direction. She offered her congratulations, but in a way that revealed this was not news to her. Malcolm was similarly reserved. They'd already talked about the engagement.

"Will you be moving to Ann Arbor?" Paul, Amy's father took a big bite of his sandwich as soon as he finished speaking.

Darcy handed Colin to Malcolm. "You're both welcome to stay here for as long as you need. The house will take some time to rebuild. We managed to salvage a few things, but the house will need to be torn down."

Though Malcolm didn't protest, he didn't echo his wife's invitation. Jordan finished chewing—he'd been starving—before responding. "Thanks for the offer, but Amy will move into my apartment for now. We'll figure out the rest after we meet with insurance and sort through what I'm sure will be mounds of paperwork."

He hadn't discussed this with Amy, but a glance in her direction confirmed that she was on board with his plan. As his little and his fiancée, she had almost no room for protest. And if she had an issue with his decision, he knew she would wait until they were alone to voice it. He loved her submissive respect. Because he couldn't help himself, he leaned over and gave her a kiss. She met him halfway, her eyes soft with affection.

"I'm going to put Colin down for his nap," Malcolm said. He stood with his son. "Grandparents, I know you're planning to leave before he gets up, so come get your goodbye slobbers, uh, kisses now."

They had a pleasant lunch, and afterward Amy's parents headed toward their RV. Jesse exited as they opened the door to board. Fran put her hand to her heart as she faced the formidable security specialist. He grinned. "I swept it for bugs and bombs. It's clean."

Jordan frowned at Fran's reaction. Jesse hadn't done anything to make her uncomfortable. Before he could say anything, Amy giggled. "She thinks he's hot."

"Your mother?"

"Um, yeah." She said it like he should have known. "He's cute, very buff, and wearing one of those tight T-shirts that shows off every muscle."

He turned that frown on Amy. "You can't look at other guys."

She rolled her eyes. "Looking and touching are two different things. You can't order me not to look any more than I could expect you not to look. That's not a realistic expectation. Frankie is cute too, and she wears tight shirts. I'm sure you've checked out her rack a few times. You can't help it. Even I've checked out her girls a few times. It's the second thing you notice about her."

Well, he hadn't. Not really. Okay, maybe he'd looked, but he hadn't stared. He appreciated tits in general, but he loved Amy's. Wait—had she said she'd checked out Frankie's rack? He stowed that though for a later date. "What's the first thing you noticed?"

"Her eyes." Amy wobbled on her good foot, and he caught her. "She has very expressive eyes."

He lifted her in his arms. "Nice job changing the subject. We'll talk about this later."

She slid her arm around his neck. "Okay, but only if you promise to put on a tight shirt and flex for me."

He was so very tempted to pinch her bottom, but instead he put her down in front of her parents so she could see them off. Next, his parents left to catch their flight home. As his father hugged him goodbye, he said, "She's very sweet, son, and I think you'll have a happy life together. You're going to have to bring her home next time you come."

"Of course." His days of traveling alone were finished.

As they waved goodbye, Frankie and Jesse descended on them. Jesse herded them toward the front door. "Get inside."

Amy limped a few steps, and he carried her the rest of the way. Once inside, she grinned at Jesse. "It must be difficult to protect someone like Jordan who is used to fending for himself."

Jesse cracked a smile. "You have no idea."

"Ha. Ha." Jordan wasn't the one who needed protection. He set Amy down in the living room next to Darcy. "We're leaving in ten minutes. I'll pack our things. You wait here."

Malcolm followed him upstairs. "You know, you *are* welcome to stay here." He spoke tentatively, and his voice trailed off.

"Just not right now." Jordan wasn't offended. In Mal's shoes, he'd do the same thing. Having him and Amy there put Darcy and Colin in danger, and Malcolm's primary responsibility was to protect his family.

"I knew you'd understand. And, given the way Amy didn't protest, I think she wants some time alone with you."

Jordan threw their things into the two bags they'd been living out of for the past week. "I'm leaving Frankie here, just in case. She's a damn good operative. I worked with her in South America. You're in great hands."

"That's not necessary. I'm sending Darcy and Colin to my parents' house, and I'm coming to stay with you. Amy means the world to Darcy, and so she means the world to me. I'm not going to sit here while she's at risk." Danger glittered from Malcolm's eyes.

Jordan chucked him on the shoulder. "Good to know she's your only concern. Here I thought you loved me like a brother, but I see how it is."

"Save the lovefest for later." Frankie came into the room and nailed them both with a firm look. "Malcolm, you can't come with us, and Jordan, I'm not staying here. Brandy hired us to protect you and Amy. That's the job I signed on for, and that's the job I'm going to do."

"Protecting Darcy is protecting Amy," Jordan said. "She'd never forgive herself if fallout from this hurt Darcy, Colin, or Malcolm." Anybody, really. Amy loved sunshine and rainbows, and he was going to move mountains and perhaps a few waterfalls to make sure her life had lots of that once this problem was neutralized. "I'll take Jesse with us."

"Nope." Frankie wasn't going to compromise. "But I can pull in Eastridge or Alloway. Probably Eastridge."

"Fine. How fast can he get here?" Jordan didn't know Frankie's colleagues, but if she trusted them, that was good enough for him.

She extracted a phone from her pocket, punched some numbers, and left the room.

Malcolm watched her go. "I'm still shipping Darcy and Colin away from the house. If there's even the slightest chance Lawrence could show up here, I don't want them here. Let's get this guy, Jordan."

"Lockmeyer wants him alive." He knew the drift of his buddy's thoughts.

"I don't give a shit about that. I want him off the streets. He's a domestic terrorist. I want this threat neutralized."

"I agree." Jordan zipped the bag. He wasn't certain he wanted to go down this rabbit hole with Malcolm, but he also wasn't sure he had a choice. If he hadn't been drugged and suffering from a concussion, would he have stopped beating Lawrence before he was sure the man was dead? He wasn't sure. "But first we need to get our families to safety."

Birds sang, and the morning sun kissed her eyelids. Amy stretched, enjoying the soft slide of the sheet over her naked breasts. Last night, Jordan had made love to her twice. The first time, he'd dressed her in a white silk nightie and treated her like she was fragile. The second time, he'd tied her up and used these huge suction cups on her boobs. Each one fit a whole breast, and the sensations they caused were incredible. With a smile on her face, she turned toward the source of heat next to her and snuggled closer. "Good morning."

He wiggled lower and rested his cheek on her boob. He might have mumbled a greeting, but his eyes didn't open. Just when she thought he was going to stay asleep, she felt his cock stir against her leg. Without opening his eyes, he groped for a condom on the bedside table and handed it to her. "Put it on."

The order wasn't mumbled, but Amy chose to let her mischievous side loose. She set it on his head. "On what?"

Just like that, she found herself face down with her ass hiked into the air. She looked back to see Jordan kneeling between her legs, sleepily donning the condom. He pushed into her without waiting for her natural wetness to ease the path. The lubrication on the condom could only do so much. She both yelped and moaned because it hurt and felt good.

"Hands above you. No coming," he said as he fucked her to a quick pace.

Her body caught up, and moisture flooded her pussy. She didn't know if it was the position or his order that she couldn't climax, but suddenly an orgasm loomed on the horizon. "Please? Daddy, please let me come!"

"No. Good girls get orgasms. Bratty girls don't. Next time do as you're told."

That light, out-of-body feeling started in her abdomen. "Daddy, I can't. Oh, please!"

He thrust one last time, and she felt his cock pulse deep in her pussy. She barely managed to keep from following him over the precipice. His softened cock slid out, and he got out of bed. "Stay there. Don't move."

She felt and heard him moving around the sterile bedroom as he dressed. The position in which he'd ordered her to stay presented her private parts for his viewing pleasure. She knew her pussy glistened with her juices, and she hoped he was enjoying this proof of her submission. As seconds passed, she felt herself falling deeper into the peace that came with giving herself completely to him.

"You can get up now. Shower and get dressed."

Popping up quickly, she ran to the bathroom. Morning sex was one thing, but she kind of wished she'd awakened five minutes earlier to gargle and use the facilities so she could be fresh for him. Though, he didn't seem to mind one way or the other.

On her way to the kitchen, she passed Frankie and Jesse in the living room, and she blushed to think they'd probably heard her begging. Oh, well. The only person whose opinion mattered was in the kitchen talking on the phone.

"Hi, Frankie. Good morning, Jesse. I hope you slept well." She knew they slept in shifts, though whoever was slumbering remained on call.

"I slept fine. I had the second shift, so your screaming didn't bother me at all." Jesse barely kept a straight face as he answered.

Frankie bent in half from laughing so hard.

Amy went into the kitchen to find Jordan listening to whomever was on the other end of the line. His expression was inscrutable, and that was never a good sign. She poured a mug of coffee and a bowl of cereal. She settled for shredded wheat because they had frosting. As she sat down to eat, he ended the call.

"What's wrong?"

He turned his face away, but not before she saw his struggle to control his emotions. Rage and sadness flashed, and then they were gone. "Frankie, Jesse, we've got a problem."

Frankie and Jesse came into the kitchen. Jordan's apartment wasn't large, and it was sparsely furnished with steel and leather furniture, which gave it an antiseptic feel. Though he'd put out a few framed photos since her last visit, this place still lacked a homey vibe. She aimed to change that.

"Judge Caldwell's house was hit with a shoulder-fired missile fifteen minutes ago. He fired from behind a natural hazard a good distance away, and so they didn't see the vehicle he was driving. Nobody was on the golf course, but two members of the grounds crew reported seeing a white van. They thought it was a delivery for a pavilion being constructed nearby."

The cereal and coffee in Amy's stomach mixed unpleasantly as the safe bubble around her burst. For some reason, she'd thought she would be out of harm's way here. With Jordan, Frankie, and Jesse, nobody could sneak up on them or drug their food. Jordan had even taken her to the doctor the day before to have her ankle x-rayed. It wasn't broken, but she had a nifty boot to wear that made it easier to bear weight.

Frankie nodded. "The parking garage is under the building, so that makes it easier to smuggle you both out."

"We've set up a safe house not far away." Jesse turned to put the plan in motion, but Jordan stopped him.

"No. Let's not react like we're in a horror movie. We're not getting in a car, running up the stairs, splitting up, or diving through plate glass windows." Jordan handed Amy a gun, and she set it on the table. "I'm sure the car will start, we have great cell reception, we're armed, and none of us are idiots."

Amy stared at the weapon. She wasn't adverse to using it, but she was sure there was more to it than point-and-shoot. "I've never fired a gun."

Frankie showed her a pin with orange on one side. "This is the safety. Make sure it's off before you shoot the bad guy. Only shoot the bad guy. Aim anywhere, though the chest is the largest target and the most effective spot for neutralizing a threat."

"Should I warn him first? Like how you say, 'FBI. Drop the gun'?" Her stomach grumbled at the interruption of breakfast, but she didn't feel like eating anymore.

"We never tell someone to drop a weapon. It's likely to go off. We tell them to move slowly, set it on the ground, and kick it away." Jordan opened his laptop and punched up a live feed of his building. "And no, you have no obligation to warn him. He's tried to murder you twice. You have every reason to shoot first and ask questions never."

He called Avery Forsythe next. She and Dustin were coming on duty to hang out in the area. Amy managed to take a few bites of cereal while he coordinated coverage.

Frankie took the seat across the small table. "Honey, I know you're afraid. It's okay to be frightened."

Amy frowned. "I'm not afraid. Jordan is here, and so are you and Jesse. Dustin and Avery are outside, and I'm assuming half the FBI will be patrolling this area soon. In addition, I'm sure the local police from every city in southeastern Michigan are out looking for this bastard. He used to be the director of the FBI in

Detroit. Cops are going to be upset that one of their own is a villain. They're not going to let him win."

The speech made her feel better on a couple of levels. She had the sense that Frankie thought she was somehow lacking in intelligence. Her naiveté, a thing Jordan loved about her, was real, but that didn't mean her faith in law enforcement was misplaced or that she didn't understand the clear and present danger Lawrence presented. Her sister might hate all cops, but Amy harbored no ill will. She'd witnessed the good things that cops and agents did every day.

Frankie studied her as if reassessing her earlier opinion. Amy continued before Frankie could say anything. "Besides, Brandy told me that you never lose and that Jesse is one of the ten best sharpshooters in the world. I'm sure taking down Lawrence is a point of pride for you two." She gestured to the gun. "I probably won't even need to pick that thing up."

Yep, the more she shared her views, the less nervous she felt. She grinned at Frankie and finished breakfast.

Nothing happened for a long time. Jordan, Frankie, and Jesse moved around the apartment, looked out windows, and talked with FBI agents on secure lines. Abandoning the gun on the kitchen table, Amy wandered the apartment and found Jordan's stash of books, most of which she hadn't read, on a shelf in his office. It looked like he had a geek bent. He had the entire collection of the Dresden files in hardcover. She grabbed the first one and stretched out on the sofa. Maybe this would keep her occupied while they did a whole lot of observing.

The book didn't hold her interest all that well. It was good, but thoughts kept intruding. She wished she had some of her things because this would be a great time to catch up on her party planning. As she thought about her business, color drained from her face.

"Babe? What's wrong?" Jordan plunked onto the sofa next to her, concern wrinkling the space between his eyebrows.

"It hit me again that everything from my business is gone. All the materials I've spent years collecting. My sample books, the flyers that I spent hours Photoshopping, all the tablecloths and banners I'd picked up on sale." She rubbed her eyes to stave off the tears. "My clients think I'm dead. I missed three events in the past week, parties I've spent weeks planning—parties that should have been a perfect commemoration of important life milestones." She sniffled, and he pulled her onto his lap.

"Babe, it'll take time and patience, but you can rebuild everything. I'm sure your clients will understand when you tell them what happened. And insurance should replace most of your stuff."

"Not my business stuff." She sat up to face him. "I never amended my policy to cover the business."

He shrugged it off. "You're a survivor, and you have me to support you ever step of the way. I have faith that you'll bounce back. Hey, didn't you save all your electronic stuff on a cloud?"

"Yes." Excitement raced through her arms, and she could already feel her fingers tapping passwords on a keyboard. "Can I use your laptop?"

"No. It's hooked up to the FBI feed. We're using it to watch the situation develop." He picked up the book she'd abandoned. "This is a good one, but it takes a few chapters to get into it. The second book is better, and by the third, it's a great series."

"I didn't know you liked paranormal stories."

"I'll read anything, especially if it doesn't make me think too hard." He flashed a boyish smile. "That makes me sound lazy."

"Not at all. You think hard all day, analyzing information for clues and motives. It makes sense that you'd want your reading material to be relaxing." She should get off his lap, but she really didn't want to. She wiggled so that he could hold her like a child, and she rested her head on his shoulder. "Will you read it to me?"

"Yeah, sure."

Jesse came in as she showed Jordan where she'd left off. "Hey, they got him. Two blocks away—he set the van on fire rather than be captured."

Relief washed over Amy. She smiled brightly. "See? I didn't have to use the gun." Jesse ducked out of the room, and Amy moved so that she straddled Jordan's lap. "Daddy, can we have really loud sex tonight?"

Cupping her face, he kissed her so deeply she thought they might have really loud sex right now. Jesse and Frankie had better say their goodbyes quickly.

Chapter Twenty-Two

Candles—check.

Lasagna—check.

Sheet, folded and converted into a tablecloth—check.

One glass of wine each—check.

Sexy pink teddy that showed off her cleavage—check.

Put the guns away in a drawer—check.

Had she forgotten anything on his list? Nope. Okay, maybe the gun thing wasn't on the list, but she didn't think guns should be left out where a child could get to them. Jordan had a gun safe, but she didn't know the combination yet, otherwise she'd put it in there. Instead, she tucked them away in an empty drawer in the TV stand. Jordan didn't have a collection of movies. He preferred a subscription to a streaming service.

She knelt in a modified pose on the pillow in the center of the living room to wait for him. The day had been inordinately long, and this late meal felt like a fresh start to the day. She was energized, invigorated by the way things had played out. Six hours ago, a man had been running around bent on ending her life. Due to the coordinated efforts of local police and the FBI team that Dustin had been running, Miguel Lawrence was no longer a threat.

Malcolm had stopped by to tell her personally, and when he'd hugged her, she'd felt the relief in his entire being.

The front door opened, and she resisted looking up, though from her peripheral vision, she recognized him. Those long, muscular, jean-clad legs stopped right next to her, teasing with their proximity. He ran his fingers through her hair. "Were you good?"

"Yes, Daddy."

"I'm so proud of you, babe. You've handled this like a champion. I know there's a lot of work ahead of you, but I'll be here to support you. I'm confident that you can achieve all your dreams. Stand up." Careful to make sure she didn't put weight on her hurt ankle, he helped her follow his order. He smiled, and the love shining from his eyes stole her breath. Of course, she was very curious about the hand behind his back.

She wanted to throw her arms around him and never let go. "I love you so much, Daddy."

"I love you too, my little one. I brought you a present." He brought the object he'd been hiding out slowly, uncertainty showing up in the way his expression froze. It was a plush clown fish, orange with black bands.

Tears blurred her vision as she hugged the stuffed animal. "I was so nervous when you said you wanted to watch that movie with me. I was afraid you'd think not nice things about me."

With a gentle nudge, he tilted her face to his. "Never. I love this part of you. I promise to always take care of you—to love you, cherish you, nurture you." With a desperate passion, his lips claimed hers. He devoured her, demonstrating how completely she belonged to him, and how completely he belonged to her.

When he broke the kiss, she was breathing hard. "Daddy?"

"Yeah?"

"Can I redecorate? Not completely, maybe just add some pizzazz here and there?"

He laughed, a joy that went deep. "Absolutely. According to my mom, my sisters, Darcy, and you, this place could use a woman's touch. You're that woman, babe."

She bounced up to her tiptoes to kiss his cheek, but her ankle protested, and she fell against him. He caught her, and lifted her in his arms.

"If this isn't the most touching sight I've ever seen, then I don't know what is."

Jordan froze, and Amy's heart raced as she recognized that voice. He put her down and turned slowly, shielding her with his body. "Miguel Lawrence, get on your knees and put your weapon down. You are under arrest. You have the right to remain silent."

Lawrence, standing in the doorway to the kitchen, laughed. "You're Mirandizing me? Seriously?" He waved the gun at Jordan. "Completely unnecessary. I'm going to kill you both, plant information that makes it look like you were setting me up, and then leave. I'll be free, and you'll be remembered as a domestic terrorist. A fitting end to this story."

He came around the sofa so that he had a clear path to both of them. His nose was bandaged, and dark circles ringed his eyes, a testament to the fact that it had been broken, perhaps repeatedly. Amy liked to think her kicks had done as much—or more—damage as Jordan's fists. He winced as he walked, but she couldn't tell what injury caused a pain that would lead to labored breathing.

"You're dead," Amy said. "They said you blew up the van while you were inside it."

Lawrence chuckled, though it was a strained laugh. "I found someone with the same build. I knew the body would be charred beyond recognition. They'd run tests eventually, but with you dead and me back in place as the head of the Detroit Bureau, the results would show that you staged the whole thing to try to kill me."

Part of that plan didn't make sense to Amy, but she wasn't looking for Lawrence to be successful. She put her palm on Jordan's back to draw strength from him.

Lawrence gestured with the arm in a cast. "Amy, I toyed with the idea of keeping you around for a little while. You're so obedient, eager to please, and compliant. I like that in a woman. My wife is that way, only she's not so kinky between the sheets. And her body lacks your very lush curves."

Amy had forgotten she was wearing a negligee. Suddenly she felt naked in the sheer material. She clutched the stuffed clown fish to her chest. Jordan moved so that he was a little more in front of her, but not enough to anger the man with the gun.

"How did you get in?" Amy was amazed. Jordan's apartment was on the fourth floor, and there was no entrance from the kitchen.

Lawrence rolled his eyes. "Fire escape. Duh."

"Why?" Jordan spat the question at Lawrence. "Why did you dishonor the badge? Why did you betray the principles we've sworn to uphold?"

Miguel seemed to consider this for a moment. He tilted his head as he thought. "Probably because the job isn't about honor. Being a successful agent is about power, as is having a fruitful career. When the leader of The Eye approached me, oh, ten or so years ago, I leaped at the chance. I've worked hard. I have more money and power than you've ever dreamed, and once I kill you, our presence here will be cemented. We own powerful people— business owners, politicians, judges—and they work to consolidate our power."

"Caldwell wouldn't do what you wanted?" Amy gasped the question. "So you hired that man to kill him at my sister's wedding. I see what you've done." Her ankle buckled, and she fell to the side. Jordan tried to catch her, but Lawrence wouldn't let him.

"Leave her where she is. Give me the access codes to your computer, and I'll kill her quickly. If not, I'll take my time, maybe tie her up and have some fun beforehand."

"You fucking touch her, and I'll kill you." Jordan took one dangerous step toward Lawrence, and Amy scooted closer to the TV stand. Using her hands to scramble back, she channeled a frightened scream queen. Lawrence paid her no mind. Jordan was the larger threat.

Lawrence fired his gun. Because it had a silencer, it didn't make much of a sound. With experience honed in black ops,

Jordan jumped clear. Amy brought up the gun she'd fished from the drawer in the TV stand and squeezed the trigger. Somehow, her eyes closed as well because she missed seeing if she hit the target. She opened her eyes in time to see Jordan catapult himself at Lawrence's midsection, grabbing the wrist of the hand that held the gun.

The scuffle was brief, and in seconds, Jordan had Lawrence pinned, and he held the bad man's gun to his head. "Amy, my handcuffs are on the dresser. Grab those and my cell."

"You can't arrest me! I own the criminal justice system. I have judges in place all over. The Eye is nationwide. I will triumph, and there's nothing you can do about it."

Ignoring the pain in her ankle, Amy skittered through the door to the bedroom and grabbed the things Jordan had requested. When she heard the sounds of flesh hitting flesh, she decided to take her time returning. While she understood that Jordan was pissed at this guy, she abhorred violence.

When she arrived, she handed the handcuffs to Jordan, and he secured an unconscious Lawrence. The man bled from multiple wounds, and she wondered where she'd shot him. "I can't believe that someone who used to be so dedicated to upholding the law turned into a rotten murderer."

"It pisses me off, that's for sure." He flipped open his phone and called for reinforcements.

That's when she noticed his calf was bleeding. "Oh, Daddy! You're hurt."

"It's nothing." He brushed her hands away when she tried to roll up his pant leg to take a look. "I'll be fine."

"You got shot. That bastard shot your leg."

"Yeah," he said. "That bastard. Don't worry about him. He's not going anywhere. You, however, need to get dressed. This place will be swarming with agents in three-and-a-half minutes."

He was a little off. They came in just as she finished sliding into the yoga pants Dustin had bought for her. By her count, that was closer to the two minute mark. And, speak of the devil, Dustin was one of the officers who responded.

Keith was as well. He surveyed the candles and lasagna, sympathy emanating from him even though his face remained stoic.

"It's still warm." She crossed her arms and leaned against the door frame. "If you're hungry."

"Looks like you two were having a romantic evening." He put his arm around her waist and helped her to the sofa. "You shouldn't be on your feet."

"That jerk shot Jordan. Make sure you charge him with attempted murder. And please make him go to the hospital. What if he has the bullet still in his leg? He won't let me look at it."

"Hush, babe." Jordan paused in giving his statement. "I'll take care of it later."

Keith and Dustin worked together to wrestle Jordan to the ground. They held him down while a medic looked at the injury. The crime scene videographer filmed the wound.

"You're going to have to go to the hospital. I don't have the equipment or the authorization to dig out the shell and stitch you up. You're lucky, though. It didn't hit bone or a major artery."

"It's fine," Jordan said.

"Wait, you said Lawrence fired once?" Dustin released his hold on Jordan, who promptly shook off Keith. Dustin crossed the room and pointed out a bullet lodged in the wall. "Did you miscount?"

"No. I didn't miscount." He sneered at Dustin. "This bullet came from my gun. I was talking him into a frenzy so I could get close enough to dive at him, and Amy went for my gun. She shot at Lawrence, but she missed. The bullet ricocheted from somewhere, I think the sofa leg, and hit me. It was friendly fire."

Dustin and Keith both had to sit down, they were laughing so hard. Heat traveled up Amy's chest, and she suddenly felt nauseous. Horrified, she scooted off the sofa and crawled to Jordan. "I'm so sorry. I swear I didn't mean it. I've never shot a gun before, and my eyes closed when it went off, so I didn't see where it went. Please don't hate me."

He petted her hair and kissed her forehead. "I'm not mad, little one. It was an accident, a fortunate one. It could have been so much worse. Now we'll have matching limps."

Chapter Twenty-Three

Amy stared at the metal and wood frame standing where her house used to be. In the past six weeks, the charred remnants of her old house had been removed, and these new beams marked the completion of the rough frame for the new house. Since it was Saturday, nobody was there working, and Amy had dropped by to see the progress.

Chicklet ran around the corner of her neighbor's house. Peggy dashed after her, but the dog stopped under Amy's hand. He looked up expectantly, and so she knelt down to give him enthusiastic scratches behind the ears. Then she fished a treat from her pocket and handed it over.

"You're going to spoil him rotten." Peggy laughed as she clicked Chicklet's leash into place.

"He saved my life. That's worth all the ear scratches and treats he wants." She kissed the mutt's head before getting back up.

Peggy hugged her. "I'm glad you're moving back in."

Amy eyed the large skeleton. "When it's finished." She and Jordan had collaborated with the architect, and the new house would be larger, with two stories and a finished basement. The bedrooms would be upstairs, and her office would be on the main floor. The basement would house a bondage and sensory room—Amy refused to call it a dungeon—and storage for her business at the other end. Jordan had promised it wouldn't look or feel at all like a basement, and she trusted him to see to those details. Otherwise there was no way she would step foot in it.

"Hopefully it'll be done by the holidays," she continued. Jordan had already extracted a promise that she'd fly to Wisconsin with him for Thanksgiving.

"Your young man came by yesterday and talked with the foreman." Peggy stroked Chicklet's head and laughed. "He's an intimidating person if you don't know what a big teddy bear he is. I'll feel better having the FBI living next door."

Amy giggled at the image of Jordan as a teddy bear, but she supposed it was an apt description. He was definitely snuggly. "Speaking of—I have to get going. He wants me to pack a picnic before he gets home."

"Oh, that's nice. Where are you going?"

Amy shrugged. "It's a surprise."

In the six weeks they'd shared an apartment, Amy had definitely put her mark on the place. The austere, minimalist furniture now featured colorful throw pillows. The walls sported photos of family and friends, and she'd recently acquired artwork from a local artist making waves with sunrise motifs. Every time Jordan came home to find something new or different, he merely smiled.

Still, it was too small to house her business and the playroom. For now, Jordan had consented to moving those toys into the bedroom so she could take over the office. She'd procured a few smaller jobs, but she was waiting until they moved to accept larger events. Until then, she worked on replenishing her stores and making new sample books. Jordan had also tasked her with designing a website for Events by Amy.

Darcy called while Amy was packing up the food according to Jordan's instructions. "Hey, Darcy. How are you?" She put the phone on speaker and set it on the counter.

"Malcolm is driving me crazy." Darcy spoke in a stage whisper. After the case against Lawrence closed, rather than accept a penalty of two weeks unpaid administrative leave, Malcolm had turned in his badge. Since then, he'd played around with consulting, but he'd only accepted two jobs. Most of the time, he puttered around the house. "I mean, it's great that he's spending so much time with Colin, but he keeps bothering me while I'm trying to work. And right now, this is our only income." She sighed, and then she chuckled wryly. "Be careful what you wish for, eh?"

Amy responded with a pity laugh. "Since his leg has healed, Jordan has spent a lot of time at work. We live together, and some days, our only communication is a text. It could be worse."

"It's worse." Darcy sniffled. "I'm pregnant, and I've been so fucking stressed that I forgot to take my birth control pills. Malcolm has no idea."

"Congratulations." Amy knew Darcy would be happy once she got over the shock. Granted, Colin was only seven months old, but that only meant the little guy would get to be best friends with his younger sibling. "They'll be even closer in age than you and me. And Mom and Dad are going to be thrilled to have another grandbaby. I'm happy for you, Darcy. You're a great mom."

Darcy blew her nose. "My allergies suck right now, and I can't take anything. I'm going to tell Malcolm tonight, and then I'm going to schedule a vasectomy. I only want two kids."

Amy wasn't going to weigh in on that issue. She heard the front door open. "I have to get going. Good luck. Let me know how it goes. I love you. Bye."

"Love you too. Bye."

Jordan came into the kitchen and kissed her on the side of her neck. "Hey, babe. Was that Darcy?"

"Yeah. She's pregnant, and she's going to tell Malcolm tonight." She leaned against his chest, and he hugged her briefly before one hand landed on her breast. They'd talked about having kids, and they'd both agreed to hold off until they felt ready. "I'd love to know where you're taking me today."

He gave her boob a little squeeze and released her. "I have a present for you."

She clapped her hands together and bounced up and down. "I love presents."

"I know you do." He turned her to face him and lifted a small paper bag decorated with hearts and rainbows. "Open it now."

Amy took the bag. She pushed aside tissue paper to find a headband with large daisies attached. It was the exact one she'd bought for herself the day her house blew up. Tears pricked the backs of her eyes. "Oh, Daddy." That title was becoming easier and more natural to say as well. "I love it. Thank you so much."

He gathered her in his arms and held her close while she got her emotions under control. "Did you get everything done?"

"Yes." When he released her, she replaced the fabric headband she'd been wearing with the one Jordan had bought. "And I stopped by the house. It's coming along nicely. Are the walls next?"

He smoothed down a strand of hair that had become caught by a flower petal. Love and affection blazed from him and bathed her in gentle rays. "By the end of next week, the exterior should be completed." He picked up a plastic container and looked at the contents. "What's this?"

"I made brownies."

His hungry grin made her heart beat faster. "I love when you bake." He brushed a kiss across her lips. "Have you done your stretches?"

First thing in the morning after he'd left for work. Her heart beat faster because his pitch had dropped, and he now spoke in his sexy Dom voice. "Yes, Daddy."

"Are you wearing the plug I left for you?"

"Yes, Daddy."

"Good girl. Leave it in until we get back. We're going for a ride on my bike, and every bump will be a reminder that you belong to me."

She didn't need a reminder for that. Being his little was a pleasure that hummed in her heart. Jumping to her toes, she kissed his cheek.

"When we get back, I'm going to put you in the swing and have my way with you."

That sounded like heaven, and juices rushed to her pussy. She put away the ingredients that needed refrigeration, making sure to show off the way her pants hugged her ass. "Unless you're really super hungry, why wait?"

"Good point. Get in the bedroom and get naked. I'll be there in a minute."

Happy beyond belief, she tugged her shirt off as she ran down the hall. She caught the headband as it fell and set it on the dresser before shimmying out of her pants. Jordan entered the room before she could remove her panties and bra. "It hasn't been a minute," she protested.

"I'm super hungry, and I couldn't wait." He tossed her on the bed and peeled her panties away. Heat rushed to her pussy as he hiked her legs over his shoulders. His mouth made her even hotter. He moaned as he slurped her juices. "Delectable. Five stars. A feast for the senses."

Her giggle was cut short when he took her clit between his lips and flicked his tongue over the tip. It was almost too much to bear. Her hips lifted from the bed.

With a groan, Jordan stopped. "You lack self control, babe. Let's get you into the swing and tied down so you can't move."

She cooperated, and a few minutes later, she found herself bound to a swing suspended from a rafter in the ceiling. Her wrists were secured above her head, and cuffs just above her knees kept her legs open and out of the way. Jordan had installed the swing a few weeks ago, and it had become one of his favorite bondage tools.

"You're going to make me beg," she breathed. "Aren't you?"

"Not today, babe, but there will be a lot of screaming. I should gag you so the neighbors don't come knocking to make sure you're all right again."

Amy blushed, and she vowed to keep as quiet as she could. Though, with Jordan in charge, that might not be possible. "Anything you want, Daddy."

"No gag." He grinned widely. "I like to hear you." With that, he licked her pussy with the flat of his tongue.

Unable to move, she relaxed against the swing and submitted to his will. Soon little sounds of pleasure purred from her throat. Jordan pushed a couple fingers into her pussy—made tighter because the plug was still in her ass—and stroked her sweet spot until she shouted her release. The rhythm of his finger slowed, drawing out her pleasure until she was a quivering mass of gelatin.

"You're mine," he said.

"Completely," she agreed. The fingers inside her flexed against her swollen inner flesh. A high-pitched squeak of protest escaped without consulting her brain.

He pulled his fingers from her and went to the toy chest. When he returned a moment later, he was drizzling lube over a vibrator that had a projection that looked like a shield. The shield part had another vibrator in it. Slowly, he slid it into her tender vagina and turned it on. Powerful pulses rocked her pussy to a new rhythm, and the shield pressed against her clit. Her will was no match for that machine, and he forced two more orgasms from her.

By the time he removed the vibrator and the plug from her rear, she couldn't form words. He took her down from the swing and placed her on the bed. As he slid into her, he looked into her eyes. "I love you, Amy."

She found the words. "And I love you, Daddy."

Michele Zurlo

I'm Michele Zurlo, author of over 20 romance novels. During the day, I teach English, and in the evenings, romantic tales flow from my fingertips.

I'm not half as interesting as my characters. My childhood dreams tended to stretch no further than the next book in my to-be-read pile, and I aspired to be a librarian so I could read all day. I'm pretty impulsive when it comes to big decisions, especially when it's something I've never done before. Writing is just one in a long line of impulsive decisions that turned out to showcase my great instincts. Find out more at www.michelezurloauthor.com or @MZurloAuthor

Re/Defined
Lost Goddess Publishing

Visit www.lostgoddesspublishing.com for information about our other titles.
Lost Goddess Publishing Anthologies

BDSM Anthology/Club Alegria #1-3
New Adult Anthology/Lovin' U #1-4
Menage Anthology/Club Alegria #4-7

Lost Goddess Publishing Novels

Re/Bound (Doms of the FBI 1) by Michele Zurlo
Re/Paired (Doms of the FBI 2) by Michele Zurlo
Re/Claimed (Doms of the FBI 3) by Michele Zurlo
Re/Defined (Doms of the FBI 4) by Michele Zurlo
Blade's Ghost by Michele Zurlo
Nexus #1: Tristan's Lover by Nicoline Tiernan
Tessa by Ali Baran
Dragon Kisses 1 by Michele Zurlo
Dragon Kisses 2 by Michele Zurlo
Dragon Kisses 3 by Michele Zurlo

Coming July 2016: Re/Leased (Doms of the FBI 5)

Here's an unedited sneak peek:

David regarded Autumn regretfully. "I didn't bring ropes. Maybe next time."

"Here." Jordan appeared out of nowhere. He handed a coil to David. "You can use mine. Amy's not one for public play. Yet."

Autumn fingered the rope. The silk caressed her back. "I'm game if you are." David didn't respond, so she lifted her arms. "It's okay if this is your first time. Everybody's a virgin once."

"It's been a while." David untied the knot holding the coil together. "You're going to need to be patient."

She encouraged with a smile. "I've got all evening."

Jordan took a few steps back to give them privacy. David worked quietly and with methodical meticulousness.

Autumn mostly watched his face, but her gaze was repeatedly drawn to the way his shoulders and arms moved. Muscles bunched and elongated, and the deeper he concentrated, the more he sucked the corner of his upper lip. Autumn was tempted to offer to suck it for him. Instead she chose to say something innocuous. "You're cute when you're concentrating."

He glanced up, surprised, and his knot-weaving fingers stuttered.

She raised her eyebrows. "Let me guess—nobody's ever told you that you were cute before?"

"You're not at all what I expected."

"You wanted a leggy blonde with huge fake boobs?"

He exhaled a laugh. "No."

"Botox lips and cherry red lipstick?"

"Hell, no. I just didn't think you'd be so forward."

"Ahh." She sighed knowingly. "I'm not demure, and that's a turn off."

"Not at all. It's refreshing. I like that you're lighthearted and that you feel free to tease and flirt. I'm having fun, and I didn't think I would." He went back to looping rope.

Autumn knew she wasn't the most beautiful woman in the world. Her looks were passable, and most of the time she downplayed them to fly under the radar. She did the same thing with her personality, though she was letting it off the leash more often tonight than she usually did. She watched him untie the knot and try again. "Maybe you want to ask Jordan for help." She used her whispering skills so nobody but David would hear. "I don't know how to tie that one either."

He looked around, but Jordan was working with another couple, so he signaled the original presenter who was walking around with his sub and giving pointers. David offered his hand. "You're Malcolm, right? I'm David Eastridge."

Malcolm nodded. "Jordan told me you were here tonight. Glad you could make it. Frankie speaks highly of you." His sub waited patiently as Malcolm talked David through making a double coin knot.

"That's it. Then do the same thing in the back. It looks good, and it'll keep the corselet from slipping too much when she moves." Malcolm and David moved behind her to work. "I hear you're looking into CalderCo?"

"No work talk." Malcolm's sub broke her silence with that hissed reminder.

"Sweetheart, you just lost one stroke of the cane."

Though Autumn couldn't see the sub's face, she could feel the palpable disappointment. Only a Painslut would be upset about one less hit with a cane. However, that wasn't what made her flinch. How, exactly, was David "looking into" CalderCo? That was where she worked as an accountant. It was her one anchor to the normal world, the cover for her extracurricular activities, and it paid for the majority of her sister's care. Did he know she worked there?

Oh, the questions she had and couldn't ask. Wait—yes she could. "CalderCo? That's a shipping company. I thought you were in analytics?"

"I am." David came around to her side. Malcolm showed him how to tie off the corselet and adjust the placement of the final knot. When he looked at her, his expression was shuttered. "How does that feel?"

She ran her palms over the ropes. "Great. And it looks fantastic." Turning around, she found Malcolm assessing the attempt with a critical eye. His sub was still pouting over her punishment. Autumn felt sorry for her.

"Malcolm, meet Bree. Bree, this is Malcolm."

"Nice to meet you, Bree." He turned to his sub. "This is my wife, Darcy. She and a few of her friends arranged this whole party."

"It's a lovely party. I very much enjoyed the first game. It revealed so much about technique and finesse."

Darcy laughed. "It did, didn't it? Amy said I'd like you."

"Amy is your sister? There's definitely a family resemblance. You're both so beautiful."

Malcolm put his arm around his wife and pulled her against his side, pinching her ass hard as he did so. "It's almost time for the next game."

Bliss parted Darcy's lips, a reaction to the pinch. "Layla's announcing this one, but thank you anyway, Master." Her eyes opened, and she focused on Autumn. "If you liked the first game, you'll love the second one. And later, there's one where your Sir will have to guide you, blindfolded, through an obstacle course, using only a crop and his voice. Then there's the gauntlet, if you're brave enough to walk down an aisle lined with sadists armed with paddles."

Malcolm rolled his eyes at his wife's near-orgasmic listing of the festivities. "Which you won't be doing in your condition."

"Congratulations." David caught on a few seconds before Autumn did. "When are you due?"

"In seven months. This is baby number two for us. Our son is eight months old. Yep, barefoot and pregnant, that's me since the day we met." From the sarcasm in Darcy's reply, Autumn couldn't tell whether the woman was happy or upset.

Malcolm grinned as he kissed Darcy's temple. "What can I say? My boys are powerful swimmers. They laugh in the face of both condoms and birth control pills."

"Let's see how amused they are when you get a vasectomy."

Autumn couldn't help but laugh at Darcy's dry tone. She clamped a hand over her mouth and buried her face in David's shirt to hide her laughter. He hugged her to him, and his chest shook with silent amusement as well.

"I'm going to get her something to eat. Pregnancy has made Darcy start hallucinating when she's hungry." With that, he dragged her off toward the barn.

Autumn looked up at David. With her body pressed to his and the way he held her, it was an intimate pose. "I bet she's a handful."

A slow grin lightened his eyes. "I bet you are as well."

She shrugged. "It's been known to happen."

The light in his eyes dimmed, and his mood grew sober. "I have really big hands."

This wasn't supposed to get serious. She dropped her gaze, severing the spell he was weaving. When she lifted it again, she attempted to make his eyes turn lighter again. She was beginning to really like that cinnamon brown color. "All men think they have big hands."

It worked. He laughed.

Made in the USA
Lexington, KY
13 May 2016